NIGHT BROKEN

NIGHT BROKEN

PATRICIA BRIGGS

ACE BOOKS, NEW YORK

THE BERKLEY PUBLISHING GROUP
Published by the Penguin Group
Penguin Group (USA) LLC
375 Hudson Street, New York, New York 10014

USA • Canada • UK • Ireland • Australia • New Zealand • India • South Africa • China

A Penguin Random House Company

This book is an original publication of The Berkley Publishing Group.

Ace Books are published by The Berkley Publishing Group.
ACE and the "A" design are trademarks of Penguin Group (USA) LLC.

ISBN 978-0-425-25674-9

PRINTED IN THE UNITED STATES OF AMERICA

Cover art by Daniel Dos Santos.
Cover design by Judith Lagerman.
Map by Michael Enzweiler.

For our good friends—you know who you are. I don't know how we ended up surrounded by so many people who are, as my father used to say, "folk to ride the river with." I especially would like to dedicate this to two people who went above and beyond for us this year as we tried to combine stupid travel schedules with horses who wait until I'm gone before turning their minds to mischief.

Dr. Dick Root, DVM, held my daughter's hand when Tilly had her foal while Mike and I were on signing tour. There aren't actually many people who will put up with a dozen phone calls at four in the morning without losing their cool. Thank you, Dick. May you and Ally (OFW Alivia) travel many happy miles together.

Deken Schoenberg also comes to my rescue, whether it be by trimming horses in triple-digit weather, lending me a hand when I get in over my head, or, as a not random example, helping when I am stuck five hundred miles away in a different country and a silly yearling decides that that is the day to get himself hurt. Magic is sorry he kicked you, especially after you drove the better part of fifty miles to come help him. He promised me that he will treat our friends better in the future.

Next time we leave town, I'm not telling the horses.

ACKNOWLEDGMENTS

This story, as all my stories do, owes much to the people who go through it and find all the oopses, plot holes, and whatnot any book collects over the months that it is being written. The mistakes that are left are mine. The following people read through bits and pieces and parts to make the book better: Collin Briggs, Mike Briggs, Linda Campbell, Michael Enzweiler, Deb Lentz, Ann Peters, Kaye and Kyle Roberson, Anne Sowards, and Sara and Bob Schwager. If you find this book enjoyable, you and I, dear reader, owe them a debt of gratitude.

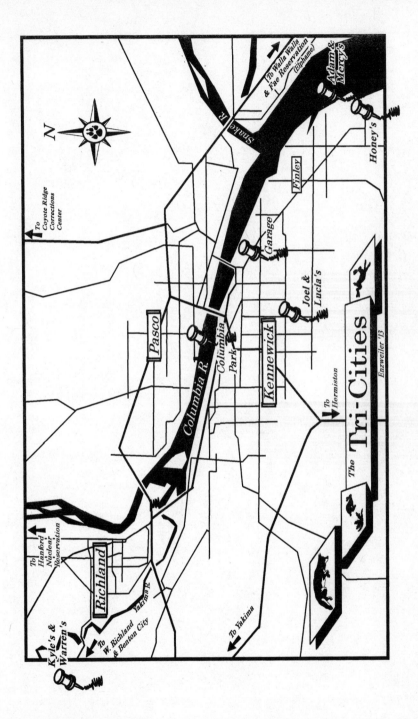

1

~~~~

THE PHONE RANG WHILE I WAS ELBOW-DEEP IN SUDSY dishwater.

"I'll get it," said my stepdaughter, Jesse, hastily dumping two glasses and a fork in my sink.

A werewolf pack that eats together stays together, I thought, scrubbing stubborn egg off a plate. Sunday breakfasts weren't attended by the whole pack—some of them had families just like regular people or jobs they worked on the Sabbath. The breakfasts weren't mandatory because that would have ruined the intent. Darryl, Adam's second, who usually prepared the meals, was a hellaciously good cook, and his food attracted anyone who could manage to come.

The dishwasher was running, stuffed full and then some. I would have let the rest of the dishes wait until it was done, but Auriele, Darryl's mate, wouldn't hear of it.

I didn't argue with her because I was one of the three people in the pack who outranked her, so she'd have to back down. That felt like cheating, and I never cheat.

Unless it is against my enemies, whispered a soundless voice in my head that might have been mine but felt like Coyote's.

The second reason for my compliance was more self-serving. Auriele and I were getting along, which made her the only one of the three female werewolves in the pack who was friendly with me at the moment.

Auriele hadn't been happy having me as the Alpha's mate, either—I was a coyote shapeshifter among wolves. She didn't think it was a good thing for pack morale. She also thought, correctly, that I brought trouble for the pack with me. She liked me despite herself. I was used to the company of men, but it was nice to have a woman besides Jesse, my teenage stepdaughter, who would talk to me.

So, to please Auriele, I washed dishes that the dishwasher could have taken care of, ignoring the burn of hot soapy water in the wounds of my trade—barked knuckles are a mechanic's constant companion. Auriele dried the dishes, and Jesse had volunteered to tidy up the kitchen in general. Three women bonding over household chores—my mother would be pleased if she could see us. That thought hardened my resolve that next week, some of the men would do cleanup. It would be good for them to expand their skill set.

"There's this kid in my second-period class." Auriele ignored the ringing phone as she hefted a stack of plates up to the cupboard with a grunt of effort. It wasn't the weight of the dishes that was the problem—Auriele was a werewolf; she could have lifted a four-hundred-pound anvil onto the shelf. It was that she was short and had to stand on tiptoe to do it. Jesse had to dodge around her to get to the phone.

"All the teachers love Clark," Auriele continued. "All the girls and most of the guys, too. And every word out of his mouth is a lie. 'Enrique cheated off my paper,' he told me when I asked him why they both had all the same mistakes. Enrique, he just gets this resigned look on his face; I expect that Clark has done this to him before."

"Hauptman residence," said Jesse cheerfully. "Can I help you?"

"Is Adam there?"

"So I told him—" Auriele stopped talking abruptly, her sensitive ears caught by the familiar voice on the line.

"I need Adam." My husband's ex-wife's voice was thick with tears. Christy Hauptman sounded desperate and half-hysterical.

"Mom?" Jesse's voice was shaky. "Mom, what's wrong?"

"Get Adam."

"Mom?" Jesse gave me a frantic look.

"Adam," I called. "Christy's on the phone for you."

He was in the living room talking to Darryl and a few of the pack who had lingered after breakfast, so I didn't have to raise my voice much. It wasn't the first time Christy had called needing something.

Dealing with Christy was usually enough to give me a stomachache. Not because of anything she could do to me or Adam. But Jesse, who loved her mother but was currently fighting to keep liking her, suffered every time that woman called. There was nothing I could do to stop it.

"He's coming, Mom," Jesse said.

"Please," Christy said. "Tell him to hurry."

Desperate, hysterical tears—those weren't unusual. But she sounded scared, too. And that wasn't anything I'd heard before.

Adam walked into the room, and from his grim face, I could tell he'd heard at least part of what Christy had said. He took the handset from Jesse but hugged her with the other arm. Jesse's eyes grew watery under his comforting hold. She gave me a frantic look before bolting away, out the door, and up the stairs, presumably to her room, where she could collect herself.

"What do you need?" Adam said, most of his attention still on his daughter.

"Can I come home?"

Auriele glanced at me, but I was already wearing my blank face. She wouldn't be able to tell what I was thinking from my expression.

"This isn't your home," Adam said. "Not anymore."

"Adam," Christy said. "Oh, Adam." She sobbed, a small, hopeless sound. "I'm in trouble, I need to come home. I've been so stupid. He won't leave me alone. He hurt me, he killed a friend of mine, and he follows me everywhere I go. Can I come home, please?"

That wasn't anything I'd expected. Auriele quit trying to pretend she wasn't listening to every word and jerked her face toward the phone.

"Call the police," Adam said. "That's what they are there for."

"He'll kill me," she whispered. "Adam, he'll kill me. I don't have anywhere else to run. Please."

Werewolves can tell when people are lying. So can some of the other supernatural critters running around—like me, for instance. Over the phone is a lot trickier because a lot of the telltale signs involve heartbeat and smell—neither of which is possible to detect over a phone line. But I could hear the truth in her voice.

Adam looked at me.

"Tell her to come," I said. What else could I say? If something happened to her when we could help . . . I wasn't sure if I could live with that. I knew that Adam couldn't.

Auriele continued to watch me. She frowned, finally turned away, and started to dry the dishes again.

"Adam, please?" Christy pleaded.

Adam narrowed his eyes at me and didn't say anything.

"Adam," Mary Jo said from the doorway. Mary Jo is a firefighter, tough and smart. "She is owed by the pack for the years that she was yours. Let her come home, and the pack will protect her."

He gave Mary Jo a look, and she dropped her eyes.

"It's okay," I said to Adam, and tried to make it not a lie. "Really."

I bake when I'm stressed. If I had to make enough chocolate chip cookies to feed Richland while she was here, it would be okay because Adam needed me to be okay with it.

If she tried anything, she would be sorry. Adam was mine. She had thrown him away, thrown Jesse away—and I had snatched them up. Finders keepers.

Maybe she didn't want them back. Maybe she just needed to be safe. My gut wasn't convinced, but jealousy isn't a logical emotion, and I had no reason to be jealous of Christy.

"All right," Adam said. "All right. You can come." Then, his voice gentle, he asked, "Do you need money for plane tickets?"

I went back to the dishes and tried not to hear the rest of the conversation. Tried not to hear the concern in Adam's voice, the softness—and the satisfaction he got from taking care of her. Good Alpha werewolves take care of those around them; it's part of what makes them Alpha.

I might have been able to ignore it better if all the wolves still in the house hadn't drifted into the kitchen. They listened to Adam's finalization of the details that would bring Christy here and snuck occasional, furtive glances my way when they thought I wouldn't notice.

Auriele took the last cup from my hand. I unplugged the sink and shook the water from my hands before drying them off on my jeans. My hands aren't my best feature. The hot water had left my skin pruney, and my knuckles were red and swollen. Even after washing dishes, there was still some black grease embedded in my skin and under my nails. Christy's hands were always beautiful, with French-manicured nails.

Adam hung up the phone and called the travel agent he used to coordinate his not-infrequent business travel: both business business and werewolf business.

"She can stay with Honey and me," said Mary Jo to me, her voice neutral.

Mary Jo and Honey were the other two female werewolves in the pack. Mary Jo had moved in with Honey when Honey's mate had been killed a few months ago. Neither of them liked me very much.

Until Mary Jo made the offer of hospitality, I'd been half planning to put Christy up with one of the other pack members because I hadn't thought it through. I knew that putting Christy in with Mary Jo and Honey would be a mistake.

Adam and I were working hard to increase the pack cohesion, which meant that I was trying very hard not to further alienate either Mary Jo or Honey. I was doing pretty well at keeping our interactions to polite neutrality. If Christy moved in with them, she would use their dislike of me and fan it into a hurricane-force division that would rain down on the pack in a flood of drama.

Once I recognized the power of Christy as a divisive force, I realized that it wasn't just a problem for my relationship with the pack, but also for Adam's. Putting Adam's ex-wife in the same house with Honey and Mary Jo would be stupid because it would force Mary Jo to take Christy's side on any tension between Christy and Adam or Christy and the pack. The same thing would be true of anyone Christy stayed with.

Christy was going to have to stay here with Adam and me.

"Christy needs to be here, where she'll feel safe," said Auriele before I could reply to Mary Jo.

"Uhm," I said, because I was still reeling under the weight of just how much it was going to suck having her not just here in the Tri-Cities, but here in my home.

"You don't want her here?" asked Auriele, and for the first time, I realized that Auriele, like Mary Jo, had liked Christy better than she did me. "She's scared and alone. Don't be petty, Mercy."

"Would you want Darryl's ex staying at your house?" asked Jesse hotly. I hadn't realized she'd come back downstairs. Her chin was raised as she flung her support my way. I didn't want her to do that. Christy was her mom—Jesse shouldn't be trying to choose between us.

"If she needed help, I would," Auriele snapped. It was easy for her to be certain because Darryl, as far as I knew, didn't have an ex-wife. "If you don't want Christy here, Mercy, she is welcome at my house."

Auriele's offer was followed up by several others, accompanied by hostile stares aimed at me. Christy had been well liked by most of the pack. She was just the sort of sweet, helpless homemaker that appealed to a bunch of werewolves with too much testosterone.

"Christy will stay here," I said.

But since Mary Jo and Auriele were arguing hotly about where Christy would be happiest, and the men were paying attention to them, no one had heard me.

"I said"—I stepped between the two women, drawing on Adam's power to give weight to my words—"*Christy will stay here with Adam and me.*" Both women dropped their eyes and backed away, but the hostility in Auriele's face told me that only the Alpha's authority in my voice had forced her to stop arguing. Mary Jo looked satisfied—I was pretty sure it meant that she thought Christy's staying here might give Christy a chance to resume her position as Adam's wife.

Though Adam was still on the phone, my pull on his authority had made him look around to see what was happening in the kitchen, but he didn't slow his rapid instructions.

"Having her here isn't a good idea. She'd do okay at Honey and Mary Jo's." Jesse sounded almost frantic.

"Christy stays here," I repeated, though this time I didn't borrow Adam's magic to make my point.

"Mercy, I love my mother." Jesse's mouth twisted unhappily. "But she's selfish, and she resents that you took her place here. She'll cause trouble."

"Jesse Hauptman," snapped Auriele. "That's your mother you are talking about. You show her some respect."

"Auriele," I growled. This morning needed a dominance fight between the two of us like it needed a nuclear bomb. But I couldn't let her dictate to Jesse. "Back off."

Teeth showing in a hostile smile, Auriele turned her hot gaze on me, yellow stirring in the cappuccino depths of her eyes.

"Leave Jesse alone," I told her. "You're overstepping your authority. Jesse is not pack."

Auriele's lips whitened, but she backed down. I was right, and she knew it.

"Your mom will feel safer here," I told Jesse without looking away from Auriele. "And Auriele's also right when she says we can protect Christy better here."

Jesse gave me a despairing look. "She doesn't want Dad, but that doesn't mean she wants anyone else to have him. She'll try to get between the two of you—like water torture. Drip. Drip. Drip. You should hear what she says about you."

No. No, I shouldn't. Neither should Jesse, but there was nothing I could do about that.

"It's all right," I told her. "We're all grown-ups. We can behave for a little while." How long could it take for a werewolf to hunt down a stalker and scare him off? A stalker, by definition, should be easy to find, right?

"Good Samaritan Mercy," Mary Jo muttered. "Shouldn't we all be grateful for her charity?" She glanced around and realized she was the center of attention and flushed. "What? It's true."

Still on the phone, Adam looked at Mary Jo and held her—and everyone else in the room—silent with his gaze. He finished his business with the travel agent, then hung up the phone.

"That's enough," he said very softly, and Mary Jo flinched. He is quiet when he is really mad—right before people start dying. "This is not up for debate. It is time for everyone to go. Christy is not pack, was never pack. She was never my mate, only my wife. That means she is not pack business, and not your business."

"Christy is my friend," said Auriele hotly. "She needs help. That makes it my business."

"Does it?" Adam asked her, clearly out of patience. "If it is your business, why did Christy call me, not you?"

She opened her mouth, and Darryl put a hand on her shoulder and led her out of the room. "Best leave well enough alone," I heard him say before they left the house.

The wolves—including Mary Jo—slid out of the room without waiting for Adam to say anything more. We stood in the kitchen, Adam, Jesse, and I, waiting until the sounds of cars starting and driving away left us in silence. All the uniting benefit of this Sunday breakfast was gone like the last of the waffles.

"Jesse," I said. "Your mother is welcome here."

"You know what she's like," Jesse said passionately. "She'll spoil everything. She can get people, can get *Dad*, to *do* things they had no intention of doing."

"Not your problem," I told her, while Adam's face tightened because he agreed with Jesse.

"She can get me to do things, too." Jesse's face was desperate. "I don't want you hurt."

Adam's hand came down on my shoulder.

"You are responsible for your own actions," I told her. Told both of them. "Not hers. She's not a werewolf, not Alpha. She can't make you do anything unless you let her."

I glanced up at the clock, though I knew what time it was. "Now, if you'll both excuse me, I need to change clothes and head to church, or I'm going to be late." I strode out of the kitchen, then gathered myself together and turned at the doorway. "Something tells me that I've got a lot of praying for patience and charity in my future." I flashed them a grin I didn't much feel, then left.

CHURCH DIDN'T HELP A LOT. I WAS STILL UNSETTLED by the events of the morning when my back hit the mat on the floor of the garage. The impact forced the air from my lungs in an inelegant sound and drove my worries away. I snarled at my attacker—who snarled back with interest.

The snarl didn't make Adam's too-handsome features less handsome, but it would probably have scared anyone else. Me? I think I have some kind of subliminal death wish because Adam's anger makes me go weak in the knees, and not in a terrified sort of way.

"What are you trying to do? Kill mosquitoes?" Adam was too mad to be aware of my reaction to his anger. "I'm a werewolf. I'm trying to kill you—and you smack me open-handed on my butt?"

Even with me on the ground, he stayed in sanchin dachi, a neutral-ready position that allowed him easy rotation for either strike or block. It also made him look pigeon-toed. Not a good look, even for Adam, but his thin t-shirt, wet with sweat, did its best to improve the picture.

"It's a cute butt," I said.

He rolled his eyes, released the stance, and took a step nearer to me.

"As for my hand on your cute butt," I continued, letting my shoulders relax against the mat, "I was cleverly trying to distract you."

He frowned at me. "Distract me from what? Your awesome, sneaky attack that left you lying on the floor?"

I twisted, catching him in front of the ankle with one foot as I put my whole weight behind the shin I slammed into the back of his knee. He started to lose his balance, and I rolled up with an elbow strike that hit the big muscle that ran up the back of his upper leg with charley-horse-causing force. As he went all the way down to hands and knees, I swung the wrench I'd snagged on my original fall and touched him on the back of the head with it.

"Exactly," I said, pleased that I'd been able to lie well enough with my body language that I'd taken him unawares. He'd been fighting a lot longer than I, and he was bigger and stronger. I was very seldom able to best him while we were sparring.

Adam rolled over, rubbing his thigh to relieve the cramp I'd given him. He saw the wrench and narrowed his eyes at me—and then grinned and relaxed on the wrestling mat that covered half the garage floor. "I've always had the hots for the mean and sneaky women."

I wrinkled my nose at him. "Sneaky I knew, but I didn't know you liked mean. Okay, then. No more chocolate chip cookies for you. I'll feed them to the rest of the pack instead."

He sat up without using his hands, not showing off, but because he was just that strong. He wasn't vain enough to realize how it made the muscles in his belly stand out under the meager cover of his shirt, and I wasn't going to tell him.

Not that I had to. His mouth kicked up at the corners, and his chocolate eyes darkened a little as his nostrils flared, taking in the change that desire had made in my scent. He stripped off the shirt and wiped his face on it before tossing it to the side.

"I only like a little bit mean," Adam confided in a low-husky voice that made my heartbeat pick up. "Withholding cookies is world-class mean."

We'd been sparring every day since I'd had a fight with a nasty vampire named Frost. Adam decided that since I was going to keep getting into trouble, the only thing he could do was try to ensure I could get myself out of it, too. I was still doing karate with my sensei three times a week, and I could feel the difference all the extra practice was making in my fighting ability. Sparring with Adam meant that I could pay attention to fighting without worrying about hurting someone (werewolves are tough). It meant that I could ignore the need to hide what I was behind human-slow movement. Today, it also meant that I could forget that phone call this morning for a little while.

I leaned forward, putting my forehead against his sweat-slicked shoulder. He smelled good: the mint and musk of werewolf, clean sweat, and the blend of scents that was Adam. "No. If I were world-class mean, I'd have told Christy to go find someone else to save her."

His arm came around me. "I don't love her. I never loved her the way I love you. She needed someone to take care of her, and I like taking care of people. That's all we had."

He thought he meant it, but I knew better. I'd seen them together when times had been good. I'd seen the damage that her leaving had done to a man who took care of the people who belonged to him and didn't let go of them easily. But I wasn't going to argue with him.

"I'm not worried about her coming between us," I told him truthfully. "I'm worried about her hurting you and Jesse. Hurting the pack. But that's better than letting her face whatever it is on her own."

He bent down and put his cheek against the top of my head. "You lied," he said. "You aren't mean at all."

"Shh. It's a secret."

He lay back on the mat and pulled me down with him. "I think you need to bribe me to keep your secret," he told me thoughtfully.

"I have a feeling I'm going to be baking a lot of cookies in the near future," I said ruefully. "I could go back on what I said and let you eat one or two."

He hmmed, then shook his head slowly, rolling me a little, so I was on top of him instead of beside him. "That would defeat the purpose, wouldn't it? People wouldn't think you were mean if you fed me cookies."

Jesse was out with friends, and none of the werewolves had ventured back after Adam sent them away.

I sat up, feeling the rise of his breath underneath me, feeling the hard muscles of his abdomen. I wiggled back a little, and he sucked in his breath.

"I don't know if I have anything else to bribe you with," I said seriously.

He growled at me, a real growl. Then he said, "See? World-class mean."

Making love with Adam was sometimes slow, the intensity building until I swore if I felt one thing more, I would burst into sparks and never feel anything again. At those times, I'd come back to myself limp and a little lost, in the best of all ways. Love means leaving yourself vulnerable, knowing that there is someone to catch you when you fall. But when I was already feeling vulnerable, I couldn't have let go like that.

Adam chose to keep it lighter this time, as if he knew how breakable I felt. He was passionate and playful, and I gave as good as I got. I wasn't the only one worried about what Christy's presence would do to us; I wasn't the only one who needed reassurance.

I cried out when his teeth nipped my shoulder, as the hint of pain traveled electrically down my spine, sending me into a climax that left me wrecked in body and whole in spirit. He waited until I was finished before starting again. I watched his face, watching him hold on to his control—and I put paid to that. I nibbled the side of his neck, then wrapped my legs around him, digging into his lower back a little with my heels. He lost himself in me, and it was enough for me to climax again.

And when we lay naked on the mats, the smell of sex and sweat in the air, his hand wrapped tightly around mine: I felt the problem of Christy shrink down to a manageable level.

As long as Adam loved me, I was sure I could deal with the worst Christy could throw at us. I pushed aside the nagging thought that the euphoria of Adam's lovemaking sometimes left me with delusions of invulnerability.

LATE THAT NIGHT, LONG AFTER WE'D GONE TO BED, someone knocked on the front door.

Adam's arm was heavy across the back of my thigh. Somehow, I'd rolled until I was curled up mostly sideways in the bed. Medea, the cat, lay behind my head, answering my question about why I was in such an odd position. She had a way of shoving me off my pillow while we slept, so she could have the high ground.

Someone knocked again, a polite knock-knock.

I groaned and pushed Medea off my pillow, so I could pull it over my head. Adam stayed relaxed and loose as I wiggled. So did the cat. She didn't protest, didn't get up and stalk off. Just kept sleeping where I'd put her.

Knock. Knock.

I stiffened, half lifted myself off the bed, and looked at Adam. Looked at the cat. I shook Adam's shoulder to no effect: something was keeping him asleep. Since it had taken the cat, too, I assumed it was magic.

I am immune to some magic, and maybe that's why it wasn't affecting me, but that persistent knock—

Knock. Knock.

—that was the one, made me think that perhaps my exclusion had been deliberate. Someone wanted to talk to me alone. Or do something to me when I didn't have Adam to back me up.

I rolled off the bed and grabbed my Sig Sauer out of the drawer in the nightstand, dropped the magazine with silver bullets, and replaced it with copper-jacketed hollow points. No werewolf I knew had the magic to keep an Alpha of Adam's caliber sleeping this deeply. That meant fae or witchcraft, and both of them could be killed by a regular bullet. I was pretty sure. Witches I was certain of—as long as it wasn't Elizaveta—but the fae were tricky.

The hollow points would do more damage than silver bullets to any of them, anyway. Silver was too hard to be good ammunition. And armed was better than unarmed when facing an unknown enemy.

I looked in on Jesse on my way to the front door. She was sleeping on her back, her arms wrapped over her head, snoring lightly. Safe enough, for now.

Knock. Knock.

The gun gave me the courage to ghost down the stairs. It was heavy. Like the daily fighting sessions with Adam, carrying the gun had become part of my routine. I wasn't human, not quite, but I was very nearly as helpless. It hadn't mattered much until I took Adam as my mate. In some ways, being part of the pack had made me a lot safer—but it had also made me the weakest link in the pack. The gun helped equalize the difference between me and the werewolves.

It was dark outside, and the narrow glass panel next to the door was opaque anyway. I had no way to tell who was there.

Knock.

"Who are you?" I asked, raising my voice without yelling.

The knocking ceased.

"We do not give our names lightly," said a man's pleasant voice. That he didn't raise his voice told me that he knew enough about me to understand that I could hear better than a regular human. His answer told me what he was, if not who.

The fae were careful with their names, changing the ones they used regularly and concealing the older ones, so that they could not be used against them. Fae magic works best when it knows who it is working upon. However, giving an enemy your name could also be a show of strength—*See how little I am worried about you? I will give you my name, and even with that, you cannot hurt me.*

Thanks to my friend and former employer Zee—iron-kissed, self-proclaimed gremlin, and mechanic extraordinaire—I knew a lot of the fae around the Tri-Cities, but the one at my doorstep was no one whose voice I recognized. Fae were good with glamour: they could change their faces, their voices, even their sizes and shapes. But all the fae were supposed to be on their reservations after having all but declared war upon the US.

"I don't open my door to people whose names I do not know," I told the stranger outside my door.

"Recently, I have been Alistair Beauclaire," he told me.

Beauclaire. I sucked in my breath. I knew who he was, and so did anyone who watched the viral YouTube video someone had filmed. Beauclaire was the fae who killed the man who had kidnapped his daughter with the intention of murdering her as he had so many other half-blood fae (as well as a few werewolves). Beauclaire was the man who had declared the fae independent from the US and all human dominion. He was a Gray Lord, one of the powerful few who ruled all the fae.

But he was more, much more than that, because he'd given up another of his names on that day.

"Gwyn ap Lugh," I said.

I'd looked up Lugh after an encounter with an oakman fae who had tossed Lugh's name about. The results of my research were confusing to say the least. The only thing for certain was that in a history of legendary fae, Lugh stood out like a lantern on a dark night. "Ap Lugh" meant son of Lugh, so at least I wasn't dealing with Lugh himself.

The fae on the other side of the door paused before saying, slowly, "I have gone by that name as well."

"You are a Gray Lord." I tried to keep my voice steady. As Beauclaire, this one had lived a long time in human guise, and he'd been, from all the interviews of his friends, ex-wife, and coworkers, well liked. No sense offending him if I didn't have to, and keeping him on the porch might just do that.

"Yes," he said.

"Would you give your word that you intend me no harm?" Not offending him was important, but so was not being stupid. Though I was pretty sure if he wanted in, a door wasn't going to keep him out.

"I will not hurt you this night," he said readily, and so

unfaelike in his straightforward answer it made me even more suspicious.

"Are you the only one out there?" I asked warily, after examining any possible harm he might be able to do without breaking his word. "And would you promise not to harm anyone in this house tonight?"

"I am the only one here, and for this night, I will ensure no harm comes to those who are within your home."

I engaged the safety on the gun, backed into the kitchen, and put it under a stack of dish towels waiting to be put away. Then I went into the front room and opened the door.

The cold night air, still around freezing this early in the spring, made the long t-shirt I wore, a black Hauptman Security shirt washed to gray, inadequate for keeping me warm. I don't sleep naked: being the wife of the Alpha means unexpected visits in the middle of the night.

I am not shy or particularly body conscious, but Adam is not okay with other men seeing me naked. It makes him shorter-tempered than usual. Adam's t-shirts were exactly the right size to be comfortable, and having me wear his shirts helped him keep his cool around other males.

Beauclaire didn't look below my chin. Politeness or indifference, either one was okay by me.

He smelled like a lake, full of life and greenness with a hint of summer sun even though he stood under the light of the stars and moon with the bare-branched trees that held only a hint of bud. Reddish brown hair, lightly graying at the temples, gave him a normalcy that the still-sleeping werewolf in my bed told me was a lie.

Beauclaire was medium tall but built on graceful lines that didn't quite hide the whipcord muscle beneath. Warren, Adam's third, was built along the same lines.

He didn't look like a sun god, a storm god, or a trickster, as Lugh was variously reputed to be. Beauclaire had been a lawyer before his dramatic YouTube moment, and that was what he looked like now.

Of course, fae could look like whatever they wanted to.

When I stepped back and gestured him into the living room, he moved like a man who knew how to fight—balanced and alert. I believed that more than I believed the lawyer appearance.

He walked into the living room, but he didn't stop there since the main floor of the house has a circular flow. He continued through the dining room and around the corner into the kitchen, where he pulled up a chair with his back to the wall and sat down.

I was fairly sure that his choice was important—the fae place a great deal of emphasis on symbolism. Maybe he picked the kitchen because guests came to the house and sat in the living room. Family and friends sat in the kitchen. If so, maybe he was trying to present himself as a friend—or point out that I didn't have the power to keep him out of the center of my own home. It was too subtle to be certain, so I ignored it altogether. Trying too hard to figure out the meaning in what the fae say or do would send anyone to Straightjacket Land.

"Ms. Hauptman," he said after I sat down opposite him, "It is my understanding that you have one of my father's artifacts. I have come for the walking stick."

2

~~~

"I DON'T HAVE THE WALKING STICK," I TOLD BEAUCLAIRE.

He should know that. I'd told Zee, and, according to his son, he had told some of the other fae to protect me from exactly this scenario.

If he didn't know, was it only because he was not from the nearby Walla Walla fae reservation? Or did that mean that Zee didn't trust him?

"Where is it?" His voice slid silk sweet and dangerous into the room.

If he didn't know, I didn't want to tell him. He wasn't going to like it, and I didn't want to enrage a Gray Lord while he sat at my kitchen table.

"I tried to give it back to the fae," I told him, stalling for time. "I gave it to Uncle Mike and it just came back."

"It is very old," Beauclaire said, and his voice was halfway apologetic. "The fae don't have it, at least none of the fae in the local reservation. Do you know where it is, now?"

He was assuming that I'd given it to the fae again. If it hadn't been for the apology in his voice, I think I might have been happy to . . . not lie, not precisely. Because I didn't know where the walking stick was, I only knew who it was with.

"Not exactly," I told him, then stalled out. Zee had been very clear that the fae would not be amused at where that walking stick had ended up.

"Then what 'exactly' do you know? Whom did you give it to?"

There was a thump from the stairs, and both of us jumped. Beauclaire focused his attention, and I felt his magic send shivers of ice along my arms.

"Hold on," I said. "I'll check." Before the first word had left my mouth, I hopped out of my chair and headed for the stairway. Whoever had made the noise was likely to be someone I cared about, and I didn't want them to get blasted by a Gray Lord.

I turned the corner, and Medea stared up at me from the fourth step from the bottom. "It's okay," I told Beauclaire. I picked her up, and, true to form, the cat went limp and started purring.

"What was it?" he said.

"I know it's a horror-film cliché," I said as I walked back into the kitchen. "But, really, it's just the cat. I thought you put her to sleep like everyone else?"

Beauclaire frowned at my cat, the magic in the air dissipating gradually. I sat down, and the cat consented to continue to be petted.

"Cats are tricky," he told me. "Rather like you, they tend to shed enchantments. I didn't expect to find one in a house full of werewolves, and magic on the fly, delicate magic, is not my specialty."

He looked at me, and there was a threat in his voice when he said, "Hurricanes, tidal waves, drowned cities—those are easier."

"Don't feel too bad about it," I told him, my voice conciliatory. His brows lowered, and I continued in a bland tone, "No one else has heard of a cat who likes werewolves, either."

Medea—maybe because dangerous men with threatening voices, in her experience, were the people most apt to drop whatever they were doing and cuddle her—decided that Beauclaire was fair game. She oozed from my lap to the tabletop and began a very-slow-motion creep across the table toward him.

"We were talking about the walking stick?" he said, raising an eyebrow. I couldn't tell if the eyebrow was at me or at my cat—watching Medea do her slo-mo cat stalk can be disconcerting.

"An oakman used the walking stick to kill a vampire," I told him. It was either the beginning of the story or a diversion, I wasn't certain myself.

I reached up and wrapped a hand around one of Adam's dog tags, which hung from my necklace along with my wedding ring and a lamb. If I was going to keep Beauclaire from destroying me and my all-too-vulnerable family in a fit of pique, he'd have to understand—as much as I did—what had happened to the walking stick.

Medea made it all the way across the table and hunkered down in front of Beauclaire. She focused on him and moaned. I'd never heard another cat do it.

"The oakman told me afterward"—I raised my voice a little so it would carry over Medea—"that Lugh never made anything that couldn't be used as a weapon." I frowned. "No, that wasn't quite what he said. It was something along the lines of 'never made anything that couldn't become a spear when needed.'"

Medea upped the volume on her yowl, then turned into Halloween kitty; every hair on her body stood at attention, and if she'd had a tail, I was sure it would have been pointed straight in the air.

Medea, who dealt with werewolves on a daily basis, was pretty much immune to fear. She even liked vampires. And she had no trouble with Zee or Tad.

Beauclaire ducked his head until he was face-to-face with Medea. He dropped his glamour just a bit, and I caught a glimpse of something beautiful and deadly, something with green eyes and a long tongue as he hissed at the cat. She all but levitated off the table and disappeared around the corner of the kitchen and up the stairs.

I felt my lip curl in an involuntary snarl. "Overkill," I told him.

He relaxed in his seat. "So the walking stick is with an oakman now?"

I shook my head. "No. It came back after that. But last summer . . . the otterkin . . ."

"I've heard about you and the death of the last of the otterkin." He shrugged. "They always were bloodthirsty and stupid. They are no loss—" He paused, looked thoughtfully at me, and said, "You killed them with the walking stick?"

"It was what I had." I tried not to sound defensive. "And I only killed one with it." Adam had taken care of the rest, but I wasn't going to tell him that. "There was something wrong with the walking stick when the otterkin died." Something hungry.

"Something wrong," he repeated, thoughtfully. Then he shook his head. "No. It is only the great weapons that are quenched when they are first made, usually in the blood of someone worthy, someone whose traits will make the sword more dangerous. The walking stick was finished long ago."

I wondered if I should mention that Uncle Mike had thought that I'd "quenched" the walking stick. Maybe I should tell him that the otterkin wasn't the only thing the walking stick had killed that day. Maybe I should tell him that I was pretty sure the walking stick had killed that otterkin mostly on its own.

But before I had a chance to speak, Beauclaire continued, "The blade you know as Excalibur was born when her blade was drowned in the death of my father." He paused, showed his teeth in a not-smile. "I understand that you might be acquainted with the maker of that blade."

I quit worrying about the walking stick for a moment.

Jumping Jehoshaphat. O Holy Night.

Siebold Adelbertsmiter had made blades once upon a time. He'd been the owner of a VW repair shop when I met him. He'd hired me, then sold me the shop when the Gray Lords decided that it was time that he admit he was fae—decades after the fae had come out to the public. I knew him as a grumpy old curmudgeon with a secret marshmallow heart, but once he'd been something quite different: the Dark Smith of Drontheim. He wasn't one of the good guys in the fairy tales that mentioned him.

Part of me, still properly afraid of Beauclaire, worried that his grudge against Zee might be turned toward me. Part of me was horrified that my friend Zee had killed Lugh, the hero of hundreds, if not thousands, of stories. But the biggest part of me was still stuck on marveling that Zee, my grumpy mentor Zee, had forged *Excalibur.*

After a moment, I started processing the information in more practical paths. That story was the answer to why Beauclaire didn't know what I'd done with the walking stick.

If Zee had killed Lugh, Lugh's son wouldn't be exchanging

kind words with him or anyone who associated with him. No one holds grudges like the fae.

"But we are not speaking of one of the great weapons," Beauclaire said, temper cooling as he pulled away from an old source of anger. "So tales of the walking stick's being used to kill a vampire or otterkin are not germane. The walking stick is a very minor artifact, for all that Lugh made it, nor is it useful for important things."

"Unless I decided to raise sheep," I said, because his disparagement of the walking stick, to my surprise, stung a bit. It had been old and beautiful—and loyal to me as any sheepdog to its shepherd. If it had become tainted, that was my fault because it had been my decision to use it to kill monsters. "Then all my sheep would have twins. Might not be important to you or the fae, but it would certainly have made an impact on a shepherd's bottom line."

He looked at me the way my mother sometimes did. But he wasn't my parent, and he had invaded my house, so I didn't cringe. I narrowed my gaze on him and finished the point I'd been making, "If I were a sheep farmer, I would have found it to be powerful magic."

"It is an artifact my father made," said Beauclaire who was also ap Lugh, Lugh's son. "I value the walking stick, do not mistake me. But it is not powerful; nor is its magic anything that would interest most mortals or fae. For that reason, it was left with you longer than it should have been."

"Point of fact," I said, holding up a finger. "It was left with me because whenever I gave it back, or one of the fae tried to claim it, it returned to me."

Beauclaire leaned forward, and said, "So how is it that you do not have the walking stick now?"

"Is it the Gray Lord or ap Lugh who wants to know?" I asked.

He sat back. "It matters?"

I didn't say anything.

"The Gray Lord is too busy with other matters to chase after a walking stick that encourages sheep to produce twins. No matter how old or cherished that artifact is," said Beauclaire after a moment. He gave me a small smile that did not warm his eyes. "Even so, had I known where it was before this, I would have been here sooner to collect it."

Which was an answer, wasn't it?

"The Gray Lord would have gotten the short answer," I told him. "Much good as it would have done him."

That mobile eyebrow arched up with Nimoy-like quickness.

"Or me," I continued. "Because the Gray Lord is not going to be happy in any case." The son of Lugh might understand why I had done what I had done because he would understand that the need to fix what I had broken was more important than that the walking stick was a lot more powerful than it had been. The Gray Lord would only be interested in the power.

He didn't say anything, and I drew in a breath.

"The walking stick killed one of the otterkin," I told him. "But saying *I* killed the otterkin with it would be stretching the truth. I did use it to defend myself when the otterkin swung a sword at me. His *magical* bronze sword broke against the walking stick, minor artifact that it is." He almost smiled at the bite in my tone, but lost all expression when I continued. "And then the silver butt of the walking stick sharpened itself into a blade, a spearhead, and killed the otterkin." In case he didn't understand, I said, "On its own. Without its intervention, I would not have survived."

The long fingers on Beauclaire's left hand drew imaginary things on the tabletop as he thought. I worried that it might be magic of some kind, but he'd promised no harm, and I could have sensed magic if he were using it.

Finally, he spoke. "My father's artifacts acquire some semblance of self-awareness as they age. But not to alter, so fundamentally, their purpose. The walking stick was a thing of life, not death."

"Maybe the walking stick is the first, or even the only one. I am not lying to you." My voice was tight. Maybe I shouldn't be telling him all of this. But he scared me, this Gray Lord who wore a lawyer's suit and seemed so cool and calm. I was under no illusions about the civility promised by the oh-so-expensive suit—the fae were masters at donning the trappings of civilization to hide the predator inside. I needed him to understand why I'd given the walking stick away, or there was a very real chance he'd kill me.

"Maybe not," he conceded after too long a pause. "But there are many kinds of lies."

"Before the otterkin died, we fought the river devil, a primordial creature that came to destroy the world. Most of the work was done by others. It was a hard fight, and we almost lost. Those who fought to kill it, all of them, except for me, died." For some creatures, death was less permanent than for others, but that didn't mean they hadn't died. "I had lost my last weapon. I was desperate, everyone was dead or dying. The walking stick came to my hand, and I killed the river devil with it."

Beauclaire didn't say anything, but his attention was so focused it felt electric on my skin. "You think it was quenched in the blood of this 'river devil.'" He sneered on the last two words.

"'River devil' was the name given to it by other people, so don't blame me for it," I told him. "But yes. Because after the river devil died, the walking stick changed. It killed the otterkin and . . . it was aware."

Beauclaire just watched me, and his eyes reminded me of Medea's when she crouched outside a mousehole. Waiting.

"I'd broken it," I admitted frankly. "And I didn't know what to do about it."

"You gave it to Siebold Adelbertsmiter," Beauclaire said, his voice cool, his body ready to rend, and his eyes hungry.

"It wouldn't let him take it when it first came to me," I told him. "It wouldn't have gone with him, so I didn't even try."

"Uncle Mike?" That would have bothered him less.

"No. Not Uncle Mike, either. I told you it wouldn't go with him. What do you know about Native American guesting laws?"

He looked at me for a moment. "Why don't you explain them to me?"

So I explained how I'd given Lugh's walking stick to Coyote.

Lugh's son looked at me in patent disbelief. "You gave it to *Coyote*? Because he was your guest, and he admired it."

"That's right," I agreed.

He shook his head and muttered something in a language that sounded like Welsh, but wasn't, because I speak a few words of Welsh. There are more British Isles languages than just Welsh, Irish, Scots, and English—Manx, Cornish, and a host of extinct variants. I have no idea what language Beauclaire spoke.

When he was finished, he looked at me, and asked, "Can you retrieve it?"

"I can try." I smiled grimly. "I have a better chance of retrieving it from him than you do."

He stood up. "I swore that I would not go from here empty-handed, and it is not in me to go back on my oath. So I will take from here your word that you will retrieve the walking stick and return it to me within one week's time."

"As much as I'd love to agree," I told him, "I cannot. Coyote is beyond my ability to control. I will look for him and ask when I find him. That I will swear to."

"One week's time." He met my eyes, and what I saw in his gaze made me cold to the bone as I remembered that he'd spoken of tidal waves and drowned cities. "If not, we will have another talk with a less cordial ending."

He walked out of the kitchen the same way he'd come in; I took the shorter path, near the stairs, and watched as he left. The front door shut behind him with a gentle click.

A car started up. I couldn't pick out the engine, though it had a low, throaty purr that sounded like something expensive. Nothing I'd worked on very much. He didn't rev it up, just drove it like a family sedan out of the driveway and down the road.

The sound of Beauclaire's engine was blending into the distant sounds of the night when I felt a tickling sensation, like someone had pulled mosquito netting off my skin. There was a half-second pause, then Adam, naked and enraged, was at the bottom of the stairs beside me. He looked at me. It was only a momentary look, but the intensity of it told me he saw that I was unharmed and not particularly alarmed. Then he was out the front door.

By the time I retrieved the gun from under the kitchen towels and checked the safety, Adam was back.

"Fae," he said, sounding calmer than he looked. "No one I've smelled before. Who was it, and what did they want with you?"

"Gray Lord," I told him because he needed to know that it had taken a Power to enspell him and successfully invade our home. "It was Beauclaire—you know, the guy who initiated the fae's retreat to the reservations. He came looking for the walking stick. Have you seen Medea? He scared the holy spit out of her."

Adam frowned. "I thought Zee knew about the walking stick. And nothing scares that cat."

"Apparently she's good with coyotes, vampires, witches, werewolves, and all the fae who've come around before, but Gray Lords are an entirely different proposition." I started up the stairs. I had to get up in a couple of hours and go to work. Tomorrow, Christy was going to be here. It looked to be a long day, and I wanted to face it with at least the better part of a full night's sleep. And first I needed to find the cat and make sure she was okay.

"Mercy," Adam said patiently as he followed me. "Why didn't Beauclaire know that you'd given the stick to Coyote?"

"As best I can put together," I told him, "Zee didn't pass it around widely, and Beauclaire and he are not speaking because Zee killed Beauclaire's father Lugh in order to quench Excalibur."

Adam's footfalls had been steady behind me, but at that last they paused. He started up again, and said, "Dealing with the fae is always full of surprises."

His hand came to rest on my back, then slid lower as he took advantage of being two steps below me and nipped at my hip. "So," he said gruffly, "what did Lugh's son say when you told him that you gave his walking stick to Coyote?"

"That I have a week to get it back."

Adam's hand curved around my hip and pulled me to a stop at the top of the stairs.

"Or?" His voice was a growl that slid over my skin and warmed me from the outside in.

"We have another talk," I told him, doing my best to make it sound a lot less threatening than Beauclaire had. I didn't want my husband out hunting Gray Lords because someone had threatened his family. "It won't come to that. I'll find out how to contact Coyote. I'll call Hank in the morning." Hank was another walker like me, though his second form was a hawk. He lived an hour and a half from the Tri-Cities and was my information source for most of what I knew about being a walker. "If he doesn't know, he should be able to hook me up with Gordon Seeker. Gordon will know." Gordon Seeker was Thunderbird, the way Coyote was Coyote. He liked to travel around in the guise of an old Indian with a thing for the gaudiest version of cowboy wear I'd ever seen.

Adam put his forehead against my shoulder. "No trouble you can't handle, then."

"I'm more worried about Christy," I told him, and it was almost true.

He laughed without joy and pulled me tighter against him. "Me, too." He whispered, "Don't believe everything she says, okay? Don't leave without talking to me."

I turned around, and said fiercely, "Never. Not even if I talk to you first. You aren't getting away now, buster."

He dove for my mouth, and when he was finished ensuring that neither of us was going to get much sleep for a while, he said, "Remember that. We're both likely to be clinging to that thought by the time this is over."

I COAXED THE BOLT OUT WITH SWEET WORDS AND steady, light hands.

I had already done all that I could this morning to find Coyote short of shouting his name into the open air—which I would have if I thought it would do any good. All I could do now was wait

32

for the phone. Not that the fae was the only thing I worried about, or even the thing I was most worried about. Adam was, just about now, picking Christy up from the airport.

Mechanicking took my full concentration, letting my worries about the fae and Adam's ex-wife fade in the face of a problem I could actually do something about.

The Beetle had been worked on by amateurs for decades, and the bolt that was turning so reluctantly was a victim of years of abuse. Her edges were more suggestions than actual corners, making getting her out of the '59 Beetle a little tricky. So far I hadn't had to resort to the Easy Out, and I was starting to get optimistic about my chances of success.

Someone cleared their throat tentatively and scared the bejeebers out of me—though I managed not to jump. He was standing behind me—a strange man, who was also a strange werewolf, my nose told me belatedly. Thankfully, he'd stayed back, waiting just outside the open garage-bay door.

Tad was twenty feet away in the office—*and* the stranger was probably only a customer who'd come around to the open garage bays instead of to the office. It happened all the time. I was perfectly safe. Reason didn't have much effect on my spiking heartbeat and the shaft of terror that was my body's reaction to being startled by a strange man in my garage.

I'd been assaulted a while ago. Just when I thought I was over it, some stupid little thing would bring it back.

I nodded stiffly at him, then visibly focused on the job ahead, no matter where my panicky attention really was. I kept talking to the bolt, finding the soothing tones surprisingly useful even if they were my own. I fought to regain control by the time the bolt came out. Every twist, I told myself, meant I had to calm a little more. To my relief, the silly exercise worked—six twists of the wrench, and I was no longer on the verge of shaking, tears, and (more rare, but what it lacked in frequency it made up for in humiliation) throwing up on a perfect stranger.

I set the wrench down and turned with a smile to face him. He had stayed right where he had been—at a polite and safe distance. He didn't look directly at me, either—he was a werewolf, he'd know that I had panicked, but he'd allowed me to save face. Points to him for courtesy.

He was neither tall nor short for a man and carried himself pulled tightly toward his core. Arms in, shoulders in, head tipped down. His hair was curly and pulled back in a short ponytail. He looked as though he could use a good meal and a pat on the head.

"I'm looking for a place to be," he said. He had a backpack slung over one shoulder that looked as old as the Beetle I was repairing. Maybe it was.

Several years ago, another werewolf had approached me at the garage, looking for a place to be. He was dead.

I nodded at this new wolf, to show him that I heard him and that I was not rejecting his almost request. But between panic attack and memory, words were beyond me at the moment.

"I called the home number of the local Alpha." He'd given me time to talk and sounded a little stressed when he had to break the silence. "The girl that answered sent me here when I told her I didn't have easy means of transport out that far. The city bus got me over here." He glanced over his shoulder as if he'd rather have been anywhere else. It dawned on me that the reason he wasn't looking me in the face had more to do with him than with my almost-panic attack. "I drift, you know? Don't like to stay anywhere long. I'm bottom of the pack, so that means I don't cause no trouble."

His American accent was Pacific Northwest, but there was something about the rhythm of his words that made me think that English was not his native tongue, though he was comfortable in it. "Bottom of the pack," like his averted eyes, meant submissive wolf: they tended to live longer than other werewolves because they weren't so likely to end up on the losing end of a fight to the death. Submissive wolves also got to travel because no Alpha would turn down a submissive wolf—there weren't many of them, and they tended to help a pack function more smoothly.

Honey's mate, Peter, who had been killed a few months ago, had been our only submissive after Able Tankersley left. A wolf I'd only been barely acquainted with, Able had taken a job offer in San Francisco. It was not only the violence of Peter's death but his absence that was affecting the pack. A new submissive wolf would be welcome.

"Bran send you to us?" I asked.

"Hell no," he said, with emphasis. "Though he gave me a list of numbers when I told him I was drifting this way. Neither of us knew I would end up here at the time." He looked out the garage door, again, at the bare beginnings of spring. "Don't think I'll stay here long, though. Hope you don't take it amiss. I don't generally stay where it's hot, and I heard tell at the bus depot that this place gets scorching in the summer."

"That's fine. Do you need a place to stay?"

He gave my garage a dubious look, and I laughed. "I don't know how much you know. I'm Mercy Hauptman, and my husband's the Alpha here. We have extra bedrooms at home—that are open to pack members who need them." Maybe with another visitor, the effects of Christy's stay would be diluted.

"I'm Zack Drummond, Ms. Hauptman. I'd be grateful for a room tonight, but after that, I'd rather find my own place."

"All right," I said. "I'm headed out there at five thirty"—usually it was closer to six thirty, but *usually* my husband's ex wouldn't have been running around in my territory that used to be hers—"if you want to catch a ride. I can't officially welcome you to the pack, that's my husband's job, but we don't have a submissive in our pack, and we could use one."

"If I can't find another way out," he said, "I'll be here at five fifteen."

He hesitated, started to say something, then hesitated again.

"What is it?" I asked.

"What *are* you?" he said. "You aren't fae or werewolf."

"I'm a shifter—Native American style," I told him. "Better known as a walker. I change into a coyote."

His eyes widened and, finally, rose to examine every inch of me. "I've heard of your kind," he said finally. "Always thought they were a myth."

I smiled at him and gave him a salute. "A few years ago, and that would have been the pot calling the kettle black, Mr. Drummond."

ZACK DRUMMOND DIDN'T SHOW UP AT FIVE FIFTEEN. Five thirty saw me fretting because the Beetle wasn't done, and I'd promised it would be finished at eight the next morning.

"Go home, Mercy," said Tad, who was on his back working on the undercarriage of the Beetle. "Another hour, and I'll have it buttoned up and done."

"If I stayed, it would shave fifteen minutes off," I told him.

One of his booted feet waggled at me. "Go home. Don't let that bitch steal your man without a fight."

"You don't even know her."

He slid back out from under the car, his face more oil-colored than not. Ears sticking out a little, his face just this side of homely—by his choice. His father was Siebold Adelbertsmiter. Tad's mother had been human, but his father's blood had gifted him with glamour and, from things he'd said, a fair bit of power.

"I know you," he told me. "I'm betting on you. Go home, Mercy. I'll get it done."

He'd been working in this shop when he was just a kid. He might be thirteen years younger than me, but he was at least as good a mechanic.

"Okay," I said.

In the oversized bathroom, I stripped out of my overalls and scrubbed up. The harsh soaps that cut through the grease and dirt have never bothered my skin—which is good because I use them a lot. Not even industrial soap could get out all the ingrained dirt I had on my hands, but my skin tones hid most of that.

A glance in the mirror had me unbraiding my hair. I ran a comb through it—braiding it when it was wet gave it a curl it didn't have normally. Nothing was going to turn me into a girly girl, but the curls softened my appearance a little.

I was almost out the door, and Tad was back under the Beetle, when he said, "When Adam's ex drives you into making sweet things with chocolate, just remember I like my brownies with lots of frosting but no nuts."

―――――――

I OPENED THE FRONT DOOR TO THE SMELL OF BACON and the sound of sizzling meat.

Adam, Jesse, and I shared kitchen duties, taking turns making dinner. Tonight was supposed to be Jesse's night, but I wasn't surprised that the only person in the kitchen was Christy. Her back was to me as she cooked in the kitchen she'd designed.

She'd been angry, her daughter had told me, that Adam had insisted on moving all the way out to Finley instead of building in one of the more prestigious neighborhoods in West Richland or Kennewick. He'd given her free rein in the house to make up for the fact that he'd wanted the house next to my trailer because Bran, who ruled all the weres in this part of the world, had told him to keep an eye on me. In addition to ruling hundreds and maybe thousands of werewolves, Bran had been the Alpha of the pack my foster father, Bryan, had belonged to. That had occasionally left Bran with delusions that he had a right to interfere with my life long after I'd left Montana and his pack behind.

Christy was shorter than me by a couple of inches, about the same size as Jesse. The body in the blouse and peasant skirt was softly curved, but not fat. Her hair, brown when I'd last seen her, was now blond-streaked and French-braided in a thick rope that hung to her hips.

"Could you find some paper towels, Jesse?" she asked without turning around. "They've been moved, and I have bacon ready to come out of the frying pan."

I opened the cabinet that held the paper towels exactly where she probably had put them on the day she first moved in. I hadn't changed the organization of the kitchen. Too many people were already using it, so it made more sense for me to learn where everything was than for me to reorganize it to my tastes.

So Christy's kitchen was exactly as she'd left it—still hers in spirit if not in truth. Her presence in my kitchen felt like an invasion in a fashion that the Gray Lord who'd been here in the wee hours of the night had not, despite his intentions.

Christy knew I wasn't Jesse, I could smell her tension—which was sort of cheating, so I didn't call her on it. Also, accusing her of lying right off the bat didn't seem like a good way to make peace with her.

"Paper towels," I said as peaceably as I could manage, setting them down on the counter beside the stove.

She turned to look at me, and I saw her face.

"Holy Hannah," I said before she could say anything, distracted entirely from my territorial irritation. "Tell me you shot him or hit him with a two-by-four." She didn't just have a shiner. Half her face was black with that greenish brown around the edges that told you it hadn't happened in the last twenty-four hours.

She gave me a half smile, probably the half that didn't hurt. "Would a frying pan be okay? Not as effective as a baseball bat, but it was hot."

"I would accept a frying pan," I agreed. "This"—I indicated the side of my face that corresponded to her damaged cheek with my fingers—"from the guy you're running from?"

"It wasn't my aunt Sally," she said tartly.

"You go to a doctor with that?" I asked.

She nodded. "Adam made me go. The doctor said it would heal okay. He gave me a prescription for pain meds, but I don't like to take prescriptions. Maybe tonight if I can't sleep."

The front door opened, and I didn't have to back out of the kitchen to see who it was; Adam had a presence I could feel from anywhere in the house.

"Hey, honey," said Christy. "I've got BLTs going on the stove. They'll be done in about ten minutes if you want to go upstairs and get cleaned up." She glanced at me, and said, "Oops. Sorry, just habit."

"No worries," I said pleasantly, as if she hadn't bothered me at all when she'd called my husband by an endearment—then could have shot myself because I saw the satisfaction in her face. My reaction had been too controlled to be real, and she'd caught it.

"Maybe you could set the table?" she asked lightly.

As if it was still her kitchen, her house to rule.

"I need to get out of these clothes," I said. "You should ask Jesse to set the table since you took over her job tonight. We might have one more for dinner—a new wolf in town."

I left before she could reply and rounded the corner for the stairs to see Adam. He walked with me up the stairs.

"Any luck hunting down the guy who hit her?" I asked, stripping off my clothes once we were in our bedroom. Even though my overalls absorbed most of the mess of mechanicking, the clothes I wore under them reeked of oil and sweat.

"No. It's not that we can't find people named Juan Flores, it's that there are too many Juan Floreses," he told me. "John Smith would be easier, though it helps that he doesn't look like most Juan Floreses. He's around six feet tall with blond hair; she said his English was good. He has an accent, but she doesn't think it was Mexican or Spanish, despite his name."

"She met him in Eugene?"

He shook his head. "Reno. She was out partying with some friends. He was a friend of a friend. Rich—with cash—not just credit cards. He talked about Europe like he was very familiar with it, but he didn't tell her if he was living there or if he just traveled there a lot."

"Cash means real money," I said. "Not just someone pretending to be wealthy."

"Probably," Adam agreed.

"Did she call the police when he hit her?"

"She called them before he broke into her apartment and started hitting her. He left when he heard the sirens, though it might have been the frying pan she hit him with." There was admiration in his voice, and I did my best not to flinch. Of course he was proud of her. It takes guts to fight back effectively after a hard hit to the head. "The police didn't have any better luck than I'm having running the name he gave her."

Adam stripped off his tie and unbuttoned the cuffs of his dress shirt impatiently. "Later that night, someone mugged the man she went out with after she returned to Eugene. Broke his neck and took off with his wallet. She's sure it was Flores, that stealing his wallet was just a cover. The police are undecided but told her that she might find somewhere else to be while they ran down leads."

"If her boyfriend is responsible, he kills pretty competently," I said, pulling on clean jeans, which were in a drawer with a stack of other clean jeans.

I'd gotten used to keeping my clean clothes folded in drawers and dirty clothes in a hamper in the closet. Adam had gotten used to calling me when he was going to be late from work. I had learned that it was those things, compromise in the form of phone calls and folded clothes, that cemented the bedrock of a relationship. I wondered what habits Adam and Christy had left over from their marriage.

"I thought so, too," Adam said, unaware of the twist of my thoughts. "My sources say that the kill was clean. Not so clean it couldn't have been an accident—but unusual in a mugging, especially in Eugene, which isn't exactly a hotbed of that kind of crime. So maybe he spent some time in the military."

"Or as an assassin or crime lord," I said.

Adam snorted as he pulled on a faded green t-shirt that said I HEART COYOTES. Yet another sign that folding my clean clothes wasn't too big a price to pay to make him happy. He didn't have any I HEART CHRISTY shirts—or I would have burned them already. "You have an overactive imagination."

"Says the werewolf," I told him. Instead of my usual after-work t-shirt, I changed into a fitted shirt in a shade of lavender that looked good against my skin and showed off the muscles on my arms. Christy wouldn't know that it was any different from what I usually wore. I didn't have her soft curves, so I'd emphasize what I did have.

"You got my text about Zack Drummond, right?" The lavender contrasted nicely with my brown eyes. Maybe I should put on eye shadow? "Seems like a nice guy. Thought walkers like me were a myth."

Adam grinned at me. "I think you're pretty special, too."

I kissed his cheek and rested in his arms for a moment before I broke away to find socks and shoes. No eye shadow. Christy wouldn't know I didn't wear makeup unless we were going out, but everyone else would. I usually went barefoot in the house, too, but with Christy in the kitchen, bare feet felt too vulnerable.

"Warren's coming over tonight to grill Christy about her stalker and see if he can learn anything useful."

"Good," I said. "Cool."

Warren had been working as a private detective for a while. He was smart about people, and he'd gotten good at finding secrets. But that wasn't why I was pleased. Warren was my friend, and Christy didn't like him. That left dinner tonight stacked in my favor—not that I *really* thought I needed the advantage.

WE WENT DOWNSTAIRS JUST AS A KNOCK SOUNDED ON
the door.

Christy dodged past us, and said over her shoulder, "I invited
Mary Jo to join us for dinner."

I decided that I was going to have to get rid of the chip on my
shoulder, or the next week or so was going to be unbearable.
Christy cooked dinner. She was welcome to invite anyone to dinner, especially one of the wolves who had a standing invitation to
the Alpha's table at any time anyway. Mary Jo was Christy's
friend.

Christy was acting as though my house were still hers. It wasn't.
But as long as she kept her actions to those acceptable in any guest,
there wasn't a lot I could do to fix it without appearing to be jealous, insecure, and petty. So I'd swallow my first reactions and
deal, until it was time to set her straight.

When Christy answered the door and let her in, Mary Jo
hummed in sympathy at the nasty bruise.

"You need to have that looked at."

"Nothing broken," Christy told her. "Just bruised, and it will
fade in time. Adam made me go to a doctor. A good thing, too,
because Mercy was about to take me to the doctor herself."

An exaggeration. Maybe.

Mary Jo apparently thought so, too, because she gave me a
cool look. "It looks like it hurts."

Christy touched her cheek, then shook her head. "It could have
been worse. A man I dated a couple of times turned up dead, and
I'm pretty sure Juan is responsible."

"Ahh jeez," Mary Jo said. "I'm so sorry."

Warren came in. He didn't knock and thus avoided the chance that Christy would answer the door again so she could make everyone think either that I was using her to do all the menial tasks or make me think she was trying to reclaim her home. Or both at once.

Probably she was just doing normal things, and I was being paranoid and jealous.

Yes, I was going to have to work on my attitude. Adam kissed the top of my head.

"Let's all move to the dining room," Christy said. "I put dinner out there. Is your new wolf coming, Mercy? If we wait much longer, dinner might get cold."

I shook my head. "I don't know. Maybe something came up."

"Let's eat without him, then," she said. "If he comes later, he can have leftovers if there are any, or I can make him a sandwich."

There was room at the kitchen table to eat there, but the dining-room table had been set with a tablecloth and good china and all. I wondered if Jesse had set it, or if Christy had done so while Adam and I were up changing. The only time I used the dining-room table was on Sunday breakfasts or holidays when everyone didn't fit in the kitchen.

I sat down on Adam's right, and Christy took the seat to his left before Jesse could sit in it. Jesse smiled apologetically at me and took the next seat over.

"All right, everyone," Christy said as soon as everyone was seated. "Dig in."

The sandwiches were all cut into triangles and set on a plate in the center of the table, a gloriously beautiful presentation with bacon cooked exactly right, red tomatoes, and bright crispy lettuce on golden toast. A huge, cut-glass bowl held a salad and sat next to a plate with homemade croutons.

Cloth napkins were folded just so, and there was a vase with the first of the spring lilies from the front flower bed. The whole table looked as though Martha Stewart and Gordon Ramsay had both come to my home to prepare a casual meal for a few friends.

Mary Jo took a bite of the sandwich and all but purred. "I haven't had a BLT this good since that picnic you had out here that Fourth of July, do you remember? You made BLTs and carrot cake. I have missed this."

That started a conversation about the better old days that eventually spread to include Adam and even Warren. Jesse met my eyes and grimaced in sympathy.

I didn't know if Christy was taking over my home on purpose or by accident, but I had my suspicions. I knew what I would do if someone else had Adam. I might use my fangs or a gun instead of a BLT dinner, but Christy's weapons were different from mine. I did know that the only way to take control back was to be a witch—and that was just another way of losing.

"Do you like your sandwich?" Christy asked me as the good-old-days talk started to wind down.

"It is very good," I said. "Thank you for making dinner."

Mary Jo gave me a look. "I'd have thought that just having flown in and being hurt, someone else could have cooked tonight, Christy."

"That was my job," said Jesse. "But Mom said—"

"I told her that I wanted to make her favorite dinner because I don't get much chance to see her." Christy looked up, her blue eyes—Jesse's eyes—swam with tears that she bravely held back. "I know that's my fault. I'm not a good mother."

She wasn't lying. She believed everything that she said. I had to give her credit for accepting the responsibility for what she'd put Jesse through—but the thing was, she was looking at Adam when she said it. Then she looked around the table. She didn't look at Jesse. This wasn't an apology; it was a play for sympathy. I wasn't the only one who noticed.

Jesse put her fork down, carefully. "Thank you for dinner, Mom. It was good. I just am not feeling well tonight. I'm going to head up and do some homework."

She picked up her plate and carried it into the kitchen and left us in silence. If I said anything, I worried she'd make Jesse's leaving or her bad parenting my fault, so I kept my mouth shut. I don't know why no one else said anything.

"You see?" said Christy huskily as soon as Jesse was out of human earshot. "I don't know why I said that, I knew it would upset her. She doesn't want to hurt my feelings—but she can't lie, either."

I'd lived through Christy's drama for a while now—*Sorry, Jesse, I know I was supposed to pick you up or you were supposed to fly down, but it just isn't convenient right now* with reasons that varied from new boyfriends to trips to Rio. Work trips, really. I knew that she was good at manipulating people, and still the expression on her bruised face made me feel bad for her.

"It's all right," Mary Jo told her. "You'll have time now to fix things between you."

And abruptly all my sympathy died away, washed away by dismay. Just how long *was* Christy planning to stay?

"I don't know," Christy murmured sadly, her fork playing with the remnants of her salad. "I'd like to think so."

Adam patted her on the shoulder.

I ate with steady determination that was not helped at all by the fact that the food was good. I could cook anything that went into the oven as long as it had sugar and chocolate in it. Beyond that, I was a pretty indifferent cook. Adam was a lot better than I, but his ex-wife was practically a gourmet chef. She'd made the mayonnaise on the BLTs from scratch.

"So," Warren said, putting his silverware on his empty plate. "If you are through eating, I've got some questions about this ex-boyfriend of yours."

"She's hurt and tired," said Mary Jo. "Can't questions wait until she's had a chance to recover?"

"No," said Adam. "We need to deal with him, so Christy can go back to Eugene and get on with her life."

Christy turned her wet blue eyes on my husband, and said, "I've been thinking of moving back home."

The food I had just swallowed went down wrong and sent me off in a paroxysm of coughing.

3

"WELL, NOW," SAID WARREN OVER THE TOP OF MY coughing, Texas thick in his voice. "I don't know 'bout all that, Miss Christy. Where you live is up to you. But the sooner we get rid of the man who is scaring you, the safer you are going to be. So I'm going to ask you to tell me how you met him and everything you can remember about him."

Christy's eyes got bigger at the solid authority in his voice, and she looked as though she were sixteen instead of the over forty I was sure of. "Okay," she said.

He reached behind him and grabbed the notebook he'd tossed on the floor when we'd sat down, and said, "Let's start with the first meeting. When and where?"

"A couple of months ago—early February, I can check for the exact date. My girlfriends and I were out gambling, a weekend in Reno. We'd gone to a show and were finishing up the night with dinner in one of the casinos. There were a lot of people around, and since we do this once a month, there were even a lot of people we knew." She played with her plate. "This man came up to our table. He was beautiful—younger than me, in a suit that . . . You know that blue-gray suit you had that was so expensive?"

Adam nodded, and I found that I was jealous of her memory of seeing him in a suit, even though he wore suits a lot. But I'd never seen him in the blue-gray suit that she was talking about.

She kept her eyes on my husband as she continued. "It reminded me of that, not in color, but in the way it was shaped. He looked . . . expensive, but not in a 'kept man' or 'I'm going to impress you' kind of way. His eyes were bright, and he ignored the others, just looked at me. Tall, golden hair, swarthy skin—not the warm tones you usually see with South American Hispanics. More like Mediterranean dark. He was big."

"How big?"

She looked at Warren. "Taller than you. Heavier—but all muscle. Like a bodybuilder." Her eyes strayed to Adam. "He must spend a lot of time in the gym because the only other man I've seen quite that muscular is Adam. And when he looked at me, he *saw* me. Intense."

She looked down and pulled her hands away from her plate. "It was intoxicating, flattering—to be the focus of such power— especially at my age." She smiled tightly, glanced at me, then away. "I'm not eighteen anymore, and he didn't look a lot older than that." She'd met Adam when she was eighteen. He'd been older than that, a werewolf already. "He introduced himself, Juan Flores, though he didn't have a Spanish or Mexican accent."

"What kind of accent did he have?" asked Warren.

She jerked her attention back to him. "European. Not French, Italian, or German. I didn't know it."

"That's not a crime," said Mary Jo, because Christy had sounded like she thought that she ought to have known.

"Maybe it was a fake accent," said Christy. "I've spent time in Europe, and I just couldn't pinpoint it. He had a little British crisp in his English, like he'd learned it in Great Britain. I thought that was why I couldn't pick it out. I didn't even ask before I hopped into bed with him. I am so stupid."

"Don't blame the victim," I told her with, I admit, a little of the irritation I was feeling. "Not your fault you didn't recognize his accent. Not your fault he singled you out."

"Adam told me that some of your friends knew him. That's why you felt safe with him," Warren said.

She nodded. "He'd done some business with Jacqui, one of my friends. She's a financial officer at Nation First Bank, works their corporate and international accounts."

"Her phone number?"

She blinked and rattled it off. At Warren's urging, she also managed a better description of Juan. He coaxed her into remembering details about his habits of speech and dress. That he liked dogs and had two hulking dogs that looked enough alike that they must have been a breed, though she didn't know what. He'd been impressed that she wasn't afraid of them—it was at that point that his desire for a little fun had changed to something more possessive. He'd insisted that she stay an extra day at his expense.

"I was flattered at first," she told us. "Who wouldn't be? A rich, beautiful, younger man who appeared passionately attracted to me."

"What changed?" I asked.

"I work," she said a little defensively.

She did, though Adam supported her. He paid the bills for her condo, her car, her insurance, and her phone bills. He told me, once, that he felt he owed it to her. I'd told him that was between the two of them and promised (hand over heart) that I'd never fuss about anything he felt necessary.

She worked part-time at a travel agency that allowed her to travel more than she would otherwise have been able to. She put together tours and business meetings, and from what Jesse had told me, she was good at her job.

"I had some extra vacation I could take, but I didn't want to use it all. When I told him that I had to go home . . . he was weird about it. Weird enough that I pretended to agree with him—and while he was in the shower, I left my suitcase, grabbed my purse, and ran. Took a taxi to the airport, where I rented a car and drove home to Eugene."

"Did he just show up at your condo after that?" asked Adam.

"No," she said. "He started calling me. I answered the first one—I didn't know it was him. I said too much. But that was the only one of his calls I took until he changed his number. After that time, I only answered calls from people I knew."

"I'll need the phone numbers he used," Warren said.

She nodded. "I have them on my phone. He sent e-mails, too. I read up on stalkers and all the advice I found said that I shouldn't respond in any way at all. So I didn't." She took a deep breath. "Then the presents started to arrive. I order a lot of things online. The first one I thought was a misorder—a red silk scarf. I called the place that had sent it and found out that someone had purchased it in person and had it sent to me. They wouldn't give me the name."

"They'll give it to me," said Warren. "Do you still have the address?"

She nodded. "On my laptop. I'll go get it." She pushed away from the table and made an escape. Up the stairs.

I looked at the stairway thoughtfully, then looked at Adam. "I thought she'd be using the guest suite."

"She was afraid to be on the ground floor," he said, and I could tell by the way he said it that I wasn't going to be happy about which upstairs room she'd taken. Warren gave him a guy look, the one that said, *I wouldn't be you in a million years, but good luck.*

"She likes the peach room," I said. It was the bedroom next to ours.

"Blue makes her sad," he told me. The blue guest room was across the hall and next to Jesse's room.

There was nothing to say that needed saying. I stood up, collecting as many dirty plates and silverware as I could. Adam touched my arm.

"Mary Jo," he said. "If you'll help Mercy clear the table, I'll grab the tablecloth and toss it in the laundry."

Mary Jo waited until we were in the kitchen loading the dishwasher to say anything to me. "It's not her fault," she said finally.

"What's not her fault?" I asked. "That Christy attracted a stalker?"

Her face flushed. "That there's tension between her and Adam. They were a couple for a long time. She called to see if I'd come and defuse the situation, so that you'd be more comfortable. She's trying."

I shut the dishwasher and started it. "Yes," I said. "She is trying." I didn't say *what* Christy was trying. I was pretty sure it wasn't what Mary Jo thought it was.

Her eyes narrowed at me, so I guess my tone wasn't as neutral as I'd hoped.

"It's okay to like her," I told her gently. "To worry and feel sorry for her. That's all just fine. I want her safe, too."

I wiped my hands off on the back of my jeans and let my voice drop into a threat. "Just be careful, Mary Jo. Be very careful. You've made mistakes before. Everyone makes mistakes. One you should not make is to imagine that Christy will ever be Adam's mate. He is mine, and unlike her, I don't throw away people who are mine."

Mary Jo met my gaze, and I held hers. Held it until she looked at the floor and tipped her chin, exposing her neck.

Jesse had told me about her mother and Adam, back when she'd been too young to know that people shouldn't share other people's pain, and I had been too . . . too involved to stop her. Her mother had told Adam he scared her, that the werewolves scared her, and that he smothered her. But I'd always thought that the real trouble between them had a lot to do with Adam's looking younger than she did. Which made her attraction to a younger man . . . something to keep in mind.

I returned to the dining room and the interested faces of Adam and Warren. Both of them had heard the conversation between Mary Jo and me, but before they could say anything, Christy was back with her laptop.

She sat next to Warren, and the two of them paged through her e-mail. Adam's phone rang, and he glanced at the number.

"I hired a man to watch over Christy's condo," he told us. "This is he." He put the phone to his ear, and answered, "Hauptman."

"It's Gaven," said a stranger's voice; in the background, I could hear sirens. "There is a situation here."

Adam stiffened. "He's there?"

"Uh, no. That is, maybe, but I haven't seen him. I've been watching your wife's . . . sorry, ex-wife's apartment building since about two this afternoon. I haven't seen anyone who matches his description, but her building is on fire—you might be hearing some sirens. The fire definitely started on her floor, and I'm pretty sure it was set in her condo. I happened to be looking up and saw a flash of color—flames in one of the windows of her place. I called it in myself—though downtown Eugene isn't exactly deserted this time of day, so I won't have been the only one. The fire department is fighting it, but it's going up fast. It's been—" There was a pause and a muffled swearword. "Sorry. Pieces of it are falling, and I was a little too close. It's only been ten minutes, and the whole place is in flames."

I glanced at Christy, who was watching Adam with a little frown that made me realize that she was the only one in the room who couldn't hear the other side of Adam's conversation.

"You've told what you saw to the police?" Adam asked.

"Gave my card to the fireman who's giving orders. Told him I'd seen something. He'll relay. I'm planning on cooperating fully with the authorities."

"Of course." Adam glanced at Christy, who had come to attention at the word "police." "They already know that there is a problem. Make sure they make the connections, all right? They have my number, but it might not hurt to give it to them again."

"They'll want to talk to her, too," the investigator said.

"What's wrong?" Christy asked.

Adam held up a finger. "Of course. She's not answering her phone directly. They'll have to leave a message for her to call them back."

"Right."

Adam ended the call and looked at Christy. "I think your stalker just burned down your condo, building and all."

She paled. "Did they get everyone out?"

Adam shook his head. "It's a big building. There is no way that they could know that this early. They're still fighting it. They'll know more in a few hours, but it could be days before everyone is accounted for."

THE WAR COMMITTEE CONTINUED TO DISCUSS CHRISty's stalker with periodic interruptions from people calling with updates on Christy's home.

Adam's investigator told us the whole building was a loss and then gave Adam a few numbers of people involved in the investigation. Once he figured out that Adam was the famous Alpha werewolf, the arson guy got almost chatty. He told Adam that they'd have to wait until the building cooled before anyone could be certain, officially, that the fire had been set. But unofficially, his gut instinct was that the fire was arson. The first police officer called shortly thereafter to ask pointed questions about insurance policies—which seemed to imply that the arson investigator had not only shared his unofficial gut instincts with the police, too, but also told them that Adam was interested in the outcome.

Courteously, Adam told the policeman that Christy had filed a report about a stalker who had assaulted her. And when Adam had recently contacted the Eugene police on the matter, he'd been told that Christy's stalker might also be involved in the death of a man she'd been dating. Adam gave him the phone number of the officer in charge of the Eugene police investigation without looking it up. The information seemed to mollify that police officer. But not the second one who called.

None of the calls I'd made concerning Coyote had been

returned, but Zack called around ten and apologized for not showing up. He'd found a place to stay and also work, but the job had
required him to start immediately. He'd come by as soon as he
could.

"I understand," Adam said. "But I'd prefer to bring you into
the pack as soon as possible for your safety. My wolves won't
bother you, but there are other things running around town that
might if you don't have pack protection."

"I'm on call this week," Zack told Adam. "I can't afford to
turn down hours, nohow. I don't know when I can come out."

"Let's dispense with the formal ceremony, then, and do something quicker," Adam said. "Where are you staying?"

Almost reluctantly, Zack gave the name of a rent-by-the-week
motel.

"Okay," Adam said. "My mate and I will be there in about
half an hour. I'll call my second. The three of us will make it
official. Meeting the pack can wait until you know your schedule."

"This could all wait," Zack said.

"No," Adam told him. "I have no intention of letting you run
around my city unprotected." He hung up before Zack could argue
further.

"I'll keep an eye on everything here, boss," said Warren. "You
go welcome the new wolf to the fold."

"Mary Jo, go home," Adam told her. "You've helped a lot
tonight, but you need to get some sleep before you go to work."

She gave Christy a worried look.

"I won't chew on her," said Warren ironically. "You go on shift
tomorrow at five in the morning. Go home, Mary Jo."

"I'll see you when you get off work," said Christy, managing
to look like she wished Mary Jo would stay while indicating just

the opposite with her words. It was quite a feat. "We can go get a manicure at that place we like in Richland."

"It closed," Mary Jo told her.

"I'm sure we can find another shop. Auriele will know someplace good."

Mary Jo grinned. "She will. Are you sure you'll be okay?"

"Mary Jo," Adam said. "Go."

Left with no choice, Mary Jo preceded us out the door. "Are you sure she'll be safe with just Warren?" She looked back over her shoulder.

"Don't be ridiculous," said Adam with more patience than I'd credited him. "Her stalker set her apartment on fire tonight. There aren't any direct flights, and it's a six-hour drive from Eugene to here. Even if he came directly to murder her in my home, guarded by one of the toughest wolves I know, Juan couldn't get here before I get back."

Adam opened the passenger door of his SUV for me, shut it, and got the driver-side door of Mary Jo's Jeep for her. She thanked him gravely, when she'd have given any other man the rough side of her tongue for his courtesy. Opening a woman's door was ingrained in Adam, but he was careful not to do it where one of her coworkers might see it. Apparently firemen, even if they were women, were supposed to be too independent to have doors opened for them—and Mary Jo didn't want to get teased about it.

ZACK'S MOTEL WAS IN EAST PASCO. THE TRI-CITIES doesn't have really dangerous neighborhoods, but east Pasco comes close. The motel was one of those old ones with little rooms that opened out onto the parking lot, the kind they don't build anymore because they aren't really safe.

The big, shiny black SUV garnered the interest of a group of boys hanging out smoking at the edge of the parking lot. They were in that fourteen-to-sixteen age category when men are old enough to feel the testosterone and too young to have acquired common sense.

"Hey, *gringo*," one of them said. "You sure you want to park that there?"

"Why don't you just leave that *chica* with us, *gringo*. 'Cus we know what to do with bitches like that. She don't need no white meat. 'Cus everybody knows white meat is bad for you."

Adam, who'd rounded the front of the car, kept walking until he was next to me. Then he turned his face a little up and out, letting the weak yellow illumination of the motel's parking-lot lights hit his features full on.

The boys had been advancing in a slow, semi-menacing manner, obviously ready to enjoy running off some poor couple in the wrong place at the wrong time.

We'd had some real trouble with gangs in the Tri-Cities a few years back, but, except for the serious drug traffickers, who were too concerned with money and keeping a low profile to be harassing tourists for being in the wrong neighborhood, most of the gang activity had died down.

One of the boys paused, squinted at my husband's face, and came to an abrupt halt. "Hey, man," he said in a completely different tone of voice. "Hey, man. It's okay, right? We didn't mean nothing by it. Just having some fun. Right, man? We don't want no trouble with you."

The rest of them paused, disconcerted by the about-face.

"It's the werewolf dude," he whispered loudly. "From the TV? Don't you idiots watch the news? You don't screw around with him."

The others turned to give Adam a closer look, then they all melted away with fake nonchalance.

"They make me feel old," Adam said mournfully once they were gone.

"That's because you are old," I told him without sympathy. He'd enjoyed backing them down. "Come on, old man. Let's go bring our new wolf into the fold."

Before we could, a sleek silver '67 Mustang pulled in next to the SUV, and Darryl got out. Darryl is big in daylight, but the night hides the intelligence in his face and the beauty of his features, which can distract from his size. In the dark, he is huge, and right then he was carrying a tide of irritation that made him even scarier than usual.

I thought of the impression Zack had given me in my garage, and said, "Hey, Darryl. If you could back down a bit? This guy isn't Peter, who might have been submissive but wasn't scared of anyone. This wolf is going to take one look at you and run."

Darryl gave me a ticked-off look. "I am not irritated with the new wolf. I'm irritated with you. You are causing me trouble, woman." Darryl's voice sounded like it was coming from the bottom of a very deep barrel. It was the kind of voice I imagined a dragon might speak in—if there were dragons. Which didn't exist. As far as I knew.

I'd thought Darryl was mostly just grumpy, but Adam growled with intent that lent Darryl's declaration more seriousness. Darryl tipped his head away from me, but that didn't make him any happier.

"What did I do?" I asked.

"You upset Christy, and that upset Auriele—who doesn't think that leaving Christy's general well-being to Adam is the right thing to do," he snapped. "I do not enjoy being put in the middle of this."

"*I* upset Christy?" I asked. "When?"

"This afternoon. You insisted she sleep in the ground-floor suite when she has a stalker after her. She's just a little bit of a thing—"

"Darryl," I said.

"I don't know what you were thinking," he said, forgetting Adam entirely. "Downstairs isn't safe. She's human and in danger from a stalker who, Auriele tells me, may have already killed a man."

"Darryl," I said again, then quit waiting for him to give me space to speak and just took it. "I admit I thought Christy would be more comfortable in the suite where she would have her own bathroom. The windows are alarmed, and there are werewolves—*werewolves*, Darryl—in the house to hear when any stranger approaches—even on foot." I tried unsuccessfully to keep the exasperation from my voice. "In any case, she's staying upstairs—and I didn't object in any size, shape, or form as I wasn't even home when she got there. I was at work."

He stared down at me, and I met his gaze. He didn't look away, and I finally threw up my hands in exasperation. "No. I am not thrilled by my husband's ex-wife moving into my house and sleeping in the bedroom next to me. But I am not making her unwelcome. I am not putting her in danger. And you know, *you know* that I am not lying."

Darryl inhaled. Looked away.

"Ah damn," he said with less eloquence than a man with a

Ph.D. who worked in a government think tank should use. "She's doing it again. I'd almost forgotten."

"I'm doing *what* again?" I asked. I was starting to get mad, too.

"It's Christy, Mercy," said Adam. "*Christy* is doing it again. She has a way of making people worry about her."

"And that's the kindest way to put it," Darryl said, sounding poleaxed. "You'd think I'd have seen it. I've had a lot of experience. I'll explain what happened to Auriele, and she'll realize that she misunderstood what Christy said. Just like the last ten times she misunderstood—it will end up being my fault because I should have realized she misunderstood what Christy told her. My only excuse is that I've had years to forget, and Auriele is blind to the faults of people she loves. I am the most fortunate man in the world because I am the beneficiary of that blindness, but I forget that other people are beneficiaries, too."

"Education and brains don't help when dealing with my ex-wife," Adam said, sounding amused, of all things. "You aren't wired to see through Christy, and neither is Auriele. Now let's go meet—"

I don't know how long Zack had been standing outside his hotel room listening to us, but, from the look on his face, it had been long enough. He saw me watching, and his face went blank.

"Zack," I said. "Let me introduce my husband, Adam Hauptman, and his second, Darryl Zao. Gentlemen, this is Zack Drummond."

"Hi," he said warily. He still looked tired and too thin. "Come in. Let's get this over with." Enthusiasm was notable by its absence.

Zack turned and walked through the open door of the motel room. Adam followed Zack, and Darryl gestured for me to go ahead. I stepped in and had to fight not to gag.

Maybe a human's nose wouldn't have picked up the odors in that motel room, or maybe it wouldn't have picked up *all* the odors. Maybe. But I didn't think even an asthma patient who hadn't smelled a scent in months could have stayed in that room for longer than ten minutes without being nauseated.

Cigar, cigarette, pipe, and every other substance anyone could smoke permeated the room, along with the smell of sex, urine, feces, and old alcohol. I've heard people complain that there is nothing worse than the smell of stale beer, but that room proved them wrong. Stale beer was the least unpleasant scent in the room. There was also mold, mildew, and mouse. All it needed was a skunk.

Neither Adam nor Darryl showed any sign of distress. Zack looked at me and gave me a faint smile. "Beggars can't be choosers."

"You can move in with us for a few weeks," I said. "As it happens, we have a freshly cleaned bedroom suite that no one is using."

"No," he said gently. "I'm sorry, but I'd rather put up with this than . . . Your house don't sound like a safe place to be at the moment. I don't like pack politics—them and me don't get along."

Darryl would have said something—submissive wolves usually do fine in pack politics because, like Christy, no one wants to hurt them—but Adam made a subtle hand gesture that meant "stop."

"That's fine," said Adam. "Welcome to the Tri-Cities, Zack Drummond. Usually, we would throw a party to welcome you—and we will—but the constraints of your schedule means that cannot happen this week. We have vampires in this town and half fae and a host of other denizens of the Forgotten and Hiding, many of which would love to find an unaffiliated werewolf to hunt."

"I understand," said Zack when Adam stopped speaking.

"Okay. My full name is Adam Alexander Hauptman. What is yours?"

"Zachary Edwin Drummond."

Adam shut his eyes and took in three deep breaths—under the circumstances in that room, it was a braver act than it usually was. Every time he breathed in, I could feel the pull of pack magic and felt it gather to his need.

My mate opened his eyes and focused his full attention on Zack. "Look me in the eyes with no offense taken or meant, Zachary Edwin Drummond."

Zack raised his chin and met Adam's gaze. "I see you, Adam Alexander Hauptman, Alpha of the Columbia Basin Pack."

"Will you join with us, to hunt, to fight, to live and run?"

"Under the moon," Zack said. "I will hunt, fight, live and run with you and yours who shall be mine."

"We claim you," Darryl said, and pulled out a pocketknife and opened it one-handed.

"We claim you," I said when Adam glanced at me.

"*I* claim you," said Adam, and he took Darryl's knife and cut a chunk of meat the size of the tip of my little finger off his forearm with practiced ease. "Alpha's flesh and blood you shall be."

He offered the bloody bit to Zack, who ate it off his fingers. Blood welled up from the wound on Adam's arm. Four fat drops fell to the carpet, and then the gouge scabbed over. In less than an hour, there would be no sign of the wound at all. A simple cut would have healed even faster.

"From this day forward," Adam said. "Mine to me and mine. Pack."

"Yours to you, mine to me," answered Zack. The smoothness of his answer told me how often he'd done this.

Magic sizzled and zipped between us, burning in my chest as if someone had set a match there. But I shared that power with the whole pack, who received Zack along with me. Zack got the whole of his end, and he cried out and wrapped his arms around his chest and sank down on the bedspread.

It would have taken more than a jolt of pack magic to make me touch that bedspread.

Darryl was made of sterner stuff. He sat down beside Zack and wrapped one of his long arms around the other man's shoulders.

"Breathe through it," he advised. "I know it burns like freaking nitrous. But it will be over before you know it."

"Better joining than leaving," said Zack in a tight voice. But the worst was over, and his muscles started to relax. Until he noticed that Darryl was holding him.

Darryl saw it, too, and released him immediately. "All done," he said, standing up.

"Now," said Adam. "Tell me about this job you have."

"I'm washing dishes at a restaurant," he said. "It's fine. I've done a lot of dishwashing jobs."

"Under the table or over the table?" asked Adam.

Zack heaved an impatient sigh. "You're one of *those* Alphas," he said in a long-suffering voice. "It's safe. I'm legal, and the job is legitimate. Not quite full-time, so I'll have to find another job to get out of this dump. But I can do that. I'm good at finding jobs. I need a pack, not a parent."

Mildly, Adam said, "It's my job to make sure all the members of my pack are safe and well fed, so they don't get desperate."

"I've been a werewolf a very long time," said Zack. "A hundred and thirty years give or take a couple. I'm not going to go out and start eating children."

"Good to know," Adam murmured. "But you aren't sleeping here, anyway. Who knows who will break in here and force you to defend yourself? The Marrok has been very clear that he doesn't want any wolf put in that sort of situation if it can be helped." He pulled out his phone and hit a button.

"Hey, boss," said Warren in long-suffering tones. "No killer stalkers or arsonists here yet. But I'm thinking that it might be a good idea to up the number of guards tomorrow. Just to make sure Christy is safe."

Maybe Christy hadn't been complaining to Warren about how no one was taking her plight seriously. Maybe Warren really felt that they needed more *werewolf* guards to protect Christy from her stalker, who was, after all, only human. Maybe.

"Agreed," Adam said easily. "We'll keep four on guard duty until we catch the stalker. I have already set up shifts for tomorrow morning. After that, we'll have to do some scheduling. In other news, Zack, our new wolf, is in unacceptable accommodations. He is working not-quite full-time and is probably willing to take on another job for an upgrade from the Nite Owl."

"I stayed there for a couple of weeks," said Warren. He wasn't lying, and he knew that Zack could overhear. "It seriously sucked. How about he come stay in one of our guest rooms. It wouldn't hurt my feelings to have another werewolf around when I can't be. Kyle just fired our yard crew and was making noises about getting the lawn mower out himself. If Zack wouldn't mind taking on the lawn, I reckon he could have room and board in return until such time as he wants to do something else. Make sure he knows that it's a big yard."

Adam tipped his head toward Zack and raised an eyebrow.

Zack made an exasperated noise, but said, "Okay. Yes. Okay."

"Uhm," I said. "Someone should let you know that Warren is third in the pack hierarchy. They should also tell you that he is gay, and Kyle is his partner. And Kyle is human."

Zack looked at me.

"Someone should tell him that, for sure," Warren drawled. "Ah reckon someone should also let him know that Kyle and me aren't looking for a third. And the house is big enough that if he keeps his door closed, he shouldn't need to worry about what other folk get up to in their bedrooms."

"And Kyle is pretty snitty if he thinks that you disapprove," I added. "He'll do his best to embarrass you."

"I'll make sure Kyle knows how much you like him, Mercy," Warren assured me.

"He knows I love him," I told Warren. "But warning the were-wolves who go to your house what the situation is so no one gets hurt has been my job from day one." An uncomfortable werewolf might take a bite that everyone would regret.

"As long as no one pees in the corners," said Zack with a wry look at the corner nearest the door, "it has to be better than this. And as long as everyone is above the age of consent and has enough sense to be able to give informed consent, I could care less what anyone does in their own space."

"Kyle and I are over the age of consent in all fifty states," said Warren, then gave in to full-out TV cowboy for the last bit. "And ah reckon ah can refrain from pee'n' in corners, though ah don't know if ah can be responsible for any'n' else."

DARRYL WAS STILL FEELING GUILTY FOR YELLING AT me because he volunteered to drive Zack over and introduce him to Kyle. When we got home, Warren was still getting information out of Christy.

I wanted to go to bed, but if I did that, then Adam would be alone with Christy when Warren left. The minute I figured out that was why I was lingering, I yawned and kissed Adam on the side of his neck.

"I've got to be up at o'dark thirty," I told them. "I'm going to bed. If some pyro decides to arson my house again, make sure I'm up, would you?"

"I'll try my best," Adam said courteously—and for just a moment I had a flashback to Adam, burned horribly and frantic because he thought I was in my trailer.

"I know," I told him, the thought of how badly he'd been hurt momentarily erasing my sleepiness.

"Mercy's a coyote, she'll be okay." Warren winked at Adam, then he said, "Just make sure you grab the cat on your way out."

"What cat?" asked Christy. "I don't like cats."

"Lock your bedroom, then," I told her. "She can open the doors. If she knows you don't like her, she'll try to follow you everywhere."

I wiggled my fingers at Adam and trotted up the stairs with a little smile warming my heart. So I'd been spiteful, but the look on Christy's face had been worth it. Tomorrow, I vowed, I'd be a better person. But tonight, I would enjoy my spite.

Jesse's light was on. I almost just went to bed—I was seriously tired, and if I hit the hay right that moment, I'd get five and a half hours of sleep.

But I knocked lightly at the door.

"Who is it?" Jesse asked.

"Me," I said, and opened the door when she invited me in.

Jesse was stretched out on her bed with schoolbooks scattered around and her headphones dangling around her neck. One of the earpieces was caught in the patch of purple hair just in front of her left ear. She didn't look up when I came in.

"I'm just heading to bed," I told her. "You might consider going to sleep sometime before you have to get up, too."

"Why did you let her do that to you?" Jesse asked tightly, without looking at me. She wrote a few numbers down in the notebook in front of her.

I shut the door and came farther into the room. I had to pick my path. My nose would have told me if there were any rotting food, but there was sure as heck everything else scattered all over the floor. My room used to look sort of like this before I moved in with Adam. Now I itched to pick up the dirty clothes and throw them in her clothes hamper. *After* I dumped out the eclectic collection of stuff already in it.

"Do what to me?" I asked absently. She had a cricket bat sticking out the top of the hamper. Why a cricket bat? She didn't play cricket. Not as far as I knew, anyway.

"Dinner was my fault," Jesse said, effectively jerking my attention back to her, where it belonged. "She wanted to make BLTs, and I didn't see any harm in it until you came home, and she was inviting people over, deciding we'd eat in the dining room, and giving orders left and right."

"Dinner was good," I said. "I've never had homemade mayonnaise before. And your mother is welcome to invite whomever she wishes to dinner—especially if she is cooking it."

Jesse sat up and tossed her pencil on the bed. She wiped her eyes.

"You *know*," she said hotly. "You understand people, Mercy.

You know how power works—I've seen you with the pack. Why did you let her take control without even fighting back?"

I sat down on the bed beside her without touching her and let air out in a huff. With the air I gave up my night of rolling in my spite. For Jesse, I could be a better person right now.

"Your mom is scared," I said honestly. "She invited this handsome prince into her life and now a man is dead because of it. She had to ask for help from your father after she'd told the world she didn't need him. She had to come here, to the home she built, and know that it isn't hers anymore, that I've taken her place."

"She chose that," Jesse all but hissed.

I patted her leg. "Yes, she did. That makes it hurt more rather than less." I gave her a rueful smile. "I always hate having to relive my mistakes, I don't know about you." Jesse's expression eased, so I continued to defend Christy. "She's scared—ashamed of how she left both of you, ashamed of how poorly she's filled the role of being your mother. So she's trying to control something. She knows cooking, knows she's good at it."

"And you let her do it," Jesse said slowly. "Because you feel sorry for her?"

I nodded, glad that she couldn't tell if I lied or not. Then I heaved a sigh because I tried not to lie to Jesse any more than I lied to her father. I might make exceptions in the case of their safety, but never just to make myself look better.

"That's part of it," I said. "I'd like to think that it was the biggest part of it because that makes me look better. Confident even. But part of it is also this—can you see me trying to compete with your mother in the kitchen while she's at her Suzy Homemaker best? I'd just look stupid—and that's what she was prepared for."

"You gave up control of the house to her," Jesse said as if it were a terrible and wrong thing. "And couldn't get it back?"

I snorted. "You obviously grew up in a werewolf pack, kid. Werewolves don't know everything. Giving her power down there did not hurt mine. This is not her home, and a dozen gourmet dinners aren't going to change that. If she is scared and needs to feel in control over dinner, I can give her that because I don't have a creep chasing after me. Ultimately, she cannot take over this house because it belongs to your father, and he is mine."

"Give her an inch, and she'll take a mile," warned Jesse.

I nodded. "That may be. But it will be okay; your mother is a good person."

Jesse snorted.

"She's a good person. She loves you." I closed my eyes because I didn't want to say the next bit very much. "She even loves your father still." I could see it in her body language. "She's a good person, but she is a weak person, too. She can't take care of anyone else because she's too busy taking care of herself." I yawned, and Jesse nudged me.

"Go to bed, Mercy," she said with a smile.

I got up and stretched. "We good?" I asked.

She nodded. "We're good."

Adam was holding the wall up outside Jesse's bedroom when I opened the door.

"Good night, Jesse," he said. "Your mom is already in bed."

"Night, Dad," Jesse said, dumping the stuff on her bed on the floor with all the other Jesse debris. "Turn out my light, okay?"

I hit the switch and shut the door.

"How long have you been there?"

He put his warm hand on the back of my neck and hauled me to our bedroom.

"Long enough to hear you defend Christy to Jesse—so, might I add, did Christy. I sent her to bed after you called her a Suzy Homemaker because she took offense at that."

I shut our door, closing us in away from Christy. If she heard something she didn't want to tonight, it was her own fault. I turned around, and Adam leaned against me, pushing me backward until the wall pressed into my shoulder blades.

"You are the opposite of Christy," he told me seriously.

I raised my eyebrows. "You don't think I'd ask for help if I acquired a stalker?"

His hard belly vibrated against mine as he laughed silently. "Maybe. Just maybe, and only if you thought someone else might be at risk. But I wasn't talking about that." He kissed me until the pulse in my neck jumped against his thumb. "She's too busy taking care of herself to take care of anyone else, you said. That's about the best description of Christy I've ever heard. You? You are too busy taking care of everyone else to take care of yourself."

He kissed me again, then put his head down to whisper in my ear. "I like your way better." And then he nipped my ear and slapped my hip lightly and stepped away.

"Morning comes early," he said lightly. "Let's get some sleep."

"Adam," I said quietly, hoping Christy couldn't hear. "That whole spiel I told Jesse about why I didn't set Christy on her ear tonight? I thought that up later. At the time, the real reason was the second one I admitted to, that I couldn't do it without looking like a vindictive, insecure witch."

He laughed, a soft sound shared by just the two of us. "I saw," he said. "Christy boxed you in, and you skated through as gracefully as possible. Don't worry, love, this was just round one, and she had the advantage with that shiner on the side of her face to gather sympathy. My money's on you for the finish."

4

"THAT BAD, EH?" SAID TAD WHEN HE CAME THROUGH
the door of the shop that next morning.

"She made breakfast," I told him, looking down at the parts
order I was putting together to hide my expression until I could
make it more cheery. I turned two sets of spark plugs into four,
stretched my mouth into an appropriate shape, and looked up at
Tad. "Homemade blueberry muffins. I brought you some." I nodded to the basket on the counter next to the till.

He shook his head. "Lots of teeth in that expression for a smile,
Mercy." He snagged one out of the top, took a quick bite, and
paused. Gave me a humor-filled sympathetic look and took
another, bigger bite. When he finished, he looked at me and
snatched another muffin. "How long is she going to be here? And
would she be interested in dating a half-fae younger man who is
currently working for minimum wage?"

"And the horse you rode in on," I groused at him without heat.

"Until she's safe, I suppose—though she's making noises about moving here. I hope she was just saying that to torment me, but . . ." I shrugged. "I don't think she'll be looking for anyone"— other than Adam—"for a while. This guy she's on the run from beat her up, and it is seriously looking like he killed another man she was dating, then burned down the building her condo was in."

Tad took a third muffin and ate it in two bites. His voice was muffled with food when he said, "Nasty piece of work, him. Are you up for this?"

I shrugged. "Sure. If it gets too bad . . . how would you like a roommate?"

"If she can cook like this, okay by me."

"I was talking about me," I told him. I was joking. But there was a cold knot in my stomach anyway.

He came around the counter and kissed the top of my head. "Poor Mercy. Let's go fix something you know how to fix. It'll make you feel better."

When I'd met Tad, a little over ten years ago, he'd only been a kid, and he'd been running this shop himself because his dad had gone on a two-month drinking binge after Tad's mom had died of cancer. He'd been nine going on fifty then, and the only thing that had changed since was that someone had rubbed off the bright and shiny cheer that had been his gift to the world. If I ever found out who had done it, I might sic a werewolf pack on them.

So it didn't surprise me that Tad was right. I found the short that kept a '62 Bus from Chitty-Chitty-Bang-Banging along the road in an hour and a half. Electrical shorts—common in old cars—were a bugger to hunt down. I'd once spent forty hours to find one that had taken me two minutes to fix after I found it. An hour and a half was good news. By the time I buttoned the Bus up, I was nearly upbeat.

Still no calls from anyone who might know how to reach Coyote. If I didn't hear from them by tonight, I'd drive over tomorrow and leave Tad to keep the shop going. Losing some production time would suck—but not as much as whatever would happen if Beauclaire came looking for his walking stick, and I didn't have it for him.

Just after lunch, one of my car guys stopped in. Keeping old cars running is my living, but there are hobbyists out there, too. I have a couple of guys and a grandmother who liked to come in and talk shop. Most of the time, they have questions for me, and sometimes I learn something, too. But really, it was about people who had car addictions looking for someone to talk with about their passion.

Joel Arocha showed up while I was elbow-deep in grease working on a Jetta that had been going through as much oil as gas for about ten years. Joel (pronounced Hoe-*el* in the Spanish style) was Hispanic, but his accent was Southwestern USA. He was my age, more or less, but the sun had weathered his skin so he looked a little older. He was about my size and weight, too. One of those tough, tough men who were all muscle and rawhide.

He worked in the vineyards, ten-hour days this time of year, with random days off. In the winter, he worked reduced hours and took other jobs to fill in. Last year I'd introduced him to Adam, and he'd done some fill-in security jobs. In his not-so-copious spare time, Joel was restoring a Thing, VW's version of a jeep, and he liked to chat with me while I worked.

Usually, Joel and I talked cars, but today he had other things on his mind.

"—so this guy comes by my house this morning, knocks on my door to see if we had any pit bulls for sale—and then he points at my wife's prizewinning bitch, and says, 'Like that one.'" Joel set the part he'd come to pick up on the nearest counter and leaned against it while he watched me work.

"That's a problem?" I asked, because he was obviously pretty hot about it. I knew werewolves, not dogs, at least not at his level.

He nodded. "It told me right up front I was dealing with someone who didn't know anything about dogs. Aruba—that is Arocha's White Princess Aruba to you—is an American Staffordshire terrier. Amstaffs look a bit like the American pit bull, but any dog fancier can tell the difference. Someone had apparently told him we had pit bulls, and he needed one to guard his house and do some fighting for him—and he gives me a wink." Joel grimaced. "A wink. Freaking dog fighters. They think it makes them macho to take their loyal dogs and get them all chewed up. To me, it just shows that they aren't worthy of having a dog. I told him not right now and asked him for his number, in case something turned up." Joel handed me an extension for my ratchet before I could reach for it.

"So he gives me the number"—he continued in the same aggravated tones—"the freaking moron. And then I ask him where he's found fighting dogs, acted as though I might want to get in on the action. Damn fool was happy to tell me. As soon as he was gone, I called the police. Second dog-fighting outfit I've turned in since Christmas. If it were up to me, I'd shoot all those bastards, no trial, no nothing."

"Or make them go fight it out in the pit with each other," Tad offered from the next bay over.

"And shoot the last man standing," I agreed. "Good for you, Joel."

"Yeah," he said. "You know what really chaps my hide, though? Someone told him to look at me for dogs. Someone, sometime got a dog from me and is involved in dog fighting. If I ever find out who it is, I'll take my dog back and hope he objects."

My cell phone rang, and Joel took a deep breath. "Yeah, I've got to get going anyway." He tipped his hat. "Catch you later, Mercy."

"Take care, Joel."

"'Bye, Tad. Don't do anything I wouldn't do."

"'Bye, Joel. Don't juggle porcupines."

Joel paused. "Porcupines?"

Tad grinned. "One bit of obvious advice for another. If I tried doing something you wouldn't do, it would be jail or the morgue."

They exchanged a few more juvenile remarks while I peeled off the sweaty latex gloves I only wore because of Christy and her manicured hands. By the time I got them off, the phone had quit ringing. The screen told me I'd missed the call I was hoping for, and I wasted no time calling him back.

"Heya, Mercy," said Hank's cheerful voice. "I got a message that you wanted to talk to me about finding Coyote. You sure you want to talk to him?"

I glanced at the garage-bay door, but Joel was safely out of sight and presumably out of hearing range.

"Talking to Coyote is on the top of my to-do list," I told him, and in the other bay, Tad straightened from under the hood of the car he had gone back to working on.

"Mmmm. And you think to call me about this why? Unlike some I could name, *I* don't turn into a coyote when I get the urge," said Hank, whose *other* form was a red-tailed hawk.

"He didn't leave a phone number for me to call," I said. "And, all joking aside, I need to find him. If you can't help, do you know how to get in touch with Gordon?"

Hank grunted. "Gordon's in the wind, kid. I haven't seen him for a couple of weeks. I called around for you, but no one else has seen him, either. You serious about it being urgent?"

"I had a fae artifact," I told him. "I gave it to Coyote, and now the fae want it back. Yesterday."

There was a short silence, then Hank said, "I thought the fae were shut up in their rez for the foreseeable future."

"Apparently some of them are still out and about," I told him after an on-the-fly decision that I owed no loyalty to Beauclaire and the rest of the fae folk. Besides, Hank wouldn't spread it around.

Hank huffed a laugh at my dry tone. "Politicians never have to follow their own laws, right? Jeez, kid. Don't do trouble by half, do you? Let me ask around a little more pointedly, and I'll get back to you, tomorrow latest."

I ended the call feeling the sharp edge of panic. It looked like getting in touch with Coyote was going to be more difficult than I'd anticipated. I hadn't really thought Hank would know how to contact Coyote, but I'd been counting on talking to Gordon, who would.

Tad asked, "Who wants the walking stick?"

"Alistair Beauclaire," I told him.

Tad blinked. "Dad was wondering what he was doing flitting in and out and about the reservation without an apparent purpose. I wouldn't have thought that the walking stick was important enough for a Gray Lord, though."

I shrugged. "Who can predict the fae? Not even the fae as far as I've been able to see. Your dad knows that Beauclaire isn't a fan, right?"

Tad gave me an oddly gentle smile. "Beauclaire would kill my father in an instant if he weren't too noble to take out the whole rez and Walla Walla at the same time. Outside of massive, wholesale destruction, my father is more than a match for him."

I took a breath. "Did your father really kill Lugh?"

Tad went back to the job at hand, but he nodded. "As my father tells it, Lugh was old, powerful, and starting to get scary. Really scary. Started out as a hero and was turning into something a lot different."

He gave me a sly look as he pulled out the battery and set it aside. "Of course, my father wasn't a white knight back then, either. He killed Lugh because he was more interested in making a cool weapon than killing someone who might be a danger to the world—but, as he likes to point out, it served both purposes, so he is happy to take credit. The fae world heaved a sigh of relief, shook their collective and disorganized finger at my dad, and then went about their business."

My phone rang again, and the caller ID said it was Hank.

"That was fast."

"I have a name," said Hank. "Gary Laughingdog. He is a coyote walker like you. Maybe he can help you—word is that he has Coyote's ear when he needs it."

"Do you have a phone number?"

"He is locked up at the Coyote Ridge facility in Connell. You'll have to go see him there."

"In jail?" I asked.

I heard the smile in Hank's voice. "He is not a violent criminal, Mercy. But he has little respect for the law or personal property, and that lands him in trouble from time to time. This time it landed him in prison for two years, of which he has served eight months. He likes women, has a reputation with them." There was a little pause, and Hank said, "Most of the coyote walkers have trouble with the law."

"At least they don't have trouble passing elementary school like the hawk walkers," I said because Hank liked to tease and could take as good as he gave.

Hank was laughing when he disconnected.

"Do you know how to visit someone in prison?" asked Tad.

"Do you?"

He shook his head. "No. When they locked up my dad, he wouldn't let me come home."

"Adam will know," I said, and dialed him.

"Adam Hauptman's phone," said Christy. "Can I help you?"

"Is Adam there?" I asked. There would, I knew, be a good explanation of why Christy was answering Adam's phone—especially since he'd told her not to answer her own phone. I'd noticed before, when she wasn't living in my home, that Christy always had good reasons for doing the wrong thing, reasons that made everyone look stupid for questioning her.

"Yes," she said. "But he can't come to the phone right now."

"I see."

"Is this Mercy?" she said brightly. "I didn't know it was you. He's on the house phone talking to the arson investigator. Can I give him a message?"

I couldn't tell across phone lines, but I was pretty sure she was lying about not knowing it was me calling in the first place. My name would have scrolled across the caller ID.

"No," I said. "It's all right."

I hung up and stared at my phone for a while. Adam had gone to work this morning the same time I had. He'd called in some of the wolves to watch over Christy. So why was he home, and why did she have his phone?

"I'd make you some brownies," I told Tad. "But she's always in my kitchen."

The expression on his face was compassionate. "I expect that the jail has a web page with phone numbers of people who can help you figure out how to visit the guy you need to see."

COYOTE RIDGE CORRECTIONS CENTER IS A MINIMUM- and medium-security facility just outside of Connell, which is about an hour's drive north of the Tri-Cities. It's a little town of about five thousand inhabitants, not including those who are incarcerated in the prison.

I didn't go alone.

I glanced at my passenger and wondered if I'd made the right choice. Not that there were a lot of pack members who'd have been free to head out on short notice, especially now that Adam was keeping four wolves at our house all the time.

Honey had lost weight since her husband's death, and she hadn't been fat to begin with. She'd cut her honey-colored hair into a severe style that framed her face with its newly hollowed cheekbones. With that and her body reduced to muscle and bone, she should have looked hard, but instead she looked fragile.

She hadn't said a word to me since I picked her up in my Vanagon. Not even to ask where we were going.

I'd told her I needed someone to come with me on an errand, and she hadn't asked any questions. I'd decided it was a subtle defiance—following the letter of the law that said I was in charge without actually making an effort to be useful. But either driving or twenty minutes of distance from Christy cheered me to more optimistic possibilities. Maybe Honey just didn't know what to say.

Or maybe she liked Christy more than she liked me, too.

"I had a fae artifact follow me home," I told her. I couldn't remember if she'd known about the walking stick. I'd tried not to talk about it too much. "It wouldn't stay with any of the fae I tried to give it to. Which would have been fine except that it started to get bloodthirsty, so I found a safe place for it. Night before last, I was visited by a Gray Lord who informed me that it would be a good idea if I retrieved it and gave it back to him."

"You gave the walking stick to Coyote," she said. And when I looked at her, she raised a cool eyebrow. "You were raised among wolves. I'd think you'd know well enough how fast and thoroughly gossip travels in the pack."

"Okay," I said. "I don't know how to get ahold of Coyote in a hurry. In my experience, he just shows up when he chooses. So I called around and got the name of another walker who might know how to find him before the fae decide to destroy the Tri-Cities in retribution."

She looked at me, frowned, and sat up straighter. "You were trying to joke—but you really believe they might destroy the whole town."

"Not *they*," I said, remembering that instant when the glamour thinned, and he'd snarled at the cat. "*He*. And yes, I think the fae are capable of anything. I'd have given them the stupid walking stick a long time ago if it would have let me."

"Was it Zee?"

I shook my head. "Zee's not a Gray Lord. Close, I think, but not. This was Alistair Beauclaire, the man responsible for the fae retreat to the reservations."

"Good," she said. "I like Zee."

She was quiet for a few miles. "Where are we going?"

"To Connell," I told her. "To visit someone who might know how to find Coyote."

She glanced down at the clothes she was wearing—rose slacks and a blue silk blouse. She buttoned the blouse another two buttons and began to shed jewelry. "They won't let you bring a weapon on-site," she said. "Not even in your car."

Interesting that she knew the rules for visiting someone in prison.

"I left the gun in the safe at the shop," I told her. "And they don't need to know that you are a weapon."

She smiled a little, and her eyes warmed.

The parking lot had a deserted feel. Coyote Ridge could hold nearly three thousand prisoners—apparently none of them had family or friends who were visiting today. Prison wasn't like the hospital, I guess. Social obligation didn't cover visiting friends and acquaintances in prison.

Like the Tri-Cities, Connell is in the heart of the desert. Not a pretty desert with sand strewn with cactus and interesting, thorn-covered plants, but shallow rolling hills that look like they needed a shave for the stubbled growth of sagebrush and cheatgrass.

Set firmly in that stark and unbeautiful desert canvas, the prison was a hostile collection of plain, rectangular buildings with cement walls and steel doors, chain-link fences topped with rolls of razor wire, and atmospheric hopelessness that lay like a weight over it all. We left everything in the van except our licenses and the keys I used to lock up.

The guards in the entrance building were professional and not unfriendly. They gave me a quarter to feed the locker where I put the keys to the Vanagon. They kept our driver's licenses—the woman behind the counter did a double take at my name, but she didn't otherwise say that she recognized it.

Honey and I carefully avoided looking at Nat, one of the pack members who was a guard here—there were two wolves on staff, but I saw no sign of Luke. We signed in, and Nat took the clipboard from me, frowning when he saw the name of the man we were visiting. I don't think anyone else noticed.

We were escorted out of the building and into one of a series of parallel chain-link-enclosed paths into the prison itself. When the doors closed behind us, my pulse picked up, and Honey flinched. We showed our visitor badges to the guard behind the glass and walked into a room that looked like my high-school lunchroom.

Dozens of gray plastic tables were set out, each with four all-plastic gray chairs. They looked like adult-sized versions of those children's outdoor picnic furniture, an effect that was not alleviated by the chessboard pattern on the top of the tables. I wondered if they could have gotten them in a less depressing color. I guess lifting the prisoners' spirits wasn't a priority.

There was room for seventy or eighty people in the room, but Honey and I and four guards were the only ones here. We sat down as directed and waited for them to get Gary Laughingdog.

It was a long wait.

He came eventually, escorted by a pair of guards, but without the complicated handcuffs and leg cuffs I'd been half expecting from TV shows.

He covered ground with the casual saunter of someone who had walked a lot of miles and could walk a lot more. He was lean and not overly tall. My first impression, skewed by too much time with werewolves, was that here in this bleak room, Laughingdog was in charge.

The guards knew they weren't fully in control. I could see their unease by the tension in their shoulders and their general air of wariness that was too much for escorting a man who didn't even rate handcuffs.

Gary looked full-blooded Native American to my eyes, though someone more experienced might have said differently. His skin was darker than mine, darker than Hank's, too. He wore his thick, straight black hair shoulder length, just a few inches shorter than I wore mine. His rough-hewn features made him interesting rather than good-looking.

Gary Laughingdog was the very first coyote walker I'd ever met, and I looked for some resemblance to the face I saw every day in the mirror because we were related. All walkers are descended from the archetypal being whose shape they take. I found the likeness in his eyes, which were the same shape and exact color as the ones that I saw in the mirror every morning.

He pulled out the plastic chair with exaggerated care and sat down with all the circumspection of Queen Victoria at her royal breakfast. His smile lit his face as his eyes, flat and unaffected by the cheer and bonhomie of the rest of his expression, traveled from Honey to me, then back to Honey, where they stayed.

"Well, *hel-lo*, ladies," he said. "What can I do for you?"

I looked up at the guards and raised my eyebrows at them. One of them walked away, and the other, after a wary glance that took in all of us, raised his eyebrows back at me. Luke was the other wolf from our pack. I jerked my chin, and he shrugged, raised his hands, and followed the first guard over to a position far enough from us that quiet talk couldn't be overheard by a human. Luke would hear every word.

Gary leaned forward, licked his lips, and said, in a low, hungry voice, "Hey, little princess, what are you doing coming out to a place like this? Gotcha some kink for a man behind bars?"

Honey raised an eyebrow, and said coolly, "Bodyguard for my Alpha's mate. And, although I haven't eaten lunch yet, I prefer cooked chicken to raw human flesh—much as your words might tempt me."

Gary took in a deep breath and shook his head in apparent wonder. "I thought there weren't any female werewolves."

She showed him her teeth in what someone else might have mistaken for a smile. "Ignorance is not unexpected."

Instead of being insulted, Gary looked delighted. He opened his mouth to say something, but then his eyes focused just over Honey's shoulder.

I knew what he saw.

I growled. A low sound that didn't carry, but it caught Gary's attention.

"She is mine," I told him. "You say *one thing* that hurts her, and I will see to it that you never get out of here." I didn't have that kind of power, but I meant it anyway. And he knew darn good and well what the "one thing" was that I was talking about.

The mask of affability dropped off his face, and he met my eyes with a blank face. I let him see just how serious I was. If he told Honey that her dead mate's ghost was following her around, I'd make sure he regretted it for the rest of his life.

The ghost that tagged along behind Honey wherever she went wasn't really Peter, anyway, not now. Ghosts were only the remnant of the person left behind, bits and pieces of people that sometimes thought they were still alive.

Something a vampire named Frost had done to Peter had kept Honey's mate here for longer than usual, kept him soul-tied to earth when his body was dead. When I'd managed to release Peter and the others the vampire had harmed, Peter had lingered for a day and night before moving on to where souls go when the body is dead. But he'd left behind a lingering, sad-eyed ghost.

It broke my heart a little when I saw his shade, and I'd be damned before Honey felt the same way.

The other walkers I'd met hadn't been able to see ghosts the way I could. It made sense that Gary Laughingdog, who was a coyote walker like me, would be able to see them as well. If I'd thought about it, I would have brought someone else here. Closed down the shop and taken Tad if I'd had to.

"He can't hurt me," Honey told me. There was something odd in her voice, but I was too focused on the coyote on the other side of the table to decipher what it was.

"*Won't* hurt you," said Gary Laughingdog, his voice softer than it had been; his eyes, which hadn't left mine, were unfocused and a little dreamy. Softer than I'd seen them up to this moment. "Not on purpose. But there's a change coming for you. I got a feel for change, and you'll have a big one somewhere near you soon." He half closed his eyes, and I felt a surge of magic that left my nose tingling and my eyes watering—it didn't feel like fae magic, or witch or anything else I'd sensed before. Gary's voice lowered an octave. "Got some choices to make, sweet Honey. Choices."

I hadn't told him Honey's name. No one knew I'd brought her with me. Her coloring was honey-toned, though. Maybe it had just been an unexpectedly accurate guess. Honey wasn't exactly an unusual endearment.

I sneezed, and Gary's eyes focused on me. He gave me a small smile, his eyes warm.

"So, little sister," he said to me. "What can I do for you?"

"Why the change in attitude?" I asked suspiciously.

"Word came only that coyote walker needs to talk to me," he said with a shrug. "Usually my brother and sister walkers are con artists, thieves, and gamblers." He tilted his head toward Honey. "Not too concerned with saving anyone's hide except their own."

Honey wiggled in her seat in an un-Honey-like fidget.

"What?" I said.

"Mercy cares," Honey said in that same funny voice she'd used before. She tapped a finger on the table. "She always cares." This time it sounded more normal.

"I saw it," Laughingdog said. "And that's why I am suddenly a lot more interested in being helpful than I was ten minutes ago. What do you need, child?"

"Child?" I curled my lip, because letting a wolf get away with patronizing me would have been dangerous. A coyote was likely to be more annoying than dangerous, but in either case, it was better to stop it before it became a habit. Not that I expected to spend a lot of time with Gary Laughingdog; however, "better safe than sorry" was my phrase of the day.

He raised a hand in surrender. "I'm a *lot* older than I look, older by a damn sight than you and your bodyguard, too. Something I can tell because of this thrice-dammed useless foresight gift *He* left me with when I was about your age." He nodded at Honey. "Said He'd come by and take it back, but He hasn't."

Beside me, Honey went still. Peter had been pretty old for a werewolf, at least two centuries. I didn't know how old Honey was—and for the moment I didn't care.

Werewolves don't age physically. I'd always assumed that, like my human mother, I'd have a normal life span, and Adam could live to be as old as . . . well, as Bran Cornick, the Marrok, who ruled the North American werewolves and sometimes talked casually about things that happened in the Middle Ages. Through Hank and his brother, I had met a few other walkers, and they seemed to come in all varieties of young and old. I had known couples, growing up, where the werewolf looked to be in his twenties, and his wife was dying of old age. I didn't want to do that to my mate. I worried about Adam because he didn't talk about it at all, and Adam was all about discussing problems he thought had solutions.

I raised my chin. "How old will I get?"

He opened his mouth, then shook his head. "It's not that kind of foresight. I don't get dates, just possibilities. And if I did know, I don't hate you enough to tell you."

"She doesn't know any other coyote walkers," said Honey. "She is married to a man who will be young a hundred years from now. She wants to know that she is not going to leave him tied to a woman who will slowly die on him."

Laughingdog looked at me. "I don't know. Most walkers age like humans—most are mostly human anyway these days. Coyote doesn't walk this ground much anymore." He smiled a little, but it wasn't aimed at me. "Most of Coyote's children don't have to worry about a long life, anyway. A fool and his life are soon parted, you know."

"I'm only half-human," I told him, mouth dry. I'd never said it before, even to myself. But Laughingdog needed to know it all so he could give me an accurate answer. "Coyote is my father. Sort of my father. He was wearing the skin of a rodeo cowboy who didn't know that he was Coyote at the time."

Gary Laughingdog tilted his face toward me. "Really?" He grinned. "Exactly half sister in truth, then." He let out a huff of air and shrugged. "You are the only real sibling I've met—but those of us closer to the magic in our heritage tend to live longer."

I sat back in my chair, feeling light-headed.

"Death could find you tomorrow, though," Laughingdog said. "So don't get overconfident. Knew a boy who was Raven's child, and he died from measles when he was six years old." He watched me, glanced at Honey, and his eyes gleamed gold from a stray glint of light off the overhead fluorescent tubes. "But you didn't come here to ask me that."

"I need to talk to Coyote," I told him.

He scooted his chair back from the table abruptly, as if to get away from my words. Both guards came to alert, and Luke had his hand on his weapon.

"No one needs that kind of trouble," the man who apparently was sort of my half brother said.

Startled by his extreme reaction I said, slowly, "I've talked to him before without the world being destroyed."

"Has he tried to kill you yet?" he asked.

I started to say "no" before realizing it wasn't true. "Not deliberately," I said instead. "I'm pretty sure it wasn't deliberate." I paused. "Either time."

Honey stared at me.

Laughingdog sucked in a breath. "Ye gods, woman. Why would you want to invite Him into your life?"

"Because I gave him a fae artifact, and if I don't get it back, the fae who came to visit me in the middle of the night might turn the Tri-Cities into a barren graveyard."

Laughingdog made a funny, high noise, then coughed. He waved off the guards and managed to tell them that he'd just swallowed wrong, and his choking became chortles while he was still trying to catch his breath.

When he could breathe without laughing again, he said, "What did you do that for?"

"Which?" I asked.

"Give Coyote an artifact some freaking fae wants," he said.

"Because at that moment it was the best thing to do," Honey said coolly. "Sometimes the only action you can take leads to more trouble. But she would have considered that when she did it. Mercy is no fool, no matter what her heritage. It is not for you to judge. Can you contact Coyote or tell Mercy how to?"

He looked at her. "Mercy isn't the only one who protects her own here, is she?" He shook his head, and to me he said, "Spent all my life trying to make sure He *didn't* visit me. Why would I want to know how to call Him? To say, 'Hi, Father, could you fuck up my life any more than I already have? Gee, thanks. I think that will work'?"

Stress made his voice sound thinner, and he glanced around the depressing room before he said, "Not that He didn't come anyway and screw with me. But at least I didn't invite Him in, you know?"

This meeting had been useful, if in an entirely different way than I'd intended. But if Laughingdog didn't know how to call Coyote, then no one did. If Beauclaire killed me, it wouldn't matter how fast I aged.

"When did he come to you?" I heard Honey ask through my

despair. "Was there any pattern? Did he say anything to you about why he came?" Funny how clearly that capital letter disappeared when Honey talked about Coyote.

Laughingdog closed his eyes. "The last time—He stopped in long enough to make sure that I'd spend a few years here in prison instead of getting safely back to my apartment when I left the bar at closing time. I was walking down the sidewalk, and there He was. He said He was pleased I was about to become interesting again." The expression on his face was suddenly horrified, and I felt a wave of the same magic that had sent me sneezing. "Don't do that," he told me as the pupils in his eyes widened until the brown was a narrow ring around it.

"Don't do what?" asked Honey.

But I knew.

"Don't 'be interesting,'" I said. "Thank you for talking to me."

He shook his head, his face bleak. "Don't thank me for that."

I reached out and touched his hand. It didn't seem too forward an action when he was my almost half brother.

"Don't worry so much," I murmured. "I have support."

He gave a bitter laugh and stood up, signaling the guards that the visit was over. "Nothing will protect you from Coyote. From . . ." His voice changed, deepened, and he said something in a language I'd never heard before. He stopped, then began again, *"He is coming and his children cry his name into the world."* He threw his head back and howled, the high, whining cry of a coyote. As the guards broke into a run, he said something that sounded like Coyote's name, but not quite, three times. It was oddly accented, making the first consonant a guttural sound and the final softer. *"Guayota, Guayota, Guayota,"* he repeated again in a soft chant that gave me goose bumps. *"His children howl his name and hunger for blood until the night is broken with their cries."*

Before the guards touched him, he fell off the chair, body writhing for a moment, then every muscle in his body seized. His back arched off the floor, and his eyes rolled back in his head. I dropped to the floor and pulled his head into my lap so it wouldn't slap the floor a second time. Honey protected his tongue by putting her fingers in his mouth. She didn't flinch when he bit down.

When he lapsed into total unconsciousness, it was so sudden that it was more frightening than his sudden fit.

Luke crouched beside me. "We've called for help. You need to leave now."

Honey and I were escorted out of the room with more speed than gentleness, but when we retrieved our IDs, Luke found us again.

"He has these fits, sometimes," Luke told us. "The doctor thinks it's the result of doing hallucinogenic drugs when he was young."

Luke didn't, quite, ask me what I'd been doing there—but only because Honey growled at him.

"Thank you," I said. "He was helpful. Treat him kindly when you can." Something in me rebelled at leaving him here, caged like a zoo animal. My half brother, he'd said. Coyote's children. I shivered and hoped that his last words were hallucinogenic remnants, but it had felt, had smelled, like magic to me. It had smelled like Coyote.

Luke nodded at me, lips disapproving, but went back to his job obediently enough.

"Some of the pack like to forget who you are when Adam isn't around," Honey said softly. "I'll have a discussion with Luke."

I gave her a sharp look she didn't see because she was watching Luke. Honey didn't like being dominant—she avoided situations in which her natural temperament showed through. I'd thought Honey didn't like me at all. So why had she just decided, out loud, to squelch Luke?

I opened the locker and collected the Vanagon's keys. I walked out the prison door a free woman, but it wasn't until I turned the van out onto the freeway that I really relaxed.

"So all you have to do to summon Coyote is be interesting," Honey mused. "Shouldn't take you long."

"You could stake me out naked in the desert near an anthill," I suggested.

She shook her head. "I don't do clichés. Besides, Adam might object."

My phone rang.

"Could you see who that is?" I asked.

She picked it up off the floor between our seats and, after a glance at the readout, answered it. "Adam, it's Honey," she said. "Mercy is driving."

"Why hasn't she picked up her phone for the past hour?" he asked.

She held the phone my direction and raised one eyebrow in inquiry.

"I've been in prison," I said in a sad voice. And left it at that. Honey flashed a grin at me, the expression startling because I was so used to the reserve she'd been carrying around with her.

There was a brief silence. "Okay," Adam said. "Was your undoubtedly brief sojourn the cause of your phone call earlier today? Christy said you didn't leave a message."

"Christy answered your cell phone, and you thought Mercy

should leave a message?" Honey's voice let everyone know exactly what she thought of that.

"No," said Adam with gently emphasized patience. "I thought that she should have told Christy to give me the phone."

"You were unavailable," I told him.

Silence followed. Unhappy silence. And then I remembered who the enemy was and what she wanted to do to Adam and me.

"I'm sorry," I said. "I let her get to me. But not to the point I did something stupid, I promise. I called Honey, and she came with me to see a man about summoning Coyote. Hank gave me his name. It was safe enough."

Adam made a man sound that could have meant anything, but I took it to mean that we were okay again. When he used actual words, the subject wasn't Christy anymore. "What did you learn from Hank's contact?"

A lot. Important things I didn't want to talk about on the phone. So I gave him the least of it. "He doesn't summon Coyote because he's pretty sure that's the stupidest thing anyone could do. But apparently Coyote has a habit of showing up when he finds one of us—his descendants—interesting."

Adam laughed ruefully. "Shouldn't take you long, then."

"That's what I told her," Honey said.

"Any word on the fire?" I asked.

"Arson is confirmed," Adam said, "though there seems to be some confusion about the accelerant used. Whatever it was, it got really hot, really fast."

"Do you think he's done this kind of thing before?" I asked.

"The fire investigator seemed to think so. We're looking for suspicious fires tied to an overzealous lover. We're also looking at the European angle. There's another trail, too. Warren got descriptions of this man's dogs out of Christy. Looks like they are some sort of mastiff. She said they were valuable and difficult for anyone except Juan—her stalker—to handle."

"That doesn't sound like a mastiff," I told him. "There's a guy in the Montana pack who was breeding all sorts of big dogs. The mastiffs were mostly big sweeties."

"I'm not sure she'd know a poodle from a sheepdog. But Juan Flores apparently took special pleasure in pointing out that both of his dogs outweighed Christy, who is a hundred and ten pounds."

Hah. Christy was at least twenty pounds heavier than that.

"Hah." Honey snorted with derision. "Christy is at least one thirty or one thirty-five."

"Big dog," I said.

Adam laughed. "I'll let you know if there is anything new, and Mercy?"

"Yes?"

"Don't do anything too interesting."

He disconnected before I could reply.

"Don't underestimate Christy," Honey said. "She's not nearly as helpless as she pretends to be."

"I know that," I said. I glanced at Honey, then looked back at the road. "I thought you liked her."

She growled. "Helpless bitch had the whole pack—Adam included—hopping to her tune. Couldn't mow the lawn, change a tire, or carry her own laundry up the stairs. Even Peter fell for it, and he usually had better sense. She didn't like Warren—I thought at the time she was worried he was going to make a play for Adam, but mostly, I think, he didn't fall over himself to be her slave. Darryl's helpless against her, but at least he knows it. All that might not have been too bad, but she played them all off each other. I had my own private celebration when she left Adam."

Her lips twisted. "I don't like you," she told me, but there was a lie in her voice, and she stopped talking, looking almost surprised. She started again, her tones softer than they had been. "I don't enjoy change," she said. "And you are change, Mercy. I am comfortable with the old ways, and you are tossing them aside whenever they don't suit you, while Adam looks on with satisfaction. But one thing I've always known is that you were trying your best to make things better. Christy, she looked out for herself first. I don't imagine that has changed. Only a fool would say the same about you—though I frequently disagree with your methods and goals."

I cleared my throat. "So. Do you want to see a man about some dogs?"

5

~~~

I PULLED INTO JOEL'S DRIVEWAY, AND OUR PRESENCE
was announced by a chorus of barking fit to wake the dead. Joel
might work in the vineyards and fix cars as a hobby, but dogs were
his passion. He and his wife bred, showed, and trained dogs. I
figured that he might be able to help us figure out what kind of
dogs Christy's stalker had. It was a shot in the dark, but I was
willing to do anything to shorten Christy's time in my house. I'd
called Joel, and he'd told me to meet him at home.

Mostly, the dogs barking at us were just excited, but I heard
the true anger of a dog whose territory is breached in at least one
bass voice.

"Maybe I should wait," Honey said. "Dogs are afraid of me."

I shook my head. "Most dogs get over their fear of werewolves
pretty fast, given a chance."

I hopped down out of the Vanagon. While I waited for Honey
to come around the vehicle, the front door opened, and a small

woman came out of the door with a leashless dog that was none-theless at heel. The dog was white, female, and looked to be a purebred Staffordshire terrier. The woman greeted me in Spanish.

I get mistaken for Hispanic a lot.

I shook my head, but didn't bother objecting to her assumption. "Sorry. *No hablo Español. ¿Esta Joel aqui?*"

She stopped when she was about ten feet away, and the dog sat as soon as she quit moving. All of the dog's attention was on the woman.

"No," the woman said, then paused. Maybe she'd had to take a moment to switch languages. "You must be Mercy. Joel called and told me what you wanted. I told him to stay at work because I know the dogs as well as he does." Her English was good, with only a touch of accent.

She gave Honey a slightly wary look, and the dog focused on her, too. "I am his wife, Lucia. Joel tells me that you are the Mercy who keeps him in parts for his old cars. Come into my house, and I will help you as much as I can."

Her house, when she ushered us in, was not fancy or large, but it was clean enough that I would have eaten off any surface. We sat on an old leather couch while Lucia retreated to her kitchen.

The big white dog who'd accompanied her outside followed her into the kitchen, leaving us under the watchful care of the three lesser dogs who were occupying the living room. All of the living-room dogs were male and all the same brindle tan. One of them ignored us entirely as he tried to destroy a hard rubber bone. One sat across the room and stared at us. I fought the urge to stare him down and nudged Honey when she started to do just that.

"We're guests," I reminded her. "Neutral territory."

The third dog, the biggest of the three, sat on my foot and put his chin on my knee. I rubbed him gently behind the ears. He closed his eyes and made snuffly-content noises. The dog who'd been staring at us heaved a disgusted sigh and wiggled around until his back was to us, not happy about the intruders but too well trained to object.

None of the dogs seemed to have an issue with having a werewolf in the house.

There was not a lot of furniture, but what there was was good. Some of it handcrafted, so maybe Joel did some woodworking. Maybe Lucia did the woodworking. On the wall across from me was a framed Texas state flag flanked by good amateur paintings of dogs. One of them could have been the big white dog that followed Joel's wife around, and the other was a yellow Lab with a Frisbee in its mouth. There was a case with a display of championship ribbons. On a bookcase were a number of trophies, some of which had dogs on the top of them.

The dogs Joel bred were expensive, well trained, and obtainable only when he was certain the person buying them was capable of taking good care of them. They were good dogs—better, he'd told me seriously, than most people he knew. He had no use for idiots who didn't respect the damage dogs could do when left untrained or put in situations where they felt they had to defend themselves.

In addition to breeding, he and his wife rehabbed the "aggressive" dogs that were brought to the local shelters that would otherwise have just put the dogs down. Joel had scars on his arms and a huge one on his leg from a terrified, half-grown Rottweiler who now, Joel had assured me, lived happily with a huge family. Mostly, they had success, he'd told me, but a few were too badly damaged to ever be safe in human company.

The Marrok took damaged werewolves into his pack, where he could control the conditions under which they interacted with the rest of the world. Joel had told me with tears in his eyes about a battered pit-survivor he'd had to put down a few months ago. He was as passionate in his desire to save his dogs as the Marrok was to save his wolves.

Joel's wife brought in three glasses of sun tea and sat down in the chair opposite the couch while I explained about Christy's stalker—and how I thought that if the dog breed he had was rare, maybe we could find someone who knew him in the dog world. I gave her the bare-bones description Christy had given me.

"Molossers," Lucia said, then gave Honey a grin. "It is a type, not a breed. It includes mastiffs and Saint Bernards. How familiar is your husband's ex-wife with dog breeds?"

I called Adam's cell phone.

Christy answered yet again. "Adam's phone," she said. "He—"

"So how much do you know about dogs?" I asked her without giving her a chance to tell me why she was answering his phone—again—and why he couldn't talk to me.

"I grew up with golden retrievers," she said.

"Do you know what a molosser is?"

"No," she admitted reluctantly.

"Ask her if she could recognize a Newfoundland," Lucia suggested.

I decided this three-way had gone from awkward to ludicrous, and I handed the phone over to Lucia. Eventually, Christy got on the Internet to look at dog breeds.

"Cane corso," Christy said. "They look right."

"Cane corso are smaller than you describe," Lucia said. "Also, they usually have nice temperaments. But poor handling can turn even a Labrador into a dangerous animal. We will keep the cane corso as a possibility. You said these dogs were black."

"Yes," Christy agreed. "Really black. In the sunlight, it looked like they were black striped on black."

After twenty minutes of questioning and checking out various breeds, Lucia's tones changed from cautiously professional to profoundly sympathetic. Christy was good, even over the phone.

"What language was the dog's name in?" Lucia's voice was soothing.

"I don't speak any foreign languages," Christy apologized.

"She's been to Europe," I murmured.

"Did it sound German?" Lucia asked. "The Broholmer might fit."

"Not German," Christy said even more apologetically. "Maybe it was Spanish or even Latin."

Lucia stared at her white dog as she thought. Finally she said, "The fila Brasileiro—a Brazilian mastiff—might fit. They are rare and very much one-person dogs. They can be very aggressive if not socialized when they are young."

Christy made her spell it out so she could look it up. After a few minutes, she said, "No. These dogs . . . their heads were more in line with their body size. And the fila Brasileiro look like bloodhounds to me. Kind of friendly. There was nothing friendly-looking about his dogs. This is sort of stupid, but I just remembered something." She paused, and said, sounding embarrassed, "The dog's breed. It sounded like a bird's name."

"Perro de presa Canario," Lucia said immediately. "Some people call them dogo Canarios, presa Canario, or just presas or Canarios." She spelled it for Christy without prompting.

After a minute Christy made a disappointed noise. "No. These dogs' ears are too small. His had long ears, like the last breed we looked at."

"Presas usually have their ears clipped—like boxers or Doberman pinschers. They do it to the American Staffordshires like my own dogs, too. I chose not to. They say it is because they are used with livestock—to prevent damage. We had a Doberman once who was not ear-clipped, and he always had trouble with his ears being sore where they bent over. But the primary reason for clipping is that it makes them look more fierce. There are people who breed presas who do not crop their ears. See if you can't find a photo of one with natural ears."

"I will keep looking . . ." Christy's voice trailed off. "There's one with unclipped ears. That's it. Presa Canario."

I took the phone back. "I'll call Warren and let him know what he's looking for."

"I'll let Adam know, too," Christy said brightly. "He'll be glad I figured it out."

"Sounds good," I responded after sorting through the things I'd rather have said to her and remembering that I had resolved not to be spiteful or petty today.

I disconnected my phone.

"So," I asked, "just how rare are presa Canarios?"

"They are rare in the US," Lucia said. "But a few years ago there was a man who wanted to breed them for pit fighting. He was put in jail, and his lawyers ended up with a pair of his dogs. The dogs had been mistreated, and the lawyers had no idea of how to handle them. The dogs killed a woman in their apartment building who was coming home with her groceries." Lucia's pretty mouth tightened, and her white dog bumped her leg to comfort her. "Do you know what happened?"

I nodded, because I remembered the incident, though I hadn't known what the breed of dog had been. "They became suddenly popular."

She made a growling noise, and the big dog who had been sleeping with his back to us turned around so he could see her. He didn't get up, but he remained alert. The dog whose head was on my knee leaned on me a little harder and sighed, groaning a little as I let my fingers search out another good itchy spot.

"Canarios are not evil dogs," Lucia told me, "any more than my Amstaffs are evil. Canarios are guard dogs, bred to protect their people, their herds—and to hunt for food by taking down big animals. Trained and raised with common sense, they are useful and valuable members of the family."

It sounded like a rant. I have a few of those, usually involving idiots who try to replace fuses with pennies, people who text while driving, and tax codes so Byzantine not even the IRS really knows what they mean—so I nodded sympathetically.

"I know that you are married to the werewolf," Lucia told me. "You understand about animals who can be dangerous under the right circumstance. If your friend's stalker has Canarios—he could train them so that they kill on command."

Honey bared her teeth and growled. All four dogs rose to their feet and surrounded Lucia—but they didn't act upset, just ready. Dogs are better than people at reading body language.

"Big dogs are just dogs," said Honey. "I am a wolf." She looked at the Amstaffs, who returned her look unafraid and ready to defend their person if they needed to.

"But you, little brave cousins," Honey said, half-amused under their regard, "you I would take with me on a hunt."

Not many people could call Lucia's dogs little and mean it. I would guess that it took a werewolf to feel that way; they looked plenty big to me.

Lucia, far from being intimidated by Honey, smiled. "Brave? Yes. They will take on anything to defend Joel or me." Her smile dropped away. "Your friend"—Christy had promoted herself from my husband's ex to my friend—"said that this man's dogs were difficult, but he had no trouble with them. That tells me that they are *his* dogs and that they are very well trained. His dogs then will be as mine. They will not know that he is a man who attacks women who cannot fight back: a man who is a coward. They will only know that this man is their god, the one they must listen to and protect. Canarios are courageous. They will not run from you just because you are a werewolf."

"I'm not actually a werewolf," I told her apologetically. "But I appreciate the insight. Do you know anyone who raises Canarios? Someone we can talk to about other breeders?"

She nodded. "I do." She left and returned with a card. "These people live in Portland and breed Canarios. They are very well-known and reputable. If Christy's stalker is a breeder or an avid fancier, they will know of him."

I CALLED WARREN AS SOON AS WE WERE IN THE VAN. He took the information and assured me that he was doing his best to find Juan Flores, so Christy could go back to Eugene.

"Thank you," I told him sincerely, and he laughed as he rang off.

Honey was thoughtfully silent on the drive back to her house. I stopped in her driveway, and she opened the door. But she stayed in the van for a moment as she looked at her house. "Maybe I need to get a dog," she said.

———————

BETWEEN THE PRISON TRIP AND LUCIA'S HELP WITH the dogs, I managed to come home very late on Tuesday and escaped quality Christy-time, for the most part. Though I hadn't planned to, I left before breakfast was made the next morning. I had a last-minute fix Wednesday night that kept me nearly an hour later than usual. The thought occurred to me that if I could avoid home long enough, maybe I wouldn't have to talk to her before she left.

I went home, confident I'd be too late for dinner, but when I came in the door, Christy met me with a smile.

"You are in luck," she told me. "Adam had an errand to run so I waited dinner for him. You have about fifteen minutes to shower." She wrinkled her nose.

"Thanks," I said, as if she hadn't just sent me off to clean up. I'd intended to shower because I was sweaty and dirty. I wasn't going to behave like I was thirteen and refuse to do it because she'd told me to. No matter how strong the impulse.

I was in my bathroom, pulling off my clothes, when I heard Adam come into the bedroom. I didn't want to have him see how agitated she'd made me, so I just continued to get ready to shower.

"Three days since Christy got here, and we've made no progress, Mercy." Adam's voice came, slightly muffled, from the bedroom. "It's not that Juan Flores doesn't leave traces—it's that none of them mean anything. It's starting to look as though he might really be someone dangerous. My connections with the DEA tell me that they have ten Juan Floreses on their watch list—none of them up high enough in the money to be Christy's Juan Flores."

He neared the bathroom, and I heard him open a drawer. "They say it might mean that he's not a drug trafficker, or that he's so big no one talks about him. I've worked it out with a few of my people so I can work from home until we find him." He paused, then said in a low voice, "You should know that Christy asked me to stay home because she doesn't feel comfortable with the wolves if I'm not here."

I turned on the shower to let it warm up as well as give me a chance to think about what I wanted to say to Adam. But when I turned, I was confronted by a large plastic see-through box covered with sparkly pink rhinestones that held a huge collection of makeup. Christy's makeup was in my bathroom, on my counter, next to my sink. At least, I thought, she hadn't put it next to Adam's sink.

"Don't we have another bathroom upstairs that Christy could use to store her makeup?" I asked.

There was a long silence, then Adam said, "There wasn't room for her stuff and Jesse's stuff in the smaller bathroom." Another pause. "I told her you wouldn't mind."

I got in the shower and stuck my head under the hot water, so I couldn't say anything I would regret. Coyotes weren't as territorial, as a rule, as werewolves, but we still had our hard lines. Having Christy flouncing in and out through my bedroom into my bathroom crossed one of my hard lines. I washed my hair and tried to let things, the ugly, unpleasant things I was feeling, slide down the drain with the rest of the grime that had covered my skin.

The shower door opened, and Adam stepped in.

"I'm sorry," he said.

I shook my head and leaned against him. The feel of his skin next to mine went a long way toward restoring my equanimity.

"She probably asked you if I'd mind," I said. "And managed to imply that only a small-minded, petty person could possibly object to her husband's ex-wife moving her makeup into the larger, brighter bathroom. If you told her she couldn't, then you'd have been implying that I was a petty, mean-spirited person."

"And jealous," he added. "I'm sorry."

I shook my head. "I love you," I told him. "I love the man you are. But her makeup is not staying here. I won't have her in our bedroom. In our bathroom. But I will take care of it." I smiled at him. "I don't care if she calls me jealous or petty. Not your worry. So still no real information on Flores?"

"No," he said, soaping up his hands and starting to wash himself off briskly. "The Reno pack sent a couple of wolves to talk to the hotel where Christy met Flores. Turns out he comes there every year about the same time, checks in under different names for which he has ID—but that is apparently not unusual despite government regulations. There's an actor who regularly checks in there under the name of the secret identity of the last superhero he played. But the staff remembers him because of the dogs—and confirmed that whatever name he's registered as, he still goes by Juan Flores."

I had followed Adam's example and scrubbed myself down as he talked. I even managed to soap my hair and condition it before the magnetic draw of Adam's skin forced me to touch him.

"He can speak native-quality Spanish, but his accent is weird," Adam told me, but his voice was a little unsteady, and he braced himself against the corner of the shower. "Not from Spain, Puerto

Rico, Cuba, or Mexico. The Argentinian maid said he sounded Colombian. The Colombian maid said maybe Venezuelan, and he used very old-fashioned—"

"Old-fashioned what?" I asked, letting my mouth follow my hands.

"Mmmm," Adam answered.

Someone knocked on the bathroom door. "Hurry up, Mercy," Auriele said briskly. "Christy's made her famous Szechuan chicken, but it needs to be eaten right now."

I backed away, and Adam snarled soundlessly.

"Yeah," I said. "Me, too."

On the way down for dinner, I collected Christy's things and set them down in front of her door.

"You aren't going to talk to her?" Adam asked.

"I don't need to," I told him. "She'll get the message." If I had to give it again, she'd be buying new makeup and a new case. But I was pretty sure this would be enough.

I ALWAYS START WORK EARLY—A HABIT FORMED IN summers when the afternoon sun can heat the garage ten degrees hotter than the triple-digit figures outside. But Thursday morning, I had left home while the sky was still dark just to get away from the breakfast Christy had been in the process of making. Nothing horrible had happened at dinner, but I didn't want to repeat it, either. Tad didn't show up at work until almost an hour after I did.

"No brownies?" he asked.

"Christy has taken over my kitchen," I told him as I wrote the last check for the garage's bills. "No stress relief for me. No chocolate for you."

"No chocolate?" he said, leaning on the counter. "That's terrible." He waited hopefully, and when I didn't say anything more, he asked, "So what did she make for us today?"

I waved him at the brown paper bag sitting next to my keyboard.

He sniffed, then opened it. "Cinnamon rolls?"

"You can eat these in here," I said, and licked the last envelope closed. "Eat them both. They have Christy cooties."

"The muffins were good," he said. "So was the apple pie. I guess I can do without chocolate if the alternative is cinnamon rolls." There was sympathy in his voice if not his words.

"Blasphemer," I told him. "There are no cinnamon rolls better than chocolate."

He sniffed again. "These might be."

I left him to it and retreated to go work on cars. In my garage, I ruled without question—and had since Zee had retreated to the fae reservation. Her makeup case wasn't going to end up in my garage.

But as soon as I put Christy out of my mind, I started fretting over my inability to find Coyote. I'd been pretty optimistic after Honey had grilled Gary Laughingdog. But I hadn't had any brainstorms about how to be interesting enough to attract Coyote's attention.

Last night I'd resorted to yelling Coyote's name to the open air (well away from home to make sure no werewolves would hear me making an idiot out of myself). I'd tried talking to Coyote as if he were in the same room to see if he would come out of hiding—and wondered if I was going to have to mastermind a bank heist in order to attract his attention.

I was contemplating criminal activities when Hank called. I

peeled off the stupid latex gloves, so I didn't get grease on my phone. Christy had done that much for me: since I started wearing the gloves—my phone was staying cleaner.

"Hey, Hank," I said.

"You talk with Gary?"

Something in his voice had me straightening my spine. "Yes."

"Hope you got the information you needed."

"What's wrong?"

"Last night or this morning, Laughingdog escaped. One of his relatives called me to see if I thought you might have had something to do with it."

"No," I said. I wondered who Gary Laughingdog's relatives were and if *they* might be able to tell me how to get in touch with Coyote. "I don't think so. Did you know that he has some kind of foresight?"

"Yes," said Hank. "And much joy he's ever gotten from it. Gets him into trouble and never out, he says. You think he saw something and broke out?"

"I don't know him well enough to say that," I said. "He had a couple of visions while we were there. Mostly a bunch of nonsense—" But he'd known Honey's name. "Something to the effect of Coyote's"—I remembered that odd pronunciation—"*somebody's* children . . . breaking the night with their cries. I don't know anyone else besides the two of us who qualify. Maybe he saw something that made his escape necessary."

"And maybe Coyote's kin don't do well in lockup," Hank said. "No more than does anyone, but Coyote was always good at getting out of places he didn't want to be. Anyway, you can expect to see police sometime. They'll talk to everyone on his visitors list, and there are about four of us up in the Yakama Nation and you.

He's not big-time, but breaking out might make him more important to them. They don't like being thwarted." "They," I knew, referred to the authorities of whatever flavor. Hank didn't like people who could tell him what to do—and he avoided them by being a very law-abiding citizen.

"Thank you for the heads-up," I said.

"Probably he's just gone walkabout. Show up with another name in ten or twenty years. He does that."

"Walkabout?" I said doubtfully. "Isn't that an Aussie Aboriginal term?"

"An Indian is an Indian, Mercy, no matter what continent they come from," he said with a grin in his voice. Before I could disagree, he disconnected.

So I wasn't surprised when the police showed up in the afternoon.

"Mercy."

"Tony?" I looked up from the Passat I was working on. There was something wrong with the injectors, but it was intermittent, and I was afraid that meant it was electronic—and probably something to do with the computer. And that would explain why the car's computer hadn't been able to tell me what was going on.

"Mercy, I need you to clean up and come talk to me."

I blinked at the tightness in his voice and focused on his face. Trouble, that expression said, and in response, I backed out of the job, pulling bolts and pieces out of my pockets and putting them on the car where they wouldn't be lost. I peeled off the latex gloves and tossed them.

"Tad?" I said.

The sound of the crawler's hard wheels on pavement signaled his emergence from under the Vanagon he was repairing.

"I'm headed off with Tony for a bit. Don't burn down the garage or run off the customers while I'm gone."

Tad glanced from Tony's face to mine, and said mildly, "Is it okay if I call in a few strippers to put on a show and charge it to the garage? I've been thinking it might pull in some more customers."

"Sure," I said as I stepped out of my overalls: in the interest of time, I didn't bother to retreat to the bathroom. I was wearing a full set of clothes underneath anyway. "Just make sure Christy makes it over in time for the show so she can tell the pack what kind of place I run here. Oh, and tell her I took off with a hot-looking man."

He grimaced. "Yeah, sorry about that."

She'd called yesterday, and, knowing how I felt about her, Tad had told her that I'd gone out for a run. Tad doesn't usually lie, though since he is only half-fae, he can, and he is a fair hand at misdirection. I had been in the garage bay, and he'd answered my cell in the office, where I'd left it.

Next thing I know, I was getting a call from Adam, who was mad because he thought that I had been running without protection. Grocery stores and other public places were unlikely spots for kidnapping the Alpha's wife. Running I had to do with company for safety's sake. I regretted it, but I understood the necessity.

I'd explained that Tad had been mistaken when he talked to Christy. I took the blame for it—thus putting myself firmly in the wrong. The pack figuratively—maybe literally, for all I know—patted Christy on the head for being so worried about my well-being.

"Not your fault," I told Tad—Christy would have found something else to make me look bad anyway. "Though this time you might mention that the handsome man is an armed police officer who will keep me safe as a fox in a henhouse."

Tad gave me a mock salute while I followed Tony out.

"Trouble?" Tony asked.

"Adam's ex-wife has a stalker, so she is living with us until we can figure out what to do about him," I told him as matter-of-factly as I could manage.

He stopped and looked at me, and finally lost the odd distance I'd sensed—as if I'd been a stranger he'd been sent to fetch. Maybe he was worried that I *had* had a hand in Gary Laughingdog's escape.

"Adam's ex-wife is living with you?" he asked incredulously.

"Her stalker is dangerous," I told him. "We are pretty sure he killed a man and burned down the building her condo was in. Until someone can find him and arrest him, Christy is staying with us because even a violent man might hesitate to face off with a pack of werewolves."

I had added the "arrest him" part because it sounded good. I was pretty sure at this point that any arrest would be postmortem. Maybe it had been a mistake because something in the last sentence put the distance right back between us.

"I can see that," he said, and continued walking to his car.

I followed and, when he opened the passenger door for me, I got in. We sat in front of the garage for a minute, and I waited for him to ask me about Gary Laughingdog's escape from prison.

"I saw what you became," he said instead. "Over at Kyle Brooks's house, when the body that was in the trunk of the car broke out, and you and Adam tried to chase it down."

I looked at him. Yep. That cat was out of the bag for sure. I'd changed into my coyote shape to go chase after a zombie and had forgotten about all the people watching. Tony hadn't been the only one who'd gotten an eyeful. I'd grown used to having more people know what I was and hadn't even thought about what I was doing and who I was doing it in front of.

In most ways, it wouldn't matter if I shouted out that I was a coyote shapeshifter, a walker, to the whole world. I wasn't alone anymore. In other ways, though, it was possibly disastrous. If the public realized that the fae and the werewolves were just the top of the anthill of Other that lived hidden among the human population, it could be bad. Bad for humans and bad for everyone else, too.

"Yes?" I said. It was a question because we weren't sitting in the car just so I could confess to being a coyote shapeshifter.

"I asked Gabriel about it."

Gabriel had been my right hand in the garage before he went to college, and Tony had been infatuated with Gabriel's mother for as long as I'd known him.

"He told me something about what you are." Tony met my eyes. "You aren't human."

"No," I agreed slowly. "Not completely."

He huffed an unhappy breath. "If there was someone in the pack murdering humans, would you cover for him?"

I sucked in a breath. "You have a body?"

"You didn't answer the question." His reply had answered mine, though.

"If we had someone going around killing people for the fun of it," I said, "I'd tell Adam."

"And what would Adam do?"

Silence hung between us. I'd known Tony a long time. Long enough, I decided, to tell him the real truth instead of sugarcoating it. "Adam would deal with it before the police could step in. The fae's sudden retreat to the reservations has put the werewolves on trial in the court of public opinion. They—*we*—can't allow a murderer to stand trial or continue to rampage."

"Are you a werewolf?" he asked. "I mean a werewolf who turns into a coyote. A werecoyote."

"There coyote." I grinned at him and received a *look*. "No. I'm not a werewolf or werecoyote—which I have never heard of, by the way. I have a different kind of magic entirely. Native magic, not European like the werewolves are. Mostly turning into a coyote is about all I manage." I wasn't going to explain to him about the ghosts or my partial immunity to magic, which was nothing I could count on anyway. "It would be best if you didn't tell everyone about what I can do, though. Best for the public, who don't need to be looking at their neighbors and worrying if they are something from a horror show. If they think werewolves and fae are it, then everyone is safer."

Tony nodded as if that thought had occurred to him, and he'd already been on board with keeping my secrets secret. "You included yourself with the werewolves, though."

I shrugged. "I'm married to one—and he made me an official member of the pack." Not just in name, but in fact—accepted by the pack magic that bound us all together. But Tony didn't need to know that. Even less than shapeshifting coyotes did people need to know that there was such a thing as pack magic. "Where are you going with this, Tony?"

He looked away, not happy. He patted the steering wheel nervously. "I need to know if I can trust you."

"For some things," I told him seriously. "You can trust me not to leave people helpless against a monster. A human monster or a werewolf monster. I don't help bad guys—even if they are someone I thought I liked or felt some loyalty to. Bad guys need to be stopped."

That, apparently, had been the right thing to say.

"Okay," he said with sudden assurance. "Okay. Yes." He turned on the car and pulled out with a squeal, switching on his lights but not his siren. "We need your help with something."

And that's all he said. But that "something" took us past the old Welch's factory, past the WELCOME TO FINLEY sign, past the road to my house that used to only be Adam's house and once was Adam and Christy's house. The semirural cluster of houses grew momentarily denser near the high school, then thinned again. We followed the main road miles farther on, out to where croplands took over from small ranchettes, turned down a rutted dirt road, and pulled in next to five police cars and an ominously unlit ambulance gathered along the edge of a hayfield.

I got out slowly as an angry man in a suit broke away from where a group of police officers were gathered and boiled over to Tony's car, glanced at me, and flushed even hotter with the rage that covered . . . fear and horror.

"What the hell are you thinking? Bringing *her* here?"

I didn't know him, but he knew me. Adam was something of a local, if not a national, celebrity—good looks are not always a good thing. That meant that lots of people I'd never met knew who I was.

"We need her," Tony told him. "If what you told me was right and this was something other than human. She can tell us what it was."

I caught a scent that bothered me, but it wasn't coming from the direction of the group of police officers. Frowning, I turned in a slow circle to pinpoint it. I glanced at Tony, but he was busy arguing with the other man, so I wandered off in the direction my nose told me to, away from the cluster of officials.

The ground was more uneven than I would have thought a hayfield would be, maybe because it was alfalfa and not grass hay. I had to watch my step as I walked along the edge of where grass had been cut. The growing crop of hay was only about five inches high—the length of a lawn that had been left a week too long. Off the cultivated field, I'd have been wading through the weeds that ruled where the ground was too rocky to be farmed.

A short distance ahead in that too-rough-to-harvest rocky area, a copse of cottonwoods grew where the ground dropped down in a natural drainage. They'd probably been planted as a windbreak because we weren't near enough to the Columbia River for the growth to be natural. By my reckoning, the source of the things I smelled seemed to be coming from the same general area.

Tony and the man had quit arguing to follow me.

"Where are you going, Mercy?" Tony called.

"Something smells bad over here," I told him. Blood and feces is bad, right?

I left the tilled ground and broke through the edging ring of opportunistic alfalfa into cheatgrass that released spiky-painful seedpods into my tennis shoes and socks as soon as I'd traveled about two steps. I followed the too-sweet, unmistakable scent of freshly opened organs and blood to a small clearing under the trees—and stopped, appalled.

"Holy shit," the stranger who knew me said in reverent tones. Then he shouted one of those words that don't mean anything except "pay attention" and "come" and are designed to carry over battlefields.

This was not a battlefield, or even the remains of a battlefield. It was the remains of a slaughter.

Bodies, blood, and pieces were scattered here and there and mixed, so it took me a moment to parse exactly what I saw. I finally decided to go with heads, because heads are difficult to eat, and the charnel-house mess was definitely missing parts and maybe whole bodies. Five . . . no, six people, all women, two dogs—a German shepherd and something small and mixed-breed—a horse, and some other big animal whose head was either missing or might have been under something.

I have a strong stomach—I hunt rabbits, mice, and small birds while wearing my coyote skin, and I eat them raw. Before this, I would have said that lots of things make me squeamish, but fresh bodies not so much. This was so far beyond anything I'd ever seen that I flinched, looked away, then turned back to stare because part of me was sure that it couldn't have been as bad as I first thought. It was worse.

Had someone in the pack done this? Or rather, given the volume of meat eaten, had several someones in the pack done this?

"These haven't been here long," I said into the silence behind me because I had to say something, *do* something. "Probably only since yesterday. It's only spring, but even so, something would have started rotting in a day or so, and I don't smell much putrefaction."

I took a step forward to see better, and Tony grabbed my arm.

"Crime site," he said. "We haven't processed this. We didn't know about this one." He looked around. "This isn't a make-out site, and there's no reason for people to be walking around here. Probably wouldn't have seen it until the guy who called us about the first body in his field came upon this by accident, too."

"How did she know it was here?" asked the angry man who knew who I was.

"I could smell them," I told him simply. "I've got a good nose—being the mate of a werewolf can bring unexpected benefits." Both were true, just not the way I implied.

"Clay Willis, this is Mercy Hauptman. Mercy, Clay Willis," said Tony. "Clay's the investigator in charge. We had one body I wanted you to take a look at because it looked like it's been eaten by something. Our guy said maybe werewolves. That kill is older than this one"—he paused and took a breath—"than these are by more than a day."

"Could have been a werewolf," I acknowledged reluctantly. If a werewolf had done this, he needed to be stopped yesterday. But, I thought with some relief, if it had been one of our werewolves who had taken this much prey, he'd been in the grips of some kind of frenzy, and that would have translated itself to the pack bonds. We all knew, on moon hunts, when one of us took down prey. It wasn't one of our pack.

"I can't tell for sure if it was werewolves from here. Maybe if I got closer." If a werewolf had been around here, he'd taken a different route to the killing field because I couldn't smell werewolf.

"Just tell us what you see," Tony suggested, and raised a peremptory hand to keep the other people spread out behind us quiet.

I looked at the pile of bodies, trying to analyze what I saw rather than worry about it.

"Someone," I began slowly, "maybe several someones—" I stopped and changed my mind. "No, it was just one killer. He had dinner, then . . . a play day, maybe? Opportunistic kills? Some predators, like leopards, will bring all of their prey to one place, where they can feed later." But it didn't really feel like that.

"Why not several someones?" Tony asked.

I tried to work that out, but my instincts said one killer, and I couldn't tell them that. When I made a frustrated sound, Tony said, "Just from the top of your head, Mercy."

"No sign of competition," I said, finally, distilling what my instincts had told me. "When a pack hunts—" Someone behind me sucked in a breath.

"Werewolf packs hunt at least once a month on the full moon," I told them firmly. "Around here, we mostly hunt rabbits or ground squirrels. Other places, they hunt deer, elk, or even moose. Just like timber wolves do, though werewolves avoid domestic animals like cattle as a matter of course."

"Point taken," said Willis, not sounding angry anymore, just tired.

"When wolves hunt, there is a hierarchy. Someone directs, others follow. I don't see any signs of that. No signs that someone got the good parts—" My voice wobbled because for all my experience with killing rabbits, they *were* rabbits. One of the women was wearing tennis shoes that looked like a pair Jesse had in her closet. I shut up for a second to recover.

"Maybe another kind of predator would hunt differently." I shrugged uneasily. "But I think this is the work of just one."

Only the horse and the other big animal—which had probably been a horse, too, because I thought I could pick out the start of a mane—had been disemboweled. Predators go for organ meats first. So why had he mutilated the other bodies beyond what he'd eaten? It had been deliberate and had nothing to do with eating because there was an intact dog leg about ten feet from me, and the dog was on the far side of the pile. I breathed in, but that didn't help. The scent of blood held no trauma for me, but the stink of terror and . . . more faintly, pain.

"I think you'll find that at least some of them were mutilated while they were still alive," I said in a low voice because I didn't want it to be true. But my stomach cramped with knowledge that the smell of pain meant someone had hurt. It was faint because pain stops when someone dies.

"A werewolf could do this?" asked Willis.

"I told—" The wind shifted just a little, and I caught another scent. I closed my eyes and took a deep breath, trying to get below the smell of the dead.

"Magic," I said, with my eyes still closed. It was subtle, like a good perfume, but now that I knew its flavor, it was strong. Problem was, I had no idea what kind of magic I was scenting.

"Fae?" asked someone who wasn't Tony or Willis.

I opened my eyes and shook my head. "Fae magic smells different than this. This isn't witchcraft, either, though it's closer to that than to fae magic."

"Witchcraft," said Willis neutrally.

I nodded. It wasn't a secret; the witches had been hiding in plain sight for a hundred years or more. In places like New Orleans or Salem (Massachusetts, not Oregon), they were virtually a tourist attraction. That human culture dismissed the validity of their claims was something the witches I know thought was a delicious irony: when they had tried to hide, they had been hunted and nearly destroyed. In the open, they were viewed as fakes—and, even more usefully, a lot of the people claiming to be witches really were fakes.

"But this wasn't witchcraft," I said again, in case he'd only been paying attention to part of what I'd told him. "Not any witchcraft I've smelled before, anyway. If you ask, Adam has someone he can send to check it out." Elizaveta Arkadyevna was our pack witch on retainer. "She won't agree to talk to you, but we can get the information for you if you would like."

"Not admissible," grunted Willis.

"Neither, probably, will Mercy's testimony be," agreed Tony. "But at least we won't be running around in the dark with blindfolds on."

Sister . . .

The whisper came out of nowhere. I glanced around, but no one else seemed to have heard it. A movement caught my eye—and there was a coyote crouched in the brush about fifty feet from where we all stood.

It could have been a real coyote—there are a lot of them around Finley. But I *knew* that the coyote was Gary Laughingdog, not because I had some sort of special way of telling walkers from coyotes—his body language said he was looking for me, and I wasn't on speaking terms with the local coyotes. He met my eyes for a full second, then slipped away: message received and understood. He wanted to talk to me; otherwise, he would never have shown himself. Maybe he knew something about what had happened here.

I blinked at the dead a moment. Could Coyote have done this? It was a useless question because I had no idea what he was capable of. There were no stories that I knew about Coyote killing like this, but I didn't know all the Coyote stories.

"All the women are wearing clothing," said one of the police officers.

"Could still have been sexual assault," said another one.

"Cougars hide their prey, so that they can eat it over a few days," the first officer offered tentatively, and someone made a gagging noise.

I don't think they realized I could hear them because they kept their voices down.

"Just for the record, you think this was done by something supernatural?" Tony asked me in a low voice.

"Yes. I told you, I smell magic."

"A werewolf did this," said Willis with authority.

I hunched my shoulders and shook my head. "The magic isn't werewolf or fae. I might be able to do more if I can get closer."

"You smell magic, and that means it wasn't a werewolf?" asked Willis, sounding like he didn't believe me. I didn't blame him.

"I am not going to make things up just to make both of us feel better," I said. "Werewolves smell like musk and mint. This smells like magic and scorched earth—and that is bad. Adam wouldn't have a lot of trouble hunting down a rogue werewolf. It would be hard for one to hide from the pack more than a day or two. We can stop a werewolf—and I'll tell Adam to keep an ear to the ground—but I don't think this is a werewolf kill."

"What if it was one of your pack?" Tony asked, almost gently. "They would know that we'd bring you in because we have before. They could hide their scent from you."

I shook my head. "Trust me. This kind of mass killing? Werewolves can smell emotion, can smell when something is off. A pack member who did this could not hide it from the rest."

"This wasn't done with a lot of emotion," said Willis.

I looked at him.

"Look at them," he told me. "The bodies are arranged for

maximum effect. The animals are on the bottom, the women on top, heads together like a macabre pinwheel." I hadn't looked that hard, but once he said it, I saw it, too. A pinwheel of dead women—and now that image was going to haunt me for a long time. "The killer felt nothing for the dead—unless you're right, and they were tortured before they died. But when he left this, he was in control. No strong emotions for your pack to smell."

He couldn't smell the fear and agony that I did. Nor could I tell him that no wolf could have hidden from the pack bonds while he killed so many.

"Maybe someone is trying to make trouble for the werewolves," Tony said.

"I think it *is* the werewolves making trouble for themselves," said Willis.

"You brought me out because you wanted my opinion," I told them. "It could be a werewolf, but if it is, isn't one of our pack. I don't think it's a werewolf. I don't smell one, but I can't get close enough to check."

"Why don't you come over to the other scene," Tony said. "They've got what they need from it?" He addressed that question to a woman in muddy overalls, and she nodded at him with a sort of studied weariness. "Maybe you can see something we don't."

I started to turn away and caught some movement out of the corner of my eye. I looked back over my shoulder and saw a woman kneeling right smack in the middle of the crime scene. Her blond hair was in a professional bun that contrasted with the jeans and tank top she wore. For a surreal moment, I thought it was Christy, and almost asked her what she thought she was doing. Then she moved and broke the illusion. It was just her hair and something in the sweep of her jawline that reminded me of Adam's ex-wife.

The kneeling woman was petting the severed head of the German shepherd. She looked up, and her eyes met mine, just as Gary Laughingdog's had. And then I realized what I was looking at and why no one else seemed to notice her. I see ghosts.

"Find the one who did this," she told me sternly.

I gave her a little nod, and Willis caught my shoulder.

"What do you see?" he asked. "What made you turn back?"

"Only the dead," I answered. "And I intend to help them as best I can."

He wasn't satisfied, but I thought he knew I was telling the truth.

6

~~~

THE ORIGINAL CRIME SCENE HAD ONLY ONE BODY, another woman. She lay in the middle of the hayfield in a section, roughly square, that had nothing at all growing in it. The soil was black, and it stained the bottom of my tennis shoes with soot. Someone had burned a chunk of field and put the dead woman in it like the bull's-eye of a target.

"Staged," I said.

"Yes," agreed Tony. "And we'll let the scene experts have their way, but, like Willis, I'm reading the other bodies the same way. Arranged for maximum effect."

Unlike the other women, this one had been partially eaten. The soft flesh of her abdomen was completely gone and most of the thigh muscles. Something with big, sharp teeth had gnawed on the bones exposed by the missing flesh.

I stopped about five feet from the body and smelled. A lot of people had been roaming around the area, and if I hadn't been looking for it, I wouldn't have scented the same magic I'd detected at the other site. Magic, death—the bare remnants of the pain and fear that had also been present with the other bodies. Over it all hung a pall of burnt grass and earth. I didn't smell any kind of volatile compound, though maybe the circle had been burned a few days earlier. Some things—like alcohol—evaporate pretty fast.

"I think it's the same killer," I said.

"We don't get so many murders around here—especially where the victims are partially eaten—that anyone is going to argue with you," said Willis. "But what are you basing that on?"

"The smell of magic is the same—and he killed her the same way he took out one of the horses," I told him. You see enough hunts, you pay attention to how prey is killed. "He tore out the throat and ate it before disemboweling her, just like he did the horse. A lot of predators develop a favorite style of kill."

I took a step closer, and the slight change in angle highlighted the ground. Paw prints, canid and huge, dug into the barren earth. They were bigger than my hand when I set it beside them. A timber wolf's paw prints would have been bigger, too—but these were a lot bigger than any timber wolf's.

"Not werewolf," I said with a relieved sigh. "Werewolves have retractable claws that don't dig into the dirt unless they are running—almost like a cougar's. These have claw marks like any other canid."

"Werewolves have retractable claws?" asked the officer who'd been still at the scene when we came here. "I'm forensics; why didn't anyone ever tell me that? I can't look for werewolves if I know squat about them. Do you have a werewolf who will let me examine him for a while?" The last question was directed at me.

"You'll have to ask Adam," I told her. Who would have to ask Bran, which I didn't tell her.

"So what was it?" Most of the cops had stayed at the other site, but a couple of others had followed Willis, Tony, and me. It was one of those who asked.

"I don't know," I told him.

I knelt beside the body and put my nose down as close to the dead woman as I could get. She had been here longer and was beginning to rot. I sorted through odors as quickly as I could.

Between the rot and the burnt smell, it was difficult.

I sat up. "I definitely smell a canid, though not coyote, wolf, werewolf, or any dog I've smelled." I looked at Tony. "I'd like to be more help. I'll recognize the way our killer smells if I run into it again. If you want, we can have some of the werewolves take a shot at identifying it."

"We are taking her word that it isn't a werewolf?" asked Willis, disbelief in his voice. "The wife of the Alpha?"

"Yes," said Tony. "We're taking her word—but we'll let forensics double-check. Would a werewolf have a better chance of identifying it than you, Mercy?"

My nose was as good as most werewolves', better than some. But Samuel was very old, and he'd run into a lot of things over the centuries. He was not a member of the pack, but he'd come look if they'd let him.

"I don't think that would be a good idea," said Willis before I could express an opinion. "If this isn't a werewolf, then we don't want to bring any in to confuse the issue. Having Ms. Hauptman here is pushing it as it is."

Willis dusted off his hands and looked at me thoughtfully. "This was not a werewolf?"

"No," I said.

He pursed his mouth. "Damned if I don't believe you. Whatever did this isn't human."

"Something supernatural," Tony said.

I nodded. "I don't know how to prove it, without anyone being able to smell this magic."

"Fae, then," said one of the other cops. "I've read all the fairy tales. The black dog is the most common of the shapes they take. Meet a black dog at the crossing of two roads or hear the call of the Gabriel Hounds, and you are sure to die."

I shook my head. "Doesn't smell like fae—and they have all retreated to the reservation, anyway."

"There are other things out there besides werewolves and fae?" asked Willis.

I got to my feet and dusted the dirt off my jeans before I answered him. "What do you think?" I asked.

He frowned unhappily.

I nodded. "That's what I think, too. I've never come across whatever did this. But judging from the tracks and the amount of meat he ate in a very short time—whatever this is, it is bigger than any werewolf I've been around. That means more than three hundred pounds."

"On the way over, you just explained to me that you didn't think it was a good thing to tell people that there were other things out there besides werewolves and fae," Tony commented.

I waved my hand toward the crowd of police officers by the copse of trees. "If something is out there doing this, then I think that it's too late to worry about what is safe for the public to believe in. This . . . I don't know what this is. Finding out and stopping it is more important to public safety than trying to not make them paranoid."

Willis shook his head and looked at Tony. "The brass is going to want this to be werewolves." He turned to me. "Fair warning. They are going to want to talk to your husband. Probably not for a few days, until the initial lab reports get back to us, but soon."

"IS THIS REALLY A CONVERSATION FOR DINNER?"

Christy interrupted me in the middle of explaining what I'd been doing this afternoon. There was an odd pause because by interrupting me, she'd made it clear that she felt comfortable correcting me. If we'd both been werewolves, I'd have been forced to make her back down—and then her supporters would have stepped in to defend her.

That I wasn't a werewolf gave me some leeway of behavior, but not much.

We were eating formally again, as we had been since Christy had moved in. Four werewolves, Adam, Jesse, Christy, and I meant eight people, which was, to give her credit, too many people for the kitchen table. Eating in the dining room with Christy cooking meant bouquets cut and arranged from the garden, good china, and cloth napkins folded into cute hatlike things or flowers.

The tablecloth tonight had been hurriedly purchased (Jesse had been sent out to the store earlier) because Christy's favorite tablecloth, unearthed from the linen closet, had a stain on it—discovered just as I came in from work. She hadn't looked at me, but the sad note in her voice had Auriele glaring at me and a few reproachful looks from everyone else, including Jesse. The other tablecloths were dirty, and there was no way we could eat at a table without a tablecloth.

I had not said a number of things—one of which was, if it was such a favorite of hers, then why hadn't she taken it with her? Another unsaid comment was that if I'd known her grandmother had given it to her on her wedding day, I would have ripped it into shreds and used a paper tablecloth before I'd put it on the table for last Thanksgiving. Instead of saying anything, I'd ignored the whole dramatic show and gone upstairs to change my clothes from work, leaving Adam to listen to Christy try to decide if there was any way to salvage her grandmother's tablecloth.

It had taken a pep talk with the mirror to get myself out of the bedroom and downstairs to eat with everyone else. Dinner had been served, the pack gossiped over, then Darryl asked me about the kill site the police had taken me to. I'd briefed Adam over the phone, but there hadn't been time to really hash the matter out.

"I mean, Mercy," Christy said, as if she hadn't noticed the rise in tension when she interrupted me, "why don't we hold off talk of dead bodies until after people are done with the food? I spent too long making this for it to go to waste."

For tonight's dinner, Christy had made lasagna (from scratch, including the noodles), and I'd been shuffling it around on my plate because knowing that she'd made the food made me not want to eat it. That it was pretty and smelled good wasn't as much of an incentive to consuming it as I'd have thought it would be.

"It's okay, Mom," said Jesse with forced cheer, trying to defuse the situation. "Dinner is kind of when everything gets ironed out. Sometimes it's hard to get everyone in the same room afterward."

Ben, one of the four werewolf guards for the night, ate a big bite, swallowed, and said in a prissier-than-usual version of his

British accent, "Mercy, when you say it gnawed on the bones, was it trying to get at the marrow or just cleaning its teeth?"

"Ben," snarled Auriele. "Didn't you hear Christy?"

Six months ago, Ben would have backed down. Auriele outranked him, both as Darryl's mate and as herself. But he'd changed, grown stronger, so he just ate another bite and raised an eyebrow at me. Silent—but not very subservient.

"Playing, I think," I said to attract Auriele's ire. She wouldn't attack me—and in her usual mode of Christy's protector, she might do something to Ben. I'd decided the best way to deal with Christy's interruption was to ignore her. "The bones weren't cracked, just chewed on. At least on the body I got close to. No cracking means no marrow. And if it was just trying to clean its teeth, it would have chewed harder."

I ate a bite of salad. It smelled like Christy because she'd washed the romaine herself. Swallowing it was an effort. Trying not to look like I was choking was an even bigger effort.

Auriele opened her mouth, but Darryl put his hand on top of hers, and she closed her lips without speaking, but not without giving him a hurt look.

Adam's hand touched my shoulder and suddenly I could swallow again. I had allies here, and Adam had my back.

"The important thing," he said, "is that we are careful. I don't want any wolf to go out running alone until we know what made those kills."

Darryl nodded. "I'll see that word gets around."

"Good," Adam said. "I've got people out looking for Gary Laughingdog. Hopefully, we'll find him before the police do—or he'll find you, Mercy."

"I'm pretty sure he wanted to talk to me," I told him. "If so, he'll find me before anyone finds him. I wouldn't worry too much about the police finding him since he's running around as a coyote."

"Did you check if Bran had any insights into what it was that killed all those people?" Darryl asked.

Adam ate another bite of lasagna, paused to enjoy it, then gave me a slightly guilty look. I decided not to tell him it was okay if he liked Christy's food. It was entirely understandable, but it was not okay, and I wouldn't lie to him. I looked away.

To Darryl, Adam said, "I called Bran. Without checking out the site himself, Bran wasn't able to pinpoint what could have done it. Taking the fae out of the picture leaves us with not much. Might even be a native creature. Bran said he once encountered a wendigo, and he believes that it was physically capable of killing this way. They smell oddly of magic, the way Mercy described them. But he didn't think that it would have left canid paw prints—or left anything except bare bones. Their curse is that they hunger in a way that cannot ever be satisfied. Also, they tend to haunt the mountain passes, not the open shrub steppe. He's having Charles do a little more research for us."

"Charles who?" asked Christy.

"Bran's son," I told her, trying very hard not to be condescending and not succeeding. Maybe because I didn't try *that* hard. She'd been Adam's wife for over a decade, and she hadn't bothered to learn anything if she didn't know about the Marrok and his sons. "He's half-Indian—Salish—and he has some people who will talk to him about things that are culturally sensitive—sacred things or stories they don't want prettied up with all the original flavor lost so that it can be more effectively marketed as a genuine Native American story."

"Have you asked Ariana?" Darryl was getting good at ignoring the almost battle between Christy and me and, at the same time, reducing the tension by changing the subject. I would never have thought Darryl would be such an adroit politician.

"No," said Adam. "Not until we've looked at everything else. I'll call Marsilia as soon as we're done here, but I don't expect her to have much for us. She might owe Mercy and need the pack to keep her seethe safe until she gets some more vampires with power here, but she doesn't like us very much."

Ben snorted. "You can say that again."

"Why not ask this Ariana?" asked Christy.

"Because her father tortured her with his fae hounds until she went mad," Adam told her before I could say something spiteful or petty. It would probably be a good idea if I refrained from answering Christy's questions.

"She is Samuel's mate," Auriele said. When Christy looked blank, Auriele added, "Samuel is Bran's other son. Samuel is a werewolf, but she's coping okay with that. However, it is still an effort for her to be around any of the rest of us. Asking her about a giant dog killing people might just knock her right back off her applecart. Not only would that be unkind to do when we don't even know if she would have useful information, but she's a power in her own right. If she goes nuts, I don't want to be anywhere in the vicinity."

Ben took a second helping of lasagna, and said in a contemplative voice, "I keep having nightmares about that night when she alternated between doctoring my wounds and wanting to kill me."

"Tad said he'd see if he can get a message to Zee," I said. "If it is fae, Zee will know what it is."

"I thought you said it wasn't fae." Auriele's voice was neutral.

"It didn't smell fae," I said. "But some of the half-breeds don't smell fae to me, for whatever reason. And Zee is old. He might have some idea even if it isn't fae at all."

"Did you tell that to the police?" Christy looked at me brightly. "That you wouldn't have been able to tell if it had been a half fae?"

"No," I said.

"Why not?"

"Because," I said gently, "there are a number of half-blood fae around here because of the local reservation. Most of them don't have enough magic to light a candle. Humans don't have a habit of treating the people we are scared of very gently. No sense getting people killed unless they are actually guilty of something."

"Mercy did the right thing." George was the fourth werewolf on duty. He was also a Pasco police officer, which lent validity to his opinion even if the kill had been out of his jurisdiction. He had that whole "I was a Marine" thing going that stiffened his posture and made even his casual movements have a certain purpose to them. "Police need the real information, not something that will send manpower off chasing rabbits when they should be hunting bigger prey."

As soon as he quit speaking, he returned to his plate. He ate with no wasted motion, and he didn't look up from his plate while he did so. George was fairly far up the pack hierarchy, but the only wolf he outranked at this table was Ben. It was safer for him to keep his head down, so he did.

"What about the new wolf?" asked Jesse. "He could have done the killing before he joined the pack." Unlike the police, she knew enough to understand that he couldn't have done it once he was bonded.

"The first victim might have been before Zack joined the pack," I told her, "but the others were more recent."

"The killer isn't Drummond," Adam told her. "I called his last Alpha, who regretted losing him. Zack stayed for six months or so, then got restless. Warren says he's pretty soft-spoken and quiet, as submissive wolves tend to be—and definitely not our killer."

"Serial killers who move around are less likely to get caught," said Jesse.

Ben shook his head. "I was over at Warren's last night. If you'd ever met Zack, you wouldn't have proposed him as your killer." He fidgeted a little, and reluctantly said, "Is there something more we can do for him? Maybe a different job? Something with more of a future."

"What's he doing?" asked Auriele.

"Dishes," I said.

"Dishes suck," said Jesse, with feeling. She was working as a waitress for running-around money and had done a couple of stints on the dishes when someone else missed their shift.

"I'd rather wash dishes than pick apples," said George in tones of non-nostalgia.

The talk around the table turned to "worse job" stories.

I excused myself when the conversation drifted to some funny event that happened back when Christy was Adam's wife, well before the pack had moved to the Tri-Cities. Even Adam got into it, had everyone in stitches about trying to find a bathroom for his very pregnant wife at 2:00 A.M. in the middle of nowhere in New Mexico. It wouldn't have bothered me if he hadn't given Christy a tender look as she threw her head back and laughed. She had a beautiful laugh. I got up from the table, taking my plate and glass.

"Didn't you like dinner?" asked Christy as I passed her, drawing everyone's eyes to my almost-full dinner plate.

"I had a late lunch." I continued on to the kitchen. "And then there were all those dead people afterward. Hard to keep the smell out of my head."

That shut her up. I think that all the talk about the dead bodies really had bothered her. I was letting her make me petty.

I kept my movements slow and even as I scraped my plate off into the garbage. I loaded my dishes into the dishwasher and walked with deliberate steps up the stairs; by then Darryl was carrying the narrative. I didn't run, didn't even move with speed, but every step was in as direct a line with my bedroom as I could manage. I shut the door behind me and caught a deep breath.

If her stalker didn't kill Christy soon, she might just drive me to it. At this point, I wasn't even certain how much of it was her fault and how much of it was me being jealous. Not of Adam, Adam belonged to me, soul and wolf. If it were just Adam, I'd have more control. It was the pack.

Pack magic, I'd learned, was real. And if enough of the pack wanted you to do something, it was difficult not to do it. When I hadn't been aware of it, some members of the pack had made Adam and me have a fight. They couldn't do that anymore, but I could feel them pressing upon me. I suspected that if enough of them wanted me out of the pack badly enough, they would succeed. What I didn't know was what that would do to Adam, but I was certain it wouldn't be good.

I walked over to my chest of drawers and unfastened the chain around my neck and set it down, so I could look at it. It had been a graceful piece of jewelry when I'd only had the lamb on it. Even my wedding ring—which I wore on my finger only on formal occasions because I didn't want to lose a finger when something caught on my ring while I was at work—was beautiful. The engagement ring had a single, large, pear-cut diamond. My wedding ring was plainer, just two small yellow topazes Adam said were the same color as my eyes when I went coyote. The rings had been brazed together so that the topazes flanked the diamond.

It was the dog tag that turned the necklace from jewelry to statement. The tag hadn't been pretty to start with, and after nearly four decades of wear and tear, it was battered and rough. Adam wore the other tag at all times.

Symbols.

I closed my hand on Adam's dog tag as the door to the bedroom opened and quietly shut again. Adam's arms came around me, and he bent so he could put his head on my shoulder. There was a mirror on the top of the dresser, so I could see his face—and his eyes in the mirror met mine.

"Thank you," he said.

"For what?"

He smiled, a peaceful expression that lightened suddenly with mischief. "For keeping the peace. You don't think that I don't know you could wipe the floor with a lightweight like Christy? You battled with Bran when you were just a kid and came out on top. Christy? She's not a tithe on Bran."

I snorted. "I don't know where you get your information, but I didn't win any battles with Our Lord and Master Bran Cornick who is the Marrok. No one does. That's why he's the Marrok."

He snorted back. "That's not what Bran says."

"Then he's doing it for his own reasons," I told him. "Don't put too much weight on his stated opinion. More than likely he's just trying to get you to do something you don't want to do."

"Peanut butter," Adam said, deadpan.

"He made my foster mother cry," I said.

"Eggs."

"That didn't work so well," I told him. "But I did learn not to arm my enemies."

"Shoes."

Shocked, I turned around, so I could see his face instead of just the reflection. "No one knows about the shoes. Bran doesn't know." I hadn't thought that Bran knew about the shoes.

"I don't know if Bran does," Adam said. "Samuel said that he and Charles cooperated to keep Bran guessing because he was really enraged about the shoes."

Charles had covered for me? I'd known that Samuel had seen me and not said anything—but I hadn't known about Charles. Truth was that in my heart of hearts I'd been a lot more scared of Bran's son Charles than I'd ever been scared of Bran. I just never believed that Bran would really hurt me. Charles . . . Charles would do whatever he had to. I was still more scared of Charles than Bran, but not *as* scared because Adam had my back.

"The shoes were not the brightest idea I've ever had," I admitted. "But I was provoked."

I met Adam's eyes, and we stared at each other for a minute, then I started to snicker. He laughed and pulled me into his body. I relaxed—and it felt like the first time I'd relaxed since Christy came to stay with us.

"The shoes didn't really have anything to do with Bran," I told him.

"Leah is his mate," he said. "Of course it had something to do with Bran. Especially when he couldn't figure out who was stealing her shoes."

I laughed again, tried to stop, while I said, "Only one shoe."

"One of each pair. At a time. Forty-three shoes gone over a five-week period. Sometimes two or three shoes in the same day. Not a scent trace to be found. Just like a wizard had conjured them away."

I blinked away tears and tried to stop laughing. It wasn't that funny—it was the release of the tension that had been building up for days. "I actually can't remember what it was Leah did, specifically. But I'm sure it was something worse than making me Enemy Number One because I let her tablecloth get stained."

"Samuel said Leah put out a bounty on the shoes and the thief."

That sent me off again.

"Her face," I managed. "If only I had a photograph of her face." Though I had a pretty good memory of it. "I thought she was just going to spontaneously combust right there in front of us—barefoot."

"When Samuel told me about it, he asked me to find out how you managed it without leaving your scent behind. He said that when he asked you, you told him that you were keeping your secret in case you had to do the same to him someday."

"Fishing pole and a big hook," I told Adam because I'd do better than shoes if I had to get back at him for something. "The hardest part was shutting the closet without going into the room." I thought about it. "Okay, the closet door and getting out of the house forty-odd times without getting caught. Thank goodness I spent a lot of legitimate time over at that house, so I didn't have to try to cover up my scent except to keep it out of Bran's bedroom."

"What did you do with the shoes? Samuel said Bran searched your foster parents' house for them."

I snickered again. "Searched every day, sometimes twice a

day—every time a shoe disappeared. Bryan got mad about it eventually, but Evelyn thought it was funny. I dumped the shoes in a glacial lake that was about three miles from our house. In between trips, because I couldn't quite manage to make it there unseen every day, I hid them in the bed of Charles's truck."

"I thought you were afraid of Charles."

I nodded. "So was everyone else, though. And he only drove that truck when he absolutely had to."

"You said you tossed all of them in the lake. I thought one of those shoes returned a few years later? Where did you hide it?" His eyes were happy.

"In the lake with the rest." I shivered in reflex. "It took me four hours of diving in that lake to find a shoe—and that was a glacier-fed lake. Most of the shoes had rotted into mush, but there was a steel stiletto with this wiry mesh stuff that looked pretty good. By that time, Bran had quit looking, so I didn't have to be so careful."

Bryan and Evelyn had both been dead then, too, and I'd been living alone in their house that no longer really felt like my own. Not even their ghosts had lingered with me. I didn't tell Adam that, he was too perceptive, and I was too prone to self-pity with Christy living on the other side of my bedroom wall.

I cleared my throat. "I had to work on that stupid shoe for months before it didn't look like it had spent two years in water. But her face at the sight of it sitting on top of the Christmas tree was so worth it."

"She'd hurt you," Adam said, his voice soft and certain.

"She couldn't hurt me," I corrected briskly if not truthfully. To earn the Christmas-tree topper, she'd made a disparaging remark about my foster father, Bryan, after he'd killed himself. "She made me mad."

"She hurt you."

I shrugged. "I was pretty sure she'd clean my clock after that one. I mean, even without evidence, who else could it have been?"

"She couldn't." Adam's face was satisfied. "Samuel told me that when she tried to bring her case to Bran, Charles swore, in front of most of the pack, that you were with him all day working on cars during the only time the switch between the star and the shoe could have been made. No one could hear the lie, so she had to leave it or challenge Charles first."

"He lied?" I said, shocked. Thought about it, and said in a hushed voice, "He lied, and no one could tell?"

"It's Charles," Adam explained as if that was enough—and it was. "You handled Bran, and you handled Leah. So don't tell me you couldn't put a stop to Christy's taunts and teach her to behave herself until she goes home."

I didn't think it would be as easy as he made it seem. But he was right that I was backing away from a confrontation.

"If she goes before there is a knock-down, drag-out fight between the pro-me and the pro-Christy factions, it'll be better for the pack." My voice was small.

"And less collateral damage," he said, kissing my nose, "Jesse has to deal with concerning her mother. She doesn't need more drama. Auriele, Mary Jo—they don't really know who she is. And that's not a bad thing."

"She's not a horrible person," I protested.

He smiled, briefly. "No. She makes people feel good for defending her, for doing things for her. Makes them feel like heroes—she made me feel that way once, too. Nothing wrong with that." He kissed me. "But I like my women less helpless."

I went limp against him, and said, dramatically, "I'm helpless against your kisses."

He laughed like a villain in a cartoon. "Aha. So that's how it's done. Well, there's no help for you, then."

"No," I said in a faint voice, putting an arm over my forehead as I arched back over his arm in the classic pose of the helpless ingénue. "I guess you'll just have your wicked way with me again."

"Cool," said my husband, a wicked growl in his voice. "Don't worry. You'll enjoy every minute of it."

I FINISHED THE WASSERBOXER ENGINE I WAS REBUILD-ing with great satisfaction. As if to make up for the chaos in my own life, the engine was going together as sweet as molasses and twice as easy. Like a gambler on a winning streak, I was worried that I'd ruin it in the last moves. But it buttoned up duck soup, as if I were putting it together in the factory instead of thirty years later.

I had an urgent brake job left (brought in about fifteen minutes before). However, I'd decided last night, after Adam was sleeping beside me and looking more relaxed than he'd been in days, that I was finished leaving the battlefield to Christy—that was giving her too much advantage.

I'd have the brakes done by lunch tomorrow, and that would have to be soon enough. I patted the wasserboxer for being such a good patient and stripped out of my overalls in the oversized bathroom/laundry room. I got a can of soda from the fridge, and, clad in civilian clothes, I ventured into the main office.

"Closing time."

"Sounds good," Tad said, looking up from the books, where he was finishing recording an appointment. Gabriel had been trying to get me to set up the appointment schedule on computer, but Tad didn't seem to mind the paper route. "You look tired, Mercy. Go home. Get something to eat. You look like you've lost ten pounds."

"Maybe I should eat more red velvet cupcakes," I said dryly. I'd brought two this morning, and Tad had eaten them both.

"Only if you make sure Christy knows they are for me or check them for arsenic," he answered, using his keys to make the till run its daily total.

I opened my eyes wide. "Oh shoot. I've just been feeding them to you. Are you feeling ill?" I peered anxiously at his lips. "I think your lips are turning blue. Do you feel faint?"

He grinned at me. "Arsenic is a metal, Mercy. Don't you remember your high-school chemistry?"

"Semi-metallic," I told him.

"And Dad is iron-kissed, a master of metals." He tucked his thumbs under his imaginary collar and grinned with lots of cheese. "I'm just a chip off the old block and safe from arsenic attacks of all kinds."

"I'll remember that the next time you drive me to attempted murder," I said. I quit joking and sighed. "She's going home soon. Then we can get on with our lives, as long as she wasn't serious when she was threatening to move here." I took a good long swig of my soda. "It's only a matter of time before Adam finds her stalker and sends him off with the fear of Adam to keep him away from her for the rest of his life."

He gave me a half smile because we both knew that it was a

lot more likely that we'd have to kill the man. I should have felt worse about it, but I'd been raised by werewolves, and the bastard had burned down a building full of innocent bystanders—four people hadn't gotten out of the apartment building before it collapsed.

"I talked to Da last night about your trouble with Beauclaire and Coyote," Tad said unexpectedly. "The mirror still isn't a good idea, but the old fae has a few tricks up his sleeve that none of the Gray Lords know about yet. I told him that you haven't had much luck finding Coyote."

"Did he have any advice?" I asked. It was unlikely that Zee would know how to contact Coyote, but I was ready for any help I could get. Today was Friday. I had two days left.

"He did," Tad told me. "He said that if you hadn't managed anything better by tonight, I was to tell you that you've been overlooking any number of avenues open to you in a way that is very un-Mercy-like." He smiled. "His words."

"What am I overlooking?" I'd called in all my markers. I'd even called Charles this morning, who had unhelpfully suggested I try a vision quest. Vision quests require fasting, which I could manage, but also a centered focus that I was never going to achieve with Christy in my home. He'd promised to call some shaman priests he knew, but warned me that, as I already knew, Coyote was elusive and mischievous. Searching and calling for Coyote was likely to result in exactly the opposite outcome.

Charles had been my last hope.

"You've been concentrating on Coyote when you should have been also looking at Beauclaire." Tad held up a finger. "Without you, it is unlikely that Beauclaire will ever see the walking stick again—and he knows it." Two fingers up. "Two: That means that you have a bargaining chip, and it also means that Beauclaire loses if something happens to you. Da also said you've been making Beauclaire the villain when he is more comfortably the hero. Beauclaire is honorable, as fae understand the word, and he has spent a human lifetime as a lawyer; he'll understand compromise. If you can convince Beauclaire that you will sincerely return the walking stick to him when and if you see Coyote, he will probably grant you time to do so. Time, Da also asked me to remind you, is less precious to a Gray Lord like Beauclaire than it is to you."

My jaw didn't drop because I had it locked tight.

Tad grinned at me. "He said you'd probably figure it out on your own if you got desperate enough. Then I told him about Christy, and he gave me permission to talk to you tonight if you hadn't worked it out already."

I don't know what expression was on my face, but Tad's gentled. "Don't feel too bad. Da knows Beauclaire, and it gives him an advantage. You'll still have to bargain hard and fast—and be diplomatic. And, Da said, whatever you do, don't mention his name, or all bets are off. Beauclaire knew that someone was going to have to take out Lugh. He was, apparently, girding up his loins to do just that when Da took care of it. That didn't mean he didn't swear vengeance."

I shook off my chagrin and gave Tad a fist bump. "Thank you. I feel like a lead weight is off my back. I'll keep looking for Coyote, but more time means that I might not be responsible for the Columbia rising up and out of its banks and wiping the Tri-Cities from the face of the earth."

"Anytime," he said. "My duties dispatched, I am off to home. Good luck with Christy and remind her that we work tomorrow, even though it is Saturday, so we'll need something tasty to get us through the day. And you need to start eating, or your plan to pretend she doesn't bother you will be revealed to anyone who looks at your ribs."

I locked up after Tad and set Adam's security system, Tad's last words ringing in my ears. I started to get my purse out of the safe when I stopped and went back into the bathroom and peered into the mirror.

I looked just like me. Native American coloring, mostly Caucasian features inherited from my mother. Except, now that I knew to look at them, the shape of my eyes was like Gary Laughingdog's. I tried to visualize Coyote's face, but I didn't know if I was imagining that his eyes were the same or not.

My hair was in the braids I usually wore to work in order to keep it out of the way so it didn't get covered in grease when I pushed it out of my face. And Tad was right. My features were sharper.

There was no question that not eating the food Christy made was making me lose weight.

There was still a brake job I could do tonight. If I stretched it out, I'd miss dinner. That would give me an excuse to pick up some high-calorie fast food on the way home, food that didn't taste or smell of Christy. I didn't want Adam to notice I was losing weight because it would hurt him—my husband took care of the people around him. I didn't want Christy to notice because she'd know she was getting to me.

I put my overalls back on, pulled on the sweat-inducing gloves, and hoisted the '94 Passat up on the lift, so I could pull the back tires and take a look.

I was working on compressing the caliper and had just got the six-sided-dice (also known as a piston tool, but only at auto parts stores) to engage the caliper when my phone rang. I'd set my phone on a nearby counter, so I didn't have to let go of anything to check the display.

Adam. Three days ago I'd have answered immediately, but the day before yesterday it had been Christy asking me to pick up a dozen apples and some butter. Real butter, no salt—make sure not to get the salted version because everyone eats too much salt.

Not a big deal at all. Stopping at the grocery store before I came home wasn't a problem. Having Christy ask me to do it was a different matter.

Pack is all about hierarchy. I understood how it works even if, before marrying Adam, I had been on the outside looking in. Humans have hierarchy, too. What Christy had done was the equivalent of the new-hire office girl calling the CEO and asking him to bring coffee for the break room—and she'd done it in front of Adam and the four attending wolves. If they hadn't known about it before, they would have known about it afterward. Pack hierarchy was one of those things I'd agreed to deal with when I married Adam, so I paid attention to make his life easier.

I couldn't do much about Christy's faux pas without looking like a jealous, arrogant bitch while Christy graciously apologized because she hadn't realized what it was she had done—though she'd lived with the pack for years. So I'd filled her order, then brought two dozen Spudnut donuts for the pack.

Spudnuts is a Tri-Cities tradition; they make their donuts with potato flour instead of wheat. I might have lost hierarchy points, but Spudnut donuts bought me credit with the wolves who were at home. The wolves doubtless knew I'd done it to buy their favor—that didn't mean it didn't work. Even Christy couldn't help but eat one.

Maybe I should bring them home every day, and that nicely rounded figure would just be rounded . . .

Dreams of petty revenge aside, she'd succeeded in making me paranoid to the point that Adam's cell number on my phone's display made me wary instead of happy. Four rings sounded before I gave in and answered. If it was Christy, I'd just say no to whatever she asked because I had to work late.

"This is Mercy," I said neutrally, bracing myself.

"Aren't you supposed to be getting home sometime soon?" It was Adam. I relaxed and felt my expression soften. "You've had the security system on for an hour, so I expected you home by now. But I see you are working still."

I waved at the corner where the tiny camera was watching my every move. The cameras downloaded themselves onto Adam's laptop as well as a backup at his office. The interior cameras ran all day long, the exterior cameras in the parking lot and around the outside of the building only turned on when I switched on the nighttime security.

"Hey, handsome. Just finishing up a brake job. Don't wait dinner. I'll grab something on the way home."

"Tad's with you?" he said smoothly. If he was watching his feeds, then he knew the answer, and that I'd broken my promise not to work alone and make myself a target to anyone looking to hurt Adam or the pack.

I cleared my throat. "Sorry, I got distracted. I'll clean up and head home."

I expected him to be unhappy with me again—as he'd been when Christy had tried to get me in trouble for going off alone. I should have thought about safety when I'd made my sudden decision to stay and work. I knew it wasn't just me at risk, but the whole pack through me because I could be used as a hostage.

"If you need a night off," he said, sounding sympathetic instead of angry, "you could go keep Kyle company. Warren is on guard duty over here tonight. Zack does fine as long as Warren is there because Warren isn't exactly flaming. But he says he can tell from what Zack doesn't say that when it's only Kyle and Zack there, it's pretty awkward."

I read between the lines that Kyle was giving Zack a hard time without Warren there to make sure he behaved. Like a kid in a candy shop, Kyle really enjoyed making people squirm. It was part of what made him such a good lawyer.

"I have no intention of deserting you for the night," I told him firmly. "Kyle and Zack will just have to manage—Kyle is good at that sort of social stuff when he wants to be. I'll be home in a half hour."

"Get food first," he said. "You need to eat, and I can see why you might have trouble eating here. I'll see you home in an hour or an hour and a half."

"I love you," I said with feeling.

"Of course you do," he agreed with a nonchalance that made me grin as he disconnected.

I let the car down and put jack stands under the rear axle. The hoist had a very slow leak that didn't matter when someone was there to raise it periodically, but overnight it would lower itself until the car was on the ground. I probably ought to get it fixed, but the garage was barely eking along in the black for once, and I was reluctant to dump it back in the red.

A blip on the monitor on the wall between the garage and the office attracted my attention as the outside security cameras switched from daylight-colored to nighttime black-and-white. The monitor sat on a shelf on top of a rectangular computer box big enough to look serious—though it and the monitor were mostly there so that anyone breaking in would think that was the whole of the security system and, after trashing the system, would quit worrying about the cameras.

No, I didn't need a system that sophisticated to watch over my garage where I repaired cars with sticker prices usually a lot less than the security Adam had installed. But Adam worried, and it cost me less than nothing to let him update the system every few months.

I stripped out of my overalls in the bathroom for a second time that day. I paused by the mirror, sighed, and washed my face because, while the gloves worked fine for hands, they still transferred grease to my cheek and mouth.

I wished I could get rid of the smell of my job as easily as I scrubbed the black smudges off my face. Christy couldn't smell it, but the werewolves all could. Christy wore some kind of subtle perfume that smelled good to werewolf noses . . . and mine, too. Apparently, Adam had found it for her while they were still married, and she still wore it—or at least she was wearing it while she was here.

I left the bathroom and reached out to hit the lights when, in the security monitor, I saw a nearly new Chevy Malibu pull into the parking lot in front of the office. I wouldn't have been alarmed—people can be optimistic about finding mechanics for cars that just have to be ready for a trip at 5:00 A.M. tomorrow—except that there was a big dog in the backseat.

It wouldn't hurt to err on the side of safety. I reached for my phone.

"Hello," said Christy cheerily. "Adam's phone."

"Get Adam," I said, watching the lights on the Chevy turn off as he parked the car. There was a bumper sticker advertising a rental car chain on the back of it.

"I'm afraid—"

"You should be," I told her in a low voice. Hungry and tired from the long hours I'd put in, I was abruptly sick of her stupid games and ready to quit playing. "Get Adam. Now."

"Don't snap at me," Christy said, all cheer gone. "You don't get to order me around, Mercy. You haven't earned the right."

The man who opened the driver's door didn't look like someone to be afraid of; he was wearing expensive clothes and slick-soled shoes. But the dog he let out of the backseat more than made up for his owner's civilized appearance.

The dog looked like the photos I'd seen of the presa Canario, but in my parking lot it seemed bigger and nastier, a male with a broad face and broader chest. Lucia had said that people trimmed their ears to make them look fiercer, but no one needed to make this dog scarier.

The dog was just a dog, though. No matter how big and fierce a dog was, after running around with werewolves, no dog scared me. So there was no reason, really, for me to be afraid of them, a man and his dog. But I was.

The image of the dead bodies on the edge of the hayfield in Finley insisted on making itself present, and I tried to shove it off to the side. The worst of the fear, I thought, was because I'd been raped here in my garage, and I no longer ever really felt safe here, security system or not.

Christy's ex-boyfriend was no one to be underestimated, but he was human and I had a gun readily available. The chill of fear that slid down my spine was unimpressed by logic.

In my ear, Christy was nattering away about manners and me being jealous for no reason.

"Christy," I interrupted her, and let menace color my voice because I refused to let her hear the fear, "if you don't give Adam the phone right the hell now, so help me, I will put you out with the rest of the trash in the morning."

From the speaker on my cell phone I could hear some shocked exclamations. Apparently, there were some other werewolves in the room when Christy answered, and they'd overheard me threaten her. I'd probably care about that later.

"I won't stay where I'm not wanted," she said tearfully. "Not even in the home that was mine before—" She squeaked, and her voice cut out, replaced by Adam's.

"Mercy?" His voice was very calm, that "people are going to die" calm only he could do. As soon as he started to speak, silence fell behind him because I wasn't the only one who knew that voice. "I see him on the camera. You stay right there, don't make any noise, and hopefully he won't be sure you are in there. I'm on my way. Sit tight, and don't let him in. I'm going to hang up right now and call the police and Tad."

Adam was fifteen minutes out—but Tad was only five. What could happen in five minutes?

7

~~~

I DIDN'T CARRY AT WORK—WITH TAD THERE, THERE WAS no reason, and a gun just got in the way while I was squirming around in engine compartments and under cars. My carry gun, the 9mm, was locked in the safe with my purse. I wasn't going into the office to open the safe because the office had big picture windows, and someone who had burned down a building that housed dozens of innocent people wouldn't hesitate to break a few windows.

Paranoia meant I had a second gun tucked in a special lockbox attached to the underside of the counter nearest the office. My fingers pressed the code, and a half second later I had the cool and heavy Model 629 Smith & Wesson .44 Magnum in my hand. I wasn't Dirty Harry, but I'd shot my foster father's Model 29 since I was big enough to handle it. My foster father's .44 was in the gun safe at home, but the only difference between it and the 629 was that the 629 was stainless steel. Both of them were too heavy for me to shoot for more than a few rounds, but I could hit a pretty tight pattern on a target at fifty feet with the gun as long as it was in the first twelve shots.

The gun was Adam's, and he'd suggested I get another Sig Sauer 9mm like my preferred gun instead because it was lighter and, being an automatic, the 9mm was faster to reload. I'd told him it was a waste of money when he already had this one.

I had made the assumption that this guy was Christy's stalker and not some poor lost traveler who stopped to use the phone or something. We hadn't managed to get any kind of photo of him, but how many guys travel in rental cars with a wicked-looking dog?

I looked at the monitor again and tried to evaluate him in the black-and-white screen. He appeared to be tallish, and his hair was light-colored. Without anything that eliminated him from the description Christy had given, I decided I was okay with making the assumption that he was the bad guy. If not, I could apologize to him later.

Why had he come here instead of going after Christy?

Maybe he had, and all the people we had guarding her had made him rethink his plan.

Maybe he thought he could take me to use as leverage to get to Christy. Or, if he was really crazy—and burning down a building was acting crazy in my book—he might be planning on killing me to get back at Adam for keeping Christy from him.

Maybe he just wanted to ask me if I'd seen Christy. My understanding of psycho stalkers was not infallible. It was also very possible that I was overreacting.

My chest hurt, and I felt the stupid light-headedness that told me I was flirting with a full-blown panic attack. Panic attacks were stupid and counterproductive, rendering me helpless to protect myself until they were over. Happily, I didn't have them as often as I used to, but now was not the time.

I reminded myself firmly that I had prepared for another attempted assault. I had a bolt-hole for the coyote to hide in. At the back of the garage, on the top of the floor-to-ceiling shelves, there was an old wooden box—a fake box. The front and most of one side were all that was left. Those I had wood-glued and screwed to the shelf so it wouldn't fall off if I bumped it. A narrow opening at the back of the side not against the wall meant I could squeeze into the box, but I wasn't trapped because the box had no lid. All the way up near the roof of my fourteen-foot-high garage meant it didn't need a top to keep me hidden, and I had about a foot between the top of the box and the ceiling.

So why wasn't I doing the smart thing and hiding up there as a coyote? He might know who I was and where I worked, but it was extremely unlikely that he knew *what* I was.

I watched the monitors as he tried the door, then looked around the parking lot. The camera angle wasn't wide enough for me to see what he was looking at, but I was pretty sure it was my van. He couldn't know I was still there unless he'd been watching the shop, but the van might make him suspicious.

That was assuming he knew what I drove, which might be giving him too much credit. Though he had apparently followed Christy from Eugene—and I knew that Adam wouldn't have advertised the trip over here if he could help it. He'd figured out she was staying with us and found my garage. It wasn't too much to assume he knew what I drove.

He walked away from the door and back to his car, the big dog pacing at his side without a leash—just as Lucia's dog had done. I had time to hide.

The security camera had its eye focused on me, recording my every move. If I hid from this human, the whole pack would know what I had done. Christy was human, fragile, and no longer the Alpha's wife. That she had gotten into trouble she couldn't get out of by herself was to be expected.

In a wolf pack, the dominant members protect—they don't need protection. I was not just the Alpha's wife, I was his mate and a pack member. That all meant that what I did mattered, and I was expected to make a better showing than Adam's fragile ex-wife, who'd driven this man off with nothing more than a frying pan. So I stood watching the monitors, waiting for him to break in, instead of hiding in safety. But the knowledge I chose to face him, that I had other options, seemed to have pushed the panic attack away.

I watched as Christy's stalker walked back over and began working on the front door of my garage. Darkness hadn't yet fallen, though the sun was low in the sky.

Five minutes until help arrived.

Five minutes if Tad was at home when Adam called him. If not, Adam would be here in fifteen.

What did it say about Christy's stalker that he risked breaking into my garage with a crowbar when it was still light out? Was he stupid? Or did he think he had enough money, enough power, to escape the consequences of his actions?

I closed my eyes and stretched my neck and rolled my shoulders to loosen them.

The front door gave with a tremendous crack—but my ears are more sensitive than most. I leaned on the front of the Passat and left the gun resting on the hood, though I kept my hold on it. Lifting the gun up too soon would cause my arms to tire, and I'd lose accuracy. I didn't worry that he would be too fast because I was as quick as any of the werewolves—and they were a lot faster than any human.

It was probably only seconds between the time he broke down the door and when he came into the garage bay, but it seemed like hours. I spent the time reminding myself that I wasn't drugged up on some fae-magic concoction that prevented me from disobeying orders. That Tad was coming, that Adam was on his way.

That if I shot him, then Christy would have to leave.

I've killed people before. If I'd felt like I had a choice, I wouldn't have killed them. No choice meant I had no regrets for those kills. Maybe I should have felt worse about that; maybe it was being a walker or maybe being a predator. I didn't think it would bother me to kill this man who had killed four innocent people—five if you counted the man who'd dated Christy a couple of times. Even so, I wasn't going shoot him unless he made me do it, I told myself sternly.

Not even if it meant getting Christy out of my home.

I concentrated on keeping my expression cool, and when he stepped into the light, I said, "Mr. Flores, I presume?"

He stopped, and the big dog stopped, too, his shoulder precisely at his master's leg. The dog's gaze was alert, intelligent, and primal. Ancient.

I blinked, and the dog was just a dog. My first impression was probably a product of the stress of the moment, an accident of shadows.

Flores smiled and raised both hands to his shoulder height, palms out, dropping the crowbar as he did so. I flinched a little at the noise of the crowbar hitting the floor.

"I see that you were expecting me, Mrs. Hauptman." He glanced at the monitors, and his smile widened. "I am not here to hurt you or yours, but your husband has something that belongs to me, and I want it back."

Looking at his face under the light, and I knew why Christy had climbed right into bed with him. If Adam was movie-star handsome—this man was porn-star material. Eyes so dark blue they could only come from contacts, skin either tanned or naturally Mediterranean dark, and even, well-defined features with sensual overtones. Bright gold hair whitened in streaks by the sun or a skilled hairdresser swept back from his face in an expensive cut. But the most noticeable thing about him, the thing that Christy had never described, was the air of sexuality that he brought with him. No one would look at this man and not think *male*, *sex*, and *dangerous*.

"Christy appealed to us for protection from you," I told him steadily. "If you know where she ran, if you know where I work, then you know what Adam is. We granted her protection, Adam and I and the whole pack. She doesn't belong to you, she belongs to us. She never *belonged* to you. You need to leave. If you leave right now, my mate won't kill you where you stand."

"I don't want to cause trouble," he said, and he lied. His dog took a step forward.

I had the big gun out and aimed before the dog took another step.

"I might regret shooting the dog, but I won't hesitate," I told Flores.

He did something with his hand, and the big dog stepped back. The air-conditioning kicked in, and the air blew past them and to my nose, bringing with it the faint scent of magic. A faint scent that altered everything because I'd smelled that scent yesterday while I stared at a dead woman in a hayfield. I fought to keep my expression from changing and angled my face a little to the camera.

"You caused a lot of trouble in Finley," I said, knowing the powerful little lens would catch my lips. Someone would figure out what I had said because there was not a chance in hell that I was coming out of this alive unless Tad or Adam made it here in time. "I saw what you did. Enjoy horsemeat, do you?"

A puzzled look crossed his face as if he were going to deny knowing what I was talking about . . . and then he smiled. His body language changed as he straightened, like an actor shedding a role. He licked his lips. "Horsemeat is not my first choice, no, but it sufficed at the time." He liked to talk with his hands. "He understands the message I left in that field, your husband, does he not? I do not recognize his territory, and I hunt freely therein. He has taken she who is mine, so I shall take from him she who is his. Balance. Only then will I take his life—and that is vengeance. There is no one safe from my—"

I shot the dog. A clean killing shot to his head. He dropped without a sound. Alive one moment, dead the next.

Flores staggered back a few steps, clutching his chest almost as if I'd shot him there instead of his dog. He twisted to look at the dog, then turned to me, crouching a little with rage in his face. "You *dare*."

"Your fault," I said coolly, aiming steadily at him and not looking at the poor dog. "You signaled, and he gathered himself for attack. I warned you."

"My children are immortal," he told me in a breathless hiss and with theatrics that belonged onstage rather than in the mundane environment of my garage. Christy had been right, there was something European in his accent, but not anything I'd heard before. Vaguely Latinish, maybe, but not any Hispanic accent I was familiar with. The accent added melodrama to his already melodramatic words. "Tied to flesh that can be killed, but that mortal flesh is easily replaced. My son will not die but rise again, and so your efforts to defeat me and mine fail. Even so, you will suffer for this before you die."

"Your children are immortal?" I asked, repeating the important part of his words for the camera to catch. The first security system had had sound, but when Adam had updated, he'd traded sound for better video. "Tied to mortal flesh. Who are you?"

"Guayota," he said.

"Coyote?" I asked, and I know my eyes widened. He wasn't Coyote.

"Guayota," he said again, and I heard once more the odd pronunciation that Gary Laughingdog had used in the middle of his vision. Not Coyote with a weird accent but another name altogether.

"With a 'g,'" I said.

But Flores, who called himself Guayota, was done listening to me. "Your husband thinks to keep the sun from me," he said. "He will regret it."

Something happened, something that smelled of scorched fabric and magic. I cried out as that heat seared my cheek. But even as the pain made my eyes water, I shot.

I aimed at Flores's face, and I kept firing until the bullets were gone. Holes appeared in his face as I shot, two side by side in the middle of his forehead, one in his cheekbone. Then I switched targets and two more holes opened up around his heart, the final one a little low and right.

Out of bullets, I grabbed a big wrench and made a backward hop onto the hood of the Passat. It rocked a little under my weight, and I thought that I'd have to remember to tell the owner that it needed work on the shocks, too. Another hop put me on the roof of the car and gave me a little space.

The bullets had knocked Flores back. He hit a rack of miscellaneous parts and sent it crashing to the floor. Flores bounced off the rack, almost followed it to the ground, but caught his balance at the last instant. I felt a cold chill because with three bullets in his face and two in the chest, *he caught his balance and stayed on his feet.*

A funny sound filled the garage; it made my throat hurt and buzzed my ears. He was laughing. A cold, hard knot in my belly told me that probably someone else was going to have to deal with the shocks on the Passat.

My shoes were soft-soled and so had no trouble sticking to the top of the Passat. The gun was of no more use except as a club, but I kept it in my left hand and kept the wrench in my right.

I didn't have much of a chance, but that didn't mean I was going to roll over and give the thing my throat. Adam was coming, and the camera was rolling. Even assuming he killed me, the longer I held out, the more information they'd glean from the recording.

Flores's face changed as he laughed, flowing and darkening, but beneath the darkness, visible in cracks in his skin, was a sullen red light. My changes are almost instantaneous, the werewolves take a lot longer than that with the exception of Charles. But none of us glowed.

Flores . . . Guayota moved his hand, still laughing, and something flew at me. I dodged, but it slid over my shirt, which caught fire, and landed on top of the Passat.

A quick brush of my hands put my shirt out, leaving me with blisters on the skin along my collarbone and a hole in my bra strap. I slid back one step to see what he'd thrown at me without having to look away from him.

It was about the size of a finger, blackened and oozing on one end. I chanced a quick glance and realized that not only was it the size of a finger, it had a fingernail. I almost nudged it with my foot to be sure, but the paint was blackening and bubbling up around it, and directly underneath it, the metal was sagging.

I'd read an account written by a Civil War commander about how he'd seen the cannonball coming toward one of his men who was wounded and down. It had been coming so slowly, and he'd just reached down to deflect it—and had lost his arm.

I didn't touch it.

Guayota had a distance weapon, however weirdly horrible, and that meant keeping back from him was no good. Time enough later to wonder at the finger and how he'd made it so hot it could melt the roof of the car; for now I had to concentrate on survival. Nor could I follow my sensei's first rule of fighting—he who is smart and runs away lives to fight another day. The bay doors were closed, and I had no way to run.

Out of other options, I attacked. There had been no more than a fraction of a second between when he threw the finger and when I jumped off the car. His burning finger meant that I knew better than to touch him with my skin. The wrench I'd grabbed was a giant-sized 32mm; it weighed about three pounds and gave me almost two feet of additional reach.

I got four hits on him, three with the wrench and one with the gun, and in that time, I learned a lot about him. He wasn't used to his prey knowing how to fight back. He had never been trained to fight hand-to-hand. He was slower than I was. Not much slower, but it was enough for me to get in four hits. He was oddly sticky, and I lost the gun to him when it sank into his flesh to be quickly consumed and absorbed.

And, finally, nothing I tried seemed to hurt him.

He continued to heat up as we fought, and before I got the next hit in, his clothes flared up in a wall of flames, then drifted to ashes. His face had melted into something with eyes and a mouth, but no other features that I could pick out in the wavy blackness of his skin.

Other than his face, his body remained in other ways human-like, but there was nothing human about his skin. It was char black and formed into a bumpy, almost barklike surface. Fissures broke open as he moved, revealing, as I'd noticed before, something deep orange with red overtones. His outer surface reminded me of nothing so much as film I'd seen of the active lava flows in Hawaii.

He touched me, a glancing blow on my hip. I slapped my hip to put out the fire and refused to look because although my face still hurt, as did the skin across my collarbone, my hip had just gone numb.

My fifth hit landed in one of those odd fissures in his skin, this one on his left shoulder blade, or at least where a shoulder blade would have been had he been human. It knocked him forward: he wasn't immune to the laws of physics. My arm and hand were spattered by hot chunks of liquid that burned.

Remembering the finger that sank into metal, I knocked the hot splatters off me, but the skin beneath them bubbled up into blisters that hurt. Flores reached out, a longer reach than he should have been able to manage, and grabbed hold of the end of my wrench. Where he touched, the metal glowed orange, and the glow rapidly spread toward my hand. I let go of the wrench before the glow touched my skin.

The air was smoky now—and not just with burning fabric. All sorts of flammable liquids spill on the floor of a garage; although I clean them by pouring on cat litter or HyperSorb and sweep them up, there was enough residue here and there to react as he brushed past them, so that there were several small fires burning reluctantly on the cement.

I spent an anxious and weaponless few moments just getting out of the way of his jabs and kicks before I could get close to something else I could use as a weapon. I tripped over the crowbar he'd dropped, but didn't pick it up: it was all metal, and I'd just learned that I wanted something that didn't transfer heat as well as metal did. But when I tripped, I knocked the big mop over on myself and grabbed it as I rolled to my feet.

The big wooden mop handle made an okay bo staff, and I used it to keep him from approaching me while occupying him seriously enough that he couldn't rip off another finger—or other body part—to throw at me. The wood kept catching fire, but if I swung it fast enough, the air put the flames out before it could burn much away. It was getting rapidly shorter, but I was only using the very end to poke him rather than using it like a baseball bat.

I managed to lure him into leading with the top half of his body and hit him in the middle of his forehead with the end of the mop handle in a lunge that would have done a fencing master proud. The wood sank a good four inches into his forehead and stuck there. When he jerked away, he took the mop handle with him.

He wrenched it out and threw his head back and howled, a noise so high-pitched that it made my ears hurt. He bent double, and parts of his body stuck together, melting or melding. I took a chance and sprinted to one of my big toolboxes and grabbed a three-foot-long crowbar off the top. This crowbar had a big red rubber handle to protect my hands.

I was running back across the garage, crowbar held up and over my shoulder, when something really big flew past me, something large enough that the air disturbance in its wake fluttered my shirt as it passed.

It hit Guayota right in his center mass, scooped him off his feet, and carried him back five or six feet in the air before he hit the far wall and the floor at the same time. That wall was covered with a plethora of rubber hoses and belts hung in a semiorganized fashion. He set the ones he touched on fire, and a new wave of toxic smoke filled the air, as the thing that hit him fell to the ground with a dull smack that resolved itself into the motor from a '62 Beetle that I'd had sitting in the office to be taken for scrap.

Adam was here.

A Beetle motor isn't huge as motors go, but it still weighed over two hundred pounds. Even I don't know all that many people who can fling an engine as if it were a baseball. But I didn't look for him because—surprise, surprise—not even being hit by two hundred pounds had put Guayota out of the game.

He rose from the ground, covered in flaming belts and hoses that he shed as he moved. He was no longer even vaguely humanlike. Instead, he had the form of a huge dog shaped much like the dog I'd shot. His head was broad and short muzzled, and his ears hung down like a hunting dog's. His mouth was open, revealing big, sharp teeth of the many, many category. The creature he'd turned into was bigger and heavier than any werewolf I'd ever seen.

This, this was the beast that had feasted on horses, dogs, and women next to that hayfield in Finley.

"Mercy is mine," Adam said softly from somewhere just behind me. "You need to leave here, right now."

"Yours?" The voice was still Flores's, though liquid splattered from the doglike monster's mouth to sizzle on the floor as he talked. "You took she who is mine. It is only meet that I take she who is yours."

"Christy Hauptman is the mother of my daughter," Adam said. "And I loved her once. She cared for me for years, and that gives her the right to ask me for protection from someone who frightens her. You have no right to her, no right to be here at all."

The dog who had been Flores, who was evidently the Guayota my half brother had warned me about, stopped and tilted his head. The dog's skin looked like it had when it was a human shape wearing it. On the dog, the charred, blackened crust resembled fur, fur that dripped molten and glowing bits of stuff onto the cement floor.

"No?" Guayota said, his voice an odd whispering hum that was almost soothing to listen to. "You are wrong. I found my love, who had been taken from me, and I celebrated the sun's countenance, warmth, and beauty. I gave her all that I was, all that I had been, all that I could be."

The hum rose to a hiss, and I shivered despite the heat because there was something horrible in that sound. It mutated into a howl that made my bones vibrate like wind chimes. The sound stopped abruptly, but I could feel the air pressure build up as if we were in an airplane climbing too rapidly.

"Then she left." He sounded like the man who'd first come into the garage, almost human. Sad. But that didn't last. "She left me, when I swore that would never happen again. Swore that never, once I finally found her, would I let her leave me."

"That's not a choice you get to make," said Adam. "You are scaring her, and you need to leave her alone. I and my pack are sworn to defend her from danger. You don't want to put yourself in my path, Flores."

"I tremble," Guayota said, smiling, his teeth white in the red heat of his mouth. "See?"

A low, groaning noise rumbled through the garage, and the floor rocked beneath me, making me stumble awkwardly to keep my feet. The cement floor cracked, and I could hear a crash of epic proportion as the earthquake sent one of the lighter-weight racks in the office area over in a crash of miscellaneous VW parts.

Guayota laughed and didn't sound even vaguely human this time. "We all tremble witnessing the might of the Alpha of werewolves." There was a popping sound, and steam escaped from one of the fissures in his back. Red glop dropped from his half-open mouth like slobber, but slobber didn't hit cement and score it.

Adam scooped up the wasserboxer engine I'd just put together and threw it. The wasserboxer engine is a lot heavier than the old Beetle engine had been, and he threw it more at bowling-ball speed than baseball.

Guayota rose on his hind legs to meet the engine when it hit, and this time it only pushed him back two or three feet, and he stayed upright and in control of the slide. Like my gun and the mop handle, the engine sank into him and stuck there, metal glowing.

Then I felt a wave of fae magic, and the engine became a shining silver skin that flowed swiftly over whatever Flores had become and covered him entirely before he had a chance to move.

"Zee?" I asked, coughing as the acrid smoke of the garage finally became too strong to ignore. I kept my eye on Guayota, but the fae-struck aluminum of the engine block seemed to be capable of staying solid around a creature who had melted hardened steel. The metal flexed a bit before settling into a motionless shape approximately the size of the creature Guayota had become.

Within the shiny skin, Guayota made no sound. My science background wasn't all that strong, but I was pretty sure the only thing keeping the aluminum from melting was fae magic.

"Nope, just me," Tad called, his voice a little strained. "Nice throw, Adam."

"Thanks," Adam said, sounding a little breathless himself.

Tad walked out from behind Adam—and he looked a little odd. The stick-out ears that had always given him an almost-comical appearance were now pointed, the bones of his face subtly rearranged to beauty as real and as human as Adam's. His eyes . . . were not human at all: polished silver with a cat's-eye pupil of purple. He was a little taller than usual, a little buffer, a little more graceful, and a lot scarier. I wasn't used to thinking of Tad as being scary.

I opened my mouth to thank them both but all I did was cough. I trotted to the garage controls to raise the garage-bay doors to let the smoke out and some fresh air in. Adam grabbed the fire extinguisher off the wall and started putting out fires. Both Adam and I were choking on the foul smoke, but Tad seemed to be unaffected by it.

As the adrenaline faded, pain took over. I'd evidently hit my right knee on something, and my cheek felt like it was, figuratively I hoped, on fire. Despite my fears, my hip was fine, just a bit achy. There was a hole burned through my jeans and underwear, but the skin beneath looked okay. The burns on my arm, hand, and collarbone hurt like fiends.

Sirens sounded in the distance, either police summoned by Adam or the fire department summoned by someone who saw all the smoke.

I put my hands on my hips, standing just outside to stay out of the smoke. "You guys better have some explanation for coming in just when I'm about to wipe the floor with him and stealing my victory."

Adam smiled, but his eyes were dark as he finished putting out the last fire. He set the fire extinguisher on the floor and stalked over to me. "Complain, complain, that's all I get. Aren't you the least bit happy to see me?"

I stepped into his arms, turning my head so the wine-dark silk shirt he wore pressed against my unhurt cheek and twisting so only the unburnt part of my collarbone touched him.

"I thought this was it," I confessed in a whisper, and his arms tightened on me until I had to tap on his arm. "Too tight, too tight, too tight . . . better."

"How long can you hold him?" Adam asked Tad, though his arms didn't slacken.

"Longer than you can hold her," Tad said dryly. "He quit struggling—probably lack of air. I could keep this up for an hour or two. If he fights like he was before, then a half hour, maybe a bit more. Aluminum is easier than steel. What are we going to do with him?"

"Jail's not an option," Adam said. "I'll call Bran—but I expect we're not going to have a choice but to call on the fae."

Tad grunted unenthusiastically. "If someone told them I'm not as powerless as most of us halfies, they would want me to join them. Maybe someone can contact my dad, and he can take credit for this." There was a metallic sound as if he'd tossed something at the metal prison he'd created from my nice wasserboxer engine.

"Hey, Mercy? Did you know there is a finger in the backseat of this Passat?" Tad asked.

I broke free of Adam and went into the garage to check out the

Passat as I started to add up the damage. I'd need to get another wasserboxer engine to replace the one that melted. The Beetle engine had been no loss . . . but the Passat was going to need some bodywork.

The finger had melted all the way through the roof, through the lining, and dropped onto the off-white leather, where it left a small puddle of blood and black ash. It looked like anyone else's finger.

"He pulled off his finger and threw it at me," I told Tad. "Do you know of any fae that pull off body parts and throw them at people?"

"I think there are some German folktales about disembodied heads," he said doubtfully. "And then there's always Thing on *The Addams Family*." He opened the back door of the car and touched the finger. "It's not moving."

I hugged myself and fought the urge to giggle. "Thank the good Lord for small favors."

Adam moved Tad gently aside and used a hanky to pick up the finger and bring it to his nose.

"I don't smell magic as well as you do, Mercy," he said, setting it back on the seat. "But this finger smells human, not fae."

"Human fingers don't—"

Tad interrupted me. He jerked his head around until he faced his metal sculpture and made a pained sound. He staggered off balance, and Adam caught his elbow to steady him.

Sweat broke out on Tad's brow, and he said, in a guttural tone, "Watch out. Something is wrong."

The whole building shook again. There was a thunderous crash as a transmission fell off the top shelf of a Gorilla Rack. Adam grabbed my hand and held on to me. It was the hand I'd burned, but I just grabbed him back. Some things are more desperate than pain.

It lasted less than a second, and it left the cement floor of my shop buckled, car parts and boxes of car parts strewn all over. The high-pitched wail of the office smoke detector went off. It went off with some frequency when I showered too long, or someone cooked bacon in the microwave, but it had ignored all the smoke and fires in the garage. Apparently, it had decided that enough was enough.

Adam dropped his hold on Tad and me, grabbed his ears, and snarled. I knew exactly how he felt—and I knew what to do. I dashed into the office, hopped onto the counter, and snagged the stool as I jumped. I set the stool on the counter and climbed on top with speed and balance hard won with practice. Reaching up to the ceiling, I popped the battery out of the alarm.

Blessed silence fell. Relative silence, broken by things that were still rolling onto the floor and the sirens that were closer now. In the parking lot, a car engine purred to life, then revved hard as someone drove off with a squeal of rubber on asphalt. I looked out the window and saw Juan Flores's rental car speeding away.

Tad was swearing in German. Some of the words I recognized, but even the ones I didn't echoed my own sentiment exactly.

"Stupid," he said to me, his eyes horror-struck. "I am so stupid. *Er war Erd und Feuer.*"

"English," murmured Adam.

"Earth and fire," said Tad without pause. "Earth and fire—and I trapped him and forgot what he was."

Earth.

Tad clenched his fist and pulled at something invisible with enough force that it caused his muscles to stand out on his arms.

With an almost-human shriek, the aluminum that had encased Flores peeled back, revealing a cavernous hole where the cement floor of my garage had once been.

Adam's head came up, and he measured the sound of the sirens. "Stay here," he said, and hopped down into the hole. He was gone less than a minute before he was back.

He looked at Tad. "You need to be out of here before those sirens get close. Can you change your appearance so no one will recognize you?"

Tad nodded.

"Change shape, then," Adam said. "You understand that it won't just be the police coming here. Even the dumbest cop is going to see that there was magic afoot here. We're going to have government agents, and if they get a glimpse of what you can do, they are going to want you. You are too powerful for *anyone* to let you run around loose: human, shapeshifter, or fae. No one but your dad knows exactly how powerful you are—let's leave it like that."

Tad changed like I do—between one breath and the next. He was a little taller than usual and a lot handsomer. He looked clean-cut and real. I wondered if he'd stolen the appearance from someone or if he practiced in front of a mirror.

"That's good," said Adam. "Go."

"Thank you," I told him.

He grinned, and Tad's grin looked odd on the stranger's face. "You aren't supposed to thank the fae, Mercy. You're just lucky I like you." Then he strolled casually outside and away.

Adam pulled out his cell phone. "Jim. Get rid of all copies of the feed to Mercy's garage after I hit Flores with the engine. Blur or get rid of anything that shows Mercy's assistant after he left when she closed up."

"Got it."

He hung up the phone and looked at me. He'd seen it faster than I had. Tad was incredibly powerful to do what he'd done. He was also young, and with his father locked away in Fairyland (the Ronald Wilson Reagan Fae Reservation's less respectful nickname), he was vulnerable: no one but family could know what he was. I looked at the sheet of aluminum, now crumpled and torn aside. It could have been an airplane or a tank or . . . We needed to keep him safe.

"The hole goes underground out to the parking lot."

"He told me his name was Guayota," I said—and that's when I saw the naked dead man lying on the floor where a dead dog should have been.

I blinked twice, and he was still there, belly down, but his head turned to the side so I could see the single bullet hole in his forehead. My bullet hole.

"Adam?" I said, and my voice was a little high.

He turned his head and saw the man, too. "Who is that?"

"I think," I said slowly, "I think that's the dog I shot." I remembered that too-intelligent, ancient gaze.

"I saw it on my laptop on the way over," Adam said. "You shot a dog."

"It wasn't a dog." I gave a half-hysterical hiccough. "They'll arrest me for murder."

"No," Adam said.

"Are you sure?" I sounded a little more pathetic than usual. My face hurt. My garage was in ruins that would make my insurance company run to find their "Acts of God not covered" clause. I'd killed a dog that had turned into a naked dead guy, and someone had thrown a finger at me.

"Flores essentially ate your gun, so no weapon for ballistics," Adam said. "And you were attacked in your garage." He didn't say any more out loud, but I heard what he left unspoken. There wasn't a member of the local police department who hadn't seen or at least heard of the recording of what had happened to me in this garage before, if only because the imagery of Adam's ripping apart the body of my assailant left a big impression.

His arms closed around me, and we both looked at the dead man. He looked like someone's uncle, someone's father. His body was spare and muscled in a way that looked familiar. Werewolves don't have extra fat on their bodies, either. They burn calories in the change from human to wolf and back, and they burn calories moving because a werewolf doesn't have the proper temperament to be a couch potato.

"Sweetheart," Adam said, his voice a sigh as the first official car pulled into my parking lot. "It was clear-cut self-defense."

I closed my eyes and leaned against him.

"Hands up," said a shaky voice. "Get your hands up where I can see them."

Adam let go of me and put his hands up. I turned around, stepping away from Adam so they could tell I wasn't armed. The man approaching us wasn't in uniform, but his gun was out. His eyes weren't on me, all of his attention was for Adam. Of course, it didn't take a genius to figure out which one of us would be the bigger threat. If I looked like I felt, I looked tired, scared, and hurt—I put my hands up anyway.

"Mr. Hauptman?" said the armed man, stopping just inside the bay door but in the middle of the open space so that the Passat didn't interfere with his ability to cover both of us. He was younger than me, and he was wearing slacks and a jacket and tie, which only made him look even younger. I noticed almost absently that true night had fallen in the short time between when I'd first thrown open the bay doors and now.

"Adam Hauptman?" he said again. His voice squeaked, and he winced.

"Keep your hands where we can see them," said another, calmer voice. This one was dressed in a cheap suit and held his gun as though he'd shot people before. His eyes had that look that let you know he'd shoot right now, too, and sleep like a baby that night. "Agent Dan Orton, CNTRP. This is my partner, Agent Cary Kent. You are Adam Hauptman and his wife, Mercedes?"

Feds. I felt my lip curl.

"That's right," Adam agreed.

"Can you tell me what happened tonight?"

"You're here in response to my call?" Adam asked instead of answering him.

"That's right."

"Then," said Adam gently, "you already know some of it. I think we'll call my lawyer before the rest."

I'd have spent the night repeating what happened endlessly to a series of people who all would hope for the real story. I've done it before. With Adam present, neither of us said anything because they weren't letting Adam call the lawyer.

Agent Orton of CNTRP, better known as Cantrip, and Agent Kent, the nervous rookie, wanted to arrest us on general principle because Adam was a werewolf, and there was a dead body on the ground. And, possibly, because they weren't happy with our not talking to them.

Luckily, we were under the local police jurisdiction, barely, because Adam's initial call had only told them that there was a man who might have been responsible for murder and arson trying to break in to my garage. Human attacking human, even if she was the wife of a werewolf, was not enough to allow Cantrip to take over the case.

We didn't correct them when they speculated that our intruder was the dead man. We said nothing about a supernatural creature who could turn into a volcanic dog and cause earthquakes because Cantrip was dangerous. There were people in Cantrip who would love to see us just disappear, maybe into Guantanamo Bay—there were rumors, unsubstantiated, that a whole prison block was built to hold shapeshifters and fae. Maybe they would just report that we had escaped before they could question us and hide the bodies. Adam, because he was a monster, and me because I slept with monsters. When I'd shifted to coyote in front of Tony a few months ago, I'd also shifted in front of a Cantrip agent named Armstrong. He'd told me he wouldn't say anything about it, and apparently, based on these two, he had not.

There were good people in Cantrip, too; Armstrong was a good person, so I knew that it wasn't just a pretend thing—like Santa Claus. But a growing number of incidents between Cantrip and werewolves or the half fae who'd been left to defend themselves when the full-blooded fae disappeared indicated that the good agents were in a minority.

The fire department arrived on the heels of the Feds, took a good look around for hot spots (none), marveled at the "damned big hole in the floor," and left with the promise of sending out someone to evaluate the scene in daylight. EMTs arrived while the fire department was still there.

One guy sat me down and looked me over with a flashlight

while the younger Cantrip agent took it upon himself to make sure I didn't make a break for it.

The EMT made a sympathetic sound when he looked at my burns. "I bet those hurt, *chica*," he said. "I have good news and bad news."

"Hit me," I told him.

"Good news is that these all qualify as minor burns no matter how nasty they feel."

"Bad news?"

"I think your cheek is going to scar. There's some chance that it will fade, but you've got dark skin like me, and dark skin and burns aren't a happy combination. Also, there's nothing to do for the burns. If the air bothers them, you can try wrapping them, but that will only be easy to do with the burns on your hands. If you see any sign of infection, take yourself down to your regular doctor."

"I can deal with scars," I said with more confidence than I felt. Who knew I was vain about my face? I wasn't beautiful by any stretch of the imagination, so I certainly hadn't expected the pang I felt knowing I'd bear Guayota's mark the rest of my life.

"It should look dashing," he told me. "Just a pale streak, and you can make up all sorts of stories about how you got it. Frostbite on your third polar expedition. Dueling scar. Knife fight in the ghetto."

"I'll keep that in mind." His matter-of-fact tomfoolery settled me. Impossible to believe in volcanic dogs when this EMT was so calmly cracking jokes as he got over the heavy ground as lightly as he could.

"I do have some advice, before I let you go," he told me.

"What's that?"

"*Chica*," he said seriously, "next time some firebug starts throwing burning things at you, run away."

"I'll take that under advisement," I promised him solemnly.

The second EMT came back from looking for other victims. "There is a finger in the backseat of the car in there," he said. "Does anyone know who it belongs to and if I should get it in ice? It might need to be reattached. Or is it evidence, and I need to leave it alone?"

I just shook my head, unwilling to talk in front of the Cantrip agent, and left the two EMTs to their debate. I wandered back over toward Adam. I don't know what the EMTs decided, but they left before the police cars started showing up.

The Kennewick police arrived while the fire department was still having a look-see, though the big red trucks toddled off soon thereafter. The local police interrupted the stalemate of our not talking and the Cantrip agents' not letting us call our lawyer. Not that we talked to the local police, either, but their presence put a damper on the Feds. Tony wasn't with the police who came, but Willis was.

"Word is that this was your husband's ex-wife's stalker," Willis told me after he'd gone inside to see the hole for himself. His suit was muddy, and so were his hands, so he must have gone down and followed the tunnel like Adam had. He sounded grumpy. "He cause this?" He glanced around the remains of my shop. "With some kind of a bomb, maybe?"

Dan Orton and his sidekick were trying to work on Adam without antagonizing the police. They were ignoring me because I wasn't a werewolf. Adam had subtly eased them farther away from me while I talked to Willis.

I looked at the Cantrip agents thoughtfully, then at Willis. "You know that site we both looked at yesterday?" I kept my voice down.

He grunted, but his eyes were sharp.

"I think this incident has a lot to do with that other. You and Tony should show up at tomorrow's deposition when Adam and I talk in the presence of our lawyer. The one we still need to call."

He looked at me, a long, cool look. "The crime you are referring to is officially a Cantrip case. And neither I nor Detective Montenegro are your puppets to call." Despite the hostile words, he sounded less grumpy than he had been.

It was my turn to grunt. "Fine by me." He couldn't fool me. Now that he knew the two were connected, you couldn't keep him away with a legion of superheroes. He'd tell Tony, and they'd both be there tomorrow.

"Does the dead body with the bullet in his forehead belong to the stalker?" he asked.

"Tomorrow, Adam and I will be happy to talk," I said, firmly keeping myself from explaining. "You mind if I call our lawyer?"

He glanced at the Cantrip agents and smiled grimly. "You aren't under arrest. Without the assurance that there was magic afoot here, Cantrip doesn't have the authority. And I am not inclined to arrest anyone without more information. Without an arrest, I don't see that I have any say over what you do."

My phone was intact, which was something of a miracle in and of itself. Willis put himself between me and the Cantrip agents while I called the pack's lawyers. Their phone system forwarded me to the lawyer on call, and the woman who answered sounded harried. I could hear kids screaming in the background, but since the screams were interspaced with wild laughter, I wasn't too concerned.

"Trevellyan," she said in a breathless voice. She cleared her throat and continued in a much more lawyerly fashion, though her voice was still very Marilyn Monroe. "Good evening, Ms. Hauptman. How can I help?"

I gave her a brief explanation—stalker, break-in, dead body. Not telling her anything Willis, who was watching me with grim amusement, didn't already know. I told her Adam wanted to get out of here tonight and give a statement tomorrow.

"Don't say anything," she said. "Don't let Adam say anything. I'll be right there."

SHE STRODE ONTO THE SCENE, A FIVE-FOOT-NOTHING warrior with iron gray hair and eyes clear and sharp blue. She took one good long look around and marched up to Clay Willis, having evidently determined he was in charge.

"Are my clients under arrest?" she asked Willis.

Adam, trailing his pair of Feds, approached in time for Willis to answer, "No, ma'am."

"We still have some questions," said Agent Orton.

"Which my clients will answer tomorrow in my office." She gave them her card. "Call that number tomorrow at eight thirty sharp, and someone will tell you when to come."

She ushered Adam and me to Adam's car.

"Now run while you can," she murmured. "I will do the same. The grandmother magic will wear off in a minute, and someone will decide that the dead body means they should arrest someone. Don't answer your phone unless you know the number and come into my office tomorrow at seven thirty."

———————

"SHE'S GOOD," I SAID. "TOUGH, SMART, AND FUNNY AS a bonus. I wonder if there really is grandmother magic."

"For what we pay her, she'd better be good," agreed Adam. "She doesn't need grandmother magic to make people scramble at her command." He pressed a button on his steering wheel, and said, "Call Warren."

A woman's voice from his dash said, "Calling."

"Boss?" Warren answered. "Everyone okay?"

"Mercy's singed, but still swinging."

"Good to hear. I got quite an earful from your security chief, who deleted a lot of interesting material."

"Then you know most of it. I need you to get everyone out of our house right now. Apparently, Christy's stalker is some kind of supernatural who can set things on fire."

"You want me to take them home?" Warren asked.

Adam took in a deep breath. "What do you think?"

"I think that our place got a lot of attention in the press when those rogue agents kidnapped Kyle."

"Suggestions?"

"How about Honey's place? It's big enough to house everyone if we don't all need bedrooms, and it hasn't been plastered all over the newspaper."

Honey's house was in Finley, too. Another large house like ours, though it wasn't built to be a pack den, so while there was plenty of room, it was short on beds.

"Sounds good. Call Honey, then get everyone out of the house."

"You two okay?"

Adam's eyes traveled to me. "Yes."

"Kyle called about ten minutes ago and said to tell you that a Gary Laughingdog is at our house and would like to talk to Mercy on a matter of some urgency."

"Tell him we will be right there." Adam pulled a U-turn. "We'll move them on to Honey's house. Call me if Honey has a problem, and we'll come up with something else."

"Right. Is Laughingdog the guy Mercy visited in prison?" I said, "Yes."

There was a little pause. "So he broke out of jail?" I said, "Yes," again.

"Kyle doesn't know that," Warren said. "If the wrong things happen, Kyle could lose his license to practice law for having him in the house."

"You get everyone safe," said Adam, "and I'll take care of Kyle."

"Movin' on it, boss." Warren hung up the phone.

"Do you think he'll go after our house?" I asked. "Guayota, I mean."

"I don't know enough about him to be making predictions," Adam said.

"Why do you think that he believes she—" I stopped speaking. "What?"

"I almost saw it then," I sat up straighter and turned toward Adam. "I'm stupid. When Tony took me to look at the crime scene in the hayfield, I thought for an instant that one of the bodies he'd left was Christy's." The ghost could have been her sister. "She was the right age, right hair color, and right body type. All of the women were, I think—though it wouldn't hurt to double-check."

"We need to find out who this guy is," said Adam grimly. "And we need to find the walking stick, so that Beauclaire doesn't kill us before Flores does."

"We have his name," I said. "Guayota. That might help. And Zee gave Tad some insight he shared with me about Beauclaire and why not running Coyote down before Sunday might not mean disaster."

He glanced my way and back at the road, inviting me to keep talking. So I explained Zee's reasoning. When I was finished, Adam gave me a short nod. "Might work. It would be better to have the walking stick, but beggars can't be choosers."

"Zee's insights into the problem with Beauclaire and the walking stick have showed me I need to start thinking outside the box more," I said.

"Oh?" Adam glanced at me, then back at the road.

"I thought we should apply that kind of thinking to the matter of Christy's stalker."

He gave me a skeptical look.

"No, really," I said. "Now that we know that Flores is really this nasty, fiery, superpowerful nothing-can-kill-me demon from hell, maybe we should consider just giving Christy to him?"

He laughed.

"I'm serious," I said. And I was. Really. If only a little bit.

"Right," he said affectionately. "I know exactly how serious you are. We've got a twenty-minute drive ahead. Why don't you close your eyes and rest up?"

It sounded like a plan. My hands hurt, my hip hurt, my cheek throbbed, and someone had thrown a finger at me—and I hadn't eaten today. Adam's hand curled around the top of my knee, and I relaxed and let myself drift off. Nothing was so bad that Adam's touch couldn't make it better. Even if he wouldn't let me give Christy to the fire-dog from hell.

8

KYLE LET US IN WITH A SINCERE, HEARTFELT GRATITUDE that didn't speak well of his guests.

He frowned at my face.

"The EMT told me the cheek will probably scar, but putting stuff on it won't help," I told him. "He also advised avoiding fights where throwing fire is involved."

"I know of something that might help," Kyle said. "I'll talk to my hairdresser and see if I can't get you some. Of course, if you keep fighting with people who throw fire at you, it's unlikely to be of any help in the long run."

"Let's get through with Gary Laughingdog first," said Adam. "And then I'll tell you what happened tonight at Mercy's garage."

"I know most of it," Kyle said. "Warren called a while ago and gave me a play-by-play. But the conversation was in my bedroom, and I haven't passed anything along just yet."

He ushered us to the ground-floor sitting room, where the defensive posture of our newest wolf put Adam on edge. Zack had pushed himself as far into the corner of the sofa as he could get. Gary Laughingdog, barefoot and dressed in jeans and a stained white t-shirt, was sitting on the back of the same couch, though right in the center of it. But he was leaning toward Zack, using body language to put pressure on the wolf.

"So," Laughingdog said as we came into the room, "do you swing the same way as your host, Zack? I usually go for women, but you're cute enough I could do you if you want."

"No," Adam said, and he wasn't answering the question Gary had raised.

Laughingdog turned to look at Adam, his posture relaxed. He'd known we were coming in, and the pressure he was putting on Zack was to see what we would do. His eyes widened as he took in Adam. "I'd do you, too." He wasn't lying. "Almost-Sister, you picked a real catch."

"It was I who caught her," Adam said softly. "It took years. And no, not interested, and neither is Zack. If you don't back off him, we may never find out just what it is that you have to tell my wife. That would be too bad."

"Zack doesn't mind me," said Laughingdog with one of those false-friendly smiles he'd used on me. "Do you, Zack?"

"One," said Adam coolly.

"You're going to count to three? Really? How old do you think I am?"

Kyle stalked over to the couch, grabbed Laughingdog by the back of his t-shirt, and jerked him all the way off the couch and onto the floor. I'd have thought such a fit of violence was completely out of character for Kyle, but somehow it didn't seem forced. Maybe Gary Laughingdog had the same effect on people that I occasionally did.

"I told you to back the fuck off," Kyle snarled. "You are a temporary guest in my house, and I am *done* with you."

Laughingdog, sprawled out on the floor, didn't look the least bit fussed. "Sorry," he said unrepentantly. "I can't help but push them when they squirm."

"Uncomfortable is one thing," said Kyle, who also tended to push people when they squirmed. "Scared is another."

Laughingdog froze and glanced up at Zack, who hadn't moved from his corner and was not looking at anyone. He was, in fact, barely breathing. Submissive wolves don't go around cringing. Peter, Honey's mate, had been a good fighter. Submissive means a wolf has no desire to be in charge.

"Ah, damn it all," Laughingdog said, sitting up. "I didn't catch it. Sometimes it's easy to get caught up and not notice what my nose tells me. I know what 'no' means, kid. No always means no."

"Mercy," Adam said. "You and Kyle take Laughingdog somewhere else and let me talk to Zack. Evidently 'no' doesn't always mean 'no.'"

Zack came to life at that. "I'm fine," he said hurriedly.

"No," said Laughingdog softly. He pushed himself across the floor until he was on the other side of the room from the couch. "I don't think so, man. But no harm will come to you here, right?"

Adam looked at Zack, then looked at me. "What do you think?"

"I think I overreacted," said Zack before I could say anything. He sounded humiliated. "I'm sorry."

"Nah, kid," said Laughingdog. "Not overreacting when you don't know me. But someone needs to teach you to do something more effective than just locking down." He frowned at me. Apparently it was my fault that he'd scared Zack.

Kyle sat down on the other end of the couch from Zack. "Give him space and leave him alone," he said.

Kyle was a divorce attorney; he had experience dealing with broken people. I'd only *been* a broken person, so Kyle was the person to listen to.

I nodded at Kyle to give his assessment my support. Adam, after looking around, pulled a wingback chair over until the back was resting against the edge of the couch. When he sat in it, it put him between Zack and everyone else in the room, and it gave Zack a barrier between him and Adam. I sat on the chair arm.

Laughingdog moved to a chair that was across the room but still gave Zack a good view of him. He looked at Kyle.

"You know," he said, "I can do a little rough since that seems to be your thing—and you look like a man who likes the boys rather than the girls."

"Not interested," said Kyle shortly.

"See," said Laughingdog to the room at large, though there was no doubt to whom he addressed his words. "That's how it's done. 'Go soak yourself in oil and light a match' in two short words."

"What did you want to talk to me about, Gary?" I asked. If I let Laughingdog keep talking without direction, someone was going to get hurt.

He looked at the burn on my cheek. "I think you met the guy I came to warn you about. If you put Bag Balm on that, it will feel better. Might even keep it from scarring. I was hoping to find you before he did, but making phone calls from"—he glanced at Kyle—"making phone calls to tell someone that an angry volcano god is going to attack her is hard enough when you know her well enough that you *do* have her phone number. It also takes me time to come off a *Seeing* like the one I had when you came to visit me. Took me a little longer to decide I had an obligation to find you and give you a little clearer warning. Getting here . . . well, for such as you and me, it wasn't a big thing, but it took time, too."

Don't tell Kyle the lawyer that the man talking to us had just escaped from prison. I got the message, not that I needed it. Adam had told me before we came in that Kyle's best defense was not to know that Laughingdog had escaped from prison.

"What do you know about this 'angry volcano god'?" Adam asked slowly.

"Some. Not a lot, but hopefully enough that you can find out more. I got a lot of random information. Do either of you know what 'El Teide' means?"

Kyle frowned. "In reference to what?"

"To Guayota," Laughingdog said.

"Coyote?" asked Zack.

"No. Guayota," said Kyle. "Starts with a 'g,' and it's the name of one of the gods of Tenerife."

"Tenerife?" I asked.

"The Canary Islands?" asked Adam. "Tenerife is one of the bigger islands in the Canaries, right?"

I'm a history major, so once Adam jogged my memory, I pulled up a few random factoids—I am a magpie of history trivia. Spain had conquered the islands that were not far off the coast of Africa over the course of a century, just in time for them to be used as supply ports for Columbus and most of the Spanish explorers of the New World.

I knew a couple of other very random things. First, at the behest of the King of Spain, Canary Islanders had settled what became San Antonio, Texas, and set up the first official government in Texas. Second, the original natives of the islands hadn't been of African phenotype. That and the local island story that there was a mysterious island among the Canaries that disappeared and reappeared had been used to fuel all sorts of Atlantis rumors.

None of what I knew appeared to be useful in the present situation, so I kept my mouth shut.

"That's right," Kyle said. "My folks used to vacation there every year—still do for all I know. I haven't talked to them much since . . . well, since. Anyway—" He spoke quickly, to get the attention off events that were still painful. Kyle seldom spoke about his family, who had disowned him when he'd told them he was gay. "There was this old woman at my parents' favorite hotel who watched kids so that the adults could go play. The native Canarians who worked at the hotel swore she was a witch—there are a lot of witches on the Canary Islands. Before I met Warren, I pretty much dismissed all of that as superstition, but now . . . anyway, the story of Guayota was one of her favorites. One hellish vacation, I heard it five times in three days." He frowned. "She's the only one I heard it from, so you should check it out somewhere else. I'm pretty sure she made parts of it up."

"Keep going," I told him. "We'll consult Wikipedia and the library later. Promise."

"It would be nice," Laughingdog said with feeling, "to hear something to put what I know in context. It might even help me make some of the odd things more useful. Please, tell us this story about Guayota."

"Okay," Kyle said. "Okay. I'll tell you what I know." He leaned forward, and I don't know how he did it, but with a bit of body language and a little warble in his voice, he called to mind a little old lady. I'd always thought that he'd had some drama training at some point. "There is a huge old volcano on Tenerife called El Teide. It's the tallest peak in Spain and one of the tallest volcanos in the world. The old people who once lived on the island called it Echeyde, which means either 'hell' or 'the gates of hell' depending upon the person you ask. Guayota lived in El Teide, either guarding the door, ruling there, or both. Only the old ones could tell you for certain, and they are gone long, long ago."

His voice softened as he talked, and he pulled an accent out of his memory and added it to the story. The chair arm I sat on was uncomfortable, so I slid off it onto the floor. The floor was better, especially when I set my back against the chair and leaned my head against the arm. I'd gotten the post-danger jitters over with while we waited for the Cantrip agents to figure out that Adam wasn't going to talk until he was good and ready. Now I was just tired. The nap in the car had made it worse, and my eyelids fought to close.

"Now Guayota was, like the Greek Titans, a violent and impetuous creature of great power. He roamed the mountain in the shape of a great, black, hairy dog with red eyes, and tragedy befell any who met him in his runs because he would eat them up. One bite for children, two for mothers, or three for big warriors who came to fight him."

Hairy? I thought about it. Maybe the way his skin had seemed to drip and crack could be described as hairy, or maybe he had another form, too.

"Charming story to tell children," said Laughingdog.

"I thought so, too," agreed Kyle cheerfully in his own voice, then there was a little pause as he remembered that Laughingdog didn't deserve a cheerful reply. He continued in a more guarded tone. "My littlest sister had nightmares. And when my parents arranged a sightseeing tour up the side of the old volcano, they couldn't figure out why she wouldn't go."

Kyle recloaked himself in the persona of the old woman, and continued, "Guayota was terrifying, but he was also lonesome. Every day, he would look up and see Magec, the sun, running her path in the sky. He thought her beautiful and wondrous and him so lonely and miserable on that mountain. So that old Guayota, he plotted to take her for his own."

Hadn't Guayota made some reference to the sun when he was talking about Christy? I tried to visualize Kyle's story, to put Flores in the place of Guayota, but all I could see was a wizened old witch with a roomful of kids that she was scaring. Witches feed off other people's pain; I wondered if they could feed off terror as well.

"So one day, he jumped, the old devil, he jumped out of the top of El Teide and captured her for himself. Loud she cried and hard she fought, but she was no match for old Guayota. She could not burn him with her fierceness, for though she was the fire of day, he was born in the fire of the earth, which is more ferocious even than the sun. Nor could she blind him with her bright beauty because his eyes were used to the molten rock of his home. And when she got too bright for his eyes, the old dog, he just closed his eyes and used his ears and his nose, which were as sharp as any shepherd's dog's and more so.

"He took her down to his home and caged her inside the volcano. For weeks, the sky was dark, and smoke filled the air. It was then that Guayota's children were born, while he held Magec in his caves. They are the tibicenas, fierce, hairy black dogs that emerged from the mountain in those days when Guayota held

Magec his prisoner. The only light that shone on Tenerife was Magec's light, escaping here and there from the caves in the old volcano, and the light of the tibicenas' eyes.

"But the people of the island were frightened that they had no sun. They called and prayed to Achamán, he who created the world. Achamán listened to the cries of the people and came down to the volcano to rescue Magec. Guayota fought mightily because he did not want to give up Magec. The volcano spewed fire and rock, and many died as the two gods battled. At last, knowing that he could not win, Guayota called up the fires of the earth to swallow the island and Magec, so that if he could not have her, neither could anyone else.

"Achamán took Guayota and stuffed him in the volcano, stopping the fire and smoke and rescuing the people of the island. He freed Magec and sent her racing in the sky once more, fierce and bright as she should be. But she is always watchful when she flies over the top of El Teide, lest old Guayota catch her once again."

Kyle stopped, smiled a little. "I told the story to my dad once. He told me that it was a primitive attempt to explain a volcanic eruption. El Teide is an active volcano, the last eruption was a couple hundred years ago. He also pointed out that the reactions on the sun's surface are hotter than any volcano magma."

Talk turned to the night's adventures, which Adam was more than capable of telling. I drifted off into a dream of a witch who changed children into great, shaggy black dogs that looked like long-haired versions of the dog I'd shot, the one who'd turned into a man. The man raised his dead head to meet my eyes with his. His eyes were the color of lava.

"Mercy," he said. "Where is my sun?"

"Mercy, wake up," said Adam.

I sat up like a scalded cat and winced because everything hurt—especially the burn on my cheek.

"Okay," said Laughingdog. "Adam's been filling us in on your night. Were you awake for all of Kyle's story?"

I yawned. "Yep. I didn't fall asleep until we got to our part. Sorry. Long day."

"Fine." Laughingdog settled back into his chair, one leg up and the other doing a restless dance on the floor. "Kyle's story makes me pretty sure that Guayota is one of the great manitous."

I frowned at him. "Manitou" was an Algonquin word for spirit, the spirit that lived in all things: in rocks, in rivers, in mountains. Great manitou . . . I made some quick jumps of logic. "When you say great manitous, you're talking about creatures like Coyote?"

"That's right. Mostly right. No." He made a frustrated sound. "Coyote, Raven, Wolf, are different than manitous. Coyote is the spirit of mischief, of second chances, of adaptation—the archetype of coyotes. It is true that he shares characteristics with the great manitous. Like him, they can take the shape of people, though they are not people. They are powerful in their sphere of influence.

"Mostly the great manitous ignore us and pay attention only to those things that matter to them. The Columbia has a great manitou, I can feel it sometimes, but I've never heard of it manifesting itself, not even in stories."

"You think Guayota is a great manitou, the spirit of the volcano," I said. "Sort of like Pele in Hawaii?"

He nodded.

"So what is he doing here? Shouldn't he be stuck somewhere within a few thousand miles of where he belongs?"

"I don't know. Maybe he grew bored." He shrugged. "If he were Coyote, that would be the answer, wouldn't it? Maybe

Guayota grew lonely. The only thing I know is that, although great manitous can manifest and travel for a time, they do need a strong connection to their spirit-home. Without that connection, they will return to their spirit shape and be pulled home."

"So we need to find out what his connection is," said Adam.

"Right," agreed Laughingdog. "But here's the part that had me—" He substituted "driven to find you" for "breaking out of jail." He was going to have to be smoother if he didn't want Kyle to realize something was up. At least he was careful to look at me and not Kyle when he changed up his words. Looking at Kyle would have been a dead giveaway. "I had a few dreams, didn't mean much to me until you showed up, and I had that freaking nasty *Seeing*. I would have let it go, but then I had a worse dream."

"What already?" I said.

"Some things you need to know about my 'gift.'" He said it with his fingers as quotes so I knew what he thought about his gift from Coyote.

"Okay."

"One. It usually comes in dreams or small bits, big *Seeings* aren't that common. Two. Sometimes I see the future, sometimes the past, most times it's the present only somewhere else where I can't freaking *do* anything about anything."

I nodded.

"Finally. When I do see the future, while it is possible to change it, the reason I see that particular future is because it has become the most likely scenario, and it's pretty close to being set in stone."

"So what did you dream?"

"There is a room with a Texas flag on the wall and paintings of dogs. On the floor is this woman lying dead. At first I thought

196

she was you, but she isn't. There's a white pit bull on the floor beside her, with its throat torn out."

I jerked my head up. "Is she a small woman, Hispanic?"

"She was dead, Mercy, and lying on the floor. I didn't have a measuring stick. Could have been Hispanic or Indian, which is why I thought it was you originally. She opens her eyes, says your name, then she's dead again."

"You know who it is," Adam said.

I stood up. "You couldn't have told me this an hour ago? Adam, it's Joel's wife, the one who talked to Christy about dogs. We've got to go, right now."

He stood up and took in the room at a glance. "You come, too, Laughingdog. We'll put you up for the night and help you get where you need to be in the morning."

"Fine," Gary said, a little reluctantly. I didn't think he wanted to do anything more now that he'd given us the information he had.

"Zack?" Adam said.

"Yessir?"

"Anyone gives you a hard time, you tell me or Warren. Or you can tell Kyle, and he'll tell us." Adam named the people Zack would be most familiar with. "We'll take care of it, okay? You are safe here."

The submissive wolf looked away, his mouth pinched in at the corners. Adam had started out of the room, but the other's lack of response had him turned back around.

"You *will* tell one of us." It was a full-on order; I could feel the stir of pack magic.

Zack threw back his head in a full temper. "Fine."

Adam nodded once, then jogged out of the house. He stopped

at the door. "Kyle? You and Zack get overnight bags packed and head out to Honey's. This place has been in the papers in connection with Mercy and the pack, and that makes it too easy for him to find."

"Okay," Kyle said. "I know where Honey lives, I think. If I get turned around, I'll call Warren."

"SOUTH KENNEWICK," I TOLD ADAM FOR DIRECTIONS as we hopped into the SUV. "Off Olympia."

"Presa Canario," he said after we were well on our way. "Warren told me a while ago that the breed originated on the Canary Islands."

"Where are we going, and why am I going with you?" asked Laughingdog.

"Lucia is a friend. She has a big white Staffordshire terrier." I glanced over my shoulder at Laughingdog. "Pit bull in layman terms. You didn't dream of her until after we left you at the prison."

"That's right."

"It was right afterward that Honey and I went to visit with her." My fault if something happened to Lucia. Why else would Flores pay any attention to her at all?

"And you are bringing me with you because?" he asked again.

"Because Kyle is a lawyer and could lose his license to practice if it comes out that you were at his house," said Adam. "I promised his partner I'd look after him."

"Partner," Laughingdog said musingly. "Warren. Right? That's the other man you mentioned. I knew Kyle Brooks was tied up with the werewolves after reading about the group that attacked him a few months ago. That's why I went there. I got turned around, and by the time I figured out where I was, his house was a lot closer than yours, and I was on foot. Four feet. I thought he'd be a werewolf, but as soon as he answered the door, I could tell that he wasn't. It intrigued me."

Adam's voice was like sandpaper when he said, "In my pack, people can date whoever they like."

"Hey, I'm not pointing fingers, man," said Laughingdog. "Just explaining why my thoughts went right to look at Zack, but a deaf and blind man could tell that there is nothing between *them*. So his partner is this other werewolf." He breathed out through his nose in a huff of amusement. "A gay werewolf. I never thought I'd see the day that a pack let a gay werewolf live."

"Gary," I said, "shut up before someone hurts you."

"Warren," said Adam at the same time, "survived a lot of idiots with that attitude." He paused. "And you ought to listen to Mercy's advice."

We made it to Joel and Lucia's house about twenty minutes after we'd left Kyle's house—most of it in silence. I'd like to have believed that we'd quelled Gary, but his silence was punctuated with amusement that was very palpable.

As soon as we pulled into the driveway, I knew there was something wrong—no dogs were barking. I knocked on the door, the men at my back. When the door opened and Lucia peered around it, my breath left my mouth in a whoosh of relief.

"Mercy?" she asked. She seemed distracted and worried.

I nodded. "Yes. Sorry to come over so late without warning you first, but the matter was urgent. I think that Christy's stalker is a little more dangerous than we thought—and I might have led him right to your door. I know it's late, but can we come in to talk?"

She gave the men a cautious look.

"This is Gary Laughingdog," I told her. "My half brother." That was a simpler explanation for his presence than any other I could come up with on short notice, and it had the additional benefit of being true. I could feel his eyes boring holes in my back, but he didn't comment. "And this is my husband, Adam."

"The werewolf," he said—and it was just exactly the right thing to say because she smiled a little. "Your husband has worked for me a couple of times."

"I thought you looked familiar. Sure, come on in." She opened the door, and we trailed behind her into the house. She saw me look around. "The dogs are back in their kennels for dinner. I'll bring Aruba back in for the night in an hour or so. The rest kennel outside."

"Why aren't they barking?" I asked. "I was worried something had happened to you."

She smiled again as she led us into the living room, but there was tension around her eyes. "No. We teach them not to bark at night unless they are put on watch. That way, our neighbors do not complain about our dogs."

"Where's Joel?" I asked, sitting down on the same couch as last time.

She shook her head, and I realized that Joel was what she was worried about, not us. "He's late."

I opened my mouth to say something as reassuring as I could, given that I didn't have a clue why he'd be late, when my eyes fell on the flag on the opposite wall. The one Gary had seen in his vision.

"Joel is from Texas," I said, staring at the flag on the wall, thinking that what had popped into my head was absolutely ridiculous. Stupid. But there was that flag staring me in the face, so I had to ask. "Is his family, by any chance, from San Antonio?"

She nodded. "That's right. San Antonio. He was up here visiting some cousins when we met. We moved to Texas first, but I got homesick, and we moved back to the Tri-Cities."

A handful of families had been shipped to Texas from the Canary Islands by the King of Spain three centuries ago. There was supposed to have been a much larger immigration, but the whole plan had stalled out for reasons that had escaped my magpie collection of historical trivia. Three centuries was a lot of time, and San Antonio was a huge city.

Assuming Gary was right, Guayota was a manitou, the spirit of the volcano, and he needed something with him that tied him to the Canary Islands. He'd said that the dog I'd killed, his "child," was immortal. Tied to mortal flesh. And when Guayota left, the dog had turned into a man. Kyle had talked about tibicenas, Guayota's children who were black dogs. What if it was the tibicenas that served as Guayota's ties to the volcano? I'd killed the "mortal flesh" his tibicena was tied to. What if he needed to find another man to bind to the tibicena? What if that man had to be descended from a Canary Islander? Maybe Lucia and Joel's troubles weren't because I'd come to them for help.

"Do you know," I asked carefully, "if Joel is one of the Canarios?" Adam looked at me sharply. "A descendant of the Canary Islanders who settled in Texas?"

She gave me a tentative smile. "His mother never lets anyone forget it. She's a proud woman, and she swears that not only were they Canarios, but her family actually was Guanche, descended from the original inhabitants of the islands before Spain conquered it about seven hundred years ago." Her smile broadened. "She talks about moving back there someday. I really hope that she does. We could vacation in the tropics and also see her less often. Win-win in my book."

"We should get out of here," said Gary, looking at the framed flag and sounding nervous. He looked at Lucia and seemed to collect himself. "Ma'am, Mercy brought us here because she is worried that Christy's stalker might be after you because you helped her."

"That's pretty far-fetched," said Lucia.

Adam looked at Gary, and said, "Why don't we take you to dinner and tell you some tall tales and you can decide if you want to believe us or not? You pick the restaurant, take your own car, and leave a message for your husband. I think that we might all be easier in a more neutral location."

She looked at Adam, because people just do. Humans are not immune to the reassurance that he brings with him like an invisible cloak; part of it is being Alpha, and part of it is just Adam.

"I think," my husband said, giving the Lone Star flag a thoughtful look, "going out might be a very good idea."

SHE LED THE WAY TO A FAMILY-STYLE MEXICAN RES-taurant off Highway 395 where there were lots of people even at nine at night. No one said anything until we'd all ordered and the waiter had brought out drinks.

Gary shot a glance at me, to see if I wanted to start. I took a chip and dipped it into salsa and gave Adam a look. If Adam told her, she'd probably believe him. It was the air of authority and no nonsense. He raised an eyebrow, and I nodded at him.

"You tell her," I said. "You're good at making this kind of stuff make sense."

So while I ate chips like I hadn't eaten in days—which was sort of true—Adam told Lucia how Christy's stalker boyfriend had broken into my garage and turned into a fiery demon dog from the Canary Islands. He combined the immediate narrative with the story Kyle had told us later and managed to make it sound plausible.

He left out Gary's jailbreak.

Food came before Adam was finished, and I ate as quickly as I could because I knew that there was a real chance that dinner would be over before I was done eating. She might try to storm out, certain that we were crazy. Or maybe she'd try to go look for Joel immediately. We'd have to stop her, for her own safety—and then there would be other things more urgent than food. Gary was eating the same way I was, maybe for the same reasons.

"So," she said carefully, "Juan Flores is really a volcanic deity named Guayota who thinks that your ex-wife Christy is—what?— some sort of reincarnation of the sun goddess he captured and raped thousands of years ago?"

"I know, right?" I said, swallowing hastily. "I had that same moment of disbelief. But for me it was when he threw his finger at me, and it burned through the top of the Passat I was standing on."

She was silent for a moment, looking at the burn on my cheek. Maybe I shouldn't have said anything about the finger, but it kept coming up in my thoughts. I've never had a finger thrown at me before. A new-and-improved addition to my creepy-hall-of-fame nightmares.

"And you think that because I helped you a little"—she pinched her thumb and index finger together to show everyone how little—"he will come after me? Because this one"—she indicated Laughingdog with a jerk of her chin—"had a dream?"

"That's what I thought when Gary told us about his dream," I told her, setting down my fork. I wasn't hungry anymore. "That Guayota might have come after you because you helped us. But now I think that because I killed the human one of his tibicenas was tied to, he needs to find another one." Immortal tibicena tied to a mortal, a mortal who was descended from the land where his volcano had fertilized the soil the people ate from. "I think, if I understand what Guayota is, the spirit of a Canary Islands volcano, that he needed a descendant of the Canary Islands to re-create the physical form of his tibicena. I think that maybe he sought Joel out because his family came from the Canaries, where Guayota originated."

She hadn't run away yet. Adam gave me a thoughtful look, a "when did you come up with this" look.

"Maybe he's coming because you helped us," I told her. "But you can't contact Joel, and Guayota is a spirit, a god, demon, or whatever from the Canary Islands. It might be a coincidence. My brother here knows a little about the kinds of spirits that dwell in mountains."

Gary kept reacting when I claimed him as a relative. I wasn't sure whether he was happy, unhappy, or just surprised by it. I just ignored him and continued on. "He told us that Guayota needs a connection to his home to function here. I think the dogs are that connection. Now that one of them is dead, he needs a replacement. I think the coincidence was that I came to ask you about the dogs." Maybe, if there was some kind of deeper connection between Joel and Guayota, maybe it wasn't such an odd thing that Joel was working with dogs. "I think, I *believe*, that your husband meets Guayota's need for a descendant of the islands—and there are probably not a lot of Canary Islanders in the Tri-Cities. I think he's taken your husband and is forcing him to become one of his tibicenas."

She paled, pulled out her cell phone, and dialed. Instead of Joel's voice telling her to leave a message, we all heard the recording advising her that the customer who had the number she dialed was not available. He'd either powered his cell phone off, run it out of battery, or destroyed it.

"We have told you quite a story," I told Lucia. "I swear to you that the danger is real. If you don't wish us to keep you safe, I understand. If you don't believe us, that's okay, too. But I think you need to find a safe place to be for a few days until we can destroy Guayota."

"I'm not sure that's possible," Laughingdog murmured, and I kicked him under the table even though I didn't think Lucia had heard.

She put her phone back in her purse with shaking hands. "I live in a city with werewolves and fae. How much more is it to believe in volcano gods?"

She wiped her face, and I saw that she was clearing the skin beneath her eyes. "My dogs like you." It wasn't as much of a non sequitur as it sounded like. "I don't want to believe you. If I believe you, then this . . . thing has my husband." She gave me a brief, tight smile, and her voice was raw. "What can I do to help him?"

"We don't know," Adam said. "We are working on it. First, we'd like to get you somewhere safe."

She examined his face, then looked at me. "Okay," she said.

"Let me stop at home and put extra food out for the dogs and get a few things packed. I am going to have to be there in the morning to feed them. Even if I could find someone willing to feed the dogs—and we have a real basket case in the rehab kennel right now—I could not ask anyone to come by if something dangerous might be hunting."

"Good enough," said Adam.

THE DOGS WERE SILENT AGAIN WHEN WE STOPPED AT Lucia and Joel's home. She'd already gotten out of her car when Adam stopped the SUV behind her. I hopped out to make sure she didn't go in alone, and that's when I smelled it.

"Blood," I said quietly to Adam, and shut the SUV door and sprinted over to Lucia.

"Hold on." I caught her arm and stopped her about two body lengths from the front door. "Shhh." I couldn't hear anything, but *he'd* been here. Along with the blood, I could smell his magic and a faint, burnt scent like scorched hair.

"What's wrong?" she whispered.

"I don't know," I lied, because if she was like Joel, the fact that her dogs were in trouble would mean I'd have to sit on her to keep her out. "We're going to wait here for Adam. He's changing, and it'll take a while, be patient. If I'm panicking for nothing, it won't matter, but if there's something here, I'd rather face it with a werewolf."

"Changing. You mean changing into a werewolf?"

"That's right." Only then did I realize that the reason I knew that was because of our mate bond. He hadn't said anything to me before I sprinted to Lucia.

"If you want to, you can go wait in your car." I didn't think she would, but it was worth trying. In her car, she might have a chance to get away if things went south.

"Is it because your brother is Native American?" she asked.

My eyes were good in the dark, and I was looking so hard they ached, but all I saw were a few bats and a squirrel. It took a moment to realize that I really didn't have any idea what she was talking about.

"Is what because he is Native American?" I asked.

"Sorry," she said. "When I'm nervous I forget to say everything out loud. Is he psychic because he is Native American?"

"As far as I know, Native Americans are no more psychic than anyone else," I told her. "My father, though, he was . . ." Was what? Coyote? "A bull rider in rodeos, but in his spare time he hunted"—vampires—"demons. He was something of a shaman, and some of that followed his children."

"You don't have visions?"

"No." I turned into a coyote and saw ghosts.

"You speak of him in the past tense," she said. Lucia asked questions when she was scared, I got that, I did that sometimes, too. More often I talked. Sometimes I laughed. It was better than crying, and it made me look braver than I was.

I nodded. "My father died. The bad guys got him." Coyote lived. Coyote always lived. The human guise he'd wrapped around himself because he was bored, the man my mother had fallen in love with, *he* had died.

The SUV door opened, and it was too soon for it to be Adam.

"I'm taking my chances out here," Gary Laughingdog said. "I got nothing against werewolves, but when they are changing . . ."

"Just as well," I told him. "They get pretty grumpy."

Gary lifted his head and smelled the air. He glanced at me, and I nodded, knowing he was smelling Guayota for the first time. He grimaced. "Just so you know, kid," he said. "I usually run when the bad things start happening."

"Me, too," said Lucia, and Gary and I exchanged quick grins because she was lying.

The sound of the SUV's door opening had us all turning to look.

Adam was beautiful as man and as wolf. His wolf isn't huge, not like Samuel's or Charles's wolves are, but he is substantial and graceful. He flowed out of the vehicle without making a sound, a blue-gray wolf with black markings. He raised his head and looked at the house.

"Okay," I said. "We're going in. Adam will take the lead, then me, Lucia, and Gary will be rear guard."

"You did hear me the first time, right?" Gary said.

"That's why you are in the rear," I told him. "To give us warning when the bad guys eat the rear guard."

He laughed, then took a good look at the door and stopped. "Someone's been inside," he said.

Lucia had locked the door when we left for the restaurant, but that hadn't stopped the interloper. The door had been forced, breaking the frame. Most of the damage was on the inside—apply enough inward force, and that happens.

Adam shouldered the door open and paused, then he kept going. I followed him, wishing for a gun, but I'd left my Sig Sauer in the safe at work and my .44 S&W at home. I hadn't wanted to retrieve the Sig with all the police and Cantrip agents running around. Maybe I was going to start leaving a gun in each car, too.

Just inside the door, I understood exactly what had made Adam pause. Something had marked territory in the house. I wrinkled my nose. It wasn't a dog. Or—and I thought about Zack's complaint about his hotel room—a human peeing in the corner.

"If that is Guayota, I'm going to completely revise my opinion on the manners of primitive gods," Gary whispered.

"You *have* heard some of the stories about Coyote, haven't you?" I asked. True, I hadn't heard any about him marking territory, but a lot of Coyote stories sound like something thought up in locker rooms by a bunch of horny teenage boys. I was pretty sure Coyote enjoyed those the most. Maybe they were all true.

Adam glanced back at us, and I caught the reproach. *He* didn't chatter when he was scared. Adam was the man in charge. Wolf in charge. So if he wanted quiet, we'd better give it to him.

The blood smell had faded once we were in the house—so nothing had died here. I didn't think. But the urine made it so rank—Lucia was coughing—that I couldn't be sure.

Nothing alive in here. Tell her to get her things, and we'll go back to the kennels. Adam's voice slid into my head like warm honey.

I'd never told him how much I liked it, because, like telling him how sexy it was when he did sit-ups when I could see his bare stomach, it could never be unsaid. He had enough power over me already. He didn't need to know how weak I was.

I love it when you talk this way to me, too, Adam told me.

"Adam says that whoever broke in is gone now," I said, trying not to smile because it would be inappropriate. "We'll have you pack something, then check on the dogs." I didn't tell her what I was afraid we'd find in the kennels. Free to run, they might have stood a chance against what I'd faced in my garage. But they hadn't been free to run. "Where is your bedroom?"

"Second door on the left," she said.

The door was closed, and I opened it because it was less likely to take damage if it was me than if it was Adam. Werewolves break things like doorknobs. As soon as I opened it, the smell of urine and musk quadrupled. I glanced inside. It looked as though a giant dog had torn the room to bits, piled everything up in the middle of the bed, and peed all over it. Which might have been exactly what happened.

I shut the door quickly. "Belay that plan," I said. "We'll find you some clothes at Honey's."

It's not fun watching someone's life get ripped to bits. Lucia didn't ask what I'd seen in the room—her nose, human as it was, could smell it, too. She just raised her chin and turned around.

Gary kept his eyes down, careful not to make eye contact with me or Adam, and led the way back through the house. I wondered what I would have seen in his eyes if he'd let me look. Because he wouldn't have hidden his eyes just to avoid offending someone; coyotes don't run that way.

As soon as we were all outside, Adam surged to the front of our little parade. He rounded the end of the house, where the gate to the back had been ripped off and thrown to the side. The rest of the fence was a thick hedge, so it was impossible to see what was in the backyard until we were right on top of it.

Gary made a noise, but Lucia just walked into the middle of the bloody mess in her backyard and knelt beside her big white Amstaff and closed the dead dog's eyes.

There were ten chain-link kennels in the yard, taking up exactly half the space. Each had a doghouse with an extended roof that gave the dogs outdoor space and still had some protection from the weather. The other half of the yard was lawn, mowed to golf-course neatness.

It must have been neat and tidy, even pretty, before someone had killed all the dogs and left. The gates of eight of the kennels had been ripped off their hinges and thrown willy-nilly. Some of them could have been rehung with new hinges, but some of them were badly damaged. One had been crumpled into a ball.

In front of the kennels, eight dogs lay on their sides, each with a single deep wound that had laid open their necks. I recognized the dog that had put his head on my knee and blinked back tears.

"I hate it when the dog dies at the end," said Gary, his voice tight. He slapped the chain-link wall of a kennel. "I tore up my copy of *Old Yeller* and threw it away."

Lucia didn't flinch at the noise, just rubbed her dead dog's uncropped ears.

Adam gave me a sharp look, like there was something I wasn't seeing. I looked again and drew in a breath. The dogs were laid out, staged just like the women Guayota had killed. But this staging wasn't for us, there was a formality here, each dog in front of its kennel.

Innocent *sacrifices*.

I called Kyle's number.

"What?" he asked. The foggy connection told me that he was on his Bluetooth connection and driving. He should have already been at Honey's.

"Did the Canary Islanders sacrifice dogs to Guayota?" I asked. "And why aren't you already at Honey's?" The dead dogs and the state of Lucia's bedroom made me sharper than I should have been.

"First," said Kyle grumpily, "we are very nearly at Honey's. We'd have left sooner if I hadn't had to figuratively hold the hands of one of my clients whose soon-to-be-ex wife called and said she was sorry for all the times she slept with other people and couldn't they reconsider their marriage. The answer to that one is no, by the way, because she darn near drove him to suicide once, and he's a good man and deserves better."

"Okay," I said. "What about the dogs?"

"I know they used to sacrifice goats to Achamán," he said. "One of the guided tours we took mentioned it. I don't know anything more."

"Thank you," I said. "I'll see you both when we get to Honey's."

I looked at the dead dogs again. They still looked like sacrifices to me. Witches drew power from pain and suffering, but also from death. Gary had said that Guayota needed a source of power. There had been dead dogs among the bodies I'd discovered out in Finley, too. But I didn't think Guayota had made sacrifices to himself.

I wasn't going to say it in front of Lucia, but I was pretty sure that what had killed the dogs had not been Guayota. Guayota could have killed them, could have twisted the gates off their hinges. But there was a possessive sort of territoriality in the destruction of Lucia and Joel's bedroom—whatever had done it had been marking his territory. And none of the dogs had put up a fight.

Maybe Guayota could control dogs the way he'd controlled the tibicena in my garage. But if he were going to kill something, I didn't think he'd use a blade—he'd have used fire.

I mouthed "Joel" to Adam because no one else was looking at my face. His muzzle dropped, then rose in a nod. He agreed.

Guayota had been here, there was no disguising his scent, but Joel had killed the dogs and desecrated his own house.

It was Adam who noticed that one of the two remaining kennels was occupied. He drew my attention to the kennel on the end, with an empty kennel between it and the dead dogs. I put my hand on the latch, and something growled from inside the doghouse.

"Don't open that," said Lucia, her voice sounding hoarse as if she'd been crying, though her cheeks were dry. "Cookie is not very friendly with humans yet."

I pulled my hand back.

"Cookie, come," she said. "Good girl."

The dog in the doghouse didn't come, though she moved around, and her growl increased in volume and general unhappiness.

I suppose that for people who don't turn into a coyote, growls might all be the same. But not for me. This growl said, "I'm scared and willing to kill you because I think you are going to hurt me."

I raised an eyebrow at Adam. He whined softly, telling the dog that no one here was going to hurt her. It might have been more convincing without all of the dead dogs.

"We need to get out of here," Laughingdog said, bouncing nervously on the balls of his feet. "If he comes back, he might just finish the job."

He looked at me, and I saw that he was frightened and wanted nothing more than to leave us here and never come back. It wasn't cowardice, any more than the dog hiding in the doghouse was a coward.

This was an expression brought on by experience—an understanding that said bad things happened, and the best way to survive was to leave as quickly as possible. I don't know what his life had taught him to bring on that look, but I could tell he was holding on by a fingernail.

"Can't leave any innocents behind," I told him. "That would be wrong. And even if it weren't wrong, it would be dumb. I think that the deaths of these dogs gave Guayota power. No sense leaving him another dog to kill."

"She's not coming out," Lucia said. She stood up. "We got her three days ago. Humane Society got her because her owner's neighbors turned him in for beating on his dog." She laughed, a sad, broken sound, as she looked down on her dog. "I ranted for an hour after I saw her. Swore that if I could hit a button and destroy the human race, I'd do it in a heartbeat. You know what my Joel said? He said, 'Niña, most people are good people. Take this dog. A lot of good people worked to save her. People noticed, they called the police. The police brought in the Humane Society, and they took her—risked getting bitten so that she could have a better life. Lots of people working to undo the work of one bastard. You know what that means? Lots more good people out there than bad.'"

"It also means bad people's works are stronger than good people's," murmured Gary, but he spoke quietly. I don't think Lucia heard him.

While the people were talking, Adam had been talking, too. The dog, Cookie, had quieted, her growls becoming whines. I figured that Laughingdog had been right about needing to get out of here and that Adam had done enough to make it possible. I opened the cage and snagged a lead and collar from a hook on the front of the cage.

I sat down on the ground in front of the doghouse. "Okay, Adam. Get her to come out."

He whined at her again and ended with something as close to a bark as werewolves get. She crawled out of the doghouse, and I found myself whining in sympathy.

She wasn't ever going to win any dog shows, wouldn't have even before someone had hit her hard enough to blind her on one side. She was a mutt. The German shepherd was pretty obvious in the shape of her head, but there was something else that gave her a heavier body. Malamute maybe. Maybe even some wolf.

She carried her head canted because of the blind eye, trying to see out of one eye and get the information she'd gotten out of both. Her tail was down, not quite tucked, and she uttered little anxious growls until she saw me. Then she barked and drew her lips back from her teeth.

I stayed where I was.

I could see when her nose first cued her in that there was something odd about me. She froze, the snarls dying in her throat. That's when Adam moved in and touched her nose with his.

It wasn't anything a real wolf or a human could have done. He used pack magic and let her feel the weight of his authority and the protection he represented. She leaned against him and sighed.

I stood up, slipped the collar on her and the lead, and she gave me no trouble, though she tried not to look at me more than she had to. Adam stayed with her. I looked at Gary, then down at Lucia, and he nodded, took her arm, and helped her to her feet.

We left the dogs' bodies because we did not have time to bury them, though it felt to me as though we should have done something. But in times of war, the care of the dead is outweighed by the need for survival.

I opened the back door of the SUV, and Adam jumped in, followed by the dog. I released her leash as soon as she was in but watched to make sure it didn't snag anywhere until she settled. Adam hopped over the seat and lay down in the luggage compartment. The battered dog followed him and curled up on the opposite side of the SUV. She put her head down with a sigh, and I shut the door.

Gary had taken Lucia to her car. He held out his hand, and she put her keys in it with the same sort of sigh of surrender that Cookie had given.

He looked at me. "We'll follow you."

Because Lucia was occupied opening the door, I mouthed *Do you have a license?* at him.

He just gave me a wink and a sly smile and got behind the wheel of Lucia's car.

9

HONEY'S HOUSE WAS FARTHER OUT THAN ADAM'S AND mine. It was maybe a little bit bigger.

There is something to the cliché that the older immortal creatures are wealthy. Not always, certainly. Warren was almost two hundred years old, and when I met him he was working at a Stop and Rob without two thin dimes to rub together. I didn't know how old Honey was—we'd never been that friendly—but Peter had had at least a couple of centuries, maybe more, and he'd accumulated real wealth. He'd worked as a plumber for the past twenty or thirty years, and that hadn't hurt anything, either.

Honey had sold the business after his death and was talking about going back to school. She didn't need a job for money, but she needed something to do—something more than random trips to visit prisons with me.

I pulled into her driveway, where there were already five or six cars including Kyle's new Jag in the parking area in the front, so

I drove around behind the house and parked by the pasture in back. Peter had been a cavalry officer, and he'd kept his love of horses. There were two of them inside the fence. One had raised its head to watch me park, but the other one kept its head down, ripping up grass as fast as it could.

I let Adam and Cookie out, catching her leash as she exited. She looked more exhausted than aggressive now, and she waited by my side as Gary pulled in beside me. Adam gave me a look and hopped back into the SUV. He'd gotten out so that Cookie would, but he intended to change shape back to human before he went into the house.

Lucia was looking as though she'd reached the end of her rope, so I decided to leave Adam to it.

"Come on inside," I told them. "Adam will join us in a minute."

Honey's house was stucco, as most upscale houses in the Tri-Cities are. In the dark, it looked white, but I knew that it was a pale shade of gray set off with dark gray trim. The rear-porch lights were on, so I led our procession to the back door into a mudroom.

I kicked off my shoes, and so did Lucia, who was only wearing sandals. She looked like a good, strong wind would blow her over. The dog was subdued, and I hoped she'd stay that way until Adam got through changing.

"Both of you stay here just a moment and take this." I handed the leash to Lucia. "I'll go find Honey and see if she doesn't have a room to put you in. No sense in throwing you to the wolves tonight."

"Joel is never coming back." Her voice was stark.

"Too early to tell," Gary said. "It doesn't look good, but saying 'it's over' before it actually is will make certain the outcome."

It sounded like he had matters in hand, so I went in search of Honey. I started toward the living room but heard noise upstairs; it sounded like cheering.

The whole upper floor of Honey's house was one room. She and Peter had used it for parties, but one wall was set up with a projection screen so it could be used as a theater. From the sounds I was hearing, she must have set up a movie or something . . . I didn't hear a sound track or anything but the voices of various pack members saying things like—"look at that jump, exactly as much effort as necessary and not an inch too high" and "triple tap, double tap, and hop."

It was that last one, uttered in Darryl's voice and rough in satisfaction that made me apprehensive. I entered the room, which was filled with a dozen or so people, in time to hear Auriele say, "Fragile my aching butt. How did she manage to avoid his swing *and* hit him with the gun? I wish we had this from a slightly different angle."

"We do," said Ben. "We have four discs. This one is Garage Cam One. There's also Outside Cam One, Office Cam One, and Garage Cam Two."

They were running the video of my fight with Guayota on Honey's projection system; the screen was even bigger than I remembered. The image was a little grainy, but I watched myself, larger than life, trip over the crowbar and land on my butt. In the background, the dog had already morphed into a man.

Most of the pack was there. I picked out Christy, Auriele, Darryl, Warren, Kyle, Ben, Zack, Jesse, Mary Jo, and Honey at a glance. Most of them were so focused on what they were watching that they didn't notice me come in. Christy, half-turned away from the screen, saw me, but I couldn't read her face.

The screen went blank, and there was a collective groan.

"Play it again." Mary Jo's voice was harsh. "I want to see that first part in slow motion. Where she figures out that he's not human."

I cleared my throat, and the room fell silent. "Honey? Is there a bedroom where I can put Lucia? Guayota paid her a visit, and she's pretty fragile. We brought her here to be safe."

"Lucia?" Honey got up from one of the couches scattered around the room, all facing vaguely in the direction of the screen on the wall. "That's the woman who told us about the dogs, right?"

I nodded, taking a half step back because once I'd spoken, they'd all twisted around in their seats to look at me, and they were watching me with *intent*. To Honey I said, "Her dogs are dead, and her husband's missing—she needs some time to regroup and a safe place to be, so we brought her here. Some clothes to sleep in and to wear tomorrow would also be nice."

"Damn, lady," said Zack, looking at me from the corner of his eye. "Damn, but you don't have any quit in you at all."

"Takes a lickin' and keeps on tickin'," said Warren. "That's our Mercy."

Christy's face was still unreadable, but she was watching me with her shoulders tight. Her eyes met mine for a moment, and I saw a flash of shame before she looked down and away.

"Why didn't you run?" asked Mary Jo, pulling my attention away from Christy. "You could have gotten away."

"Because I thought he was human," I told her, all but squirming. I felt like they'd all seen me naked, though all they'd done was watch a video I'd known was running while I fought Guayota. I wanted to get out of there, but Mary Jo was waiting for more of an answer. "By the time I figured out that he *wasn't* human, it was too late, and I was trapped in the garage. Where did you get that disc, anyway?"

"One of Adam's security team dropped them off," said Honey. "I thought it would be a good thing to see this man in action before we had to face him." Honey got up and went to the projector system. I thought she was going to turn it off, but she hit REPLAY, then grabbed my arm and urged me back down the stairs while a larger-than-life-sized me got the gun out from under the counter and waited for Guayota.

"Do them good to see it again," Honey said as we started down. "They like to dismiss you as a liability. Let them see you fight."

"I'd have lost if Adam and Tad hadn't shown up," I told her.

"That lot, most of them, would have lost when the dog started his attack," she said, unperturbed. She gave me a laughing glance. "What I really wish, though, is that there had been a camera at your house when Adam tore a strip off Christy when she wasted time playing stupid games with his phone when you were calling for help. I'd pay a lot of money to have gotten to see that."

"She wouldn't have done it if she'd known I was in danger," I told her—and it felt odd to be defending Christy.

"Maybe not," said Honey, "but I'd sure have liked to have been there to see Adam dressing her down. He never did before. She was too good at making everything someone else's fault."

She led the way back into her kitchen and did a double take when she saw Gary. "I thought you were in—"

Honey hadn't been with us when we'd discussed his jailbreak and my seeing him at the crime scene in Finley. Apparently no one had mentioned it to her.

"I decided to follow you," he broke in with a good-old-boy smile before she could say the "prison" word. "The most intriguing, most beautiful woman I've ever seen. I thought, if she would just *look* at me, I would never need to eat again because that look would sustain me for the rest of my life."

"Do those kinds of lines ever really work?" Honey asked coolly, having gotten over her surprise. She glanced at Lucia and warmed her expression as she gave the rest of us a discreet nod. She wouldn't talk about the jailbreak in front of anyone else. "Lucia, come with me, and I'll get you set up."

"What do you want me to do with Cookie?" When Honey looked blank, Lucia clarified. "With the dog?"

Honey looked at the battered dog, glanced at me, then went to her cupboard and pulled out a mixing bowl. "We'll send someone out for dog food in the morning. There's a bathroom off the bedroom you'll be in, and we'll fill this with water there."

The two of them left, and I caught Gary by the arm before he could follow.

"You'd better cool your jets," I told him, because although he might have interrupted her to stop her from blurting out where she'd last seen him, there had been real intent in his flirting—as there hadn't been when he'd been messing around with Kyle and Zack. "Honey will wipe the floor with you."

His eyes went half-mast, and his voice dropped in evident pleasure. "I know."

I threw my hands up in the air. "You've been warned. Don't come looking for sympathy here."

The outside door opened, and Adam came in. He stomped the dirt off the bottom of his shoes on the mudroom mat with determined slowness. I recognized the careful movement as an attempt to keep his still-agitated wolf under control.

His calmness in the back of the SUV had been more of the same: my wolf didn't like being helpless when someone he felt responsible for was in trouble. Joel had done some work for Adam, and that was enough to make him Adam's responsibility.

I leaned against a counter and relaxed deliberately. Gary raised an eyebrow, looked toward the mudroom. Then he proved he was a lot better at reading people than he liked to pretend because he copied my position on the far side of the kitchen from the mudroom. He left a lot of space between me and him.

Adam came into the kitchen after he was satisfied with the state of his shoes. He saw Gary and me, and came over and leaned on the counter, too, close enough to me that his body pressed against my side.

He focused his gaze toward the opposite wall, where a cabinet displayed antique dishes, very carefully not looking at Gary on the other side of me.

I broke the silence. "Tad," I said, because it should have occurred to me earlier to warn him.

"I called before I came inside. Tad said he'd take the opportunity to visit his father," Adam told me. "Guayota is welcome to try to find him in Fairyland." He frowned. "I'm not sure how voluntary his going is; it sounded like someone noticed him using magic, and he has to go talk to them."

"Can he get back out again?" I didn't bother to hide my anxiety.

"Tad didn't think it would be an issue, not with his father there. Though he said if we don't talk to him in a week or so, we might see what we can do to break him out."

Zee would be hard to hold if he didn't want to stay somewhere. He'd gone to the reservation voluntarily—hostilely voluntarily, but voluntarily nonetheless. "Maybe not," I said.

We subsided into silence again.

Adam said, "Guayota has Joel. Only a man who had those dogs' trust could have killed them, sacrificed them that way, one after another without their fighting back."

"I know," I agreed.

"You think that he's found a way to turn Joel into one of his dogs, the tibicenas, like the one you killed who turned back into a man."

"I do."

He bowed his head and growled. It took him a few moments to find his words again. "Joel is a good man. He would never have killed, have *sacrificed* those dogs of his, given any kind of choice. He'd have killed a person before he killed those dogs."

"Agreed." Anyone who'd talked to Joel about his dogs knew that.

"We hit the trail at Joel's backwards," Adam told me. "Joel and Guayota went to the kennel first. Joel killed the dogs, then, in the shape of one of the tibicenas, he destroyed his bedroom."

"Yes," I agreed. The destruction in the house hadn't been Guayota. If he'd been as angry as the animal who had attacked that room, he'd have burned the place to ashes. "He was hunting his wife, and she wasn't there. He responded like a territorial animal in a rage." Rage at Guayota redirected at the things he loved most.

I blinked back tears at the wrongness of that.

"Some sacrifices are worth more than others," said Gary.

Adam still didn't look at Gary, but he nodded. "Whatever tore up that bedroom was a lot more lethal than the dog you shot. Bigger."

"They are shapeshifters like Guayota." It wasn't a guess. I'd seen the size of the claws on the walls.

"There is probably no way to get Joel back," Adam said.

I heard the guilt in Adam's voice and knew that this was the issue at hand. I narrowed my eyes at him. I could argue all night about why he shouldn't feel guilty about Joel and how we didn't know enough about Guayota to know that Joel was lost. We had a lot of alternatives to explore before we gave up. But sometimes taking another tack worked better.

"If I hadn't killed the male tibicena, then he wouldn't have needed a replacement. If I hadn't gone to talk to Lucia, maybe he wouldn't have tracked down Joel." Unless he had some way of finding the people who were tied to the Canary Islands.

"If you folks are done with me," Gary said, "I think I'll get going."

Adam glanced at him. "You wait a moment." To me he said, "You know it isn't your fault."

"I know it," I agreed. "But if we're accepting blame, I think that I'm closer to the cause than you are."

He grunted irritably. "Fine."

"Fine."

Adam took a deep breath, and I could sense the cloak of civilization that he pulled over the beast who wanted to kill something, anything, because Adam and his wolf were united in their dedication to justice, and its defeat could send them off in a rage. He took a second breath, and the mantle settled more firmly in place.

To Gary he said, "You have been very helpful. Of course you can leave whenever you wish. Do you have a place to go?"

Gary spread his arms and shook his head. "I'm fine, man. I'm used to going my own way. Don't take offense, but trouble is looking for the pair of you, and I'd rather be a long ways away."

"Stay here for the night." Adam looked tired. It wasn't the time—it wasn't much past midnight—it was all the dead dogs, the guilt he shouldn't feel, and the effort of controlling himself. "We'll get you money and maybe a ride out of here in the morning. On the run is tough. Take shelter when you can find it."

"You don't want me here," said Gary. "You've got trouble, and I'll just bring you more."

"We have pizza coming in about fifteen minutes," Honey said briskly, returning to the kitchen on the heels of Gary's words. She'd probably heard Adam, too. "Eat. Stay the night—and then no one will stop you from running as far and as fast as you want."

"I'm not a coward," he said defensively. "Just prudent."

He hadn't cared what Adam and I thought of him.

Honey's eyebrows rose. "I never said you were. I also don't think you are stupid. Eat. Sleep. Run. Works better in that order because you can run faster on a full stomach and a real night's sleep."

"Okay," he said. "Okay. I'll leave tomorrow, thank you."

It had been Honey, I thought, who had made him decide to stay. She was too smart not to see it, but she chose to ignore him.

Instead, she spoke to Adam. "Warren told us about what happened at Mercy's garage tonight, and we've watched the video." She looked at me and smiled but continued to talk to Adam. "When your security man brought the disc of Mercy's fight with Guayota for you here, I thought it would be useful for all of us to see what we're facing. I've got it running upstairs if you want to watch it again."

"Tomorrow," he said. "I watched enough of it while it was happening. Tomorrow is soon enough to see it again for me."

Honey looked at me but spoke to Adam. "For a fragile almost human, she did well."

"Any fight you live through is a fight well fought," said Gary. "That said, I might wander upstairs and see what it is I'm running from." There was a faint bitterness in his tone, and Honey looked at him. He raised both hands in surrender and grinned. "Tomorrow. Running from tomorrow. Tonight, I'm in the mood for a movie." He turned around, winking at me along the way, and headed toward the stairway, almost bumping into Christy, who was just coming into the kitchen.

"Hey, pretty lady," he said. He hesitated, but when she didn't acknowledge him in any way, he just grinned and kept going.

Christy went right for Adam as if none of the rest of us were there.

"This is your fault," she said viciously. "I felt so horrible, bringing my troubles here, and it was *your* fault."

"Careful," I murmured, but she didn't pay any attention to me—which was foolish of her.

"I should have known when Troy was killed." It took me a second to figure out who Troy was, I'd never heard the name of her boyfriend who'd been killed. "The only time bodies start appearing around me is when there are werewolves involved," she continued.

"Juan Flores isn't a werewolf," I said, but again I spoke quietly, and she didn't appear to have heard me.

Adam didn't say anything. He took a deep breath and just— accepted what she said. It was the first time I'd ever seen a real fight between them. Watching him as she spewed guilt all over him, I realized that he enjoyed *our* fights almost as much as I did. When we fought, he roared and stalked and fought back. He didn't let his face go blank and wait to be hit again. Being willing to accept responsibility for the well-being of others was part of being Alpha, part of who Adam was, and she was very, very good at using that against him.

Tears leaked artfully down her face. "I tried. I tried, then I had to run. But I can't get away from you, can't get away from the monsters. They follow me wherever I go, and it is your fault."

Adam wasn't going to defend himself. Honey wrapped her arms around her stomach and turned away. Honey believed herself to be one of the monsters, too, and so Christy's venom spread over Honey as well.

Enough.

"Adam didn't make you go sleep with some complete stranger because he was handsome and rich," I said coolly, but this time at full volume. There wasn't a wolf in the house who hadn't heard Christy, so they could listen to me, too.

"Stay out of this," she snapped at me, wiping futilely at her cheeks. "This isn't your business."

"When you blamed Adam, whose only fault that I can see is that he has poor taste in wives, you made it my business," I told her.

Honey cleared her throat. "You do know you are one of his wives, right?"

I raised an eyebrow. "Happily, he doesn't know how bad off he is with me—and I intend that he never will."

Life came back into Adam's eyes with a wicked glint, and I saw a hint of his dimple. *Better,* I thought, *better.*

Christy knew she'd lost control of the scene. Her eyes narrowed at me, and she lost the tears. "Juan came after me because of Adam."

"You slept with a complete stranger," I said. "Not Adam's fault you"—Jesse had come down the stairs, with Ben and Darryl trailing behind her, so I didn't call Christy a slut—"made a poor choice."

"He was a friend of my best friend," she said. "Rich, charming, and handsome, he wasn't a 'complete stranger.' I had no way to tell that he was a monster."

"You didn't know enough about him for Warren to find him. You didn't know where he lived, what country he was from. I bet you didn't even check to see if he was married or not before you chased after him. How long did you know him before you hopped into bed with him? An hour?"

It probably wasn't fair to use what Jesse had told me about her mother's dating habits against Christy, but she hadn't been playing fair, either. The tears had been cheating, and when she'd realized just how many of the pack had started to filter into the kitchen behind her, she would doubtless use them again.

"He approached me," she said defensively—not to mention falsely.

"Are you stupid? How long did you live with the wolves?" I asked her incredulously. "You do know that most of the people in this room can tell that you are lying, right?"

Stupid. She wasn't stupid, just self-absorbed and unwise. She didn't like people thinking badly of her, so she lied.

I stalked away from her, incensed that most of me wanted to play fair instead of just ripping her to shreds the way she'd ripped into Adam. It felt disloyal to Adam. It felt like I might be letting her manipulate me into feeling sorry for her.

As I turned back toward Christy, I saw Jesse standing a little behind her. Jesse was Christy's daughter, and I wouldn't do anything to hurt Jesse. With a good reason not to destroy my enemy, I paced back until I was face-to-face with Christy again.

"Look." I tried to keep my voice gentle. "No one cares if you sleep with a football team, none of whom you know and all of whom are half your age." I repeated it so she could hear the truth in my words. "We don't care."

Christy went pale in genuine hurt, making me reexamine what I'd just said.

"That doesn't mean that we don't care if one of them hurts you. That's another matter entirely. Call us, and we'll go take care of it. But you have to quit flinging blame around."

"It wasn't my fault," she said, quietly, believing it. But then she aimed her venom at me and increased the volume. "Not my fault. It wasn't."

"Juan came after you because you slept with him, then you ran," I told her, but then I started thinking about what that meant. "If you had waited and told him you weren't interested, he might have left you alone." I worked through the germ of the idea. "If he'd been leaving bodies everywhere he went, Warren would have figured it out. But there weren't bodies, there weren't fires until you ran." I knew there hadn't been bodies, because Warren had looked for bodies left the same way as his victims here in the Tri-Cities. Why hadn't there been any other bodies? "That's not your fault," I told her, "but it is interesting."

She stared at me, her fists clenched.

"Had your friend slept with him before?" I asked.

Christy was competitive. I knew, because Jesse talked to me, that Christy had slept with her best friend's husband just to prove that she could. Maybe she'd done the same thing with her best friend's lover, assuming that Flores had been her friend's lover. I didn't care. I just needed to know if Flores had slept with women other than Christy.

Christy didn't answer, but her clear skin flushed pink, telling me I'd hit the mark. All the marks.

"He didn't stalk her?"

"No," she whispered. "He didn't stalk her. One night, and he was done with her. She was pretty bitter about it. But she doesn't have an ex-husband who is a werewolf."

Guayota hadn't sounded like he cared if Adam was a werewolf, he sounded like he wanted Christy back. Why stalk Christy and not her friend? What was different about Christy?

The question rang in my head while I answered the nasty venom in her last sentence. "The only thing Adam has to do with this is that you bragged about being an Alpha werewolf's ex-wife to catch Juan's attention." Juan had known that Adam was a werewolf and that he was Christy's ex-husband. Could have been that he'd researched it, but there was a hint of competitiveness in the way he'd confronted Adam. The kind of competitiveness that happens when a man's lover brags about a previous lover.

She didn't answer me, so I knew that my shot in the dark was right that time, too.

"This guy has nothing to do with werewolves," I told her. Guayota hadn't cared that Adam was a werewolf, hadn't cared about Adam, really, except that he stood between Christy and Guayota and that he had been Christy's husband. "Congratulations, Christy. You just met one of the weird things in the world that don't fit neatly into the fae or werewolf category."

"Weird like you," said Christy.

"Well, yes," I agreed. "I thought that went without saying. Weird things like me."

"What are you, exactly?"

I hadn't realized she didn't know, but I wasn't going to let her change the direction of the conversation. Not when I'd been getting some interesting information about Guayota, and not while Christy was still trying to make the situation be someone else's, be *Adam's*, fault.

"This isn't about me," I said. "Ask me some other time, and I'll tell you. So you got Juan's attention, and maybe because you know to look for odd things and don't discount them the way someone who hadn't been married to a werewolf might, you realized he wasn't just some rich guy on the make, not just some guy at all. He scared you—but not because he was so possessive. He scared you the same way Adam scared you. If Juan Flores had been exactly what he presented himself as—a bored young businessman not opposed to sleeping with any pretty woman who threw herself in his path—it would have been okay. Instead, you got a man who was a lot more than he appeared to be on the surface. It scared you, and you ran."

"He cut his hand," she said, in a low voice. "And it healed like Adam's cuts and bruises healed."

I closed my eyes. She'd known he wasn't human, she'd known, and hadn't warned any of us.

"Why didn't you tell me that?" asked Adam, sounding, of all things, hurt. "Did you think that we wouldn't help you?"

I wasn't hurt. My hands curled with the effort of not smacking her because she'd put everyone in danger—and hadn't told us everything she knew.

"I didn't know there was anything else out there," she said.

"The fae are locked up where they belong. He wasn't a vampire. I thought he was a werewolf."

"Then why not tell us?" asked Mary Jo from the doorway of the kitchen.

Christy looked around and realized it wasn't just Adam, Honey, and me who had been listening. Jesse, Ben, Darryl, and Auriele were in the kitchen, but behind them, in the doorway, in the little hallway beyond, and standing in the stairwell, the rest of the wolves had been a silent audience until Mary Jo had spoken.

"Because that would have meant that she put her foot in it," I told Mary Jo, and everyone else. "Because, until she saw the video, she really did think he was a werewolf and that the reason he was coming after her was because she told him that Adam was her ex-husband, Adam the famous werewolf. She believed that knowing about Adam was why he came after her—as a strike at the Alpha of the Columbia Basin Pack. She thought that if she hadn't told him about Adam, he wouldn't have come after her. She thought it was her fault he knew her connection to Adam, and she didn't want anyone to know that." And she'd thought that if it hadn't been for Adam, Juan Flores would have just let her run away—which made it Adam's fault again. She believed it was Adam's fault because otherwise she'd have to admit her guilt.

"But he wasn't a werewolf," Christy said. "So it *wasn't* my fault he killed Troy, burned down my building, and killed all those women here."

"No," I said, tiredly. "It wasn't anyone's fault, Christy."

"Between your looks and running, you triggered some sort of psychotic episode. He fixated on you and gave chase. Not your fault." I looked at her until she dropped her eyes. "Not Adam's fault, either."

Auriele bustled over and put her arm around Christy's shoulders. "It was a good thing that you had us to run to," she said. "Another woman might not have."

"It *is* my fault," said Christy, believing it because that was the attitude that would win over the most people. That was one of Christy's gifts, her ability to shift her worldview whenever it was to her advantage. She turned her head into Auriele's shoulder and burst into heavy sobs. "I was so stupid to trust him."

Shoot me now, I thought. I'd known that she'd turn on the tears once she had the right audience. Jesse gave me a tense smile, then turned and slipped out of the kitchen and away from her mother's theatrics.

I found Adam.

"*I* blame her," I muttered grumpily, if softly. My voice hadn't been quiet enough to escape wolf ears, but none of the people gathered around Christy looked my way—even with very good hearing you have to be listening first.

Adam kissed my head and dragged me closer until my back was tight against his front. He dropped his mouth to my ear. "Okay. As long as you keep in mind that just because you blame her doesn't mean it *is* her fault." Though he'd put his mouth to my ear, he didn't bother whispering.

"Only if you remember that while she is drumming up sympathy for her heaping helping of guilt—she doesn't really feel responsible," I said. "Just for now responsible."

"Sounds like you know our Christy as well as those of us who lived with her," said Honey, leaning a shoulder lightly against both of us in a gesture of solidarity. She looked at the pack, and said, "Some of us, anyway."

On the far side of the werewolf pack trying to comfort Christy,

Ben shared a cynical smile with us. He wasn't petting Christy, either.

The pizza guy came after that and broke up the comfort-poor-Christy party. Pizza places don't usually deliver that far out in the boonies, but Honey, it turned out, had an arrangement with a place in Kennewick—an arrangement that included a huge tip for the driver and a surcharge on the pizza.

The food was a signal, and as soon as the last scrap of pizza was gone, everyone retreated to their Honey-assigned sleeping places. Adam and I got the formal living room. Jesse opted into the giant upstairs room with her mother, where they'd decided to watch some disaster film from the seventies that had just made it to video.

"THE UPSIDE OF THIS," ADAM TOLD ME AS WE STOOD next to the air mattress, which had a fitted sheet already stretched over it, a pair of pillows, and a blanket, "is that we get this room to ourselves."

I dropped down to sit on the mattress and gave him a look. "No door, no fun." The sounds of the movie filtered down the stairs and into the room. Everyone in that room, everyone who was something other than human, at least, would hear whatever we said—or did—in here.

Adam smiled and plopped down beside me. The air mattress bucked under his sudden weight and tried to toss me off, so I lay down for more stability.

"I'm too tired to do anything anyway," he said, lying back beside me. He reached over and took my hand. "If it's any consolation, we're not going to get a whole lot of sleep before we have to head to the lawyer's."

"I'd forgotten about the lawyer," I said. "Somehow, that seems a long time ago."

His hand clenched on mine, hard enough to hurt before his grip gentled. "I thought he'd kill you before I got there," he said.

"Yeah," I agreed, trying to sound like it hadn't bothered me. "Me, too."

"Don't do that again."

"Okay," I said agreeably. "How often can I get attacked by a volcano god in my shop?" I groaned. "Not that there is a shop."

"You have insurance," Adam said.

I sighed. "I'm not covered for acts of God," I told him. "I wonder if they'll try to find a way to make that mean volcano gods as well as God God."

"God God," Adam said, sounding amused. "I'll remember that. Speaking of things to remember"—and now he didn't sound amused at all—"I like it when you defend me. I haven't gotten a lot of that."

"That voice," I said, and he laughed happily, though even his laugh held that rough sexual overtone. He rolled until he was on top of me, and he nibbled along my jawline.

"You like my body," he told me, "you like me sweaty, and watching my belly when I do sit-ups."

"Hey," I said, trying for indignation, "I never told you that."

He laughed again. "Sweetheart, you tell me that every time you can't look away, and you know it. But"—he laughed again, then said, in that deep growly voice that was his own personal secret weapon—"you really like it when I talk to you, like this."

"No door," I squeaked. "She'll walk in on us and make sure Jesse is with her."

Adam froze and growled for real. "You're right. You're right. And I almost don't care."

"Jesse," I said.

"Jesse," he agreed with a groan, then rolled up—abdomen flexing nicely—and onto his feet. He began to strip, not bothering to hide his arousal. If Christy walked in, she'd get quite a show of what she'd thrown away.

"You might as well get ready for sleeping," he told me in grumpy tones. "Morning is going to come early."

"I'm keeping my clothes on," I told him, equally grumpily. "Without doors, everyone will feel pretty free and easy stopping in to bring you their complaints." Everyone being Christy. "I'm not taking chances."

"They come in, they deserve what they get," Adam told me and, naked, spread the blanket over the mattress and me.

I wiggled until I was right way around. Then I pulled the blanket off my face while he climbed under the covers. He planted himself right next to me, and his scent spread over both of us.

I was well on my way to sleep when a thought occurred to me. "He's broken," I told Adam.

Adam grunted. Then, when I didn't say anything more, he laughed once. "Okay, Mercy. Who is broken?"

"Guayota, Flores, whoever," I told him. "He was doing okay in the modern world before he ran into Christy. Before she reminded him of someone he lost a long time ago."

Adam was thoughtful for a moment. "Because there weren't any other bodies."

"Warren would have found them if there were, right?" I asked.

"Warren or my buddies in the DEA," he agreed.

"The women he killed, the ones Tony brought me in to look at, they all looked like Christy," I told him. "Do you believe in reincarnation?"

Adam reached over and pulled me closer. "I believe that Guayota is very old and that Christy was his trigger. You know better than most how it is with the very old wolves. They'll do fine—until suddenly they snap."

"I still think we should give him Christy," I said.

"No, you don't," he told me firmly. "I was there for your speech in the kitchen, remember?"

"If we gave him Christy," I said persuasively, "we could visit them in the Canary Islands."

"Like Lucia wants to visit Joel's mother?" he asked. "Giving him Christy won't fix him, Mercy. There's no reasoning with the old ones once they are broken. He's started killing and he'll keep killing. And then there is Joel."

I sighed. "I suppose you're right. I think we're going to wish that we'd had Tad come over here instead of going to Fairyland."

"Tad didn't have much of a choice," Adam said. "We'll figure something out."

That meant he didn't know how to kill Guayota, either, but that wasn't going to stop him. I'd known that Christy was going to try to break us up, but I hadn't considered that she might get Adam killed to do it. I lay tense and miserable beside him. Much as I wanted to, I couldn't place the blame on Christy. It was just bad luck.

"So," Adam said brightly, changing the subject, "have you planned what you're going to tell Beauclaire when he comes looking for his walking stick two nights from now?"

"Yes," I told him. "I'll tell him to go ahead and take out the

Tri-Cities, as long as he makes certain he takes out Guayota when he does. Then you, Jesse, and I can drive to my mom's house in Portland for a surprise visit."

"Mercy," he said reprovingly.

"Okay," I told him, "we don't have to go to Mom's. Montana would work, too."

"Mercy," he repeated. "We've been in tough places before. It will be okay. You're just tired, or you wouldn't be so upset." He pulled me all the way over on top of him and patiently waited while I wiggled until I was comfortable.

"Go to sleep," he said. "Things will look better in the morning." I was almost asleep when he murmured, "And if it doesn't, we'll invite your mom down to deal with Guayota *and* Beauclaire."

———————

AT SOME POINT IN THE NIGHT, I ROLLED OFF ADAM, off the air mattress, and onto the floor. Maybe it was the rolling that woke me up. Maybe it was dreaming of Guayota eating at my kitchen table with Christy and my mom. They'd been talking about the flower garden and eating an avocado salad, so I don't know why I was so scared, but even awake my heart was pounding, and I'd broken into a light sweat.

I sat up and rubbed the back of my neck to dispel the tension of the dream—and to rub away the lingering sting of my head hitting the hardwood floor.

"Mercy?" Adam's voice settled me more than my rubbing hand had, wrapped around me like a warm coat on a cold night.

"Bad dreams." My throat was dry.

"Do you want to talk about them?"

I rolled to my hands and knees, leaned over and down to kiss him. I pulled back and decided to revisit the kiss. Adam's kisses were always worth a second pass. If we had had a door between us and Christy . . .

Even so, I was more than a little breathless when I answered his question. "Not necessary. I'm going to get a glass of water, then I'll be right back." I kept my voice to a whisper, so I wouldn't wake anyone else.

He nodded, wrapped a hand around my hair, and pulled me down for a third kiss. Then he smiled, let me go, and closed his eyes. I really, really wished there was a door—or that I was more of an exhibitionist.

I was still dressed from earlier—without privacy I wasn't going to strip and give Christy a chance to say something we might both regret. All I had to do was zip up my jeans, and I was ready to face anyone who might be wandering around the house at this hour.

In the kitchen, I drank some water and glanced out the window—and froze. A man sat on the roof of Adam's SUV with his head thrown back, a bottle upended over his head as he drank. He wore scruffy jeans, boots of some sort, and a white t-shirt.

He was too far away for me to see him swallow, but the bottle stayed there for a while. I could tell by the way he pulled the bottle down that he'd drunk it dry. He wiped his mouth with the back of his hand, then, glancing my way, casually saluted me with the bottle.

With the moon at his back, he should have had no way to see me tucked safely behind glass in the dark kitchen. I dumped the rest of the water out of the glass and set it quietly in the sink. My shoes were still in the mudroom where I'd left them. I slipped them on and walked out to talk with Coyote.

10

$\sim\!\!\sim\!\!\sim$

"GARY LAUGHINGDOG SAID THAT I SHOULD TRY TO BE interesting if I wanted to see you," I told Coyote as soon as I was reasonably close to the SUV.

Coyote laughed. "That one has been trying to avoid me for most of his life." His white t-shirt set off his long black braid, tied with a pink scrunchie.

"Maybe if you didn't get him sent to prison when you visited, he'd be more interested in seeing you," I suggested, trying not to stare at the scrunchie. It had a white lamb dangling from a chain, and I was pretty sure he'd worn it just for me. I didn't reach up to touch the lamb on the necklace around my neck.

"Gary needs his life shaken up," Coyote told me, then he belched with more sound and fury than a thirteen-year-old boy with a roomful of girls to impress.

"If you get me or mine sent to prison, I'll hunt you down," I told him seriously.

He grinned at me and half slid, half scrambled down the back of the SUV to end up standing on his own feet. He left the bottle on the vehicle's roof. He began moving off down the driveway at a brisk walk. When I didn't immediately follow, he turned around and began walking backward and waving his hands for me to join him.

His braid swung around when he did, the little lamb flapping with his movements. I was not going to say anything about the stupid lamb if only because I was certain he wanted me to say something about the stupid lamb.

"Come. Come," he said. "Come take a walk with me."

If I hadn't needed a favor from him, I might have stayed behind. But I did—and I wasn't opposed to some exercise to get rid of the miasma of fear and despair my nightmare had left me with. Our feet crunched on the dry dirt and gravel.

"I don't understand why you are so determined to hang around with werewolves. They are all about rules. And you"—he slanted a laughing glance at me—"like me, are all about breaking them."

There was something about walking down a deserted road in the dark that made for thoughtful silences. Especially when the deserted road was too long, too unfamiliar, and even at this hour of the night, too deserted. Coyote probably had something to do with that.

Finally, I said, "I don't know about that. The werewolves' rules are all designed to keep people safe."

"Safe." He tested the word. "Safe." His nose wrinkled. "Who wants to be safe? I haven't noticed you running to safety."

I bit my tongue. I liked being safe. Being in Adam's arms was safe. Talking to Coyote was anything but—and where was I? I supposed he had a point.

"Safe is good," I told him. "Not all the time, no. Sometimes, though, it is better than water in the desert."

He made a rude noise.

I thought more about rules and werewolves. I glanced over my shoulder, but I couldn't see Honey's house—or any other house for that matter. Coyote was definitely doing something. I hoped that Adam went right back to sleep and hadn't heard me open the back door. He'd be worried.

"Rules keep the people I love safe," I said, thinking about Adam. "It is important to me that *they* are safe."

He nodded like I had said something smart. Then he said, "And when rules don't keep them safe, we break the rules."

I could agree with that—and almost did. If it weren't for that little bit of smugness on his face, I would have. I wonder what rules he was contemplating breaking.

"Admit it," he said when I didn't say anything more. "Admit it. Keeping all the rules is boring. Tell me you don't want to short-sheet Christy's bed—or put ipecac syrup in some of that too-delicious food she is always cooking."

"I'm not childish," I told him. "And I'm not petty."

"No," he agreed sadly. "More's the pity."

"And how do you know how good her food is?"

He just smiled and kept walking.

I took a deep breath. Time to ask him about the walking stick. I'd given it to him as a gift, and he'd taken it as a favor. I wasn't sure how he'd react when I asked for it back.

"There he is," Coyote said, sounding delighted, and he broke into a sprint, the stupid lamb bouncing with his stride.

I ran as fast as I could, but Coyote stayed ahead of me. I couldn't see who it was, but I wasn't surprised when, after a minute or two, the path turned, and there was Gary Laughingdog sitting in the middle of the road with his back to us. I stopped beside him, but Coyote had walked around so Gary couldn't avoid looking at him.

"I hate you," Gary said with feeling. He threw a small rock and nailed a T-post on the side of the road. He picked up another, tossed it into the air, and caught it on the way back down.

Coyote threw his head back and laughed. "I wondered how much longer you'd stay locked up in the gray box. You didn't used to let them hold you for so long."

"Knowing I was safe from you there," Gary said, throwing the rock in his hand with barely controlled violence, "I planned on staying inside as long as I could. My conscience drove me out before then."

"Conscience," mused Coyote. They looked alike, he and Gary Laughingdog. "I wonder where you got that?"

"Quit tormenting him," I said sternly.

Gary twisted half-around to look at me. "Go tell the sun not to rise." He stood up and dusted off the back of his jeans. "Looks like you got too interesting, Mercy. But did you have to let him include me?"

"I have a gift for you both," said Coyote grandly. "Come along, children." He started off down the road.

"We might as well," said Gary in the voice of experience. "If we don't, something horrible will come out of the night and chase us. We'll end up dead, or doing exactly what he wanted anyway. Cooperation saves all of us a lot of trouble."

Coyote snickered.

"What?" Gary said, sounding aggravated.

Coyote turned around and walked backward. He held up a

hand. "You." He held up another hand as far from the first as he could. "Cooperation."

Gary sneered at him. Coyote sneered back, and I saw that Coyote's eyes and Gary's were the same shape. Then the moment was over, and Coyote turned around and faced the way he was going.

Gary started to follow, but I stepped in front of him and stopped, shaking my head. I waited until Coyote was far enough ahead of us so we could talk in relative privacy before starting down the road. Relative, because I was certain Coyote could still hear us; he wasn't *that* far ahead.

"Why aren't you asleep?" I asked Gary.

"Because I'm a fugitive from the law, and there was a lawyer sleeping in the same room with me," he said with feeling.

"Kyle wouldn't have turned you in."

Gary shook his head. "Eventually, he'll realize who I am, and, if he doesn't want to lose his license to practice, he'll *have* to turn me in." We walked a little while, and he said, "I don't really want to get any of you in trouble for harboring an escaped prisoner. I've done what I needed to do, told you what I knew, and it is time to make myself scarce. It isn't the first time I've been on the run from the law."

He looked down at his feet, then gave me a rueful smile. "Though most of the time I've deserved it more. I can head over to one of the Montana reservations, and they'll let me stay until the state of Washington decides it isn't so concerned with some idiot held on a nonviolent crime. If I'd walked while on parole, they might not even look for me. Once the fire dies down, I'll get a fake ID and show up somewhere else as someone else. About time to do that anyway."

"All that was true earlier when you said you'd spend the night," I said.

He looked at me, then away. "One of your wolves saw me looking at Honey and told me about her husband. That's who she's got following her around, right? She's not going to be able to see anyone else until she lets him go."

I'd had the thought that it was Honey's fault that Peter's shade was still hanging around, too. "Probably not, no," I agreed. "He died not very long ago."

"She's interested in me," he said. He flashed me that grin again, but I saw behind it to how alone he was. "I'm not just being vain, though I own that as well. But it hurts her that she's interested, and I think she's been hurt enough. It was time for me to leave."

Coyote began whistling a song that sounded suspiciously like "London Bridge Is Falling Down."

"Screw you and the horse you rode in on," Gary yelled, and Coyote laughed. To me Gary said, "So I'll leave. I'll become someone else and maybe stop by in a few years." He didn't mean that last sentence, I could tell, and he knew it—so the lie was for himself and not me.

"Fingerprints?" I said. "DNA? Facial-recognition software? Hard to lose yourself in this day and age." That had been the main reason that the werewolves had finally come out to the public.

He raised an eyebrow. "You mean you don't know how to fix those?" Then he shrugged, gestured with his chin toward Coyote. "He taught me a trick or two. He can teach you, too. Gary Laughingdog is no more. I'll pick a different name and be someone else."

"Sounds lonely," I said.

He shrugged again.

I saw a beer can that looked like one I'd passed earlier. I kicked it gently and sent it rolling to the side of the road. "If you'd gotten me up, I could have taken you to the bus station and bought you a ticket."

"Hitchhiking is safer." He looked at Coyote. "Usually. If Honey didn't live out in the middle of freaking nowhere. I had to go looking for a less rural area that might have someone who'd pick up a hitchhiker—"

Coyote briefly interrupted his whistling to say, "Or a car to hot-wire."

Gary clenched his jaw. "Or a car to hot-wire," he agreed. The clenched jaw told me it bothered him to steal a car—and that he'd have done it if necessary. Oddly, both of them made me like him a little more. I've done some hard things in the name of necessity.

"If I had started earlier or not had to walk so far, maybe I could have just gotten a ride instead of walking the same half mile over and over again until I finally realized that the reason the road looked the same wasn't just because around here a lot of roads look the same. I probably hiked two hours before I noticed. I have a little experience with odd happenings; mostly it means that matters are out of my control. Again. So I sat down and waited for Coyote to show up."

Sympathy didn't seem the right response, so I just kept walking.

Eventually, the stiffness left his shoulders, and he seemed to mellow a bit. He asked me, "Did you get a chance to ask him about the fae artifact you need from him?"

"No," I said.

"Shh," said Coyote, trotting back to us. "Time to be quiet now. This way. Come with me." He stepped off the road into the darkness.

We climbed a little hill—a hill I hadn't noticed until Coyote took us off the road. It was, like most uninhabited places around the Tri-Cities, covered with rock and sagebrush. We crested the hill, then followed a trail down a steep gorge. At the bottom of the drop, a thicket of brush grew, the kind that occasionally flourishes around water seeps that are sometimes at the center of ravines around here. The brush covered the faint trail we'd been following. Coyote dropped to his hands and knees to crawl through. After a deep breath, as if he planned on diving underwater instead of under a bunch of leaves, Gary did the same.

I followed. The soil under my knees was softer than I expected. No rocks, no roots, no marsh, nothing with stickers—not that I was complaining. But if I hadn't already known Coyote was manipulating the landscape, the lack of nasty plant life would have proved it. There were no signs of any other people or animals despite the way this trail looked like some kind of thoroughfare for coyotes or raccoons.

A high-pitched wailing cry broke the silence of the night and sent unexpected, formless terror through my bones, leaving me crouching motionless under the cover of bushes like a rabbit hiding from a fox. The first howl was answered by another.

I wasn't the only one who froze; Gary had stopped, too. Coyote sat down and turned to face us.

"His children break the night with their hungry cries," Coyote said. "That we hear them in this, my own land, means that they have hunted this night, and there are more people on their way to the other side."

"Dead," said Gary. "You mean Guayota has killed more people."

Coyote nodded, as solemn as I'd ever seen him. "You need to understand this, both of you. Once Guayota took the first death, he can never stop. He will kill and kill and, like the wendigo, never be free of the terrible hunger because death never can satisfy that kind of need. He cannot stop himself, so he needs to be stopped." He lifted his head and closed his eyes. "They are quiet now. We need to keep going."

The pitch of the trail changed to an uphill climb, gradually getting steeper and steeper until I was scrabbling up a cliff face. I could no longer see Coyote or Gary, and I hoped they were still ahead. I dug in my fingernails and shoe edges and hauled myself up. Sweat gathered where sweat generally gathers and rolled in jolly, salt-carrying joy all across the burns I'd acquired fighting Guayota.

Eventually, I chinned up over the edge of the cliff and rolled onto . . . a lawn. In front of me was a hedge, and under the hedge were Coyote and Gary, lying side by side. There was space between them, and I elbow-crawled forward until I was even with them but still under the hedge. Beyond the hedge was a manicured lawn just like the one I'd crawled over.

That cliff edge had been a barrier between Coyote's lands and the real world. I hadn't noticed the transition on the way out here, but now, lying beneath the hedge, my senses were crawling with information that hadn't been available—the sounds of night insects and the scents of early-spring flowers.

Coyote's road had looked and smelled exactly as I expected— but real life doesn't do that. Real life is full of surprises, big and small. I'd keep that in mind the next time Coyote showed up.

That we were out of Coyote's place meant that the hedge we lay under was real, as was the yard and the house it surrounded. The back of the house was lit by bright lights. I saw the silhouettes of trees and bushes. Between us and the house was a kidney-shaped pool encased in a walkway of cement. In the night, with the house lights shining in my eyes, the water looked like black ink.

The house was a high-end house, not rich-rich but nothing that a mechanic's salary would have touched. Maybe there were some distinguishing features on the front of the house—like an address. But from my viewpoint, the house looked like any of a hundred other expensive houses. The deck, jutting out fifteen or twenty feet from the house and three feet off the ground, was the most interesting feature, that and the dogs.

The two dogs were chained at opposite ends of the deck, each chewing on rawhide bones as long as my calf. At least I hoped they were rawhide bones.

Coyote shoved something in my hand. I didn't have to look down to know that I held the walking stick, but I did anyway. It looked much as it had the last time I'd seen it: a four-foot-long oak staff made of twisty wood, with a gray finish and a ring of silver on the bottom. The silver cap that sometimes became a spearhead was covered with Celtic designs. It looked like something I could have bought at the local Renaissance fair for a couple of hundred dollars.

The last time I'd held it, I had felt its thirst for blood, and its magic had thrummed in my bones. Now, the wood was cool under my fingers, and it might as well have been something I bought at Walmart for all the magic I sensed.

"It knows how to hide itself better," Coyote murmured, sounding like a proud parent.

I watched the dogs, but they didn't seem to hear him as he continued talking. "I taught it a few tricks and gave it an education. It helped me out of a few jams."

I was going to have to return the walking stick to Lugh's son, and tell him that Coyote had taught it a few things. Why did I think that might not go over too well?

"Do you remember what the walking stick's original magic was?" asked Coyote.

"Makes sheep have twins," I told him. The dogs didn't react to my voice, either.

"And?"

"That was it," I told him. "Lugh made three walking sticks. This one makes twin lambs. One of them helps you find your way home, and the third allows you to see people as they really are."

"Hmm," said Coyote. "Are you sure your source was reliable?"

"Yes," I told him.

"I think," said Coyote, "that you should recheck your source. Maybe there were three staves that all did the same thing, or maybe there was only ever one. Or maybe"—he gave me a sly look—"I was just able to teach it to ape its brethren. I suppose it doesn't really matter. Look at the dogs."

I tightened my grip on the walking stick and looked. "It's hard to see anything with those stupid lights," I complained.

Coyote gave me a look, then glanced at Gary. "Okay. But look fast."

I frowned at him—and Gary sighed, rose to his knees. In his hands he rolled two small rocks, like the ones he'd been playing with when Coyote and I had first come upon him. He lobbed them, one right after the other, and took out the big lights.

Both dogs surged to their feet, glanced at the lights, then right where the three of us crouched.

"Gary," said Coyote conversationally as he turned around and raised his butt in the air until he was crouched like a runner in a sprint at the Olympics. "You should stay until the end of this story. Sometimes the end of the adventure is much better than the beginning. Besides, you might be more useful than you know if you stick around."

Gary answered something, but I'd finally remembered that I was supposed to be looking at the dogs. Under my hand, the staff warmed, and I realized it was happy to be back with me. Then I looked, really looked at the dogs, and the walking stick's affection and Gary's and Coyote's voices were abruptly secondary.

The dog nearest me was female; I could see her form inside the dog's body—sort of wrapped in the flesh of the larger animal. She had a woman's body, naked and made more disturbing by a head that was a smaller version of the dog's. She had dog's paws from her ankle on down. She crouched on all fours. Binding magic wrapped her from head to paw in a shimmering pinkish fabric—since joining the pack, I was getting pretty good at spotting those. Pack bonds were part of my daily life, and what held her was a magic very similar but not the same. If the pack bond was spider silk woven into a chain, this was a Mandarin's robe used as a straightjacket.

That was not all I saw, though, because my seeing of her was not limited to what I could sense with my eyes. Age. She was so old, this dog. Older than the structures around her by millennia or more.

Her eyes glistened red in the night and focused on us. She opened her mouth, displaying sharp teeth that were too many and too long to fit in her mouth. She barked at us, the noise bigger than it should have been and with an odd whistling sound to it that made me want to cover my ears—it wasn't that unearthly and terrifying sound that Coyote had said was the tibicenas, but it was something akin to it. Everything about the tibicena was bigger, more powerful than the lines of the body she presented to the real world.

The other dog . . . the other dog was Joel. If the woman's binding magic was a robe, his were silk ties. They wrapped securely around him but did not envelop him completely. They weren't part of him yet.

Like the female, he saw us, too. The dog's body that encompassed him was poised on the deck, watching us, but silently. While the dog was motionless, Joel was not. He pulled and tugged at the bindings, peeling them back and leaving gaping wounds that bled behind. As soon as he cleared one place and started on another, the bindings grew back.

I wondered how old the man I'd killed when I shot Juan Flores's dog had been.

Coyote leaned forward, and whispered into my ear, "When it looks like a mortal creature, the mortal flesh encompasses the tibicena and may be killed as any mortal creature. When it is wrapped in the tibicena's form, it cannot be harmed by mundane means."

And when he said the word "tibicena," the head of the walking stick sharpened into the blade of a spear. My eyesight sharpened, too, and I saw that there was a third layer I had not been able to distinguish before. Surrounding each dog was a shadow that grew more solid as my hand clenched tighter on Lugh's walking stick, a shadow that was large and hairy with red eyes, as in the story Kyle had told. Huge—polar-bear huge. Four or five times as big as any werewolf I'd ever seen. Gradually the other, smaller forms disappeared inside the giant dogs—both of whom were looking directly at me.

Coyote slipped back, grabbed my ankle, and dragged me backward, out from under the hedge like I was a rabbit he'd caught. He dropped my ankle, grabbed my elbow, and hauled me to my feet. Before I could catch my balance, he all but threw me down the cliff face we'd come up. I managed to stay on my feet, using the bottoms of my shoes like skis and leaning my weight back on the walking stick for balance in a mockery of glissading.

As a kid, glissading down steep, snow-covered mountain slopes had been an upgrade in difficulty and fun to simply sledding. "Fun" wasn't a term I applied to glissading down a cliff that had no snow for padding in case of accident and using an ancient artifact that might break—and wasn't that a lovely thought? I had a pretty good idea about what would happen when an old fae artifact was destroyed. At least the spearhead had returned to its more usual form, so I wasn't likely to stab myself with it, too.

I didn't fall until I was almost at the bottom. So when I rolled, I hit that improbably soft ground and emerged not much worse for wear. Gary landed on his feet beside me, and on the other side, Coyote grabbed my arm—exactly where he'd grabbed me before so I was sure to have bruises—and hauled me to my feet, again.

"Run," he said.

Gary grabbed my hand and pelted down the path, pulling me in his wake. The path still had its cover of greenery, but now the ceiling of leaf and stem was tall enough for us to stand upright in.

As soon as I was running all out, Gary dropped my hand. I tucked the walking stick under my free arm, put my head down, and ran as the howls of the dog became baying and a second dog joined in the chorus. Joel had evidently lost his battle for control—and Coyote's trick with the landscape didn't stop the dogs from hunting us in it.

Speaking of Coyote . . . I glanced over my shoulder in time to see that a four-footed coyote had stopped in the middle of the path behind us. He was a little bigger than the usual coyote, but if I'd seen him out my window, I wouldn't have given him a second look. He gave me a grin and a wag of his tail before running the other way.

"Stupid, stupid, stupid," Gary chanted as he ran. "Stupid freaking Coyote. Always getting me in trouble."

I bumped him with my shoulder. "Accept some responsibility for your own life," I panted, finally. "You could have stayed sitting in the middle of the road. You *chose* to come with us."

Gary gave me an irritated look. "Whose side are you on anyway?"

He wasn't as out of breath as I was. Maybe he had more practice running.

"I didn't know there was a side to be on," I grunted.

I could still hear the dogs. No. Not dogs. I thought of the giant forms, the ones that Coyote said could not be harmed by mundane means. These were Guayota's children. They were tibicenas.

"They sound like they're getting closer," Gary said. I wished he hadn't, because I'd been thinking the same thing.

"I thought Coyote was going to divert them." My voice was breathy because I didn't have much air to spare.

"Right," said Gary. "Just like he diverted the police when I ended up in jail. I think *we're* the intended diversion here."

"He dumped me in a river where there was a monster killing things," I told him.

"There you go. That's the Coyote I know and hate."

The woods and brush thinned, and we were running on the hill down to the gravel road we'd traveled before.

"Which way?" said Gary.

I looked frantically, but there was nothing to distinguish one direction from another. Although the moon had been in the sky when we ducked into the tunnel of brush, there was no sign of her now. I felt down the pack bonds and the bond I shared with Adam. Though I could tell they were *somewhere*, I got no sense of where they were in relation to me. The connection was foggy, as if they were a lot farther away than an hour's walk.

"You pick," I said, as we hit the bottom of the hill—and he jerked my hand and pulled me to the right.

I made the mistake of looking up the hill and caught sight of one of the tibicenas cresting the top—the female. She saw us and bayed twice before plunging down the hillside after us. I quit looking back and concentrated on running—and on hoping that she didn't give that cry we'd heard before, the one that had frozen me in my tracks.

"Isn't that walking stick supposed to take you home?" Gary asked. "Why don't you say the magic words? 'There's no place like home. There's no place like home.'"

Where did he get enough breath to be sarcastic? If he wasn't being sarcastic, then he didn't know fae artifacts as well as I did.

"They aren't Dorothy's ruby slippers," I said. "Fae artifacts have a mind of their own, and this one is particularly contrary."

I'd turned my head to glance at him, and I noticed that there was a house in the distance—the first house I'd seen all night.

"Look, Gar—" I ran full tilt into something solid planted right in front of me. I lost my balance, and my feet skidded sideways to tangle with Gary's. Everyone fell, tumbling and rolling on a gravel driveway because Gary and I had been running really fast. And the solid thing hadn't been a tree, like I thought, it had been Adam.

"Hi," I said, panting, sprawled out on top of my husband, who'd done the chivalrous thing and taken the brunt of the fall. "A funny thing happened when I went to get a glass of water." He smelled so good, warm and safe and Adam.

Coyote had dumped Gary and me right in front of Honey's house, at the exact spot where my husband stood . . . had been standing until I hit him running full out when he wasn't expecting an attack from the ether.

Still lying flat on his back, Adam looked over at the walking stick that had missed clocking him in the head by an inch, maybe less. Coyote hadn't fixed the walking stick entirely, or possibly at all, because I got the distinct impression that the walking stick had tried to hurt Adam but hadn't quite managed it. I tightened my hand on the old wood, and the impression faded until it was only a stick in my hand. The effect Adam had on me was such that it was only then I remembered that I should be afraid.

I lifted my head and listened as hard as I could. But I couldn't hear them.

"Are they still following us?" I asked urgently.

"We're not dead," said Gary, who hadn't moved from his prone position on the ground. "I'd guess that we lost them when we got dumped back here. It's too much to say that we're safe, not when Himself is about—but safe for now."

"I take it you met with Coyote?" Adam said politely as he sat up so I was sitting on him instead of lying on him and glanced at Gary. "Both of you?"

Gary got up and started pulling goathead thorns out of his arm. "I hate Coyote," he said without aiming the remark at anyone.

I ignored Gary and answered Adam. "Was it the walking stick

that gave it away?" I asked with mock interest that would have worked better if I weren't still trying to catch my breath. My heart was beating so hard that the force of my pulse almost hurt.

"No, I figured it out earlier, when your scent trail disappeared into nothing. Mostly. The walking stick just meant my suspicions were correct." Adam closed his fingers on my shoulder, not quite hard enough to hurt. "*Don't* do that again," he said. "My heart can't take it."

"I didn't *intend* to do it the first time," I half whined. I would have all-the-way whined, but it was suddenly too difficult to whine. Why was it that I could run and run—but a minute or so after I stopped, I couldn't breathe anymore?

I could happily have stayed safe in Adam's arms all night if it weren't for the fact that I was covered with sweat, and I had to straighten and give my diaphragm a fighting chance to force my lungs to start working properly.

I stood up, and Adam's hand loosened, sliding from my shoulder to my arm until he had my hand.

"I'll certainly try not to wander off with Coyote again without your knowing about it. But 'try' is all I've got," I told Adam when I had control of my breath again.

He looked up at me. There was heat in his gaze—there is always some spark of heat when Adam looks at me, but there was also need that was deeper than sexual. I could see the shadow caused by worry, possessiveness, and a vulnerability that allowed him, the Alpha wolf, to stay on the ground when I was standing. That vulnerability (and the possessiveness) meant that Adam would never let me leave him, as he'd let Christy leave him.

I didn't like him vulnerable to anything, even to me. I pulled on Adam's hand, and he stood up.

"I love you, too," I told him, and he smiled because he'd let me see what he felt. I cleared my throat. "I think Coyote was trying to help."

Gary made a derogatory noise. When I looked at him, he was staring down the road. He didn't trust in his safety, even when the danger couldn't be heard or scented. I wondered if he wanted to be safe, or if he was more like Coyote. Like *me*, he was covered with sweat, but he seemed to be breathing better than I was. He must have stayed in good shape while he was in prison.

"Where did Coyote take you?" Adam asked. He had kept my hand.

"Let's go find someplace to sit down," I said. I needed a shower more than I needed to sleep—and I needed to sleep, now that the adrenaline charge was dying down, like a bee needed flowers.

Honey had a picnic table in her backyard. Sitting on the table, Gary and I took turns telling Adam what had happened. I don't know why Gary sat on the table, but I was still so jumpy that I didn't want to chance trapping my legs if we had to run again. Adam paced. I envied his energy: he hadn't been chasing after Coyote all night.

Before we'd gotten very far in our narrative, Darryl, then Mary Jo, joined us. Mary Jo gave me a full glass of water. I drank half of it and dumped the other half over my head to rinse away the sweat that was still dripping into my eyes with stinging force. The water helped my eyes but not my cheek.

"You can turn into a coyote between one breath and the next," said Mary Jo when I got to the bit about running from the tibicenas. "I've seen you do it. You are faster that way, so why didn't you change when the tibicenas were chasing you?"

"Clothes," said Gary. "You try changing when you're wearing your clothes, and the next thing you know, you're tangled up in your jeans."

"At least you don't have a bra," I agreed sourly.

"While you were out running around, you got an interesting phone call," Adam told me, pulling my cell phone out of his back pocket. He hit a button. "Wulfe wants to talk to you."

I put it up to my ear. If he'd said that last before he'd hit the button, I'd have objected. Jumpy and exhausted are not a good state for talking to Wulfe, Marsilia's right-hand vampire. The last time I'd seen him, he'd been trying to kill me—and Marsilia, the vampire who ruled all the vamps in the Tri-Cities. There was an outside chance that Wulfe had actually been trying to protect Marsilia, but I had no trouble assigning him as much villainy as seemed to want to cling to him—and a bit more.

"Mercy?" Wulfe's voice was enough to wake me right up.

"You wanted to talk to me?" I wished I had more of Mary Jo's glass of water left.

"Mercy," he whispered. "Mercy. I can still taste you in my mouth." I pulled the phone away from my ear because I didn't want his voice that close to me. "I long for your blood on my tongue, little coyote-girl."

Creepy. Of all the creepy people and monsters I've encountered—and a lot of monsters are pretty creepy—Wulfe is the one who gets to me the worst. I think it's because he scares me the most. I had been thinking about drinking, and he started talking about it, as though he was reading my mind. He does that kind of thing a lot. He knows it bothers me, and that just encourages him.

"And I can see you turning to dust in the middle of the afternoon under the hot summer sun," I told him, trying to sound bored. I did a pretty good job. Exhaustion and boredom sound a lot alike. "If your dream comes true, then mine gets to come true, too."

"Life is not so fair, Mercy," he said, and someone in the same room with him made a noise.

Any adult who has ever watched a porn flick knows that noise. It's the one that real people don't make unless they are faking something.

"If you just called to flirt, I'm hanging up."

He drew in a shaky breath, then moaned.

I hung up.

"Who was that, and why was he having phone sex with you?" asked Gary.

"I need to wash my brain," muttered Darryl. "Next time I see that vampire, I'm going to squish him like a bug."

"I feel violated," I said, half-seriously.

The phone rang, and I set it on the table. It rang again, and we all looked at it.

Adam picked it up and hit the green button on the screen.

"Mercy, you spoil all my fun," Wulfe said, sounding less psychotic and more petulant. "You keep killing my playmates. It's only fair that you take their place."

I don't know which playmates he was talking about. Andre? Frost? Frost was the last vampire I'd killed.

"No," said Adam, as if Wulfe had been asking a question.

"I told you I'll only talk to Mercy," said Wulfe, dropping into singsong. "I know something you don't know."

"What?" asked Adam.

"I have news about a man who was looking for a house this week with room for his dogs. He paid cash. Lots of cash."

"Where?" asked Adam.

"Oh dear," Wulfe said. "You don't think I'm going to tell *you*, do you? I could have told *you* an hour ago."

Adam looked at me. I took the phone. Coyote said that Guayota and his dogs had killed again tonight. This wasn't just about Christy anymore. Guayota needed to be stopped.

"It's me," I said. "But if you keep screwing with us, I'll call Stefan and see if he can't figure out what your news is."

Marsilia, the mistress of the local vampire seethe, was courting Stefan with as much delicacy as a Victorian gentleman courted his chosen lady. He'd been her most loyal follower for centuries, and she'd broken the ties between them with brutal thoroughness in order to maintain control of her seethe. Now that he was finally talking to her again, if he asked her for information, she'd give it to him. Even if it was for me.

There was a little silence on the line. Then Wulfe said, sounding hurt, which was absurd, "I have no reason to help you, Mercy. One of my sheep brought me some interesting-for-you information. But if you aren't going to be nice, you don't get it."

Vampires.

"Nice how?" I asked.

"Come to my house tonight," he purred. "You remember where it is, right? I'll give you my information if you play well enough."

"She isn't going alone," said Adam.

"Oh no," agreed Wulfe. "Nothing says fun like an Alpha werewolf. Just you two, though."

I was going to be a zombie for the meeting with the lawyer and the cops tomorrow. Adam would have to do all the talking for me—he'd had about ten minutes more sleep than I had. But if Wulfe knew something, anything that would give us an advantage over Guayota, we needed to find out what it was. In less than a week, he'd killed who knows how many people. The official report, according to Adam's private investigator in Eugene, was that four had died in the fire Guayota had started in Christy's condo. There were all those women in the field in Finley and however many he'd killed tonight. Coyote had said Guayota wouldn't stop until he was stopped.

"Fine," I said. "Give me time to shower, and we'll be there." I hung up my phone and looked at the time.

"When's daylight?" I asked.

"About three hours," Adam said. "About a half an hour before we're scheduled to meet with the lawyer."

"I could take Warren or Darryl," I said. "You could sleep and go meet with the lawyers. I'd join you later for the police and keep my mouth shut. Possibly drool on your shoulder and snore."

He shook his head. "No. I'll drool and snore on you, too. The one thing that is not going to happen is you visiting the court jester of the evil undead alone."

11

〜〜

WULFE'S HOUSE WAS IN A HOUSING DEVELOPMENT
that had been an orchard ten years ago. The houses in this one
almost escaped that "we were all designed by the same architect
and you can pick one of three house plans" sameness. It had been
in place long enough for hedges and greenery, but not quite long
enough for big trees.

The neighborhood was firmly middle-class, with mobile bas-
ketball hoops in front of the garage doors in driveways and swing
sets in the backyards. The people who lived right next door to
Wulfe had a giant cedar kid's activity center—it was way too huge
to be merely a swing set—and an aboveground swimming pool
in their side yard. The side yard right next to Wulfe's house. Those
hadn't been there the last time I'd visited.

Wulfe's neighbors had a yappy little dog that started barking
as soon as we pulled into Wulfe's driveway. No lights turned on,
and I bet that it yapped at cars driving by, cats trespassing in its

yard, and bugs flying past the window. There is nothing more useless than a watchdog that barks at normal things the same way it does at a thief at the door.

"This is where Wulfe's home is?" asked Adam, turning off the engine.

"I know," I told him. "Blew my mind, too."

He looked at the swimming pool. "I feel as though I need to warn them about what occupies the house next door."

"If it helps," I said. "They are probably the safest people in the Tri-Cities. He's not going to feed so close to home—and you can bet that nothing else is, either. Unless their yappy dog drives Wulfe crazy; then all bets are off."

Adam shook his head and hopped out of the SUV. I jumped out of my side, too. I couldn't see the ghosts. Vampires' lairs always have ghosts, but they only show up when the vampires are asleep. I could feel them like a dozen eyes watching me from the shadows.

I met Adam in front of the house and let him approach and knock on the door while I kept an eye out behind us for an ambush. The man who opened the door had a line of big hickeys on his neck and wore nothing but a pair of jeans. When Adam wore nothing but his jeans, it was sexy; this guy was just disturbing. He wasn't fat, but there was no muscle on him, just loose skin and softness where muscle should be, as though someone had siphoned all the muscle out and left him . . . dying. His eyes were dead already.

He didn't really look at us. All of his attention was focused behind him even though his eyes were on us. "My master says you are to follow me," he told us.

We entered the house. Though it looked spotlessly clean, the interior of the house smelled. I remembered that from the first time I had visited here, but it was worse than I remembered, as if I'd filtered some of it out in my memories. My nose caught the charnel-house odors of blood, meat, feces, urine, and that odd smell of internal organs. Faintly but pervasively, I could smell an underlying scent of something rotting.

Adam took point, and I followed, watching behind us as I had on the porch. Wulfe's sheep led us into the kitchen, where we were treated to the sight of Wulfe lying down on top of one of those 1950s chrome and green Formica kitchen tables. There were three chairs that matched the table: two of them were knocked over, and the third was tucked in where it belonged on the side of the table where Wulfe's head was.

Like the guy who was ushering us into the house, Wulfe was naked from the waist up. Wulfe had been about fifteen when he was made a vampire, old enough to hint at the man he would never become. His ribs showed, and his skin was almost powder white, a shade paler than his hair. Last time I'd seen Wulfe, his hair had been buzzed, but it was longer now, maybe half an inch long, and it had been shaped.

He lay faceup, back slightly arched and eyes closed. One foot, wearing a purple Converse tennis shoe, was flat on the table, pushing his knee up. The other leg was outstretched, that foot bare and pointed like a ballet dancer's. He'd painted his toenails green, and they matched the color of the Formica tabletop. I didn't know if that was on purpose or not.

The light over the dining-room table was on, and someone had put daylight bulbs in the fixture because the tabletop looked more like an operating table than a place people might sit down and eat breakfast.

"Wulfe," Adam said dryly. "It's what's for dinner."

"*Yes!*" Wulfe said, suddenly sitting cross-legged and facing us. "See, Bryan? I told you he would get it!"

"Actually, you said *she* would get it, master," the man who'd let us in said.

Wulfe looked at him thoughtfully. "Am I still allowing you opinions?"

The man blinked at him.

"How long have you belonged to me, Bryan?"

Bryan had been the name of my foster father. There were lots of people named Bryan. It shouldn't bother me so much that they shared a name, this man who was the victim of a vampire and my foster father.

"Two days?" Bryan sounded unsure.

"That's right," said Wulfe. "I let you think until the third night. What happens on the third night, Bryan?"

Bryan's heartbeat picked up. For a moment I thought it was fear, but then I caught the scent of arousal. "You drink me dry," he said in the same breathless voice that six-year-olds talk about Christmas.

"Go away, Bryan," Wulfe told him. "Go sleep until tomorrow."

"Tomorrow," Bryan agreed, and hurried eagerly past Adam and me. After a moment, I heard a bedroom door slam.

"You feel sorry for him," Wulfe accused me.

"You intended me to feel sorry for him," I assured him. "Mission successful. What do you want in exchange for the address?" I couldn't rescue the vampire's victims without starting a war, and it was too late for this Bryan anyway. If I were sure that war would confine itself to Marsilia's seethe and our pack, I might try it—but my connection to Bran and Marsilia's to the Lord of Night who ruled vampires the way Bran ruled the werewolves held the danger

267

of escalation. If there was a war between werewolves and vampires, everyone would lose.

Still, if one of their victims ever asked for help . . .

Wulfe lowered his eyes as if he were a little shy. "I want a drink, Mercy. Just a little sip."

"No," said Adam, and the word was echoed by another *No*—Stefan's voice in my head.

I'd let Stefan bind me to him once, because another vampire had been feeding from me, and I didn't want to belong to that one. Belonging to any vampire was bad—all anyone had to do was look at Wulfe's victim, his Bryan, to understand that. Belonging to a vampire the other vampires called the Monster would have been worse than bad, so I'd asked Stefan for help and he'd tried. But Stefan's hold had been broken when the Monster had taken me again. When he died, all of the ties between the vampires and me were gone. Stefan had told me so. I'd known him a long time, ten years and more. Until this moment, I'd have sworn he wouldn't lie to me.

I wanted to be shocked at proof that he'd lied—but . . . he'd spoken in my head a few months ago, when I was fighting the vampire Frost, who wanted to take the city from Marsilia. I'd been hoping it was a leftover effect, a glitch, something that wouldn't happen again, so I hadn't talked about it to him or Adam. When nothing else happened, I decided it wasn't worth worrying about.

I'd evidently been wrong.

Adam heard that second *no* as well, because he looked at me, his eyes widening. Before he could say anything, though, Stefan was just suddenly there in the kitchen, standing between us and the vampire on the table.

There are some powers all vampires have. There are others that only a few gain as they age. Stefan could teleport. As far as I knew, he and Marsilia were the only vampires who could do that.

He had gained weight since I saw him just a month or so ago at one of the bad-movie nights Kyle and Warren hosted. Not enough to bring him back to where he'd been before Marsilia had nearly broken him, but close. He wore a dark blue t-shirt and faded jeans.

Wulfe started giggling as Stefan grabbed him by the throat and growled, "Mercy is off-limits."

Shivers slid down my spine, and my knees weakened. All this time, Stefan had been listening in. Could he call me, too? Make me come to him, no matter what I wanted to do?

"No, she isn't," Wulfe said triumphantly. Stefan's hold on his throat didn't seem to be having any effect on his ability to talk. "She'll never be off-limits to you, isn't that right?"

"His tie to her was broken," said Adam.

"It must have been a strong link," said Wulfe, hanging limply from Stefan's hands. "It must have been strong if the Monster couldn't take it. But then a lot of people underestimate our Soldier, our Stefan. Even so, a stronger vampire than Stefan should be able to supercede the blood bond he has with you, Mercy—we could fix that for you. Who would you rather serve, Mercy—Marsilia or me?" Wulfe giggled some more.

"Stefan?" I asked, wanting Wulfe to be wrong about the tie between Stefan and me, but empirical evidence suggested otherwise.

Stefan's back was to us. He set Wulfe down on the table. Wulfe quit laughing as soon as he was free. Face abruptly expressionless, he confronted Stefan. "Did you think that I wouldn't tell her? You think to keep her, and that keeps you from rejoining Marsilia because through you, Marsilia would have access to Mercy."

Adam's arms came around me, and he pulled me to him as I absorbed what Wulfe had just said—and that Stefan was not protesting. This was why Wulfe had insisted we come to his house—because he wanted to confront Stefan. I hadn't missed that Wulfe watched me as much as Stefan. He'd also wanted me to attack Stefan for lying to me—to give Stefan no one to turn to except Marsilia.

"I will not betray her," whispered Stefan, eyes on Adam.

"We know that," Wulfe said, but he'd been watching me, not Stefan when Stefan spoke. Wulfe thought Stefan was speaking of Marsilia, but Stefan's eyes had been on Adam. He'd been talking to Adam about me. "Come, Stefan. With you in the seethe, Marsilia will fight to protect Mercy because she is needed to keep you in line. You have been Marsilia's Soldier for four centuries and more. Marsilia needs you. You've been hiding your secret bond from the coyote-girl. Now that she knows, you have nothing more to hide. Marsilia will give her word that she will not touch the bond you share with Mercy, won't try to claim her for herself—no matter how useful a tame walker would be."

"I will not take that chance," Stefan said. He raised his head and met my eyes. "Mercy," he said. "Never say yes when Wulfe asks if he can bite you. It will open doors you do not want open. I am sorry I didn't tell you the blood bond between us wasn't gone. I didn't want you to know because I knew it would chafe, this tie between us. If the Monster couldn't sever it, then the chances are good that neither Wulfe nor Marsilia could do it, either. Though, as Wulfe pointed out, they could probably take the tie from me and tie you to them." He hesitated, then said, "With you bound to me, Marsilia would not dare kill you because her actions hurt so many of those I protect—I would kill her, or she would be forced to kill me."

"They are sheep, Soldier," said Wulfe contemptuously. "Sheep are for using." He started to raise his hand, and I felt magic gather. Then Stefan moved, drawing a blade from somewhere and bringing it down over Wulfe's hand in a swift, overhand chop. Wulfe's unattached hand dropped to the floor.

"Not on my watch," said Stefan.

"Darn it," said Wulfe mildly, looking at his severed hand while grasping the maimed limb with the hand that remained useful. He squeezed to slow the bleeding. "Look what you've done. It will take them all day to get the blood off the floor."

"How did he lure you here?" Stefan asked. *I don't listen to you all the time,* his voice in my head told me. *Wulfe called me on the phone five minutes ago and told me you were in trouble.*

It was as if he'd picked up just what was bothering me the most—which I guess he had. Not surprisingly, that understanding didn't make me feel any better.

"Wulfe promised us information," Adam growled, shaking his head as if he'd heard that secondary message from Stefan, too. "We need an address."

"I'll get it," Stefan promised.

"I counted you my friend," Adam said, his voice icy.

"I am," said Stefan. "We'll speak of this later."

"Yes," said Adam. "We will. There is one way to cut such a bond."

"No," said Stefan sadly. "No. I would only take her with me at this point. She accepted the bond willingly, and that makes it a lot stronger than one that is forced on someone. Go now, Adam. Morning is near. I'll come by tomorrow night, and we can talk."

He and Adam stared at each other, Adam with near violence and Stefan with patience. If what he'd said was true, I could almost understand the lies he'd told me because he was right: knowing that we were tied together was going to bother me a lot.

"I TIED THE WHOLE PACK TO A VAMPIRE," I SAID NUMBLY as Adam drove us back to Honey's house.

"No," Adam said. "He can't use you to influence me. The bonds will not be superceded like that." He glanced at me, then back at the road, but his hand took mine. "I have your back on this one, love."

I grunted.

Adam laughed.

I frowned at him, and he said, "Sorry. That's my grunt you stole. I've been thinking, and you should have, too. If Wulfe is right, and I see no reason to doubt that, the tie between you and Stefan has been going on a long time now. And he has never used it—except this once, to protect you." Twice. He had used it twice. "Stefan tries to be honorable, as honorable as his condition allows."

"Condition?" I said wryly. "That makes it sound like he has rabies or distemper."

"Rabies has a lot in common with vampirism," said Adam.

I grunted again. He was being too casual about all of this despite the growly interchange he'd just had with Stefan. "You knew," I said. "You knew it wasn't gone."

Adam was still, then said, "Yes. I've been around a little longer than you, dealt with the vampires more." He glanced at me, then away. "And I can smell him on you sometimes, just a whiff now and again when I know you haven't seen him in days or weeks."

I thought about that for a while. "And you didn't tell me?"

He shrugged. "What good would that have done? Stefan is more than a little in love with you, you know that, right? It's what makes Marsilia hate you so much. If he had known a way to break it, I think he'd have told you. I know that such things are not easily destroyed—and that if the Monster had really held the reins, you'd have been in worse shape when he died."

Adam was right. All that Stefan had done with our link was to help me twice. But Stefan was right, too. Knowing that the tie was still there chafed. Knowing that Adam had known about it and not told me . . . that chafed me even more.

OUR LAWYER, MS. TREVELLYAN, WHO HAD TOLD US TO call her Jenny, watched the disc Adam had handed to her. It was from Camera Two in the garage and showed pretty much everything I'd seen when Guayota had come to visit. It also showed, to my relief, the dog changing into a man in the background while Guayota and I fought.

She watched it from beginning to end, and her poker face was flawless. If I didn't know better, I'd have thought that she saw fights between volcano gods and mechanics on a daily basis. Her assistant, a bright young thing, had yet to acquire a mask that could cover her fascination.

"Good one," the assistant breathed at the point where I stuck the mop handle into his head. It looked more disturbing on-screen than it had been at the time. I suppose I'd been worried enough about survival to get too squicked then.

When the disc finished, she added, "You've done a lot of karate, right? That looked like an outtake from some of the old martial arts shows—before they learned to get the actors to slow down so the audience could see what they were doing."

Jenny Trevellyan cleared her throat. Gently.

A light flush rose in her assistant's face. I hadn't caught her name, and now I regretted it because I liked her. "Sorry. But you're lucky you survived. Seriously, that guy was scary."

Jenny folded her hands and stared at Adam. "Okay. What happened later that made you erase the end of the video?"

"An unfortunate glitch in the equipment," Adam murmured. "We have three discs from different cameras, but something, maybe the excess heat, made them all quit recording around the same time."

The lawyer's assistant, who was scribbling down notes, lit right up. "Magic is supposed to affect electricity like that. I've read that wizards can't be in the same room with things like computers and stuff."

I knew where she'd read that. I bit my lip. It was to our advantage to spread a little misinformation whenever we could.

"Convenient as that explanation is," said Jenny dryly, "I would like to know what would happen if Cantrip *magically* figures out what the cameras would have shown if they hadn't . . . glitched. I am your lawyer; I can't help you if I don't know the truth."

"Someone came in with Adam and saved my skin," I told her. "The means that someone used would make that someone very valuable to the military or any number of other disreputable types who might resort to kidnapping to get that kind of power under their control. I'm just glad that the glitch happened when it did. That way, we can just give the credit to my husband and ensure that a Good Samaritan doesn't suffer for saving my bacon. We'd like to leave that person out completely."

"Okay," she said. "If the opportunity comes up, I might remind Cantrip that there is already one video in existence showing exactly what Adam is capable of." She wasn't looking at me, and I was glad. Adam had, in a graphic fashion, destroyed the body of the man who'd assaulted me. The video of that had been released so that neither Adam nor I was charged with murder. It was only supposed to go to certain people, but it had been seen more widely than it should have been. "And," she continued, "that a second example wasn't wanted. That way, no one will be looking for another reason for the glitch. Is that acceptable?"

"Fine," said Adam.

"You gave me a brief statement before we watched the video. Now tell me again who this is that broke into the garage and why he attacked Mercy."

I folded my arms and put my forehead down on the desk while Adam talked. The next thing I knew, Adam had gathered my hair in one hand and tipped my head sideways. I blinked at him.

"She needs to see the burn on your face," Adam said.

It took me a moment to process what he said, then I sat up and showed her myself. I showed her the burns on my hands and arms and the one on my ribs. I'd put Bag Balm on them, and they felt better, despite what the EMT had said.

"You shot the dog first," Jenny said, "the one that . . . er . . . turned into a man? Then he threw some sort of fire magic at you and burned your cheek—that's not on the disc I saw, but Adam told me that it's on the second disc. Then you fired five times at him, three to the head, two to the chest. You jumped on the car, looking for a way out, and when it became obvious that there was nothing available, you engaged in battle with Juan Flores, who apparently is a Canary Islands volcano god named Guayota?"

She was scary good. She got out the last part of the sentence without any inflection.

"Almost," said Adam. "First, he broke into the garage with a crowbar. We have that caught on the outside camera."

She nodded. "Okay, I'd like to wait until I've had a chance to review all the discs available, but, as you've pointed out, there is the worry that in the meantime some poor law-enforcement officer will run into him without knowing what he is. We need to let the law-enforcement agencies know what they might be dealing with. With that in mind, and with your permission, I'll send copies of the discs to the police immediately."

"And," I added because it seemed an important part of the narrative, "he admitted to me that he'd killed seven women whose bodies were discovered yesterday . . . no, sorry." Just because I hadn't slept didn't mean that time hadn't passed. Her assistant handed me an ice-cold bottle of water. I took it and drank a quarter of it down. "It was the day before yesterday, Thursday. The police took me out to the crime scene to see if werewolves were responsible for the massacre."

Her right eyelid twitched. "That's the first I've heard of this. When did he admit that? I didn't see it."

"That's the 'trouble in Finley' I was talking about," I told her.

She took in a deep breath. She made me go over all that I knew about the seven women and assorted horses and dogs that Guayota had killed near the hayfield in Finley. At some point, her assistant took over the questioning, though I'm not sure she was supposed to.

"You mean all the dead women looked like Mr. Hauptman's ex-wife? That's . . . that's right out of a profiler's book."

Jenny snorted her coffee, wiped her nose, and gave her assistant a quelling look. "You might curb your enthusiasm over the deaths of seven women, Andrea. It isn't really appropriate."

"Poor things," said Andrea obediently. "But this is like being in the middle of an episode of *Criminal Minds*." She paused. "Okay. That's dorky. Sorry. But most of our cases are like somebody's kid got drunk and hit a fence and wants to make reparations but would rather not lose their driver's license. The only murders we've been involved with have been those 'everyone knows who did it,' and our job is to get our client the lightest sentence possible . . . and I'm talking too much." She blinked at us. "It's just that I moved here hoping I might get the chance to see a fae, because the reservation is just over in Walla Walla. And here I am talking to a werewolf about a fire demon who is killing people and burning down buildings."

Jenny covered her mouth, and when she pulled her hand away, her face was stern. "She actually is very, very good in court." Her voice became very dry as she said, "You wouldn't recognize her. And, in case you were worried, nothing comes out of her mouth in public that she doesn't want to say."

"I am discreet," agreed Andrea.

"So," Jenny said in a we're-getting-back-to-business manner, "you want me to set up a meeting with Cantrip and the police."

"That is correct," Adam agreed.

"Okay. I'll get something set up for this afternoon, hopefully here, but probably down at the Kennewick police station." She looked at us and smiled. "In the meantime, I suggest you get a few hours of sleep."

IN THE END, WE CHECKED INTO A HOTEL. HONEY'S house was filling rapidly with even more pack members as the story about last night's fight got out. Sleeping there during the day was out of the question.

Adam put us in the hotel nearest the airport. The room was clean and quiet, and for the four hours we were there, it was perfect for sleeping. Well, after we remembered to put out the DO NOT DISTURB sign—and after I put the fear of me into the second maid who apparently couldn't read the sign.

I wasn't exactly chipper when we woke up to head in to our afternoon appointment with Cantrip and the police, making a quick stop at the mall to grab clean and appropriate clothing. Apparently, Cantrip was still jockeying for position and fighting with the local police, so our lawyer's office was acceptable neutral territory.

The Cantrip agents, Orton and Kent, were waiting for us, smugness radiating off them both. Jenny and her assistant Andrea were there along with a gray-haired man who was balding and so thin and fit that he must have made a real effort at keeping in shape. It was hard to tell for sure, but I thought he was maybe twenty years older than our lawyer, which would put him in his late sixties or early seventies. His face looked slightly familiar, and he exchanged courteous nods with Adam, so I assumed he was someone from the firm whom Adam knew. Jenny didn't introduce him, beyond his name, Larry Torbett.

Jenny gave us a small, controlled smile. "I suggest that we start. I have the originals of three discs from the security video at Mercy's garage from the night in question for you, gentlemen. I have copies for my files and, of course, I have already sent copies over to the police as well. Detective Willis called to tell me that they found the video enlightening, but that they would, regrettably, be late.

"The outside camera clearly shows Mr. Flores, who is wanted

in connection with murder and arson in Eugene, breaking into the garage with a crowbar after hours when only Ms. Hauptman was inside. The other two are views from two different cameras in the garage. I will show you one, the one that shows, more or less, Ms. Hauptman's view of the events. The last camera shows Ms. Hauptman's actions better. They are time-stamped."

At the conclusion of the video, Orton looked grimly satisfied and the younger Cantrip agent, Kent, triumphant (presumably because any altercation between the wife of a werewolf Alpha and a fire demon put the case in their jurisdiction).

"Well," said Larry Torbett, "wasn't that something watching the agents come, Jenny?"

"There is more," she said. "There is no sound in this recording, and Ms. Hauptman has a lot of pertinent information that is not apparent. Ms. Hauptman?"

By this time I could have told the story in my sleep, but four hours of napping had removed that temptation. I told the whole thing from beginning to end. The Cantrip agents didn't ask for any clarification, which bothered me. Only when I had finished entirely did the Cantrip agents stir.

"Ms. Hauptman," said Agent Kent genially, "I know that you are on record any number of places stating that you are not a werewolf."

I narrowed my eyes at him. "That's right."

He tapped the discs. "Are you human?"

"Are you?" I asked.

"You move very well for a human," said Agent Kent, who didn't seem nervous or green today. The change was so great that I wondered if the appearance of being a rookie was one he used for effect.

"Thank you," I told him. "I'll tell Sensei that you were impressed."

"My wife takes lessons in Shi Sei Kai Kan. Additionally, we spar in various styles several times a week. I do not intend that anyone hurt Mercedes again." Adam's tone was cool, and the warning in his last sentence was clear to anyone who was listening.

"We are familiar with the . . . alleged assault," said Agent Orton.

"Have you seen the security footage from that?" asked Torbett before Adam could speak.

I got my heel on Adam's foot, but he'd cooled off considerably and frowned at Torbett.

"No," said Orton. "However—"

"I have." The older man's voice was cool. "I assure you that an assault took place, and the bastard got what was coming to him." It was nice that he agreed there had been an assault, but was there anyone in the whole world who hadn't seen me assaulted? Anyone except Orton, that is. Maybe we should have just put it up on YouTube. I forced my hands to unclench before anyone noticed.

"The issue remains," said Agent Kent, taking up the charge as the senior agent stalled out. "That we believe, Ms. Hauptman, that you have not been entirely forthcoming about whether or not you are human."

"Are you?" I asked again. Because my nose told me that he was not.

"Yes," Kent said, believing he told the truth. "How about you, Ms. Hauptman?"

"No, you aren't," said Adam, intrigued. His head tilted, and he took a deep breath, so everyone would know what sense he was using to determine it. "Fae. Though you aren't even a half-blood. Maybe one of your parents?"

Agent Kent just stared at him.

"You might talk to them and ask," I suggested. "Do you have trouble with metals?"

"I have a nickel allergy," he said defensively.

"This isn't about Agent Kent." Orton had had time to recover. "We've determined that Ms. Hauptman is a potential threat to the public safety, and we are bringing her in as a murder suspect who has supernatural powers that make her too dangerous to be incarcerated in the usual ways."

"Under what authority?" asked Jenny.

"Under the Humanity Act that established the agency I work for, Ms. Trevellyan, and the discretionary detention provisions in the Patriot Act. We can detain Ms. Hauptman indefinitely as a possible terrorist." Orton's tones were smug.

I wasn't afraid of their taking me. But I was terrified of what Adam would do to ensure that they did not. Adam, though, wasn't tense at all. I frowned at him. Why wasn't he upset?

"Are you acting on your own, sir?" asked Larry Torbett.

"I have my orders," said Orton repressively. "Ms. Hauptman, you aren't going to give us any trouble here, right?"

"I'm not," I said, still watching my husband, who seemed pleased. "But I wouldn't go counting your prisoners before they are safely in your detention cell."

Larry Torbett smiled at me. "Well said, Ms. Hauptman. Mr. Hauptman, you should know that I have in my possession documentation that someone in high places would like a pet werewolf and was not opposed to kidnapping to achieve his desires. How presumptuous of him to try to use the law to enable him to do so. Who is your supervisory agent, Agent Orton?"

Orton frowned at him. "Supervisory Agent Donald Kerrigan. Ms. Hauptman, I would advise you not to resist arrest. That will only add to your troubles."

"Allow me to clarify matters, before this goes too much further, gentlemen," said Jenny. "Agent Orton, Agent Kent, Mr. and Ms. Hauptman, this is Larry Torbett, Ph.D. Dr. Torbett is teaching a four-day seminar at WSU Tri-Cities on fae-human relations. He retired two years ago from a government think tank in Washington, D.C., though the president called him back to help deal with the mess last year when the fae retreated to their reservations. He was also my law professor, which is why he is staying with me. He asked to join us out of curiosity and boredom, I suspect." She smiled at the continued clueless looks she was getting. "But the layman would better know him as L. J. Torbett, editor of the *Watchdog Times*."

The *Watchdog Times* was an influential Web-based magazine that wrote and recirculated pieces about government mischief. Recently, it had engineered the forced retirement of a state judge in Pennsylvania caught giving harsh jail sentences in return for kickbacks from the privately run state penitentiary and was responsible for the highly publicized trial of a federal official who was spending ten years in jail rather than the cozy estate in the Bahamas he'd used tax dollars to pay for.

The *Watchdog Times* had also cleared the name of a conservative senator who was accused of having sex with a minor. They hadn't saved his marriage, but they'd saved his career, mostly, and certainly rescued him from a jail sentence when they proved the whole thing had been set up by his political rival—and that the boy in question had been a very young-looking twenty-three-year-old who'd been well paid to act his part.

If he said he had documentation, L. J. Torbett had documentation.

"You were asleep when Jenny asked if I'd mind if her old friend joined us," murmured Adam to me. "Jenny said he'd thought that it was odd that Cantrip Agents were first on scene, and asked to sit in this afternoon."

I leaned against him and watched the old lawyer turned journalist wipe the floor with the Cantrip agents.

"This," he said, "is a disgrace. That government agents who should be above reproach lend themselves to such a scheme is appalling."

"You can say what you'd like," said Orton with dignity. "But that doesn't change my orders."

"Yes," Agent Kent said heavily. "Yes, it does. Unless you want to be dropped to junior-janitor rank for the rest of your tenure in Cantrip, it does. Kerrigan is a political rat, and if he's behind this, he'd sell us down the river without a qualm. If he's not behind it and it is from higher up, he'll sell us even faster."

Torbett nodded at the younger agent but looked at Orton when he continued talking. "There are larger issues at stake, too, gentlemen. Do you know that the fae are talking to the werewolves, trying to gain their support for an alliance against the government of the US?"

Orton gave a short nod. It wasn't a secret.

Torbett said, "What do you think would happen if you forced the Alpha of the Columbia Basin Pack, one of the most prominent packs in the US"—that the humans knew about, anyway—"to defend his wife against government agents? The man who gave you your orders doesn't understand what he's messing with. A man like Hauptman, a werewolf, will die defending his mate. He would never have let you leave with her. He tried to tell you that. Did you miss the part where Mr. Hauptman said he wouldn't let anyone hurt his wife?"

He gave them a moment to digest that. Then he said, "Do you want to be famous, gentlemen? I assure you that your names would have gone down in the history books as the *idiots* who forced the werewolves into a confrontation with the federal government." He leaned forward. "Do you know that Hauptman has been doing his level best to keep our relations with the werewolves from reaching the boiling point, as they did with the fae?"

"I think that we are going to regret not eliminating the werewolves while we have a chance," said Agent Kent.

I thought about Bran and wondered what made Agent Kent think that they ever had a chance at eliminating the werewolves.

"Whatever you might think of the legality, Dr. Torbett, I believe this is a matter of survival. Having Hauptman and his pack under our control would have been the best thing for everyone—even the wolves," Kent said heavily.

"Under whose control?" asked Torbett genially. "And do you know what they were planning to do with the werewolves? I do. I have"—he smiled—"interesting documentation that is eventually going to see some public servants and an elected official in jail."

"It sounds like Mr. Hauptman is trying to blackmail us," said Agent Orton, his voice gravelly. "We can't take his wife in because he'll start a war?"

"Is it blackmail to tell a child that he'll burn his hand if he puts it in a fire, Agent Orton?" asked Jenny. "This is, I think, the same thing."

"Orton," said Kent, sounding tired, "we are done here."

"We have orders," the older agent said.

"No," Kent told him. "This isn't the army. We were given instructions and gathered new information that made those instructions unwise."

"Gentlemen," said Jenny, "I trust we are finished here. If you have further questions, please feel free to call me rather than bothering the Hauptmans."

That's when Detective Willis came in, looking exhausted. "Sorry to be late. We've found three more dead women, and the press has found out about all of them." He looked at Adam. "We've watched that video and read the letter Ms. Trevellyan sent with it. We are satisfied that this Juan Flores is our killer, whatever he is. I'm supposed to tell you that if you have any more information on him, we'd like it, including where he can be found. For my part, I just hope you have more of an idea of how to handle this thing before it kills again than we do."

12

~~

ON THE WAY TO HONEY'S, WE DECIDED TO DRIVE BY the house to check on the cat and grab another change of clothing. Warren had left Medea with a mixing bowl filled with cat food and another with water because they'd spent an hour looking for her everywhere. He figured if he couldn't find her, then neither, probably, could Guayota. There was a cat door in the house, so Medea could come and go as she pleased. If Guayota came and burned the place to the ground, hopefully she'd escape.

But I intended to stick her uncooperative rump in a cat carrier and take her with us. I wasn't taking the chance of leaving her vulnerable.

I quit worrying about the cat when I saw the car parked in front of the house. A gray Acura RLX, a luxury sedan with horsepower, was sitting in Adam's usual spot.

Adam slowed a little. "Do you know that car?"

I started to shake my head, then reconsidered. "No. But I bet it belongs to Beauclaire. I didn't see what he drove, but I heard it, and the RLX fits what I heard."

The SUV resumed its usual speed. "He's early, and you left the walking stick at Honey's house."

"He can follow us to Honey's—"

"I won't take him to Honey's house," Adam said. "We've already exposed her enough by moving the pack there."

"Fine. We can meet him at a place of his choice in an hour."

Beauclaire was leaning against the front door, reading a book. A battered old copy of *Three Men in a Boat*; I'd had to read that in college. Twice. Now I couldn't remember if I'd liked it or not. Beauclaire looked up when we drove in.

"Let me deal with him," Adam said.

This wasn't a John Wayne–esque "let the men deal with the situation, little lady." There was a bit of sandpaper in Adam's voice: he was still unhappy that the fae had invaded his house and made him sleep through it. He wanted to go establish dominance. Over Lugh's son. Because that was a really smart idea.

While I'd been processing, Adam had already gotten out of the SUV. I shoved open my door and scrambled out, nearly tripping over the walking stick that fell on the ground as if it had been in the SUV and I'd kicked it when I hopped out. Which it hadn't been, and I hadn't done.

"Adam," I said. "I've got the walking stick."

He stopped halfway between the SUV and the house. He looked at me, and I trotted up to show him.

Beauclaire straightened, tucked the book in his suit-jacket pocket, where it didn't bulge. Either he'd used glamour, or the suit was as expensive as it looked.

Adam put a hand on my back as I passed him in an unvoiced

request, so I stopped next to him. Beauclaire came down the stairs to us, his movements so graceful I wondered how he had passed for years as human.

He paid almost no attention to Adam and me. His eyes were fixed on the walking stick. I couldn't tell what he felt for it, and I expected to. I expected him to be . . . something more decipherable.

He stopped several feet away and for the first time looked at us. Looked at Adam.

"I will not apologize for coming into your home and making her retrieve my father's walking stick," he said. "It was necessary."

"If," said Adam, "if you had come to my house and knocked on the door, Mercy would still have done everything she could do to find Coyote and get the walking stick back for you. You have, as Lugh's son, a just claim on the artifact. If you had done that, matters would have been even between us."

"No," said Beauclaire. "I would have owed you something for the service you had given me. I will not owe a *human* for anything." Substitute "slimy toad dung" for "human," and he might have said it the same way.

"Neither my mate nor I is, strictly speaking, human," said Adam. "But you made your choices. And so the consequences will follow in due time."

Beauclaire bowed without looking down or losing Adam's gaze. His bow was almost Japanese in all the things it said and didn't say. *I accept that there will be trouble between us, though I will not seek it more than I already have. I disturbed your peace deliberately, and the consequences are upon my head.* It was a long conversation for such a simple gesture.

I held out the walking stick. "Here. Coyote said he taught it a few things."

Beauclaire looked at me. "I don't know Coyote," he said. "Maybe I will have to remedy that."

Adam's lips curled up in satisfaction. "I would pay money," he said.

Beauclaire, who still hadn't reached for the walking stick, narrowed his eyes at my mate.

"Oh?"

"You never get quite what you expect from Coyote," I told him. "He was amazingly helpful this time, so I expect that something horrible will happen to us in the near future." I wished I hadn't said that as soon as the words left my mouth. I already knew that something horrible was coming. I wiggled the walking stick. "Would you take this already?"

"Of your free will," he said.

I rolled my eyes as I repeated the phrase. "Of my own free will, I give you this walking stick"—and I kept going, though that was the end of the usual phrase I'd spoken every time I'd tried to give the walking stick back to a fae—"fashioned by Lugh, woken by the oakman, and changed by blood, changed by death, changed by spirit. Change comes to all things until the greatest change, which is death. This I entrust to your care."

I tried to pretend that I'd intended to say all that from the very beginning, tried to ignore the way the walking stick was warmer than it should be in my hands and felt almost eager, as if it wanted to go to Lugh's son. Adam knew I was acting, I could tell because the pressure of his hand on my back changed. Other than a sharp look, Beauclaire didn't seem to have heard anything he wasn't expecting.

I wished I knew whether it had been the walking stick or Coyote who had put those words in my mouth. It might even have been Stefan, for all I knew, but he should be asleep, and it hadn't sounded like something he'd have said.

Beauclaire took the walking stick, closed his eyes, and frowned at it. "This is a fake."

"No," I said. Coyote could have passed a fake walking stick to me, though that wasn't quite in his character. But a fake walking stick would have stayed safely at Honey's, tucked inside the locked tack room in the barn, where I'd left it.

Anger built in his face, and he tossed the walking stick back at me. He didn't mean to hurt me because he didn't throw it like a weapon. I could probably have caught it—but Adam caught it instead.

"Are you implying that we are lying to you?" Adam asked gently. He twirled the walking stick like a baton.

I put a hand on his and stilled the stick. "Thank you," I told him when he let me stop him. "The walking stick has been just a little too happy to hurt people lately."

He sucked in a breath as I took it out of his hands, then he opened and closed them a couple of times. He glanced up at the sky. "A few more days until the full moon," he told me.

Werewolves were edgy around moon time. Edgier, anyway. I couldn't help but wonder if the walking stick hadn't helped his anger along just a bit.

"Mr. Beauclaire," I said. "This is the walking stick that Coyote gave me after he showed it how to hide itself better. I left it this morning in a safe, locked in a place miles away from here. It fell out of my SUV just now."

I handed it to him again, but I thought that it wasn't as happy to go to him as it had been before. It felt rejected. Sulky.

"Behave," I told it. Adam looked at me.

Beauclaire turned it around in his hands, felt over the silver knob, then ran his hands over the stick itself. He half closed his eyes and did it again. He gave them another of his indecipherable looks. "I told you that I would not apologize, but that was before I rejected the prize I sent you to get. This is my father's walking stick, though it has changed from the last time I held it a thousand years ago, more or less. I did not expect that it would. His small magics tend to be more stable than the larger ones, which have, up to this point, showed themselves to be more adaptable."

He met my eyes. "Mercedes Athena Thompson."

"Hauptman," added Adam.

"Hauptman. I apologize for my disbelief. I apologize for not recognizing the truth of what you told me. I apologize for not listening." He paused, looked at the walking stick again, and his eyebrow rose, almost as if it had said something to him.

He gave me a faint, ironic smile. "My thanks for retrieving this one from the"—he paused—"sanctuary that you had found for it. I owe you a favor of your choice."

"No," I said. "No. You don't. I know about favors from the fae."

"That," he said austerely, "is not for you to accept or reject."

"Information, then," I said. "Do you know anything about Guayota?"

He shook his head. "I have heard about your trouble. The fae do not live on the Canary Islands, and I know nothing more than that he is a volcano spirit taking flesh. Zee's young one has been asking around without luck, I believe." He hesitated. Gave me a look that said, *There is another question to ask me here. But I can't tell you unless you ask.* Something about Tad.

"If I ask you to help us defeat Guayota?"

He smiled grimly. "If I were the Dark Smith of Drontheim, I would offer to help and leave you so far in my debt that you would be my puppet until the end of your days."

"That's what I thought," I told him. "But I needed to ask."

"Information would be a reasonable balance," he told me. "You know that the Smith's son has been requested and required to attend the fae court in the reservation. So that would not be new information to you."

That there was a fae court was new information. I wondered if it was a court in the sense of a court of law, or a more traditional fae court. And what the answer to that might mean in the future.

But he'd told me the information he was willing to give us. "In repayment of the favor you owe me, is Tad being held prisoner?"

He smiled as if I'd been clever. "I was asked not to speak of this to you, but as I owe you a favor, I can disregard the earlier request. Tad is unhappy, and those who hold him are not listening. He is being held against his will, but those who hold him don't know Siebold Adelbertsmiter as I do." He said Zee's full name with distaste. "I may not like him, but no one can hold such a one as the Dark Smith of Drontheim when he is unwilling. There are too many old fae who forget what they once knew and believe in the old quarrelsome man they see. There will be no need for a rescue attempt, and indeed, such an effort might backfire. You will not be able to contact them, however, until matters play out." He raised an eyebrow at me. "I think that there is now balance between us. Though I include this as part of our bargain: if you have not heard from the Smith's son in two months' time, you may cry out the name you know me by and I will come and tell you how matters stand. I would not be surprised if it takes at least that long."

Then, walking stick in hand, he gave Adam a respectful nod, got in his car, and drove off.

I took a deep breath. "That's done."

Adam shook his head. "Let's hope so.

We collected our clothing, but it took a while to find the cat. Tracking a cat through a field? No problem. Tracking a cat through the house where the cat lived? That was miserable—and to add insult to injury, when I looked in our bathroom, I found that Christy's shampoo and conditioner were in our shower. She hadn't, however, put her makeup back on the counter. Maybe it was because she took her makeup with her to Honey's house.

Adam found the cat eventually, on top of a bookcase in the living room where she'd been watching us look for her. Crouched behind a large copper pot filled with silk flowers, she was nearly invisible.

I gave the flowers, beautiful dusty gray-blue blooms that contrasted and complemented everything else in the room a little too well, a baleful look.

"Yes," said Adam, petting my cat as he held her like a baby in his arms. She caught his hands and sank her claws into him just a little before her purring redoubled, and she snuggled deeper against him.

"Yes, what?" I asked.

"Yes, Christy picked out those flowers. The pot, however, was my mother's. Feel free to fill it with something else. If you leave it empty, it collects dust and dead spiders." His voice was so full of patience that I knew he found me funny.

Normally, our bond fluctuated on how much information I got from it, swinging pretty widely during the length of a day. But even within a few minutes there was some variation, like a swing moving up and down. One second, I was getting grumpy because he was laughing at me, and the next, I was flooded with this mix of tenderness, love, and amusement all mixed together in a potent bundle that meant happy.

Hard to get grumpy over that.

His smile grew, and the dimple appeared and . . . and I kissed him. I rested my body against him, at an angle so I didn't squish the cat, and thought, *Here is my happiness. Here is my reason to survive. Here is my home.*

"I never forget," I murmured to him when I could.

"Forget?"

"Forget who you are to me," I said, petting him with my fingertips because I could, because he was mine. "I'll be fretting about Christy, worrying about the pack, hoping Christy trips and spills her cardaywatsafanday stew—"

"*Carbonnade à la flamande*," said Adam.

"—all over the floor, then I look at you."

"Mmmm?"

"Yep," I said, putting my nose against him and breathing him in. "Mmmm."

I was just considering the empty bedroom upstairs and weighing it against the possibility that Guayota would choose that moment to attack when someone knocked at the door.

We broke apart.

"You have the cat," I said. "I don't want to spend another hour looking for her. I'll get the door."

"Be careful," was all Adam said.

I checked through the peephole, carefully, because there had been that one movie on bad-movie night where someone had been killed because he'd put his eye to the peephole, and the bad guy had stuck a fencing sword through the hole and into the victim's eye. We'd stopped the film to argue whether or not it was possible to do—and I remained forever scarred by the scene.

It was Rachel, one of Stefan's menagerie, one of his sheep. Stefan was gentler on the people he fed from than other vampires I'd come into contact with. He found broken people or people who needed something from him so that the exchange—their blood and the course of their lives for whatever a vampire might provide them—was, if not even, a little more balanced. Most members of a vampire's menagerie died slowly, but Stefan's people, mostly, thrived under his care. Or they had until Marsilia had happened to them.

I opened the door.

Rachel, like Stefan himself, had gained a little weight back. She didn't look like a crack addict anymore, but she didn't look really healthy, either. Her skin was pale, and there were shadows in her eyes. She didn't look young anymore—and she was around Jesse's age. But she was back in her goth costume—black lacy top, black jeans, and long black gloves that disguised the two fingers Marsilia—or Wulfe—had cut off her right hand.

"Hey, Mercy," she said. "I've been chasing all over looking for you—I assume you know that someone tried to blow up your garage? I gave up about noon, did the shopping and a few errands, and decided to try again before I drove home. This is for you." She handed me an envelope with my name in elegant script.

I opened it and found a lined note card with an address: 21980 Harbor Landing Road, Pasco. And, underneath the address, in the same flowery script: *Sorry.*

"Hel-lo, handsome," purred Rachel. "Man with cat is one of my fantasies."

I didn't look up. "He's taken, Rachel, sorry. She's underage, Adam, and—you're taken. Rachel, this is my husband, Adam. Adam this is Stefan's—" His what? "Sheep" wasn't any word I'd ever use to describe someone I liked, no matter how accurate it was. "Stefan's."

"'Sheep' is the word you're looking for," said Rachel. "I'd better get going before the ice cream melts. 'Bye, Mercy. 'Bye, Mercy's husband."

She turned and trotted out to her car, a nondescript little Ford I hadn't seen before. She waved and took off in a peel of rubber and gravel that made me wince a little as the splatter of small rocks rained down on the SUV.

I twirled the card in my fingers before handing it reluctantly to Adam.

"Here," I said, more casually than I felt. "I think we'd better call Ariana and Elizaveta, don't you think? Someone has got to know how to make werewolves fireproof."

WARREN MET US AT THE DOOR TO HONEY'S HOUSE.

"Hey, boss," he said, drawling like there was nothing wrong, but I could tell that he was upset by the set of his shoulders. "We were taking Gary Laughingdog to the bus station like you asked— and Kyle says to tell you thank you for making him aid and abet an escaped convict like that—when he started having convulsions in the backseat. We pulled over, and he was unconscious, so we brought him back. He hasn't woken up, and Kyle is pretty well resigned to losing his license to practice law."

I gave the cat carrier to Adam and set down the bag of Medea necessities I carried. The cat box and kitty litter were still in the car, and so was my .44 S&W, which I'd retrieved from the house. "Here. You take the cat and Warren. I'll take Kyle," I said.

Adam gave me a look.

"Sorry. You heap big Alpha dog," I told him. "I'll let you call it next time. But I'm right, and you already know it. Kyle will just make you mad on purpose—and Warren will listen better to you than me about relationships because he'd feel comfortable storming away from me when I said something he didn't want to hear. Where is Kyle?" I directed my question at Warren.

"Down the hall, third bedroom on the left. Watching over Laughingdog, who is still unconscious." He frowned at me. "Before Christy came, I never thought about how much you manipulate the people around you—it doesn't feel like manipulation when you do it."

"The difference is," I told him, "that I love you and want everyone to be happy. And"—I lifted a finger—"*I* know what's best for you."

"And," said Adam, "Mercy's not subtle. When she manipulates you, she wants you to *know* you've been manipulated."

I'd already crossed the living room toward the wing with the bedrooms, but I turned around to stick my tongue out at Adam.

"Don't point that at me unless you are going to use it," he said.

I smiled until I was safely out of sight.

THE DOOR TO THE BEDROOM WARREN HAD INDICATED was shut, so I knocked.

Kyle opened the door. I'd seen Kyle angry before. But I don't think I'd ever seen him that angry. Maybe it was because that anger was directed at me.

I slipped through the doorway, though I was pretty sure he'd intended to send me on my way. But I'm really good at sticking my nose in where no one wants it.

The room was one of those bedrooms that builders throw into huge houses because they know the kids aren't going to get a vote about what house their parents buy. Honey's house was huge. This bedroom was maybe ten feet by nine feet. Just big enough for a twin bed and a chest of drawers. I hadn't seen Honey's suite, but I was sure that it wasn't ten feet by nine feet.

The bed that someone had tucked Gary into was a queen-size bed, and that meant there wasn't room for a chest of drawers of any size and that Kyle and I were very close to each other. If he'd been a werewolf, I'd have been worried.

"So," Kyle said mildly as he shut the bedroom door. "We're driving to the bus station in Pasco with the guy who had stopped at my house to look for you. Warren, I want you to know, told me that he was a distant relative of yours. I don't know if that's the truth—and at this point, I don't think I care. But I digress. The important part is that while I'm driving Gary to the bus station, I'm still at the point where I trust that what Warren tells me will be the truth. I'm just beginning to get a funny feeling, though, because I can't figure out why Warren has been so concerned about ID. Even to get on a bus, Mercy, you need ID, but everyone has ID. Why is Warren worried if this guy—you know, your relative—if he has ID?

"I've just finished driving over the cable bridge when suddenly, Gary screams in my ear like Girl Number Two in some horror flick. It sounds like he is dying, so I pull right over on the side of the road instead of putting my foot on the gas and ramming the guy in front of me, which is that first reflex impulse I have when someone screams in my ear." He paused, looking at me.

I figured that only a stupid person would say anything until he'd wound all the way down, so I stayed quiet and tried to look sympathetic.

Kyle's foot tapped a rapid tattoo as he waited for me to respond. Finally, he said, "Warren gets out and opens the back door like he isn't surprised. Like he expected *Gary Laughingdog*"—he bit out Gary's name with special emphasis, separating the last name until the "Laughing" and the "dog" were really two separate words—"to break out screaming at any time. Warren whips off his belt and shoves it between Gary's teeth because, Mercy, this relative of yours that we were just going to shove on a bus is having a grand mal seizure.

"So here I am, busy worried about what kind of people I'm associating with who are callously throwing a relative on a bus who has grand mal seizures so often that my *partner* isn't surprised by it—when my brain catches up with what the newscaster on the radio has been announcing. Can you imagine my amazement that Gary Laughingdog escaped from the Coyote Ridge Corrections Center? All this time when I thought I was escorting your relative, I've really been harboring an escaped convict." He waited again, but I wasn't that dumb.

He rocked forward as if he wanted to pace, but there just wasn't room. "I explode all over my partner because it is instantly obvious to me that you and Adam both knew where he'd come from—because you'd talked to him before he came to my house. Imagine my surprise when I found out that Warren had known, too. I'm the only one left out of the 'hey, this guy is an escaped convict' knowledge circle."

This is when I could have spoken, after he enunciated his problem, but he didn't stop talking so I could explain.

"I told Warren when he lied to me about what he was that I don't like lies," he said. "Liars can't be trusted. He told me that he would never lie to me again."

He stopped talking then, but I had no words. I'd forgotten. I'd forgotten how much he hated to be lied to. How could I have forgotten, when he and Warren had broken up over it? Not over Warren's being a werewolf but over Warren's not telling Kyle what he was. They'd gotten back together, but it had been rough.

Gary moved his arm over his eyes. "Drama, drama, drama," he whispered.

"You shut up," I snapped. Warren and Kyle were going to break up, and it was my fault.

"You quit yelling while you're in the room with the guy with a migraine," Gary told me. "Look, Kyle. I get you. We've been trying to keep the whole escaped-prisoner thing away from you—give you plausible deniability—but that's obviously done. You go call the police and let them know you found me, and I'll go quietly. You'll keep your license—because you called them as soon as you found out, and we'll all support you on that. But if you do, you have to know that it means that Warren and Adam will die."

Kyle's whole body turned to face the man on the bed. "What?"

"If I'm not here when the pack faces off with Guayota," Gary said, very slowly and clearly like people do when they are talking to young children or people who don't speak English, "then Guayota wins by killing all the wolves. That's what this last *Seeing* was about."

He pulled his arm off his eyes and squinted at me. "Let this be a lesson to you, pup. Do not deal with Coyote. He'll screw you over every time. Had I had this vision while lying in prison, I'd have let everyone die because, hey, what did I care? Bunch of werewolves I don't know bite the big one, big whoop. But Coyote waits until I meet everyone first. I *like* Adam. He's what an Alpha is supposed to be and so seldom is. I like Warren, and I really, really think Honey is hot. I can't just go back to jail—no matter how safe from Coyote—and let them all die."

"Coyote?" asked Kyle. He looked at me and frowned.

"Dear old Dad," said Gary. "Mine and hers. That's how we're related."

"Not mine," I snapped. "My father was Joe Old Coyote who rode bulls and killed vampires. The vampires killed him and made it look like a car wreck. If my father was Coyote, then he abandoned my mother when she was sixteen and pregnant. If Coyote was my father I'd have to hunt him down and kill him."

My father was Joe Old Coyote, who died on a road in the middle of nowhere in Montana before I was born. He didn't know that he was just a shell Coyote wore because Coyote had grown bored. He wouldn't have left us if he'd had a choice. After he died, my mother had to leave me with werewolves because she didn't know what to do with me and because she was too young to work at most jobs full-time. So she'd left me. And I was a freaking grown-up, so I could just deal. I was happy. My mother was happy.

And my father was dead. And if my father was Joe Old Coyote, I didn't have to kill him.

Both Gary and Kyle were looking at me oddly, and I realized that I must have said all of that out loud. I cleared my throat. "So, yes, daddy issues. Both of us, Kyle. Gary was in jail because Coyote managed to facilitate his breaking the law, then left him to be picked up by the police." I looked at Gary. "You know, if you wanted to be really paranoid, you might consider that Coyote wouldn't be excited about having Guayota here, in Coyote's playground. You might think that maybe you were in jail so that you were somewhere I could find you when I needed to ask someone how to get it touch with Coyote."

He closed his eyes and nodded. "I've had the same thought. But didn't you come find me because some fae dude wanted the walking stick you gave Coyote? He'd have to have manipulated him, too."

I dropped to the floor because it was just barely possible. Here I'd been complaining about Christy's manipulations. But she was minor-league next to Coyote.

"It wouldn't take much, right?" I mused. "Beauclaire isn't fond of humans. And here is one of his father's artifacts in the hands of a human despite all the fae who'd tried to take it from her. I'm sure Coyote knows a few of the fae who might whisper in Beauclaire's ear." I looked at Gary. "Tell me *I'm* just being paranoid."

"The thing you have to ask yourself is this," Gary said. "Is it Guayota Coyote wants to rid the world of, or us? I *can* tell you that he won't care if we die. Death doesn't mean the same thing to him as it does to us. Possibly it's a test of strength. Survival is one of those Catch-22s. If you live through one of Coyote's games, it delights him because then he can push you into one that is more dangerous. On second thought"—he opened his eyes and looked at Kyle—"*please*, call the cops."

"Why were you in jail?" asked Kyle.

"Seriously? Do you know how many guilty people are in jail? None." Gary's voice rose to imitate a woman's voice. "Honest. I didn't kill him. He fell on my knife. Ten times."

"I saw *Chicago*," said Kyle. "You won't lie to me because Mercy can tell if you lie. And I'm a lawyer, and, current circumstances aside, I'm pretty good at hearing lies, too."

Gary stared intently at him for a moment, then shrugged, letting the tension in his body slide away. "I guess it doesn't matter to me. I could tell you that I got drunk, stole a car—though I'm pretty sure that was Coyote, but I was drunk, so who knows. Then I stole four cases of two-hundred-dollar Scotch—I'm pretty sure that might have been Coyote, too, but all I remember is watching him opening one of the bottles. Finally, I parked the car in front of the police station and passed out in the backseat with all but one of the bottles of Scotch until the police found me the next morning. That I am sure was Coyote. If I told you all of that, it would be true."

He looked at Kyle, his eyes narrowed in a way that told me his head was still hurting. "However, the real reason I went to prison was because a few months before I woke up in front of the police station, I slept with the wife of the man who was later my state-appointed lawyer. I didn't know that *he* knew I slept with his wife until *after* I was serving my sentence, when another of his clients was happy to tell me." Gary closed his eyes. "That the car we stole was a police car didn't help."

Gary laughed, winced, then said, "The funny part is that I had not had a drink of alcohol since I went on a five-day bender in 1917 and woke up to find I'd volunteered for the army." He smiled and moved his arm back over his eyes. "It's not safe, you see, to get drunk when Coyote might be watching."

"He's telling the truth," I said, after it became obvious that Gary was through talking.

"And you escaped because you knew that we were about to get hit with some kind of volcano god when we were expecting Mr. Flores the stalker," Kyle said.

Gary grunted. "I didn't know about Mr. Flores. All I knew

was that Mercy was trying to get an artifact back from Coyote. But then somehow this volcano manitou was going to kill someone, and it was connected to Mercy." He looked at me and then away. "And Mercy was my sister."

Kyle rubbed his face, drew in a breath, and looked at the curtain covering the window. Then he said, with a sigh, "Plausible deniability, eh?"

"If you didn't know Gary had escaped from prison, you couldn't be held responsible," I said. "Warren was pretty mad at us for putting you into a situation that could hurt you like that. Adam told him that he'd take care of you and see that you wouldn't get hurt."

"And if you go with the pack to deal with Guayota," Kyle said to Gary, "Warren survives."

Gary shook his head very slowly, like it hurt. "Not how it works. All I know is that if I don't go, they all die. Maybe if I go, we all of us die much more horribly than they would have otherwise." He moved his arm so he could see Kyle's face and grimaced. "Yes. I recognize that expression. Anyone who deals with Coyote wears that expression eventually. And no, I don't know why my going makes a difference."

Kyle stretched his neck to relieve tension and gave a miserable half laugh. "I suppose if Warren's possible death makes me feel like this, I should give him the benefit of the doubt, right?"

"People make mistakes," I said. "Even people we love."

"Hell of it is, I'm not sure where the mistake was," said Kyle.

"Not killing Coyote the first time I saw him," said Gary. "Not that he'd have stayed dead, but I think the experience might have made the rest of my life more bearable."

"Kyle," I said. "I love you like a brother. Go out and make up with Warren before he heads out to try to get himself killed."

———

CHRISTY MADE DINNER WITH LUCIA'S AND DARRYL'S help: baked herb-and-flour-encrusted stuffed chicken. I ate it and had seconds. It was very good—and right now I was too scared to be jealous.

Honey didn't have a table big enough to seat the whole pack—and Adam had called the whole pack together. Samuel and Ariana showed up toward the end of dinner.

Elizaveta could have made a spell to make one werewolf resistant to Guayota's elemental fire magic—her term, not mine—but she would have needed a piece of his hair or fingernails. If I'd stuck Guayota's finger in my pocket, she could have used that, but I didn't think we'd have much luck getting it back from the police.

Ariana said she could help. With fireproofing, not finger-stealing.

We all settled down in the big upstairs room to see what she had to offer. She and Samuel stood in front of the big-screen TV.

Dr. Samuel Cornick was tall, compelling but not handsome, and when I was sixteen, I'd thought he was the love of my life. He'd thought I was someone who might be able to give him children that lived. It was a relationship that was doomed to make neither of us happy, and his father, the Marrok, had seen it before we'd fully committed tragedy and so had sent me away. For a long time, I'd compared every man I met to Samuel—Adam was the only one who had stood up to the comparison.

Samuel's mate, Ariana, stood in his shadow. Where he drew the eye, even in a crowded room, she could go unnoticed. Her hair was blond, her eyes gray, her skin clear, and her entire aspect unremarkable. But that was a fae thing. Being too beautiful or too ugly made someone interesting, and mostly, the fae would rather go unnoticed. I'd seen what she really looked like under her glamour, and she was spectacularly beautiful.

"Okay," she said when everyone was in the room. She held Samuel's hand with white-knuckled strength because she was afraid of us, all of us. To say she had a canine phobia was a masterly understatement. "I command earth, air, fire, and water— though not as well as I once did. That I command fire means that I can protect you, some of you, from this demon-god. I don't know how many I can spell. I think it unlikely that I can do more than ten, but probably at least five. Adam, you should pick the ones you need to take with you in order of the most useful in battle."

Adam nodded and stood up, but before he could speak, Samuel said, "I'm going, and she's already tried out the spell on me."

Adam gave him a look.

"This is not my pack," Samuel said to Adam's unspoken comment. "But Mercy is part of my family by my choice, and that makes you, by extension, my brother by marriage. I'm going. You don't get a choice."

So the fear I'd seen in Ariana's eyes hadn't just been because she was in a roomful of werewolves.

Adam said, "I would not have asked, but I'm very glad to have you on our side."

Then he looked around the room, his gaze touching each of us as he spoke. "Guayota is our enemy. He is not our enemy because he hurt one of our own, though he has. He is not our enemy because he violates our territory, though that is also true. He is not our enemy because he attacked my mate. He is not even our enemy because he is evil. He is our enemy because he kills those who cannot protect themselves against him. Because he will not stop until someone stops him."

He paused and took a deep breath. "I have seen him fight—and so have you. I am not sure this is a fight we can win. But there is one thing I do know, and that is that we will not, we cannot, wait around until he kills another innocent. We might die fighting him, but if we do not try and stop him, we are already defeated."

The room was silent and at the same time it echoed with the power of his words.

He looked at Darryl. "We don't always see things the same way, but you have always put the pack first and foremost. I have fought Guayota, and I tell you that without Tad's help, he would have defeated me. Ariana can make us invulnerable to his heat—but you saw the video. I don't know that he can be killed, or if he can, how it might be done. I have spoken to Bran, and if we fail here tonight, then he will send Charles. But Guayota invaded *my* territory. This is my fight. You should also know that Ariana told me what she could and could not do, and I've had time to think. Darryl, I need you to protect the pack if this fight doesn't go well."

He looked around at the whole room, and we were all silent, even Lucia, Jesse, and Christy, who were not pack, even Darryl, who wanted to protest. We were silent because he wanted us to be so, and he was the Alpha. His eyes lingered on mine, and if there was grief in them, I think it was only our mating bond that let me see it. He didn't think he was going to survive this—or he'd have taken Darryl with him.

"I will take the walker Gary Laughingdog, who brings a prophecy that he must come," Adam said into the silence. "Then myself.

The rest of you are volunteers. Feel free to say no because the estimate that Ariana gave me was six wolves. If you would rather not die tonight, or rather wait until another night, there is no shame. Warren?"

Warren drawled his "Yes, boss" without hesitation.

The wolves stirred and began to howl. Emerging from human throats, it was not as pure or carrying as it would have been out of the wolves, but the emotion was the same. There was respect and a celebration of his bravery in accepting and in the honor of being chosen to fight beside his Alpha.

It took Warren entirely by surprise. He grabbed Kyle's hand and held on as his eyes brightened with tears that threatened to spill over.

Warren had spent most of his very long life alone, when wolves are meant to live in packs. I'd first met him while he worked at a gas station near here. I'd introduced him to Adam—who I resented at the time but couldn't help but respect. As Gary had said, Adam was what an Alpha should be, and I'd known it. Adam had welcomed Warren into the pack, but the pack had taken him in with mixed feelings.

Their support told him that there were no mixed feelings left. Not at this moment.

When the howl faded, Adam said, "Honey?"

There was another stir in the pack; this time it was more shock than approval. Women didn't fight, not in traditional packs. Honey was now unmated, which should have left her rank at the lowest of the pack, even below Zack, our new submissive. But Honey wasn't a submissive wolf, not even close.

Honey didn't need *their* approval. She raised her chin, looked at me—because Adam's call had as much to do with me as it did with the pack. She'd resented it when I had refused to leave the traditional relegation of women alone. She'd liked that being married to Peter meant she was low-ranking.

She gave first me, then Warren, for whom she'd always had a soft spot, a savage smile. "Yes, boss," she said.

Me. I thought hard at Adam—and I knew he heard me. *Pick me. If everyone who goes is going to die anyway, why not pick me?*

I need you to survive, he answered me without speaking, without looking at me. *I need to know you survive.*

I need you to survive, too, I thought, but I tried not to send it to him. There was a faint chance he'd listen—and what if one werewolf instead of a coyote made a difference? What if I was the reason he died? So I kept silent.

"I'm sorry," said Christy suddenly, before Adam could name anyone else.

Adam gave her a tender look that she didn't deserve. *God help us and keep us from receiving what we deserve*—it was a favorite saying of my foster father, Bryan.

"It's not your fault, Christy," Adam said. "It is just a case of being in the wrong place at the wrong time."

She got up from the couch where she was sitting next to Auriele. "No. Not that, Adam. I'm sorry that I wasn't strong enough to live your life. I left you—you would never have left me." She looked at me and looked away. The tears on her face weren't crocodile tears, they were the real, unattractive thing complete with runny nose. She still was beautiful. "I'm glad I left, for your sake. You found someone who can stand beside you. I couldn't live with what you are, but that's my problem, not yours." She looked down, then straight into his eyes. "I love you."

If she hadn't done that last part, I would have kissed her—

figuratively speaking—and cried friends. There are some things that honest, honorable people don't do to the people they love. They don't propose marriage on TV. They don't bring home small cuddly animals without checking with their spouses first. And they don't tell their ex-husband they love him in front of a crowd that includes their daughter and his current wife right before he goes off to almost certain death. It didn't help that most of us could tell that she wasn't lying.

Adam said, "Thank you." As if she'd given him a great gift. But he didn't tell her what, exactly, he was thanking her for.

She caught the ambiguity. She gave him a rueful smile and sat down. Auriele hugged her fiercely.

I pulled my legs up and wrapped my arms around them.

Maybe they won't die, I thought. *Maybe something Gary does keeps them from dying.*

All this time, since the first time he kissed me, I'd been worried about growing old, about leaving Adam alone. And it turned out that it was going to be the other way around.

"Paul," Adam said. Paul's name wasn't a surprise, not like Honey's.

Paul nodded, looked at Warren, shook his head, and said, "Yes, boss," with graveyard humor. Paul had tried to kill Warren once because Warren was the wolf just above him in rank and because Warren was gay. Now he was going out to a battle that Adam didn't think they would come back from, and he, like Honey, was telling Warren that he had his back. People can change.

"George."

"Yes, boss," said the quiet policeman.

Maybe I should have kept the walking stick. It had worked against a vampire, against the river devil—surely the river devil had been as powerful—more powerful with its ability to remake the world—and it had been the walking stick that had brought it down.

"Mary Jo?" he asked.

"Fighting fires is what I do," she told him. "Yes, boss."

Mary Jo loved my mate, too. She'd protect him if she could. I was glad that she was going. My grief was so huge that I had no room for jealousy.

The walking stick . . . was made of wood and silver, and no matter how magical it was, wood was wood. I had no doubt that someone could throw it into a campfire and it would emerge unscathed, but a campfire was not a volcano. If the walking stick could do some great magic that would kill a fire elemental like Guayota, Coyote would have told me. I was pretty sure Coyote would have told me.

"Alec?" I didn't know Alec as well as I did some of the other wolves. He was a friend of Paul's, and Paul didn't like me much.

Maybe Coyote would have told me if the walking stick could kill Guayota. He'd told me that mortal means could not harm the tibicenas when in their tibicena form. Did he mean that the walking stick might?

"Yes, boss."

I was pretty sure that the walking stick had served Coyote's purpose by showing me what lay within the tibicenas. If it would have been effective against them, he'd have told me—or couched it in some kind of riddle that I'd still be puzzling out when one of the tibicenas killed me.

"That's enough," said Adam. "If Ariana has more magic when she has dealt with us, then I will call for more volunteers."

Because of her fear of the wolves, Ariana worked with them

one at a time, in the kitchen. I thought Samuel was going to go with her, but he came and sat next to me instead.

"We don't have any idea on how to kill this thing," Samuel said. "Ariana tells me that as far as she knows, the only way to kill a primitive elemental like Guayota would be to destroy his volcano, and even then, he would not die for centuries."

"El Teide is the third highest volcano in the world," I told him, pressing my cheekbone into my knees. The burn reminded me that turning to my other cheek would have been smarter. "I think it's a little beyond our capabilities. Killing the tibicenas, his two giant dogs, might do it. But you can only kill their mortal forms, when they look like mostly normal dogs instead of polar-bear-sized monsters. I suspect they are not going to be fighting werewolves in their mortal forms."

"Ariana would come with us," he told me, "but she doesn't have the power she once had, not even a tenth of it. And fire-dogs are too close to her nightmares; there is no guarantee that she wouldn't do as much damage to us as she would to Guayota and his beasts."

"I'd come with you," I said, "but Adam doesn't want me to die, and for some reason, he seems to think that's his decision to make."

Samuel hugged me. "Don't mourn us until we're dead," he said.

"I'll spit on your graves," I told him, and he laughed, the bastard.

"Nice," said Adam, crouching in front of me. "I had to watch you go up against the river devil."

"That sucked, too," I told him without looking up from my knees. "But we had a plan that we thought might work."

"Based on a story," he said roughly. "It wasn't a plan; it was a suicide mission."

I looked up and met his eyes. I didn't say, *So is this*. He knew it; it was in his eyes.

"Honey has made her suite available to us," he said. "Will you come?"

I unlocked my fingers from around my legs and rose out of Samuel's embrace and went into Adam's.

"Yes, please," I whispered.

No one in the room spoke, but they watched us leave, knowing where we were going, and I didn't care.

Honey's suite was a bedroom, office, and bathroom, all done in shades of cool gray. It surprised me until I remembered that this had been Peter's room, too. The gray suited the man he'd been.

We didn't speak. All of the words had already been said. When he stripped my clothes off me, I noticed that Honey kept her house a little cooler than ours because I was cold—or maybe that was just fear.

Naked, I took off Adam's clothes and folded them as I set them down, as if taking care with his clothing might show him how much I longed to take care of him. Unusually, his body was slow to awaken, and so was mine—but that was okay because this was about saying good-bye. About impregnating my skin with his scent so that I would have him with me after he was gone. About remembering exactly—exactly—what the soft skin just to the side of his hip bone felt like under my fingertips and under my lips. It was about love and loss and the unbearable knowledge that this could be the last time. Was probably the last time.

I could feel Ariana's magic on him, and I hoped that it would be enough to keep him safe.

He lay on his back on Honey's bed and pulled me on top of him as he'd done the first time we'd made love. He let me touch him until his body was shuddering, and sweat rose on his forehead. He pulled my face up to his and kissed me tenderly despite the speed of his pulse.

"My turn," he whispered. I nodded, and he rolled me beneath him and returned the favor, seeking out *his* favorite places and the ones where I was most sensitive. He brought me to climax, then lay with his head on my stomach, his arms around me, catching his breath before he started to build the pace again.

We ended as we'd begun, with me on him, watching his face as I moved on him and he in me. The expressions he wore told me to speed up or slow down until his bright yellow eyes opened wide, and he grabbed my hips and helped me take us both where we were going.

I lay down on him and put my face in his neck, and if I cried, I didn't show him my tears. He ran his hands up and down my back until I could pretend I hadn't been crying.

"I suck at this," I told him. "I suck at words when they count."

He smiled at me. "I know."

"I understand," I told him. "I understand why you have to go and why I have to stay. I think that you are doing the right thing, the only thing you can do. I wish . . ." My stomach hurt and it would have been kindness to put me out of my misery, but I wasn't going to share that with Adam.

I know, he said.

"You weren't supposed to get that," I told him.

"I know that, too," he said, his voice tender. "You should know that you can't hide things from me."

"Good," I said, my voice fierce. "Good. Then you know, you *know* I love you."

We showered the sweat off our bodies in Honey's shower,

wordless. His hands were warm, and he was patient with my need to touch and touch. I wished futilely that this time would last forever, but eventually he turned off the water and we dressed.

"Willis asked you to call the police if you figured out where Juan Flores was," I said, jerking a comb through my hair.

Adam took the comb away and took over the job. His touch was gentle and slow, as if there were all the time in the world to do the job properly. As if untangled hair mattered.

"He did," Adam said. "And I saw enough cannon fodder in 'Nam to last me a lifetime."

He saw my flinch and paused in his combing to kiss me. Neither of us talked again until he set the comb aside.

"I love you," I told him rawly. "And if you don't come back, I *will* spit on your grave."

He smiled, but not enough to bring on his dimple. "I know you do, and I know you will. Mercedes Athena Thompson Hauptman, if I have not said it, you should know that you brought joy into my life when I thought there was no joy left in the world."

"Don't," I said, tears spilling over as I frantically scrubbed them away. "Don't say things like that when I'm going to have to go out there and face all of them. Don't you make me cry." Again.

He smiled, this time with dimple, and mopped my face with the shirt he hadn't put on yet. "You're tough, you'll deal," he said. "And at least I didn't leave you a letter."

13

~~

THEY LEFT AT DUSK. ARIANA HAD ONLY MANAGED TO magic the wolves through Mary Jo, so Alec was with those of us who waved them out. When they were gone, most of the pack dispersed to their own houses. Lucia busied herself cleaning up the havoc that the pack had made of Honey's house, and Christy and Jesse helped her. I understood the need to do something.

"Mercy." It was Ariana, but it was something more, too, so I was careful to move slowly when I turned around.

"I have to go," she said. "I wish . . . but I cannot stay with my magic depleted and so many wolves about."

I wrapped my arms around myself. "I understand. Thank you, Ariana. You gave them a chance."

She looked down. "I hope so," she said in a low voice. "I hope so."

I didn't know what to say to her fear, not with mine so wild in my heart. So I watched her get into Samuel's car and drive off, and tried not to remember that I knew the address.

I went back into the house through the back door. Christy was cooking with Lucia and Auriele. They looked like they were making enough food for an army, even though everyone was gone.

"Where's Jesse?" I asked.

"Upstairs with Darryl," Christy said. "She doesn't want to talk to me, but maybe you'll have better luck." Christy looked tired and worried. Her eyes were red. I hoped mine weren't. "If I had stayed here, where I was needed, everyone would be safe now."

I wiped my hands over my face to cover whatever expression might have crossed it. She wasn't trying to shut me out, she was trying to save Adam and the rest.

"If I had married a doctor, like my mother told me to, then I wouldn't have Joel to grieve over," Lucia said unexpectedly. She was good at being quiet and unobtrusive. "And that would be a waste. If you had stayed here, this might not have happened, but maybe you'd have gotten in a car wreck and died." She shrugged. "It does no good to play with what-ifs."

"Well said," Auriele told her. "'Play the hand you have,' my papa liked to say."

I left them to their conversation and trotted up the stairs, where I could hear a movie running quietly. Darryl sat on one side of the couch nearest to the TV and Jesse on the other.

I sat down in the middle. "So," I said to Darryl, "do you think Korra is going to be as good an avatar as Aang?"

"Who's Aang?" he asked.

"You started him with Korra?" I accused Jesse. "That's not okay. It's like reading the last chapter of the book first."

"Honey doesn't have *The Last Airbender* series," Jesse said in a low voice. "It was Korra or bust."

"I think I should check on the cooks," Darryl said. He left with cowardly haste.

I reached over and turned up the volume of the show until I was pretty sure we had privacy.

"I like Korra," Jesse told me in a melancholy voice. "She's not perfect, but she tries hard."

"Like your mom," I said.

She nodded. "I love her."

"And she loves you back," I said.

She nodded. "She does. She's not perfect, but she's my mom, you know?"

"You've met my mother," I told her, and she laughed. I loved my mom, too, but I was very glad she lived in Portland.

"I'm glad I have you and Dad," she said. "That way, it's okay that Mom is . . ."

Flaky? Selfish? Horrible?

"Mom," she concluded.

We watched Korra for a while longer. Darryl rejoined us as soon as we turned the volume back down.

"I am not wanted in the kitchen," he said. Darryl loved to cook. "Christy says that men can't cook."

"You're a great cook," Jesse told him.

He smiled at her, a gentle smile he saved for Auriele and Jesse. "I know. I'm better than any of them, but they won't listen to me."

"I think I like Korra better than Aang," I said after we'd watched another five minutes. "She gets to go do things instead of waiting around for other people."

"I hear you," agreed Darryl.

"I think I'm going to go check on Medea," I said.

———————

WITH LUCIA'S BIG DOG IN THE HOUSE, WE'D SHUT Medea in the tack room out in the stables. The horses in the pasture whinnied at me when I walked by. I threw them a couple of flakes of alfalfa hay, though there was plenty of grass in the pasture. A couple of extra flakes wouldn't hurt them.

Medea greeted me with frantic purrs. I sat down on the wooden floor next to her and petted her, trying not to think.

There were two Western saddles bedecked with silver on wooden saddle racks and another pair that were more everyday trail saddles. Blue ribbons and big, oversized awards plastered one wall. Everything was covered with dust, as if, like the horses, they had not been used since Peter died.

Eventually, Darryl came out to talk.

"Hey, girl," he said from the doorway.

"Hey."

"Jesse was summoned as taster in the kitchen," he told me. "They should be over at the house by now, in the middle of changing." Adam's plan had been to find a quiet spot near Guayota's place so that all the wolves could change. Then they would wait until the small hours of the night and take what advantage surprise might offer them.

I'd been keeping track of the time, too. "I'll let you know if our mating bond tells me anything," I told him, my attention firmly on the way Medea's rabbit-soft coat rippled under my fingers.

"We'll all feel it if anyone dies," Darryl told me after a very long moment. "Why don't you come into the house? I'll keep Christy in line."

I looked at him and raised my eyebrows. He smiled sheepishly. "Okay. But I expect she'll behave in front of everyone, anyway."

"It's not Christy," I assured him. "I just don't have any comfort for anyone left in me, Darryl. And if someone even looks at me with sympathy . . . no. I'll wait here for a while more."

He hesitated. "I told him I would look after you." His voice was soft, as soft as I'd ever heard it.

I wiped my eyes angrily but managed a half laugh. "Shut up. Samuel told me not to mourn until I had something to mourn about."

"Yeah," Darryl said softly. "Yeah."

He leaned against the doorframe and kept me company for a few minutes before returning to the house. It would be hours before we knew anything, anything at all. Tibicenas could be killed, temporarily, if they caught them in dog form. They were going to try to take them out as early in the fight as they could, and if that didn't destroy Guayota or send him back where he came from, they would then concentrate on Guayota. Seven werewolves and a walker against a god.

I curled up around Medea and prayed as fervently as I ever had. I had faith that it would help. But death isn't a tragedy to God, only to those left behind.

I finished, and only then realized that Stefan was sitting on a hay bale on the wall on the far side of the stable aisle, where he could look through the tack room door and see me.

"I didn't want to interrupt," he said. "I told you I'd come talk tonight, but I had some trouble finding you." He paused. "I talked to Darryl at the house. He told me what's going on. A volcano god, eh? If I'd realized exactly what that address meant . . . I'm not sure I'd have gotten it for you." He looked away. "I think the talk I promised you ought to wait until—until later, I suppose."

I'd forgotten about the talk. Somehow, it didn't seem important to fuss about something he could have done nothing about. Any other day, I might have gotten self-righteously angry. I'd worked really hard not to freak at the bonds I shared with Adam and the pack. I wasn't sure I had it in me not to freak about a bond with a vampire, even one I liked. But today I couldn't find the energy to lie to myself and believe that blaming Stefan for the mess would make anything better.

"It's okay," I told him. "It wasn't your fault. I understand why you didn't tell me that the bond was still real. I agreed to it in the first place, and I'd do it again, even knowing the consequences. Lies aren't always destructive, are they? Sometimes a few lies hurt no one. You have nothing to apologize for, and I have nothing to be mad about."

He patted the hay bale beside him. I picked up Medea, got to my feet, and stepped down into the stable aisle. He smelled like popcorn, and it was subtly reassuring. I sat down next to him, and Medea deserted my lap for his.

His fingers found the favored spot under her ear, and she closed her eyes and purred. I leaned against his shoulder, and he waited with me.

The barn was dark, the only light came from the bare bulb in the tack room. It smelled of leather, hay, and horses. I could hear the two horses eating outside and Medea's purring. An owl hooted from somewhere nearby. In the distance, very far distance, I could hear a car's engine. Someone coming home from a Saturday shopping expedition or an early movie.

I closed my eyes. Stefan's arm tightened and loosened under my temple as he petted Medea. I couldn't hear his heartbeat or listen to him breathe. Usually when he forgot to make himself humanlike, the oddness made me uncomfortable, but tonight it was peaceful. I only wanted one heartbeat in my ear.

Adam's.

The horses took off running, their hooves a rapid thunder in the night. I pulled my head off Stefan's shoulder to see if I could hear what spooked them.

"The wind changed, and they smelled me," Stefan said. "That's all. They'll be back in a few minutes because they aren't really scared." He leaned his head back against the wall. "I remember when all I wanted was to ride a horse. We had four at my home when I was growing up. Two were plow horses. One was a pony my mother used to go to market. The fourth was a riding horse that just showed up one day wearing the remains of a saddle. One of his knees was enlarged, and it was sore for months afterward. It never really went down, but it didn't seem to bother him much after he rested up. We kept waiting for someone to come claim him, but no one ever did. I learned to ride on him."

The car was getting closer though still probably a couple of miles out. Something about it made me nervous—I stood up. It sounded like the car Juan Flores had been driving when he broke into my garage.

"Stefan," I said. "How many people can you do your instant transport with, if we're only talking a couple of miles?"

"Four. Maybe five if I don't need to be conscious after the last one. You need me to take you somewhere?"

"Not me," I said. "There are only three other houses on this road, and the rest of the land is farming. I've heard a Toyota V6, two different Chevy trucks, a Ford truck, and a Mercedes while I've been here. There is a Chevy Malibu approaching us right now, and Guayota drove a Malibu when he attacked me at my garage."

"You think Guayota is coming here," Stefan said.

"Yes, I do."

If Stefan could get Jesse, Lucia, and Christy away from here, they might make it out alive. I didn't think I could convince Darryl to go. Or Auriele.

I put Medea down. If the worst happened, I didn't want her trapped in the stable. I grabbed a pitchfork that was leaning against the wall and set off for Adam's SUV at a brisk walk, my ear tuned to the still-distant car. "Would you take four people from here to—" Where? "My house." The Vanagon was still at the ruins of my garage, but Jesse's car would be there. "Once you get them all there, call Adam's cell phone. You'll probably get a man named Gary. Tell him what happened. Then get everyone into Jesse's car and drive."

I opened the passenger side of the SUV and retrieved the S&W 29 and a box of ammunition from under the front seat. The car was still coming, so I headed for the house at a sprint.

Stefan stayed beside me. "I could take you out of here."

"You do, and I will never forgive you." I opened the back door but didn't go in. "I'm second in the pack, Stefan. That means I don't desert anyone. If you can get the humans out of here, I will owe you for the rest of my life. Take Auriele if you can."

He looked down at me, then did the strangest thing. He kissed me. A quick butterfly kiss that gave me no chance to react. "I'll do my best to keep your lambs safe, Mercy. If I can get them all to safety, I'll return."

"No," I said. "Vampires and fire don't mix. Don't throw yourself away, Stefan. Let Adam know that Guayota is coming here— Ariana magicked him, and some of the wolves, so they can survive fire. They'll come as soon as they can."

———————

THE PITCHFORK WAS A WEAPON OF LAST RESORT, AND I set it under some bushes, where, hopefully, I could grab it in a hurry, and the bad guys wouldn't notice it. I'd left Darryl and Christy arguing with Auriele, but Jesse and Lucia had already been taken to safety.

I wasn't out front long when Darryl came out the door, turning off the porch and yard lights as he did so. He strolled out to me and listened to the car. The driver had been driving back and forth a bit. Country roads can be tricky when all you have is a direct line to your target—was Guayota tracking Christy somehow?

"How sure are you about this being Guayota?" Darryl asked.

I shook my head. "Could be a lost tourist. Could be a couple of kids out exploring. Could be a neighbor who bought a new car. Did you talk Auriele into going?"

"No," said Darryl. "That took Christy." He started stripping off his clothes and began his change at the same time. I could tell by the sparkly feeling in the werewolf magic that followed all the wolves around. Tonight, it felt especially obvious, as though all my senses were on high alert. "Never thought I'd be grateful that Christy can lead people around by their noses before. Your tame vampire took Christy and promised to be back for Auriele. I am very grateful that all vampires can't jump places like that. They'd rule the world, no doubt."

Darryl dropped his shirt to the ground and started shedding wristwatch and rings. "If this is Guayota, we don't have a chance."

"I know." All day I'd had this feeling of impending doom. Usually, I'm the optimist in the party, but today was different.

"It's going to take me about twelve minutes to change even

pushing it, and whoever that is, they'll be here in two. I called Adam's phone, but no one picked up. Likely right about now they are all in the middle of changing, and no one will be able to listen to the message. Stefan said to tell you that he'd keep calling until he got hold of someone. He said that if he had the juice left, he'd come back and help. But from the looks of him when he vanished with Christy, I think it'll be a while. If that car is Guayota, it will be too late for the two of us. I watched that fight in the garage, and Adam says you'd both have been toast if it weren't for Tad."

"Yes," I said. "It's too bad Tad is locked up in Fairyland."

"We could run," Darryl said.

"No," I told him. "The tibicenas are faster than we are. Gary and I ran from them, and if Coyote hadn't pulled one last trick, they'd have caught us. This is pack territory—" I tapped my foot on the ground. "That helps, in a fight." Not much, but we were going to need everything we had.

"I'm going to the barn to finish changing. It will be safer if I have a few seconds to orient myself. My wolf is aggressive when I first change." He kicked off his shoes and dropped his slacks. "I'll come help as soon as I can."

"If—" I said. "If there is no use, you run, okay?"

Darryl shook his head, his eyes bright gold in the moonlight. His teeth were sharper than they'd been a second ago. "My wolf won't leave you, Mercy."

He left, a dark shadow among darker shadows, almost invisible to my eyes, but I heard his rapid footfalls as he ran for the barn.

I saw the headlights of the oncoming car for just a moment before the engine cut out, and, a moment later, the headlights went dark.

Night is seldom really silent. The light wind rustled the branches of the trees in the yard and the grass in the nearby fields. Spring frogs croaked, and the night hunters added their calls. But, gradually, the other sounds died and left only the wind.

The odds that the car was Guayota's skyrocketed into the certainty zone. Our best chance was for me to kill the tibicenas, one of whom was my friend, and then to hold Guayota off in the hope that, somehow, someone was able to reach Adam. Gary could answer the phone. Maybe that was why he'd had to go with them.

Maybe Guayota would finish off Darryl and me, then head back to his home, where he'd find Adam and the others waiting for him. Probably he'd track down Christy, if that's what he was doing. It must not be a perfect method of finding her, because she was gone and he was still coming. Maybe Guayota would manage to kill us all—it felt like that kind of night.

From the house, I heard Cookie bark an alert. She was answered by two hunting howls, high-pitched and hungry, one on either side of me. Judging by what I had learned while Gary and I had been chased by the pair of tibicenas, they were maybe a hundred yards apart. The sound they made wasn't the same one that had made my blood freeze when Coyote had taken Gary and me out. Maybe that meant they were still in a vulnerable form, something I could kill.

A darker shadow moved where there hadn't been a shadow before, and Juan Flores, who was Guayota, stepped out where I could see him. I didn't bother aiming my gun at him, though I remembered that he'd staggered back when I'd shot him before. He stopped at the edge of the lawn.

"Where is she?" he asked. "Where have you put her?"

He looked so human—but so did I, I supposed.

"She's gone," I told him. "We sent her away when we heard your car."

"I don't understand you," he said, a faint frown between his eyebrows.

"I know," I told him. For a moment I wasn't scared, just sad. He was so lost. "She's not who you think she is."

"Yes," he said, and, for a moment, the sadness in his voice echoed mine. "Yes, she is. Do you think that I would not recognize the face of my beloved? I looked across the room, and there she was—she knew it, too. I come to you this night, made strong from hot new blood, but I need her to feel complete. Without her by my side, I am always hungry."

More bodies somewhere, Tony, I thought.

"We are ready to renew the hunt, and she cannot be hidden from me," continued Flores in this creepy, reasonable voice I remembered from before. "But she might be hurt if we are forced to continue to hunt her, that is the nature of a hunt. I don't want to hurt her. If you tell me where she is, I won't hurt her."

He was sincere. He didn't want to hurt her. I thought of Kyle's story and wondered if perhaps he had not meant to hurt the goddess he'd kidnapped and raped. Intention and results are often different.

"No," I said.

As soon as I refused, Flores's eyes flared red, and his face, though still human-featured, lost any resemblance to a real human expression. "Take her," he said.

Something dark and hot moved in the darkness, and I raised the gun and fired at the tibicena charging from my right as rapidly as I could, though even with my night vision, all I could see were its red eyes, as if it somehow drew the darkness around itself like a cloak.

This was not the dog that I'd killed in my garage; this was the bigger, faster version I'd seen the possibility of when Coyote had taken me to visit Guayota's house. As Coyote had promised, the bullets—and I knew from the bright spots that appeared and vanished on the tibicena's body that I was hitting it—didn't even slow it down. When I felt its too-hot breath, I dropped the gun and dove for my pitchfork.

And then we danced.

I could not trust my sight to tell me where it was, but the coyote knew, and I let her guide my steps. The pitchfork was a better weapon against the tibicena than the mop, crowbar, or wrench had been against Guayota. The long wooden handle didn't heat up, and the metal ends didn't burn as long as I didn't leave them on the tibicena too long, because it had quickly become apparent that the tibicena, like Guayota, was a creature of fire, of the volcano where it had been birthed. As a test, I hit the beast hard, sinking the tines in a few inches, then jerking them out.

The wounds glowed red, and something bubbled out for a moment, but it took two seconds—I counted—for the holes to close. I didn't dare hit it any harder, or I'd lose my weapon. The wounds also disturbed whatever it was that kept me from seeing the tibicena, and I caught a glimpse of it, huge and hairy.

Guayota was turning in a slow circle, ignoring my fight with his tibicena as he searched for something—Christy.

I danced faster.

For a few minutes, we were at a stalemate, the tibicena and I. I couldn't hurt it, but I was moving too fast for it to hit me. As long as I could keep the speed up, and my coyote could sense its attacks, I was okay. A few minutes is a long time in a fight—and all I had to do was hold out long enough for Darryl to come.

But there were two tibicenas. I caught a glimpse of the second one when it slapped me on the head with its paw.

———

I STOOD ON CRACKED BLACKTOP IN A SCHOOL YARD. There was a swing set in front of me, and Coyote sat on the only swing, moving it back and forth a few inches by wiggling his bare toes on the ground. It was one of those swings you see in parks and schools, with thick chains attached to a big, flat strip of rubber. The pink scrunchie was gone, his braid bound by a strip of white leather.

"I'm dreaming," I said flatly.

"You're dying," corrected Coyote, lifting his head from where he'd been watching his feet, to meet my eyes. "Your neck is broken. Do you feel any different? I always wondered what other people feel when they are dying. For me it is usually like this—" He let go of the chains and clapped his hands once. "And I'm back to normal except not quite where I was a moment ago."

"How do I kill Guayota?"

He shook his head and backed up slowly, letting the swing ride up his back. "You can't. It isn't possible. Besides, you are dying." It didn't sound like my death bothered him very much. He tilted his head, and said, "Do you know that burn on your cheek looks like war paint?"

"Gary thinks you're just playing with us," I told him.

Coyote nodded soberly as he hopped gracefully on the swing and let it carry him forward, then back. "Gary has reason to, but he doesn't think like you do. He thinks—Coyote hates me and has me thrown in jail." He leaned into the swing and used his legs and back to build momentum. "You think—what good comes from Gary Laughingdog in jail with the gift of prophecy he hates so much? Could it be that perhaps, just perhaps, both of Coyote's children have a chance of surviving if they are working together?" He gave me a sly look. "Not that it wasn't funny to see his face when he realized we'd stolen a police car, and he was parked in front of the police station."

I thought about what he'd said. "Why did you show me the tibicenas?"

"Didn't you want to save your friend Joel?"

"You answer a lot of questions with questions."

"Do I?" His smile turned smug, and he leaped out of the swing, landing on his feet but letting his body fall forward until his hands rested lightly on the ground. He lowered his eyelids and suddenly there was nothing lighthearted, nothing funny about him, just a primordial fierceness that burned down my spine.

"I guess you aren't dead yet, are you?" he whispered, and the words wrapped around me as my vision went dark. "Good thing coyotes are hard to kill."

I OPENED MY EYES AND REALIZED I WAS CRUMPLED on the cool damp grass, and there was a tibicena crouched over me, licking the long wound in my arm. I couldn't move. My body knew that moving would hurt, and it just wouldn't respond to my urgent demands that it do so.

I could hear fighting, but it was Auriele's battle cry that let me take my eyes off the tibicena guarding me.

I'd never seen Darryl and Auriele fight together, and they were beautiful. For the first time in my life, I wished I were a singer like the Marrok and both of his sons were because only music would do them justice.

Auriele was still in human form and she held my pitchfork as a weapon. Her clothes were burned, and, I imagined, hidden by the night, there were also burns on her skin. She was muscle and grace and speed as she stabbed and pivoted, jumped and dodged around her husband.

Darryl's brindle coat made him nearly as hard to track as the tibicenas' magic made them. Most wolves fight with instinct. Some, as I had tonight, fight with instinct and training. But a rare few hold on to enough humanity to use strategy. And that strategy was what made him and Auriele so impressive. He charged and leaped, she struck and rolled, and somehow neither of them was where they'd been when the tibicena who wasn't guarding me lunged and tangled herself up with Guayota.

If it had only been the tibicena they fought, I would have had no fear.

Guayota, even in his fiery-dog form, was not as large as his tibicena, but there was no question who was the nastier predator. While the tibicena, Darryl, and Auriele fought with everything in them, Guayota played. Darryl bled from a dozen small wounds and, as I watched, Guayota struck him again, and a shallow cut stretched from Darryl's shoulder to his hip. It was a wound from Guayota's claw only, without the heat he could generate, though the wet grass smoked, and he left blackened patches wherever he stood for longer than a breath.

Are you going to let them die while you watch? Impossible to tell if the voice was Coyote's or my own.

My muscles would just not move. I struggled like a bodybuilder trying to lift weights that were a hundred pounds too heavy, and the effort built up to a growl in my chest and out my throat.

The tibicena quit licking my arm and growled back.

I stopped struggling as I met its eyes briefly and saw Joel in them. The tibicena shook his head, and the long, rocklike hairs that ruffed his neck rattled together. The connection broken between us, he went back to my arm. He had worked a piece of skin loose and was tearing it away, swallowing it.

I had a terrible, wonderful idea.

"Joel," I said, and the tongue that had been traveling back to my arm paused, and his eyes met mine, again, eyes that were a dark, sullen red that was more like garnets than rubies.

Didn't you want to save your friend Joel? Coyote had asked me when I asked him why he'd shown me what the tibicenas were. And I'd seen that the spells that tied Joel to Guayota's immortal child were a lot like pack bonds.

I didn't have the walking stick, but I could see the struggle that Joel still fought. Stefan had said something about bonds when he'd been apologizing for not breaking the one between us. He'd implied that a bond taken willingly was stronger than one that was forced.

"Answer the questions I ask you, and I can help," I said, my tongue thick in my mouth. I had practice drawing on my mate's power, and now I drew it around me, finding that I could borrow a little strength. That was useful, but the important part of Adam's power that I preempted was his authority. "You don't have to say your response out loud. Joel Arocha, I see you."

Garnet eyes glittered with borrowed light.

"Will you join with us, the Columbia Basin Pack, to hunt, to fight, to live and run under the full moon?" There were ritual words, but I'd been taught that the ritual was secondary to intent in all werewolf magic. I thought of Joel—tough, thoughtful, and big-hearted—and welcomed him into my family.

I paused but held his eyes. "I claim you," I told him, feeling the familiar gathering of pack magic until it burned in my throat, until the next words were determined more by the magic than by me. "We claim you, Joel Arocha, son of Texas, son of the Canary Islands, guardian of four-footed cousins. By my flesh and blood that is the flesh and blood that belongs to the Alpha of the Columbia Basin Pack is our bond sealed. From this day forward, you are mine to me and mine."

Pack ties, mating ties did not break the bond between Stefan and me because they were two different magics: vampire and werewolf. But the spells I'd seen wrapping around Joel were similar to pack bonds.

The first sign that what I'd done had worked was the now-familiar burn in my chest as the pack absorbed another member. Joel staggered, and for a moment his weight pressed down on me unbearably. I think I blacked out because my vision did that weird jump thing, where one moment I was staring at one thing, then the next I was looking at something different, though I couldn't remember moving my gaze.

The tibicena who was Joel was no longer standing over me, but fighting with the other tibicena. I couldn't see Darryl, but Auriele was lying with a knee bent in the wrong direction, and she wasn't moving.

"What did you do?" Guayota's voice was oddly slurred, but I could hear the anger in it. I couldn't turn my head, but Guayota moved into my field of view.

The huge fiery-dog form that Guayota wore was oddly

lopsided. His left side looked exactly as I remembered. Glowing red eye, crackled skin that showed the moving currents of molten substance that flowed just beneath. The other side was dark, the light beneath wholly extinguished, and as he staggered, half dragging himself from the battleground to where I lay, the outer surface of the dead side began to lighten to gray and crumble when he moved.

"How did you steal—" said Guayota—and then Adam was there, a great blue-silver wolf. Adam and Warren and Honey, who landed on Guayota at the same time, their fury as bright and shining as Guayota had ever been.

"Screw me and stake me out." Gary's voice was in my ear. "I think she's dead. How could she be burned this badly and not be dead?" He was talking about me, I realized, but I didn't remember getting burned. Coyote had told me my neck was broken. Gary was still talking. "I've sent back steaks that were this overdone. Mercy?"

There were other noises in the background: growls and howls and cries of pain.

"Not dead yet," I told Gary. I had to say it again before he understood me.

He huffed half a laugh. "Finally found a sibling I could stand to talk to for more than ten minutes, and . . ." He didn't finish that sentence. "I gotta tell you, you look bad, Mercy."

I licked my lips. They cracked, but I talked anyway. "Got here sooner than expected. You did, I mean. Did you get a call?" Is Adam here? I'd be safe if Adam was really here. But that wasn't true, was it? Coyote had told me I was dying.

"No, but someone's phone was going off every two minutes until one of the werewolves killed it. Please save me from being trapped in a car with that many angry werewolves ever again. They were all mostly changed to wolf, barely, when I had another *Seeing*, one of the big ones. *Saw* you and a couple of werewolves fighting Guayota on Honey's front lawn and realized why I had to go with the wolves. Took me a while to get them to understand. And once they did, I had to drive because they were all too much werewolf already—and let me tell you, oncoming headlights when you have a migraine are no kind of fun."

A cry, the same kind of bone-chilling cry that Gary and I had heard once before, cut through the sounds of battle and Gary's soothing voice like a knife.

Gary turned to look, and that let me see one of the tibicenas bite deep into the other and shake it until it turned into a much smaller thing. I recognized the mutated woman that the walking stick had once shown me. Joel, the tibicena who was Joel, dropped her to the ground. She writhed once, then was still.

"Look," Auriele said, and I was happy to know she wasn't dead. "Look at Guayota." I strained my eyes to the side until I could see the wolves fall away from the thing that had been Guayota. One of those wolves was Adam. Something inside me loosened. Adam was alive.

Guayota's dog form dissolved around the man whom Christy had known as Juan Flores.

Though there were wolves all around him, it was my eyes Guayota sought. "I'm so hungry," he said. "Where is she? She was supposed to be here." And then there was just nothing where he'd stood. Nothing. No wisp of clothing falling to the ground, no dust or ash. He was just gone.

Adam turned to look at me, and I tried to get up. But the movement sent sparkles through my vision, and I was lost in darkness.

THE SMELL OF CLEANING SOLUTION WOKE ME BRIEFLY.

". . . broken neck blah-blah-blah." It sounded like Samuel, but there was something wrong with his voice. He sounded so sad, so I tried to listen. Maybe I could cheer him up. "And the burns . . . I'm sorry, Adam—"

Adam said something, and I sank into his voice like it was a warm sea.

"IT'S PROBABLY BETTER IF YOU TALK TO ME AND DON'T pay attention to all of that," said Coyote.

I was lying on a thick field of new-mown grass that smelled a lot better than the cleaning fluid had. I watched the sky where small groups of clouds chased each other like little ducks.

"Mmmm," I said dreamily.

Coyote chuffed a laugh. "They do have you on some strong stuff. But you'll remember this anyway. Guayota isn't dead. You can't kill one of his kind unless you destroy what he represents. That need not concern you—although I wouldn't be in a hurry to go visit the Canary Islands for a while. A few years, and he'll forget. He shouldn't have worn a human-seeming for so long."

"Like you did when you became Joe Old Coyote," I said.

"Not at all," he told me indignantly. "That cloud looks like me, don't you think?"

"The bigger one?" I asked.

"Yes, that one that looks like it's about to eat an egg."

"No. That one's a rabbit."

"*Rabbit,*" he said indignantly. "That's a coyote."

I laughed, but that was a mistake. My vision went black for a few minutes, then, slowly, the sky, clouds, and grass were back.

"Don't do that," said Coyote. "It makes it difficult to hold you here. I break things, a lot of things, but I don't want one of them to be you. So just rest here."

"What about . . ." It was difficult to be worried; most of me wanted to just watch the clouds drift by.

"Let me talk," Coyote said. "You don't know what questions you want to ask. Unusual decision to bring Joel into the pack. You could have used the walking stick to cut the threads of Guayota's spell, and that would have done the same thing as you managed to do with the pack spell." He paused. "Maybe. Maybe it would have just burned to ashes. I don't know. It'll be interesting to see what happens to the pack with a tibicena in it."

"I didn't have a choice," I told him. "I gave the walking stick back to Beauclaire."

"Did you?" said Coyote. "Hmm. *Anyway,* Guayota, being separated from that which gave him life—the volcano—needed two anchors to hold him in his human-seeming and allow him his power. Two anchors who were connected to his island. Why two? Why male and female? Who knows. Doubtless there is a reason, and if you meet him again, you might ask because the answer interests me."

"Never," I told him. "I am never going to the Canary Islands."

There was a little silence beside me, and I realized that he was lying in the grass, too. "It's supposed to be beautiful in the Canaries," he said a little wistfully. "There's this underground lake lit by torches . . ."

"No," I told him.

"Maybe Gary will go," Coyote said contemplatively. "But in any case, when you claimed Joel, tibicena and all, it threw the magic that allowed Guayota to live away from his island out of balance, and it unraveled."

"Then Joel will go back to being just human?" I asked.

"That depends," Coyote said.

"On what?" I turned my head, glimpsed his face, then my world went black again.

———

"WHY DON'T YOU JUST DIE?" HISSED SOMEONE IN my ear.

After a moment, I realized it was Christy.

"I know it was you. I know it. And now I look like a freak." Something dripped on my cheek and touched my lips with salt.

"*Mom,*" said Jesse. She sounded appalled and . . . amused.

"She's nasty and vindictive," Christy said. "Everyone thinks she farts rainbows—and look what she did to me. I'm *blue.*" She wailed the last.

Christy had used the bottle of shampoo she'd left in my bathroom. I hoped the dye hadn't stained the tile, but it would be worth it if it had. There were some noises, then Jesse's breath was warm on my ear.

"She's gone to get coffee, Mercy," she told me. "I love her, but—the dye was inspired." She giggled. "You are terrifying. I can't believe you got her while you were . . ." She cleared her throat. "While you were in the hospital." She laughed again. "I told her she should leave it. I'd dye my hair blue again, and we could be twins. Even Auriele laughed at her expression, though she turned her head so Mom couldn't see."

There was a long, peaceful silence, and then Jesse said, "I want so badly for her to be happy. But I can't make her happy. All I can do is love her. Do you think that's all right?" She patted the pillow beside my head. "You need to wake up pretty soon, though. Dad needs you. So do I."

THE SHEETS WERE VERY WHITE AND SCRATCHY AND the blankets too thin. My toes were cold, and I was lying on my side. I wiggled to try to pull my feet up and get them warm.

"Mercy?" Adam said.

"We need to get new blankets," I told him, and he laughed.

"Whatever you want, sweetheart."

I took a deep breath and realized that I really was awake because it hurt. The sun was shining, the AC was on too high, and I was in a hospital bed.

Adam leaned forward and kissed me. Then I kissed him back. With interest. He laughed and rested his forehead on mine, and I felt his whole body go limp.

"You are so stoned, baby," he said.

"Am I fried?" I asked.

"What?" He rolled his head a little so he could see my face.

"Burned like a crispy steak," I clarified.

"No. Not as bad as it could have been." He hesitated. "Not as bad as it was, I think, is a better answer. The cheek scar will have a companion on your forearm, and I'm afraid the shotgun-pellet scars have some company. Might be a while before you are happy about walking on your left foot, but that was just blisters, and Samuel says it should heal with no scarring."

"No modeling contract," I said mournfully.

"Not in your future, no," he said, and his dimple flirted with me. "You'll have to make do with me."

"Coyote said I was dying," I told him. "And Christy wanted me to."

"Coyote, eh?" He gave me an odd smile. "I went to grab some coffee that first night you were here, and when I got back, he was sitting on the edge of your bed. As a coyote." He rubbed his face and took a deep breath. "Samuel said the first X-rays showed that you'd broken your neck. He . . . wasn't optimistic. But after Coyote had his visit, things got better. As for Christy—" His skin next to mine flushed, and his eyes lightened to amber for just a moment. His voice was calm, though. "Christy has been banned from the hospital. She decided to stay at Auriele's until she figures out whether she is going to move back to Eugene or job search over here. They managed to get the blue off her skin, but she had to dye her hair black. You are not her favorite person."

"Auriele's okay?" I asked, suddenly anxious.

"Shh," he said. "Auriele is a werewolf. She was down for a couple of days, but, as of yesterday, she's fine."

The muzzy feeling was retreating. "How long have I been out?"

"Three days," he said. "And you've only been mostly out. Samuel said you wouldn't remember much of it, though. He also said that they'd probably let you out tomorrow morning. Since there are now no signs of a broken neck."

"Joel?"

He laughed, a happy uncomplicated laugh. "And I thought *I* threw the fox in the henhouse when I brought you into the pack. Joel is . . . yesterday he stayed human for almost an hour."

"Coyote said something about Joel." But try as I might, I

couldn't remember what it was. "Coyote also said we should avoid visiting the Canary Islands for a couple of years."

"I'll bear that in mind." He was quiet for a while, resting his upper body alongside mine. Eventually, he sat up. "If I don't move, I'm going to fall asleep," he said. He looked tired. Beautiful, but tired. "I'm going to go find some food, and I'll bring some back for you, okay?"

"Sure."

"Don't cause any trouble."

"Me?"

The dimple came out again. "I'll be back soon."

As soon as he left, I sat up and started unwiring myself. I had to pee, and I had no intention of letting my bathroom activities be a public event ever again. I wasn't as bad off as I had been after the fight with the river devil. As long as I didn't need a wheelchair— everything else was gravy.

I sat up and swung my legs down—and realized that Adam's recitation of my injuries had limited itself to the burns. My left leg was encased from my toes to about six inches above my knee. My right forearm was bandaged, but my left elbow was immobilized by something with more structure. That I hadn't felt them meant that I was still on a lot more drugs than I'd figured. I gave the IV still hooked to my right hand a look of respect and decided not to pull those out the way I'd intended to. The IV stand was on wheels—it could come, too.

I slid off the bed and got about six feet when it occurred to me that this might have been a bad idea. I wobbled, recovered, wobbled again, and would have fallen if I hadn't grabbed the walking stick at the last minute.

"Well, hello," I told it. "I didn't expect to see you here."